Seven Blades of Legend

FIRE BURNING

KYLE CANADY

authorHOUSE®

AuthorHouse™
1663 Liberty Drive
Bloomington, IN 47403
www.authorhouse.com
Phone: 1 (800) 839-8640

Published by AuthorHouse 09/09/2017

ISBN: 978-1-5462-0661-3 (sc)
ISBN: 978-1-5462-0660-6 (e)

Library of Congress Control Number: 2017913483

Print information available on the last page.

TABLE OF CONTENTS

23

A NEED TO LIE

Darkness. A mother's voice heard faintly in the distance. Slowly Christian opens his eyes and looks up at his bedroom ceiling. He yawns and stretches for a minute, laying comfortably in his soft bed. A relaxed grin spreads across the young Prince's face while his eyes remain half open. He notices the eerie silence and sits up.

"Mom?" he called out.

"Christian, breakfast is ready." Natalia replied from out of the room.

The prince arose dressed in royal attire with his hair parted just like he prefers. Christian walked through his bedroom door and into the dining room. At the breakfast table he saw Alisha seated with Grechov and Carmon, all of which were eating bowls of cereal. The young prince sat down as his mother brought him a bowl of cereal. He looked down at the bowl, but instead saw a stack of buttery pancakes with syrup and jellied toast with bacon on the side of a large dinner plate.

"Thanks momma." he smiled happily.

"I love you." Natalia responded lovingly.

Christian noticed the queen walking towards a closet door and knew she was in imminent danger. "Momma, NO! Don't open tha door." he warned.

"Why baby? What's wrong?" she asked curiously.

"There's a monster in there with a glowing eye. The royal mystic put it in there so it wouldn't get out." Christian explained.

"Oh, I forgot. Thank you baby." his mother replied without caution of the danger lurking on the other side. She kissed her son on the forehead and sat down.

"Where's dad at?" he questioned.

"He's looking for the armor."

"Oh yeah, I forgot. I'll help him out, I know where it is." he said walking away from the table without taking a bite of his breakfast. The prince turned to assist his father, but glanced back only to witness that everyone was gone except his mother. Natalia laid dead on the floor of an empty room. The prince panicked and ran through the doorway to warn his father. Christian entered the courtyard where he witnessed his father fall to the ground lifelessly. The prince began to cry and noticed Raziel and Fire starter standing over his deceased father smiling and laughing.

The two were engulfed in flame, but stood unharmed, taunting the saddened boy with their laughter. Christian fell to his knees, his head began hurting and a rhythmical beeping sound began to ring from somewhere. Everything began to fade as the continuous beeping became louder and louder.

Christian had woken from a haunting dream, but this time not in the comfort of his own home, but rather in a hospital bed. His vision cleared and adjusted to his surroundings. He raised his arm feeling the I.V. needle in his arm, the patient wrist band on his right arm, and the plastic tube through his nose and down his throat. He sat up feeling weak and a tad dizzy.

Christian was horribly disoriented and all alone in the room. The young prince looked up at the television hanging on the side of the wall. The Vailstone Community News channel reported chaos and murder at the Vailstone castle. The young prince shivered as he witnessed Pip Gordan's words in text at the bottom of the screen reporting the death of his mother and father.

An overwhelming empty void circulated through Christian's entire body. The young prince began crying without making any sound. His sorrow was so strong he felt the urge to throw up, sob uncontrollably, and found difficulty gasping for air. He sat quietly, paralyzed in his bed mourning his loss.

A family destroyed, a young man left behind in an uncaring world, orphaned, Christian felt as if his soul was ripped from his core. Pain too powerful for words, the overhead view of a boy weakly sitting up in a hospital bed………

Back at the Vailstone castle authority personnel struggled to maintain peace. News reporters stood outside struggling to capture any possible video or photograph that they could use to make themselves relevant. Seth sat in his living room with a mug of hot chocolate watching Pip Gordan report information about the supposed death of the royal family. The reinstated detective sipped more of his hot chocolate and looked to his sword resting in it's scabbard in the corner of the room. He thought for a moment before setting his mug down on his coffee table. Seth stood from his recliner, grabbed his police issued hand gun, picked up his black sword, and left his home driving his car away rather quickly.

In the demolished ballroom Raziel remained sitting on the ground in regret of his actions. King Dorian's corpse lay beside him, a gaping hole in the floor leading to the burning room below, and soldiers standing by uncertain of how to take action. Hikaru remained cowering behind the debris, watching Raziel.

The current head of security, Major Tydus Collins, reached the room passing by the guards. He took a few steps closer to the grand duke, who was still motionless.

Tydus looked at the grand duke in awe, looked at the deceased king's body, then back at Raziel.

"What have you done?" he asked in disbelief.

Camron ran through the guards frightened of what to find of her father. She noticed all of the aftermath and looked at Raziel, "Dad?" she asked in a scared whimper.

Raziel removed his hands from his face and stood up, "Carmon?" he asked troubled.

The scared teen hurried over to her father in tears. Raziel embraced Carmon carefully as not to crush her. The brunette feared what the consequences would be for her father. She hugged Raziel tightly before looking at King Dorian's bloodied body. The girl stared for a moment and slowly stopped crying, "I love you dad."

"I love you to bud."

Major Collins walked over to Raziel and placed his hand on the grand duke's forearm, which went unnoticed by Raziel. The sound of handcuffs cackled together once removed from Collins' back pocket.

"I have to place you under arrest sir." Tydus informed unsure of himself.

He moved forward to cuff one of Raziel's wrists which caused Carmon to panic. She pushed Tydus back, "NO STOP! YOU CAN'T! IT'S NOT HIS FAULT! STOP!" desperate to protect him.

Raziel, guilt and grief stricken, moved forward and placed his hand on Carmon's shoulder cautiously, "Carmon." he stated in a calm voice. He kneeled down as she turned around. "I messed up, I messed up really bad."

"No." she weakly inturrupted.

"I need to go with them now. I need to try and somehow make things right of this." he told her as he kissed her forehead softly.

Raziel stood up and surrendered to Major Collins. Carmon stood nervously with tears in her eyes while the Major hesitantly approached Raziel and placed him in handcuffs. Hikaru slowly stepped out from the ruble and witnessed the grand duke willingly be taken into custody. Soldiers quickly approached the ambassador to assure his safety.

A tiny bird flew into the castle and perched near the ceiling in which the king was in. It twitched its head quickly noticing all the details. At that time General Grechov speedily barreled through the castle entrance in a terrain dosser with the retrieved terrain dosser close behind him. The mechanical monster came to an abrupt halt. The side door flung open and slammed against the side of the vechicle. The general hurried out of the terrain dosser and down the side latter as quickly as humanly possible. News reporters and Vailstone police officers as well as soldiers swarmed the angry general.

"What tha hell's going on here?! I'm gone for one day and everything goes straight ta hell!" he complained while asking soldiers for information.

Camera's flashed in the General's face relentlessly, trying to forever instill his first reaction to the tragedy. The military leader was bombarded with questions left and right from reporters extending microphones and cell phones near him for answers.

"Who exactly is responsible for the attack on the kingdom?"

"Is it true that this was an act of terrorism?"

"Have the king and queen actually been murdered in cold blood?"

"Did Raziel act on his own accord or has he been acting as a double agent?"

"Where were you during the attack on the kingdom? Do you believe you could have stopped this had you of been present?"

Grechov was overwhelmed by the hysteria and began brushing reporters aside to find the answers to their absurd questions.

"Move! Outta my way you damn vultures!"

Lieutenant Brookes hurried after Grechov to help try and assess the situation. Chase and Lee, however, remained inside the terrain dosser.

"General Grechov was furious the second he found out about what happened." Lee stated.

"Yeah, and it didn't help that it was all over every radio station." Chase replied.

"I wonder what the REAL story behind this is."

"Well......." Chase enticed.

"Well what?"

"Well, why don't you go down there and find out?"

"Cause whatever killed them might still be in there." Lee explained.

"So you're chicken." Chase taunted with a smug grin.

"Pfftt! I ain't die'n." Chase quickly brushed off.

Lee glared at his hypocritical friend.

Grechov stormed into the celebration hall which was transformed into a final resting place. It took him a moment to absorb the sight, the crumbled stone pillars, the fiery hole beneath them, and off to the side he noticed Major Collins throwing a blanket over the body of the late King.

The general rushed over to the major and grabbed his coat pulling him closer, "What tha hell happened here?! I left you in charge during our absence and THIS is what I come back too!"

"I'm sorry sir, the grand duke began fighting against the king in the Kamisama armor and..." Tydus regretfully reported before being inturrupted by the general.

"The grand duke? Raziel. Where is he now?!"

"He's been put into our holding cell."

"Brookes!"

"Yes, sir!" Miranda responded readily.

"Help the major clean up this mess." he ordered leaving her behind with Collins as he marched out.

"Yes, sir!"

Raziel sat on a rickety old bench in the royal holding cell reliving the horrible moment of the look on his friends face as he punched through his body, killing him. He lowered his head and closed his eyes trying to forget the screams of the queen as she was crushed by the giant pillar. He heard the jail room door crack open slowly. He looked up and noticed the general had finally arrived to the castle.

"Grechov....." he addressed with an empty tone before looking down at the floor again.

"Sir, what happened? Why is the king dead?" Grechov interrogated softly and quietly.

Without an answer Grechov stepped closer to the cell while the grand duke still hung his head in grief, "Sir?"

"I'll tell you why," a familiar voice resonated, "because Raziel refused to give Dorian the armor."

Grechov turned to see Hikaru had entered the room behind him, "What? Because of the armor?"

"NO! It's not like that." Raziel quickly corrected, "It's complicated."

Grechov stood between the two, "Well somebody needs to explain what tha hell happened and stop side stepping the answer."

"Raziel entered the celebrations wearing the armor knowing full well he wasn't about to strip down and hand it over to the King in front of the entire kingdom. He presented himself as if the armor was his own rather than Dorian's." Hikaru explained.

Grechov looked at Raziel curiously, wondering why he would do such a thing.

"This obviously infuriated the king, making him look out to be a fool in front of the entire world. So he ordered Raziel to remove the armor, of course he refused which only made things escalate from there. Dorain was so quick to turn on Raziel at that point that he even summoned Arda fravas."

"He turned that thing on Carmon." Raziel defended.

Grechov looked at Hikaru for confirmation in which Hikaru agreed with a slight nod verifying that truth.

"There's more to it than what it seems." Raziel added.

"Oh? Really, could you be so kind as to enlighten us then?" Hikaru chimed.

"I couldn't figure out how to break it to Dorian. I thought maybe if I presented the armor as my own to everyone that he would have no choice but to let me keep it as my own."

"So, it was for the armor." Hikaru figured.

"No. I was going to break it to him after the ceremonies were finished." Raziel confessed.

"Break what to him? What are you not telling us?" the ambassador impatiently asked.

"Fire starter told me before the celebrations even began, that if the armor was worn by someone who didn't have the heart of a true warrior that the armor would turn against who wore it and they would die that instant."

Grechov and Hikaru stood beside themselves with this new information.

"We all know Dorian wouldn't have survived wearing the armor." Raziel sighed, "It's only until now that I could admit that to myself. He was my best friend, but he wouldn't have listened to me."

Hikaru walked over to a desk chair near the wall on the other side of the small room and sat down. The three were silent, curious what to do from this point.

"So what now?" Grechov asked.

"I'll give up the armor and await my punishment." Raziel paused, "It's the right thing to do."

"The hell you will." Hikaru quickly snapped back, "You can't take off that armor now! If you do then somebody at some point will eventually put it on, and then what? Who's to say their going to be any better than you? If anything they'll be worse I guarantee it." Hikaru proclaimed, bringing his point of view to light. "We don't have a king nor queen, nobodies in charge of the kingdom except for their children. Let's face it, we're safest while you're in that armor cause the second, the very SECOND that's off and you're vulnerable, we're vulnerable and we WILL be attacked by something for it."

"Everyone out there will turn on us if something isn't done about this. We can't just explain that the king everybody looked up to was a big fake and would die if he wore the armor. They'll look at it as a lie." Grechov reasoned.

"That's it, maybe that's what we need. A lie." Hikaru answered back having an epiphany.

"Hm?"

"Everyone knows the royal mystic betrayed us and is actually this Fire burner fellow, right?"

"Fire starter." Grechov corrected.

"Okay, well what if he put a spell on Raziel, to assassinate the king and queen?" Hikaru suggested.

"But, nothing can happen to me while I'm in the armor, it won't work." Raziel reminded.

"Well look before you take it off then cause there aren't many options we have here and if we don't have a good answer for what happened, people will revolt, riot, all hell will break loose." Hikaru pleaded.

"We need to arrest that Fire starter anyways." Grechov reasoned.

"But to lie? Like it wasn't my fault?" Raziel stated. "I don't know. Honesty should be our course of action."

Hikaru looked straight at Raziel's eyes, "A lack of honesty is what's gotten us here in the first place."

Raziel lowered his head and looked away.

"But yes Raziel, sometimes the best course of action isn't the right path. If you want to prevent a violent revolution, you'll need to lie with us."

Major Collins entered the room breaking a moment of silence, "General sir, the bodies have been retrieved, but there isn't any sign of the prince nor princess."

This information gained everyone's attention.

Hikaru stood from his seat, "We need to find the children, especially before things get worse. I'll figure things out on my end, General Grechov you devise search parties and find them. As far as it stands right now, Christian is our new king."

General Grechov agreed and left the room following Ambassador Hikaru. Major Collins began to close the door, but stopped for a moment and thought to himself.

"You know, the people of this kingdom used to look up to you." Collins scolded Raziel, before quietly adding under his breath, "I used to look up to you."

"I was trying to protect him." Raziel shamefully stated.

"You've sure got a funny way of going about that." the Major replied coldly.

He began to shut the door before a small bird swooped through the door and into the hallway startling the Major. Without anyone's knowledge the tiny bird had been present through their entire converstaion.

"How tha heck did that get in here?" Collins asked himself before closing the door and locking the entrance to the royal holding cell.

24

IF IT LOOKS LIKE A KIDNAPPING, AND SOUNDS LIKE A KIDNAPPING...

Seth slowly came to a stop in front of the Vailstone police department before taking a deep breath. He closed his eyes and recalled dark moments of the past, being ripped of his badge, the embarrassment of being cuffed and booked by his fellow officers, and the condescending look of judgment. He gasped as he returned to the present. Seth regained his nerves and placed his sword in the backseat. After turning off the car engine the black haired detective locked his car door and proceeded up the police department entrance stairs.

The entire department was all a frenzy. Officers rushing to the aid of the kingdom's castle while others maintained peace in the panicked streets. Detective Notch walked through the glass doors calmy and passed the front counter. Seth began walking to a metal detector, which was mandatory to walk through once entering deeper into the police headquaters, yet all officers were being issued out for aid at the castle and to deter rioting on the streets, so Seth quickly took more advantage of the situation and rushed around the metal detector. He noticed a few staff members taking destress calls while he scanned the room, recalling a few familiar faces. The pale man hurried before being noticed and down a narrow hall before reaching a room full of old case files. Seth stood before the door and looked both directions to see if anybody was watching him before he swiftly entered the cold dusty room.

He hesitated from turning on a light as not to bring attention to his presence so he pulled a small flashlight from his pocket and searched for a particular filing cabinet. He proceeded twelve steps in, through a labrinth of documents, filing cabinets, and boxes of cold case files, until eventually it was before him, Seth's old case files. He opened the filing cabinet and fiddled his fingers through the documents while holding his flashlight by his teeth. Seth finally stopped searching and withdrew a small stack of folders. He looked around before stuffing the folders inside his coat, shutting the cabinet door, and leaving the room quickly.

His heart began to race as he tried exiting the police station, but as fate would have it an old friend of Seth's started running his direction and he had little time to avoid the meeting. Seth darted into the nearest room narrowly dodging the old friend. Seth exhaled heavily, a chance meeting like that would certainly ruin what he had planned. An old friend would know for certain that Seth didn't belong in the police department. Seth lifted his head slightly and smiled with a tiny bit of relief.

A woman officer was washing her hands staring at Seth with curiousity, "You lost?"

Seth smirked embarrassingly, "I could have sworn this was tha men's room." he explained shrugging his shoulders and exiting the women's restroom. The black haired man walked faster and passed the metal detector once more.

The female officer began drying off her hands before recalling, "Notch?" She hurried out of the restroom looking both ways for any sign of him, then decided to try the front entrance. She ran through the metal detector setting it off and approaching the front desk. "Nancy, did you see a white man with long black hair and a brown coat pass through here?!"

The older woman at the front desk, who was being overwhelmed with phone calls herself, sat up, "Yeah, he just walked out tha door a moment ago. Wasn't he rushing to help?"

The female officer watched Seth's car speed away, uncertain of his purpose for being there.........as did a patient masked swordsman.

On the other side of the kingdom Wade and Amanda finally arrived to Smith manor. The two entered Wade's mansion nervous and uncertain. The butler approached the two as they stood inside behind the closed door breathing heavily.

"Is everything alright, sir?" the butler asked with concern.

"You don't watch a lot of T.V. do you?" Wade exhaled.

"No, sir. Can't say that I do." he paused. "Do you need anything?" he continued taking note of his and Amanda's distress.

"I could use a drink." Amanda and Wade replied simultaneously catching the butler off guard.

"Certainly, what would you prefer?"

"Anything!" the two continued answering at the same time.

As the butler walked away to obtain their drinks Wade and Amanda slowly walked into a large living room filled with comfortable seating arrangements, a marvelous grand piano, an over sized wide screen television, and trophies placed all about the room ranging from acting awards, accomplishment awards, and women's photos.

"What the hell happened back there?" Amanda further questioned.

"I don't know. It's like I told you in tha car, Raziel had that armor, the king freaked out on him, and the whole thing went bat shit crazy."

"There's gotta be more to it than just that." she assumed.

Wade pulled out his cell phone and selected a name in his phone's contacts list.

Amanda grabbed the remote for the television and turned it on to catch the news reports of the chaos at the kingdom's castle. The first news station she came across was Vailstone Community News with none other V.C.N.'s Pip Gordan.

"As Vailstone enters such a severe crisis one can't help but wonder if all of this is a result of some kind of alien mind control."

Amanda changed the channel to another news station, "I don't even know how that guy still has a job." She turned her head looking at her friend, "Who are you calling?"

"I'm trying to get a hold of Gloria Humphrey." he answered back realizing Amanda had no idea who he was speaking of by the puzzled look on her face. "Gloria? The sparkly red dress Gloria, some benefit for hungry people Gloria?" he noted trying to help jog his friend's memory. "Ugh! Back of the limo on the highway in that traffic jam Gloria!"

"What? Wait, are you calling some chick for sex right NOW?!" Amanda pieced together.

"Yeah, I need to distract my mind from all of....that." he motioned at the T.V. with his free hand.

"Well I could certainly use an escape right now too, but you don't see me calling somebody for a hook-up!" she sniped.

"Is that an offer?" he asked.

"NO!" she answered raising her voice.

Both stopped squabbling and directed their attention to a random news broadcaster reporting the death of the king and queen.

Amanda gasped, "Oh my God."

Wade finally got an answer on the other end of his cell phone, "Hey this is Wade. I need you to wear that red dress and come over."

he paused for the woman's reply, "Okay, thanks." he said before hanging up the phone and returning it to his pocket.

The reporter certainly snarred both friend's attention with her next startling message, "This just in," she said pausing and placing her hand to her ear as the information was fed to her, "Prince Christian and Princess Alisha have gone missing, presumably kidnapped, eyewitnesses have given statements to police and kingdom officials stating the young royals were seen being taken against their will by young individuals with swords. These individuals were identified as part of the royal ceremonies today. Supposedly five of the special guests had a sword of their own, it is speculated that this was in fact an ochestrated event amoungst the accused five and are considered armed and dangerous........I've just been told a sixth guests was suspiciously absent during the ordeal. A randsome note is speculated to present itself within the coming hours as well as a list of demands. Perhaps mercenaries? Revolutionaries? Or simple terrorism? For now we sit in aggonizing anticipation awaiting the ugly truth."

The reporter listened intently to the news feed through her ear piece. "We're being informed now that sources are working diligently to discover the names of the accused six and will soon be presenting us with photo identification, stay with us for more as this story develops."

Amanda and Wade slowly looked at each other with great worry.

Deep with in the forest surrounding the Vailstone castle Wraith carried the distraught princess with her smeared make-up and tear soaked top while Vincent leading the way. Wraith was confused to a degree with in himself. He was attracted to the beautiful girl, yes, but his heart was also weighing on him. Wraith has never been the kind of guy to feel remorse for another, so why now? He felt a pain in his chest as he watched tears drip from the young girls eyes.

After an hour or so of traveling deeper and deeper into the forest the white haired teen came to a stop, looking all around and uncertain of which dierection to travel in next. He was frustrated for many reasons, but being lost was a the top of his list for the current moment.

"Why are we stopping?" Wraith questioned.

"Just gimmie a minute will ya?" Vincent snapped back, "Just where are we going anyways?"

"What?! You were leading us without direction?! Now we're just lost in the freak'n woods?" Wraith griped.

The princess struggled in Wraith's arms, "Put me down." she cried, "Put me down!"

The princess was placed softly on the ground, Wraith and Vincent watched painfully while the girl tried standing and walking in an aimless direction. She fell to knees crying, "WHY! What I'm I supposed to do now?!" she pleaded looking at the boys with watery eyes.

Vincent and Wraith both slowly looked at each other without a single clue of what to do or say to console the emotionally injured blonde. Wraith nudged Vincent on the back and tilted his head towards Alisha, indicating for Vincent to stop her crying. Vincent's eyes glared at Wraith showing his dissaproval, so Vincent nudged Wraith on the back and tilted his head towards Alisha indicating for Wraith to console the princess. Wraith shook his head and began pulling Vincent's arm in Alisha's direction. Vincent resisted and started pushing Wraith's back to force him at her. Alisha showered the ground with salty tears while the two teenagers silently bickered amoungst each other as to whom was supposed to help her feel better about the death of her mother.

Several feet away from the squabbling boys a small pair of beady eyes watched from underneath a mound of upchurned soil. The creature noticed the crying princess and the two boys standing in front of her before slowy and quietly returning underneath the ground.

Wraith and Vincent began wrestling with each other until Vincent lost his footing and was pushed down directly in front of the princess. She looked up at his face as he was kneeled before her. The white haired orphan figured he was the last person on earth to turn to for sympathy and hadn't any clue what to say to help her feel any better. He nervously smiled at the crying beauty.

"Hey......." Vincent struggled.

The princess lungged forward and hugged Vincent tightly, dripping her tears over his shoulder. Vincent was startled by the sudden act to recieve compassion and left his arms open wide before slowly moving inward and hugging her back. The teen slightly blushed for a brief moment, it was the first time in Vincent's life that anyone has ever hugged him before. Even though the circumstances were tragic, it was a nice feeling that gave Vincent a small warm feeling inside. Wraith stood behind them somewhat jealous, he didn't realize she wanted someone to hug. He had thought she wanted deep caring words of healing and compassion, which Wraith knew he was terrible at giving.

A pinecone flew across the ground from the direction of the mysterious spy and popped Vincent in the back of the head.

"Hey! Whad'ya do that for?!" Vincent sniped looking back at Wraith.

"Huh? I didn't hit you with that." he defended. "If was going to hit you I wouldn't use a pinecone. I'd use one of THESE!" he declared waving his fist at Vincent.

"Oh yeah!?" Vincent asked standing up from his hug with Alisha to face against Wraith.

"Yeah!" Wraith agreed stepping forward.

"Ya know, I hate little punk ass pukes like you acting tough on the street like people give a damn. Everybody knows shits like you are just compensating cause you always act tough in numbers, but it's never the case one on one." Vincent insulted clintching his fist.

"Think your big? Come say that over here and I'll kick your ass, turds like you always annoy the hell outta me anyways. Mommy and daddy were never around so now I'm a big tough guy." Wraith stated buckling down preparing to fight Vincent.

As the two of them glared at each other readying to fight the beady eyed creature, who was still spying on them, began moving at the both of them very quickly from underneath the ground. Vincent cursed at Wraith hatefully then charged at him swinging while Wraith backed away trying to dodge his blows. Alisha's tears began drying up while she watched the two attack each other in shock. Wraith stepped back further from Vincent moving away from another punch.

"Stop running from me!" Vincent complained.

At that moment the spying creature emerged from the ground causing rocks and pebbles to fly about. It jumped from the ground far enough just to bite onto Wraith's sword handle and jerk it away from him completely. Right after doing so it dug back into the ground swiftly. All three teenagers were surprised by the mysterious creature.

"My sword!" Wraith yelled. "Get it!"

Vincent followed behind Wraith as he chased after the creature disturbing the ground from below. Wraith lunged forward attempting to tackle the thief but only landed face first in the grass since it darted another direction at the last minute. Vincent stepped on Wraith's butt and back adding insult to injury while chasing after the creature.

Wraith lifted his head furiously, "Hey!" the ex-convict wanted to bitch but instantly noticed he was being left behind in the chase. The purple haired teen lept off the ground and ran after to catch up.

Princess Alisha was distracted by her severe pain, watching the mysterious chase. "Wait! Look it's coming back." she announced.

Wraith stopped in his tracks as the underground creature made a sharp u-turn and began making its way back with Vincent following right behind.

"I've got it this time." Wraith muttered until noticing the shark fin emerge from the disturbed earth, "A shark?!" Wraith started to sweat on his forehead thinking nervously as he imagined a ground shark emerging from the ground and ripping him apart!

"GET READY!" Vincent shouted.

At the last moment, however, the creature completely submerged underground and vanished entirely.

"Hm? Where did it go?" Alisha asked subtly.

Vincent stopped right in front of Wraith. The two looked around the ground for any new movement, but saw nothing. After a small moment Alisha started screaming and kicking her leg.

"It's got the princess!"

The two quickly ran over to her rescue. Wraith lifted Alisha's dress quickly with Vincent readying his sword for the attack. The two teenagers faces blushed, seeing nothing but panties.

Alisha slapped both in the face swiftly as an 'innocent' ladybug flew away from underneath her dress, "Perverts."

Wraith looked at the stunned white haired teen smugly, nodding his head slightly, and offering a fist bump at the pleasing sight.

Vincent looked at Wraith like an idiot which immediately killed his offer.

"Well, let's go." Wraith ordered.

"Go where?" Vincent questioned.

"Go find my sword, I'm not losing it just like that."

"You can go, it's your sword. I've got mine."

Wraith was agitated, "Well gimme one of yours so I can fight it then."

"No, screw that. You lose swords. I'm not losing mine."

"What's it matter? Your swords don't even do anything special anyways. It wouldn't be any different than me holding a big stick anyways." Wraith mocked.

"I'll give you a big stick you can do something with!" Vincent insulted.

"You wanna fight punk?!"

"Yeah, you gonna run like last time?!"

"Alright turd! Put your swords down and we'll do this then!" Wraith ordered.

"With pleasure." Vincent replied stabbing both of his swords into the ground and walking over to the purple haired agitator.

"Stop! Why do you two keep insisting on fighting each other? I'm an emotional train wreck over here and all you two can do is think about how much you want to pound the other's face in! UGH!" Alisha flustered.

Both teens looked at Alisha and endured her words, "She's right." Wriath said walking over to the princess quickly and passing up Vincent, who still wanted to fight.

"Look, I'm sorry we ca," Wraith pretended to apologize then quickly grabbed one of Vincent's abandoned swords stabbed in the ground, "Ah ha!"

"You bastard! Gimmie back my sword!" Vincent hurried over to Wraith to take his sword back until all of a sudden the creature from underground emerged once again.

The being was small and furry, a tan colored puppy with a shark fin on the back of its head, a shark tail, and razor sharp rows of shark teeth! As quick as the little shark dog appeared it had already latched onto Wraith, biting his hand with the sword in hand.

Everyone was stunned and confused for a slight moment until the silence was broken by Wraith's screaming in terrible pain by the shark dog's teeth digging into his hand. The teen shook and waved his arm wildly attempting to shake loose the adorable beast. Wraith let loose the sword, allowing it to drop to the ground before trying to punch the shark dog in the face. The little tan pup released Wraith's arm in time to dodge the punch and retrieve the dropped sword. The pup bit the sword handle and began running away.

Vincent watched as one of his swords were being stolen and immediately grabbed his only remaining sword and chased after the small tan dog. The chase ended once the little pup cornered himself by running to a massive tree in the woods. It turned around to face off againt the orphaned boy.

"Give me back my sword or I swear I'll make puppy tuna outta you."

"Hee hee hee, bet'cha think you're real funny coming up with that ol' joke don't cha?" the little pup replied with Vincent's sword in it's mouth.

"So, You can talk? Hand it over." he ordered taking a step closer to the cornered dog.

"No! One more step and I'll snap this blade in two. I can do it." the pup warned. He started biting down on the sword to show Vincent he wasn't bluffing.

Wraith and the princess finally caught up to the two and their stand-off, standing behind Vincent.

The teen with silver hair gripped his sword while watching the small puppy threaten his other half, "Stop, that's my sword!" he shouted out while reaching outward to his sword.

At that moment the sword began to shake and quiver within the little pup's teeth. The small shark dog began to wonder what was happening. He had known he wasn't biting down hard enough to shatter the blade yet, when suddenly to everyone's amazment the other blade of Vincent's completely burst into metallic shards, handle and all! The dog opened his mouth allowing the other shards to lift from out of his mouth and somehow hover in the air overhead. All were surprised by the hidden ability of the Vincent's swords.

Vincent was greatly concerned with the well-being of his sword until he realized he had awoken his swords ability. The teen smiled happily, "Hey look, my sword does have powers." A small metallic shard floated before Vincent grabbing his attention. "Huh?" He slowly reached out to touch the shard, but it drifted away and out of his reach each time he tried.

"Try to use your sword." Alisha advised.

Wraith and Vincent both looked at Alisha, "Huh?"

"I mean, use your sword to touch it." she clarified.

Vincent turned and faced the single shard hovering directly in front of him. He lifted his sword and pointed it to the metal shard. The boy slowly moved the tip of his blade forward penetrating the metallic shard somehow making the tip of his sword appear through another metal shard that hovered several feet away above the small shark dog. The further he extended his sword, the further the sword extended through the shard floating around the small pup. All were excited to witness this unforeseen ability of Vincent's sword except for the thieving pup who was pinned to the tree.

The blade grew closer, "Ah! Please don't kill me! I'm sorry." the pup pleaded.

"Where's my sword?!" Wraith shouted, ignoring his bleeding hand.

The dog turned his head and ignored the purple haired teen's question until Vincent pushed his sword closer to the pup's body. The pup gasped, "Okay, I'll show you" he said in defeat.

The little shark dog lead the three teens to his secret hiding place with Vincent's sword blades still hovering above him. The trail ended at a large hollowed out tree with a huge hole at the base.

"It's in there." he pointed.

Wraith walked over to the base of the tree and poked his head inside noticing the small stolen 'treasures' of the little canine. A small top, an action figure, a few fruits, a pile of very small bones, and his stolen sword.

The little pup looked over to princess Alisha and apologized, "I'm sorry I couldn't save you."

"Huh? Save me? From what?" she asked.

"From your kidnapper's, I didn't know the white haired guy's sword could do that."

Alisha was stunned, she realized the small dog misunderstood the entire situation. Her being carried into the woods, her tears, their weapons, it was all a huge misunderstanding. Wraith walked back over to the group, he and Vincent menicingly looked over the frightened shark dog.

"Let's see, what punishment is suitable for a little bitting sword thief?" Wraith grinning wickedly.

The princess picked up the little puppy boy and held him tightly, "Nobody's hurting a hair on this little guy's head."

"The hell I'm not." Wraith repiled.

"Hurt his legs then." Vincent advised.

Alisha turned to the side holding the pup, "No! This little guy tried rescuing me. He's a hero."

"He failed." Vincent said quietly.

"He's a monster." Wraith tried reasoning.

"He is not a monster. He's a, he's, um." she tried arguing.

"I'm a shark dog." the little pup answered back. Alisha placed him back on the ground, "My momma was shark an' my poppa was a dog."

"Still a little monster." Wraith grimaced, causing the little pup to growl.

"So how exactly is this little dog a rescuer of yours?" Vincent questioned.

"He thought you guy's were kidnapping me."

"What?" Vincent disbelieved.

"Yeah, I heard a bunch of commotion at the castle today and saw all the panic, then the news people and cop people started saying the prince and princess was kidnapped by guys with swords. It doesn't take a genius to put two and two together." the dog explained as if pittying the minds of the two boys.

"WHAT!? We didn't kidnap her!"

"Sure, now ya tell me. Well, that's what everybody in Vailstone thinks, so you guys are in BIG trouble." he said proudly crossing his little arms.

"So what now?" Wraith asked.

"We just go back with Alisha and explain." Vincent said.

"I'm not going back there. Raziel killed my mother and my father for all I know. I don't know who he is anymore." the princess confessed.

"I'm not going back. I just got out of prison and am being set up for kidnapping a princess. Do you have any idea how fast I would end up back behind bars?! I'm not going back to jail, forget that." Wraith informed everyone.

"So what then?" Vincent asked. "I'm not becoming a fugitive because of all this."

"I know a place back in the city where we can lay low until we figure out what to do. That's where I'm going." Wraith stated as he began walking off.

The princess began slowly following after Wraith, "You're going to?" Vincent asked.

"I don't know what I'm supposed to do right now, but I can't go back home. I need to gather my thoughts. Laying low sounds good to me for now until I can figure out what needs to be done." Alisha explained.

"Alright, let's go." the little shark dog chimed in.

"You're coming with us?" Alisha asked.

"Of course, these two obviously can't get along and work together. So I'll come with you to ensure your safety." the pup smiled.

The princess smiled back, "Alright. Hm, you never told us your name."

"I'm Bo. Nice to meet you princess."

"The pleasure is all mine Mr.Bo." she complemented.

Vincent rolled his eyes following them all while Alisha and Bo bonded with each other.

25

SCORNED FIRE

Completely oblivous to all of the misinformation that's been spreading through the news channels like wild fire, Kaz roared his motorcycle into the parking lot of his usual biker gang's hangout near the outskirts of the Vailstone kingdom. The muscular biker looked at the bar and smiled before turning off his engine. Kaz was known for being a badass throughout motorcycle gangs, so when the black haired man thrust open the poorly lit bars doors open it was not unusual for many to quieten down upon his arrival, but for his own gang it seemed at bit awkward.

"Hey." he merely muttered expecting a welcoming cheer from his own members. Kaz looked to the bartender, "Woody, gimme a beer would'ya?"

The swordsman began walking over to his group, "It's Kaz! He's back." his black haired bombshell mistress announced running over to him. She ran over to Kaz and was lifted by her lower back by one arm before he kissed her passionately while the other bikers cheered his return. "Baby what happen out there?"

"I'll tell ya what happend, I slayed a mountain monster and got THIS baby!" he yelled revealing his impressive sword and gaining more cheers. He accepted his beer and began guzzling it down.

"No offense Kaz, but I think she meant with the whole dead royal family thing." a friend of his corrected.

"Hm? Oh, that shit went sour so I got the hell outta there." he nonchalantly explained taking another drink and finishing his beer entirely.

"But what about tha kidnapping? Is it for money?" his mistress questioned.

"Kidnapping? What are you talking about?" he inquired looking at her in his arm.

"The news is talking all about it, saying you and five other guys that got swords kidnapped the royal kids. Said you, that Wade Smith guy from all those porn movies, some fired cop guy, and three others."

"It was a set up from the start?!" Kaz wondered to himself.

"Hey Kaz, I think these guys are here to talk to you." one biker near the window announced.

Kaz and his friends approached the smoke stained tinted windows, "Vailstone soldiers, just like when that general came here looking for you." Kaz's mistress stated.

"Yeah, but this times gonna be a lot different." Kaz warned.

"Hey Kaz, here, take my ride. It's out back." his friend request offering his keys.

"Pht, I've got my own set of wheels." Kaz explained looking at his bike around the five soldiers outside.

"Be careful baby." the black haired babe requested.

"That's not how I play." Kaz said before walking through the doors and approaching the soldiers outside near his bike. "That's a sweet ride." he stated referring to the soldiers jeep.

A soldier in charge looked up and noticed Kaz with a sword strapped to his back in a sheath. "We're looking for the owner of this motorcycle here, but something tells me that would be you. Is your name Kaz by any chance?"

"Oh? You must think that because I've got this big long sword here that I'm one of those kidnappers you're looking for from the news, huh?" he questioned sarcastically with a coy attitude while unsheathing his broad sword.

The five Vailstone guards began forming a circle around Kaz to easily apprehend him. As they grew nearer and nearer for the pounce the large biker countined.

Kaz looked around at the surrounding guards and smirked, "It's gonna take a lot more than five'a you guys to take me down." he boasted.

The Vailstone guard in charge waved his hands as he slowly stepped closer, "Now sir, there's no need to get rough now." he explained trying to defuse the situation.

"Hm, that's NEVER been my policy." he said swinging his massive sword around in the air before stabbing it into the ground causing a massive lightening bolt to strike where he stood and the five men around him which launched them all flying in seperate directions.

The soldiers lay motionless where they landed as the crowd of bikers rushed out cheering and praising Kaz for taking on five guys at once without effort, not to mention the impressive sword he had collected along his way. Kaz's mistress watched as he climbed onto his motorcycle and revved his engine.

"Kaz! Where're you goin'?" she called out.

"I've been set up by cops." he answered loudly, "So I'm gonna get some answers from one I know." he quietly said to himself as he speed off in the direction back into the heart of Vailstone.

Mean while, deeper into the kingdom of Vailstone a strange looking man clocked out from work. Drove his average looking car home while listening to the propaganda over the radio and taking a draw off of his cigarette to calm down. He slowly came to a stop as smaller children evactuated the not so near by school in light of the kingdom's recent events. The man watched each child cross the street with the crossing guard on duty before driving on through and arriving home. He parked his car, walked up a five step porch to his apartment building, and entered his home.

The strange man was stunned to find his home had been trashed. It appeared someone had broken in somewhere looking for something. He pulled a handgun from his work bag and quietly placed the bag on the floor next to the open door before creeping into his house further. As the man began to approach a corner to peer into a nearing hallway the front door slowly began to close. As the door creeked shut the man turned around and noticed a tall man who had been standing behind the door the entire time. He wore an old trench coat and had long black hair. As the owner of the apartment saw, upon a more detailed inspection, the intruder had in his hand a long black bladed katana in his right arm.

The man was nervous, "Who are you? What'da you want?"

"Me? I simply want justice." the intruder barely whispered to a hearing volume.

"Justice? What'da you talk'n about?"

"Maybe this will help jog your memory." the man in shadows answered and flung a manila folder with a police report and picture of an innocent little child paper clipped to the top of the report. The man's demeanor altered upon seeing the girl's photograph. "Remember now?"

"I don't know what this has gotta do with me?" he man lied.

"Tha hell you don't. You remember that little girl's face cause I personally made sure you'd NEVER forget. You sat in that interrogation room for nearly eight hours dodging questions, clamming up, eating up the attention. It's a shame I never found that small knife you used on her. Or maybe it was just the district attorney's fault, who knows. But I've always put the blame on myself for any shits like you that evaded justice. I usually got justice for my victims, but, something with your case, you just walked away. It killed my faith in the system a little that day." Seth exposed.

"Detective Notch? I'll see that you lose your badge for this." the man happily threatened.

Seth walked out of the shadows completely and stepped closer to the justice system cheating murderer. Seth's black blade glimmered slightly in the low housing light. "I've lost something more precious." he paused, "My soul." he announced looking up directly at the man.

The man smiled and pointed his gun towards Seth after noticing his only weapon on hand was a black katana, "You're about to lose your ass screwing around like this with me cop. See you broke into my house without a warrent. Now, I can tell 'them' that I just got off work and was ambushed my some lunatic with a sword in his hand. Shoot you dead, and not have broken any laws at all." he advised almost excitedly.

"True, but do me one favor first......Why? Why'dya do it?" Seth wondered.

The gunman raised his arm and pointed the gun straight at Seth's chest and smiled, "Because, she was a HOT little thing. Cutting her open was practically enough to make me climax without even a stroke." he smirked, "Oh, and you were wrong. I didn't use a small knife, I used a box cutter." At that exact declaration the man shot Seth in the chest extremely close to his heart which forced the man to fall instantly with his fresh open chest wound, due to Seth's katana being unsheathed.

The evil man dropped the gun as he fell to the floor dying and bleeding out. Seth sheathed his black katana on his waist, opposite to his handgun, in perfect health and slowly walked over to the bloody man. "Oh, and do me one more favor. When you go to hell, tell'em I sent you. That way it'll be easier for Satan to tally my score card." Seth walked out of the building as the man breathed his last breath.

The vengeful detective sat back down behind the driver's seat in his car and glanced at the passenger seat, looking at only three police case files left remaining from his stack he had taken from the police headquaters. As Seth started his car and drove away to his next destination, the masked mercenary Cain walked out of an area of the apartment and looked at the lifeless man's body. He picked up the case file in his gloved hand and had realized what Seth was attempting to do during the midst of all the chaos, why he was doing it, and now he knew how the detective had murdered the other nine victims before this criminal without so much as a scratch upon himself.

Better yet, the masked murder knew how and why he was cut when sword fighting against Seth in the cave inside the forest of darkness. Cain stepped back into a dark area to vanish quickly. The mercenary was determined to confront the vigilante detective once more.

Back at the Vailstone Doltan hospital Christian remained motionless and unresponsive while propped up in his bed. His eyes strained, dried out, tired. The teenager was an emotional wreck.

Rufus walked into the hospital room, "Hey? I heard you were finally awake." he said without a reply. "How ya feeling? You feel'n better?"

Christian's glassy eyes glanced at the news channel slowly then looked forward into nothingness once again.

"Oh, you heard, huh?" he said reaching for the remote to turn off the televison.

Christian grabbed Rufus' wrist and made him drop the remote control, "NO! I want to know everything." he snapped in a crackling hoarse voice.

"Okay." Rufus complied. He pulled up a nearby seat and sat down beside the prince's hospital bed. "Yeah know," the large teen struggled,"if you wanna talk." he offered reaching out. "I know what you're going through. When I lost my dad,..."

"THIS HAS NOTHING TO DO WITH YOUR DAD! It's NOT tha same! GET OUTTA HERE! GET OUT!" Christian lost himself and freaked out on Rufus.

Rufus was surprised and scorned at the prince's uncalled for response. "Forget it." he muttered silently before walking out of the room.

The prince was left laying in his bed alone with his eyes open wide, glued to the television, absorbing all of the painful information reported to the public when suddenly a new announcment began stirring up everyone.

At the Vailstone castle courtyard Major Tydus walked out before the crowd of reporters and upset civilians and cleared a path for the ambassador. Hikaru walked out into the courtyard calmly with concern all over his face. As the ambassador prepared to inform everyone of the lie that was concocted within the holding cell black birds of all variety and size flocked around landing on nearby ledges, gates, statues, and even stood by on the ground as if waiting for something.

Soldiers created a perimeter of protection for the ambassador. Hikaru stood tall as he prepared a speech. He looked about the cameras before starting, "My fellow Vailstoneians, our dear neighboring kingdoms, people of the world,...a great tragedy has befallen our beloved kingdom. It's true....an evil wind did blow through our fair kingdom." reporters started yelling questions and interrupting Hikaru, which he merely raised his hands to quieten them down once again. He took a deep breath before continuing, "I'm sure in the event of this dire moment in our lives you've heard many stories formulated already in such a small amount of time, but I am here to set things right. Yes.....it is true that our dearly beloved king and queen have passed on." he announced causing a huge uproar.

Given a moment the crowd quieted down and stopped asking questions to further listen to the ambassador. "The manner of their death's is irrelevant. The event of their death is what truely matters here. As many of you may have already known, the castle walls were attacked by a ghastly specter a few nights ago, which led to the venture that would forever change the course of our futures. A venture that resulted in finding the legendary armor of Kamisama. Upon this quest were six voluntary individuals, the grand duke,..", whos very mention excited booing and jeers amoungst the crowd, "and our very own royal mystic."

"We are all human....and as so we build bonds....believe and hope with in each other, which at times those of an unscrupulous nature take advantage of to misguide our trust. We placed our faith in the magic of the wrong man. The Vailstone kingdom's royal mystic was in actuality an individual by the name of 'Fire starter'. I believed in this man, the grand duke believed in this man, King Dorian believed in this man. Yet....he abused that trust to try and cripple our kingdom...shake the very foundation of our civilization.... and force us to crumble as a society. In the assassination of our fair king and queen, this Fire starter's goal was not only to destroy us as a whole, but also to obtain the armor of Kamisama."

One reporter spoke up, "Excuse me Ambassador Hikaru, isn't it true infact, that it was actually Raziel in the armor who murdered King and Queen Doltan? And if so, what's to become of the armor now?"

Everyone grew silent listening with severe anticipation for Hikaru's response.

The ambassador stood quietly with his hands by his side until he lifted his right arm, "Rather than tell you, allow me to show you."

At that que Raziel walked from the castle doors freely and stood beside Hikaru. Major Tydus stood by keeping upset people at bay, despite his growing loss of respect for Raziel. Cameras blinded Hikaru as flash photography went crazy. Questions as well as threats roared throughout the crowd. Hikaru waved his hands in the air trying to quieten everyone down. Eventually the mass of people began to listen with the assisstance of the crowd control.

Christian was at full attention while watching them on his hospital room television.

"Yes, it is true! As an instrument through the orchestration of Fire starter through the use of black magic, our Grand Duke, Raziel, was manipulated in carrying out the orders of our traitorous mystic against his will. But this mind controlling magic has been dispelled." Hikaru announced to the world.

Raziel raised his arm, "I am not innocent. I will never forgive myself for what has occured this day. It is true,.." Raziel paused, regretting his agreement with Hikaru to lie, "through the Fire starter's mind controlling magic, I was used to carry out his bidding. I, Raziel, was powerless to stop myself. I will regret this day til the day I die, yet, I do not seek your sympathy nor expect your forgivness."

"Ambassador Hikaru, will Raziel continue to wear the armor of Kamisama?" a reporter questioned.

"Yes. Soley for the protection of the armor Raziel will continue to wear the armor. With the mind control spell broken he is back to his normal self and is devoted to protecting this kingdom as well as you and myself."

"What's to stop this event from happening again?"

"The mind control spell from Fire starter was placed upon Raziel before the armor was put on. He is protected from harmful magic while wearing the armor, before that was a different story. Luckily, a counter spell for his well being was somehow effective. It is truely a mysterious armor with much to learn from it. Next question please." Hikaru carried on.

"What has become of the prince and princess? Are they still alive?"

"Yes, they were last seen alive. However, I have been recently informed by eyewitnesses and Vailstone authority that the six individuals mentioned earlier have been sighted in what at this time is speculated to be abduction. The authorities including Vailstone's own General Grechov are locating these individuals and the royals as we speak. It is unknown whether they are working in tandem with the Fire starter at this time but we will keep everyone informed as the information develops itself." Hikaru answered professionally.

One reported shouted louder over the flurry of questions, "If the royal mystic is this Fire starter person as you've claimed, then is it safe to say that the kingdom is without a mystic advisor at this time, and if so, then who is the one who lifted the magic spell from the grand duke?"

Raziel looked to Hikaru for the answer, Hikaru was a professionl lier so the moment of shock for not having an answer wasn't noticeable to anyone, yet Raziel knew this question was not covered yet. At that time, however, all of the birds in the area began flying at once and circling in the sky with each other. All who stood in the courtyard were startled and confused by the massive swarm of birds blocking out the sun light. Then, all of a sudden the black birds began flying into one spot close to the ground, forming a mass of black darkness until eventually a single entity began to emerge. From the birds, a tall, muscular, black haired man in an extremely dark black dress and high heels stepped forward. He wore a feathered cape and his dress was feather trimmed. The black lipstick and dark eye shadow on the man made his eyes appear more intense.

The mysterious stranger stood as if expecting a hero's welcome, "Crow."

Raziel stood beside the confused Hikaru, "Excuse me?"

"I answered the gentleman's question, Crow. I am the one who saved the grand duke from the evil spell of the royal mystic." Crow fibbed.

The crowd loved his showmanship and absorbed as much video and photography of the stranger as possible. Raziel and Hikaru were speechless, unaware if the other had known of this stunt.

"It is true. I saved our kingdom's Raziel from the clutches of Fire starter's evil magic. As you now all can see, I can manifest into many birds and those many birds can remanifest into me, yet while I was in my bird form I was trapped by this royal mystic. Locked away in a bird cage for some of his witchcraft no doubt. I was helpless and could do nothing but watch his trickery, but thankfully I witnessed the measures in which he created this mind control spell. Eventually, I was able to break free of my cage and free Raziel from this terrible spell, but sadly I was not quick enough." Crow lied fooling everyone who listened, aside from Raziel and Hikaru.

"But as Hikaru has stated, we are strong and will not allow this evil wind to blow our great kingdom down. So we must stick together and be united as one more now than ever. And so, for that reason, I have also accepted Hikaru's offer to become the next mystic advisor for the Vailstone kingdom!" Crow announced happily as he walked over to Hikaru and forced his hand shake, both smiling for the cameras.

As the crowds attention was focused on Crow and Hikaru a massive brust of flame exploded within the mass of people. Spectators ran in a panic while other scurried while on fire. Fire starter stood before the three liers with Grunt by his side. "Well, that's a hell of'a story ya got the'ya." he confessed.

"Fire starter?! Come to turn yourself in? Or back to try and finish the job?" Hikaru asked loudly.

Fire starter's rage burned as he refused to stand by as he was being framed as responsible for the death of the king and queen and even worst, blown his cover to the whole world, announcing his location to all enemies of his which may have been watching the news. "Ya lil snot!" he insulted blasting a fire ball from the end of his staff towards Hikaru.

Raziel blocked Hikaru and Crow from the fiery attack, "Fire starter! You're under arrest for treason." Raziel warned.

"Oh? Is that how it is, huh? Well, ol'friend ya seem ta be confused, let'n that arm'a get to yar head!? I've helped ya this whole time n this' what becomes it? Fine, if ya insist n tell'n stories then lemme give ya reason ta tell anoth'a." he said spraying a massive ring of fire around himself and Grunt which protected them from the kingdom soldiers before continuing. "If ya don't confess, n tell everyboda that I'm not ta blame in this whole thang, then I WILL burn this kingdom to tha ground. I'll unleash ALL my summon'ngs to destroy anythin' n' everythang until ya tell tha truth!" Fire starter declared cackling with his terrible laugh.

"Fire starter WAIT!!" Raziel called out.

But it was too late, Fire starter and Grunt both burst into a massive flare that allowed them to vanish. The entire world witnessed the promising threat by Fire starter thanks to the news cameras. Raziel regrettably looked back at a surprised Hikaru, worrying of the coming dangers to be unleashed upon them all.

26

CHRISTIAN'S MOTIVATION

Christian's heart was revived as he witnessed Fire starter's televised threat upon his late father's kingdom.

"I've gotta stop him!" he exclaimed sitting up in his hospital bed. The young man's will for life had returned, with his mother and father passed it was HIS responsibility to protect his birthright. The youthful prince pulled the long plastic tube out of his throat and nostril making him gag. He then removed his I.V. needle out of his forearm, making him bleed a little. Christian stepped out of bed feeling just a tad dizzy, he walked along side his bed with his right arm propping him up. Once he reached the end of the bed he had managed to fully regain his balance, but felt a slight cool breeze. Christian's firm butt was completely exposed thanks to his hosptial attire. The brown haired teen blushed as he tied the back of his hospital gown better.

Christian walked over to an ugly bland dresser in the room and opened each drawer looking for his clothing, but was unsuccessful. A commotion was heard down the hall which intrigued him into peering outside. Through opening his room door a little he saw general Grechov down the hallway with several Vailstone guards surrounding Rufus and asking him many questions. Rufus appeared intimidated, suddenly the entire group began walking swiftly towards Christian's room. The prince closed his door and began panicking. There were too many questions left unanswered and with the state the castle was in he was unaware if Grechov could be trusted or not?!

Christian rushed and looked into the restroom noticing not even an inch to hide, he glanced under his bed and realized it was a terrible spot to hide. He stood up and saw the window and figured that was his only chance. Christian hurried over and tried opening the window but no luck, the hospital window could only be opened 3 inches from the wall for safety purposes. The speedy footsteps of the general could be heard approaching. The prince scanned the room with his eyes wondering where to hide, where to escape? The royal youth's heart skipped a beat as the door began to open.

General Grechov opened the door and instantly noticed the empty bed. He was surprised and angry, he turned his head looking at Rufus, "Where is he?"

Rufus was stunned to see the prince had vanished, "Huh? I dunno? He's supposed to be in here."

"Take him anyways." Grechov ordered.

Kyle Canady

The soldiers accompanying the general arrested Rufus and ascorted him away while Grechov looked about the room. Grechov opened the restroom door, looked underneath the bed, and inside a small closet before walking over to the cracked open window. Grechov felt of the window and could tell it wasn't capable of moving out any further.

"Sir?" a soldier by the door asked questioning for orders.

"He's not here. Scan the building. Search every room, this is our new king we're looking for. Find him!" Grechov ordered.

The soldier had taken his orders and left as Grechov began leaving the room. Christian stood breathing nervously above the ceiling tiles, balancing carefully on small narrow metal strips to support his weight. Grechov began to leave the room until noticing a small drop of Christian's blood on the tile floor. The general touched it with his gloved finger, noticing it was still fresh. He looked near the area for anymore drops of blood and noticed one on the floor near the dresser and even a drop on top of the dresser.

Grechov looked up to the ceiling tiles and saw one of them sitting adjacent to all of the others like it. He climbed the dresser and stood up, unlodging it from its given spot and looking above the ceiling tiles. Grechov squinted his eyes to try and see, giving his vision a moment to adjust to the darkness. After a minute he clearly saw a person balancing through the darkness.

"Christian? Is that you?" Grechov called out.

The prince turned his head quickly seeing Grechov looking directly at him, "No! Stay away! I know what happened!"

General Grechov hoisted himself above the ceiling tiles after Christian, "Don't worry son, it was all the Fire mystic's fault. You can trust us, trust me." Grechov took a few steps in Christian's direction before falling through the ceiling and into the hallway below, which startled everyone.

Soliders and nurses rushed to his aid, but Grechov brushed them away. "Get away from me damn it! The boy's in the ceiling! Get'em, he's above the ceiling! Go!" he ordered his troops after standing his sore butt up from off the ground.

Soldiers began running down the hallway not entirely understanding Grechov's instructions clearly. Christian however, freaked out and tried hurrying which made his footing sloppy.

Eventually, the prince stepped down on the narrow weak metal incorrectly, lost his balance, and broke the metal frame and ceiling tiles below him forcing him to crash down to the hallway floor below. The prince's arm was bruised as he lay on the floor in pain, yet he couldn't stop lest he be taken as Rufus was. A scream was let out as the prince fell through the ceiling only announcing his presence.

A nurse ran over to his aid and grabbed his arm for the soldiers, that way he couldn't escape. Christian stood up, hurting from his fall, and pulled his arm away.

"Let go, let go of me!"

"Don't worry, it's okay. He's over here!" the nurse yelled.

Christian pushed the man down while pulling his arm away, successfully freeing himself. Christian ran over to the elevator doors and pushed the button repeatedly hoping for the doors to open faster. His bloodpressure began to rise as the soldiers spotted him and began persuiting. Christian was hopelessly cornered until the elevator door finally opened. He lept inside finding the button to close the doors and pressed it as soon as he could. A moment sooner and he certainly would have been caught, unfortunately the chase wasn't over just yet.

Grechov stood at the end of the hallway and witnessed his soldiers miss the elevator doors, "Did he go up or down?" he yelled.

"Down, sir! Most likely first floor."

"Take the stairs, beat him. Meet him down there!" Grechov ordered.

The soldiers obeyed their general without hesitation. They burst through the emergency door stairwell running down the stairs. One troop jumped down two flights of stairs, beating the others down to the bottom floor. He ran into the hallway and awaited the elevator doors to open. As soon as the elevator opened the soldier was confused, seeing an old woman connected to her breathing apparatus.

Christian peeked around a door watching the soldiers. He slowly closed the door to the room he had entered. The prince still needed to hide, it wouldn't be long before they came looking for him in this room as well. He turned around seeing multiple rows of church pews, stained glass windows, and a statue of Jesus Christ in the front and center of the room. Christian walked towards the staute looking for somewhere to hide securely and safely. There, beside the staute, sat many beautiful potted plants and a piano nearby. The prince began to hear voices coming from a room connected to his and layed down behind the many plants.

An emotionally scarred mother and father walked out of a room with a blond man dressed in black and white robes. The father held some folded clothing in his arms and slowly handed them over to the man in robes.

"Here, father. These were his favorite clothes, please give them to another young man who will appreciate them." he asked woefully.

"I will. God bless you brother." the blond man replied. "How about one last prayer before you go?"

The mother and father bowed their heads with the man in robes as Christian watched through the plant life.

"Dear heavenly father, we ask that you help guide brother and sister Ramos in their time of pain. Help them to understand your plan and to assist them in finding forgiveness to the lost soul who crashed into them the other day, taking their only son. I ask that for the holy spirit to help them in strength, and help them to stay true to their paths. We ask that....." the reverend was inturrupted as the hospital church doors flew open, startling the recovering parents. "Amen, I'm sorry, is there a problem gentlemen?"

General Grechov marched into the room with three soldiers looking under the pews and inside a utility closet, "Go check that room in there." Grechov ordered.

"Excuse me, what's going on here?" the reverend wondered.

"Have any of you seen a young brown haired boy running around in a hospital gown?" Grechov questioned.

"No sir, we were right in the middle of prayer here."

"Pray I'm forgiven." Grechov replied rudely. He looked to the soldiers that entered the other room and was notified it was clear. "Back into the hospital then." he ordered while motioning them to leave with his two fingers.

"We'll be back father." the husband informed as he left the church with his wife.

The reverend nodded "God bless you."

As the husband and wife left he turned to the impatient general.

"What's the matter? What has this young man done?" the reverend inquired.

"We're looking for the prince. If you'd turn on the 'devil' everynow and then and watch the news, you'd know what's going on." Grevoch sarcastically answered.

"Trouble with religion brother?" the pastor asked.

Grechov smirked while walking towards the exit, "I don't have a problem, I just have a hard time talking with imaginary friends." he smarted back before leaving the church.

"Asshole." the reverend answered back under his breath. He started walking back to his study while holding the deceased boy's clothes in his hands until he noticed Christian's naked butt pop up on the other side of the arrangements with his peripheral vision. "Hello?" he called out.

The prince stopped not to cause suspecion.

"Could you please stand up." he paused. "Um, I can see your butt."

Christian quickly stood to his feet in embarrassment.

"Prince Dalton?"

"You gonna tell Grechov I'm here?"

"Should I?"

Christian shook his head answering 'no'.

"You running because of what happened at the kingdom this morning?"

Christian nodded his head 'yes'.

"Did you come here to talk to me about it?"

"No, I came in here on accident." Christian told him.

"If that's what you want to believe." the reverend replied.

"What do you mean, 'what I want to believe'?" Christian asked.

"Perhaps you were guided here by something? Rather than just, stumbling here on accident?"

"I need to go." the prince said.

"You won't get very far in those hospital clothes there." he said grabbing the prince's attention. "I 'just so happen' to have an extra pair of clothes over here, 'if that's what you'd like yourself to believe'. I mean, you're welcome to them if you like."

"I thought those people wanted you to give them to somebody in need?" Christian wondered.

"Yes, someone who I felt would appreciate them and I can't think of anyone else who would appreciate some nice clothes than a half naked prince. Besides, I think the previous owner would think it pretty cool for, of all people, a prince to wear his outfit now." he smiled.

Christian walked over to the reverend and was given the clothes, "Thanks. Why are you being so helpful?" he asked.

"Do you not appreciate my helpfulness?"

"I do." Christian answered.

"And that's why. Oh, you can change in there if you like." the reverend stated. Christian began to walk into the other room before the blond man spoke again, "Also, ya might wanna be more cautious about saying that in a church ya know."

The prince looked back, "What?"

"I do!" the man said laughing from his own joke. "Because you're in...a church! Marriage, 'I do'." he chuckled. He could see the joke was lost on Christian, "Never mind, you'll laugh later." he said wiping away a tear.

The prince closed the door to the study and undressed completely, he looked at the outfit and noticed an interesting spiral shell necklace. He thought it was neat and wore it around his neck before dressing in the remaining clothes. Christian put on the last article of clothing, a dark gray jacket and looked in a fancy mirror inside the study. He judged himself from front to back, "I like it."

Christian walked out of the study and looked at the reverend, "It's a perfect fit."

"I figured somehow it would be." he admitted smiling. "Now what will you do?"

"I have to go, I need to fix whats happened somehow."

"And how will you do that?"

"Um, I dunno. I just know I have to stop Fire starter and Raziel, I'll figure something out."

"Raziel? The grand duke?"

"He killed my parents. I have to find a way to make things right."

The sound of many people running down the hallway began to grow closer and closer to the church entrance. The reverend pushed Christian inside the study and locked the door from the inside.

"What's going on?" Christian wondered.

"It sounds as if your friend is back for you again."

"Grechov!" Christian announced.

The pastor hurried over to his stain glass window, "Here, you can get out through here young prince."

Christian ran over to the window, "Thanks for all your help, I never even got your name." he realized.

"Luke Winters, now hurry." he stated as Grechov began pounding on the studyroom door.

Christian climbed out of the window, but Winters grabbed his wrist at the last moment, "Huh?"

"Young prince, keep in mind, revenge is a dark path, if traveled, it won't lead you to happiness." Winters warned before releasing Christian's arm.

Christian paused for a brief moment absorbing the man's warning, but soon after ran along the side of the building until he was able to turn a corner and disappear inside the city. Soon the doors to the study room burst open.

"Where is he? Where's the boy?" Grechov questioned.

Winters moved away from the window, "What ARE you talking about?"

"Security footage showed the prince ran into the church."

"Then I would advise searching the church, wouldn't you agree." Winters replied.

General Grechov motioned for his soldiers to search the church and study for the prince, "What are you doing by the window?"

"Talking with my friend until you showed up." he replied sarcastically.

Grechov glared at the reverend while the rooms were searched.

"It's entirely clear sir, he's not here." the soldier informed.

"Then find him elsewhere." Grechov ordered in a stern voice without looking away from reverend Winters. He then turned away and followed the Vailstone soldiers out of the church once again. Slamming the door on his way out.

27

HOUSE ARREST

Raziel and Hikaru left the courtyard, returning inside the castle with Crow. Firefighters had immediately arrived to extinguish the fires caused by Fire starter. News stories of the event went viral all over the internet and T.V.

"I can't do this, Fire starter isn't bluffing. He WILL send out whatever he's got and he WILL burn Vailstone to the ground. I have to tell everyone the truth." Raziel explained.

The grand duke began marching outside to confess, but Hikaru jumped in his way to stop him. Without any effort what-so-ever Raziel accidentally knocked Hikaru to the ground.

"Oh! I'm sorry Yotameshii." Raziel apologized reaching out to assist the ambassador up from off the ground.

"You can't NOW! It's much too late for that. You want us to appear as murderers and liers? We'll either have to call out Fire man's bluff or stop him once he attacks." Hikaru demanded.

"I agree with Hikaru." Crow inturrupted.

The grand duke and ambassador both slowly turned their sights on the man in the black dress simultaneously.

"And you. Who in the hell ARE you?" Hikaru addressed.

"My name is Crow, I'm new around here. I'm your new mystic advisor." he responded with cold eyes, not even looking Hikaru's direction.

"Why in the hell do you think YOU'RE our new mystic advisor?" Yotameshii questioned with attitude.

"Um, because I know you lied to those people. I know the spell on Raziel didn't happen and you want to give me this cushiony mystic job to keep me quiet." Crow threatened.

"URGH!!!! You think you can blackmail ME and just get away with it?!" Hikaru warned.

"What will you do about it?" Crow tested.

"Yes, Hikaru. What are you going do?" Raziel asked as well, except his tone of question was more of a warning to Hikaru, not to lose his head. "It only seems right, we can't lie without expecting consequences in return."

"Alright! Fine." Hikaru caved and adjusted his coat and tie, "So? How are you so sure we misspoke anyways?"

"Please, spare me the political phrases will you?" Crow answered, "Anyway you spin it, a lie is a lie."

Hikaru was even more put off by their new mystic advisor, seeing through the ambassador's political safety words.

"So how did you know we lied?" Raziel asked bluntly despite Hikaru's concern.

"Let's just say, a little birdie told me." Crow explained as a small bird, which was in the chamber room Raziel was locked in, flew to him and into the darkness of his black cape.

"Well, that explains that then doesn't it." Hikaru snubbed. "It looks like we'll need to figure out a story so we're all in sync with each other."

"We certainly wouldn't want to misspeak incorrectly now." Crow poked.

"Yotameshii, sir! A message from General Grechov, he says he has obtained one of the swordsman and is close to cathing the prince as well. The prince had escaped but is nearby, most likely confused and scared by recent events." a solider ran up informing.

"Christian." Raziel stated under his breath with sympathy.

"Excellent, Grechov already has one of them." the ambassador stated pleased.

"One of them? 'The seven chosen'? What's the point in bringing them in? So our stories line up?" Raziel inquired.

"Partly, I'm just a little worried about those swords of their's is all."

"Why is that?" Raziel wondered Hikaru's meaning, "You seriously think they'll run wild with those swords of theirs?"

"As far as I'm concerned they're Vailstone property. They were found during our mission and with the use of our army. Secondly, those seven swords were with that armor for a reason, I'm sure of it. If we're not careful, those seven swords might actually be able to counter act the power of that armor of your's." Hikaru warned, "I don't like loose ends, that's why Lieutenant Brookes is on her way now to bring us another of those swords." he smiled.

"Where have you sent her?" Raziel asked.

Outside Wade's estate two Vailstone kingdom offical jeeps pulled up to the gate. Lieutenant Brookes drove one while Chase and Lee sat in the back seat.

"No, no, no. I'm saying Fire starter probably has psychic powers and THAT'S how he controlled the grand duke." Lee explained in serious converstaion with Chase.

"Yeah, well I heard that Fire starter is actually the grand duke's REAL father and that he carried out the hot head's orders to please his dad." Chase informed.

"No way."

"Yep."

"And just where did you hear that dumb story?"

"I'll have you know it was reported by none other than Pip Gordan himself." Chase stated.

"Oh wow, you really think it's true? Now that I think about it, I've never recalled meeting his father before." Lee realized.

"You wanna know something weird? Me neither." Chase replied with a straight face.

"Would you two idiots keep quiet and stay focused. Ugh." Miranda scorned, "That doesn't prove anything, neither of you have ever met my dad either. Doesn't mean Fire starter is my father too."

Chase and Lee both sat in complete shock, mouths open, and eyes widened soley focused on her as they began wondering who was truely the lieutenant's real father!

As soon as the Vailstone vehicles parked the lieutenant and her soliders were at the mansion's front doors. The Smith estate butler answered the door normaly, but he was certainly surprised to have guests of the royal family's army present. Without hesitation the butler acquiesced the lieutenant's request and lead her and the soldiers to Wade.

"Master Smith, Lieutenant Brookes of Vailstone is here to see you sir."

Wade stood from his couch quickly, "What!? Lieutenant Brookes from the castle?! What. Why? Um, ugh, just tell her that I'm a sleep. No, that's dumb."

"You're out or something." Amanda joined in.

"Yeah, that's better." he exclaimed snapping his fingers, "Tell her that I'm out or something like that."

"I probably won't believe that one as much." Miranda answered back stepping from behind the butler.

"Of course not." Wade chuckled embarrassingly. He walked over to greet Miranda with her troops behind her, "A true pleasure. Not the female company I was expecting, but a true pleasure non-the-less." Wade announced holding the lieutenant's hand and giving it a gentle kiss.

"Wade Smith, I am here on behalf of the authority of the kingdom of Vailstone. Your presence is requested at the castle immediately." Brookes stated.

"Hold on, by who's authority exactly? The king and queen are dead! Who's calling these shots now? The..the duke?" Amanda questioned without hast.

"I'm sorry, but who are you?" Miranda asked.

"Amanda Jones, and if he goes, then I'm going as well."

"I'm sorry Mr.Smith, but your girlfriend must remain here."

Wade and Amanda both instantly began correcting the lieutenant's error at the same time.

"Whoa, time out there. We're not a couple." Wade laughed.

"Oh, you misunderstood, I'm single."

"I've just known her for a long time. Since I was a kid in fact."

"Well there is this cute guy that works behind the counter at one of Wade's clubs, but I don't know. I mean, I'm the manager so don't you think that would be a little taboo?"

"She's not like my other female friends, we've never even slept together."

"Besides, Wade is a really good friend and all, but he's too much of a leture."

"I'd only gotten as far as touching her boob, and she got all mad at me about it. Then again she was unconscious."

"I have standards and too much self-respect to allow myself to be with somebody like him."

"It's not like I killed anybody. I just like boobs."

7 Blades of Legend

Everyone stood silent and lost while hearing the rambles of the two friends. Chase and Lee's eyes slowly glanced at each other before focusing back on Wade and Amanda.

Miranda closed her eyes and shook her head as if returning back to her cognitive senses. She extended her hand outward towards him, "Mr. Smith, if you would please?"

"Right now? In front of everyone?" Wade asked.

"Uh, yes." Miranda answered a tad confused.

"Well, okay." Wade began walking over to Miranda.

"Wade?! Hold up, how do you know you can trust th..e....." Amanda stopped her reservations about Wade leaving with them once she noticed Wade walk over to Miranda and squeeze on her boob.

Wade smiled happily, "Thank you, you have no idea how badly I wanted to do this."

"What are you doing?" Brookes questioned.

"Accepting your offer. Oh, or better yet, 'following orders'." he winked.

"I meant for you to come with us, not touch me." she clarified.

"Oh!" he laughed, "I thought cause I said. Cause I like boobs. I totally misread you there." he struggled explaining while laughing with embarrassment.

"Idiot." Amanda said to herself.

"Amanda I'll be back, just watch over everything for me while I'm gone will ya?"

"You can't be serious? You're leaving with them?"

Wade leaned in Amanda's direction, "If any thing is wrong I'll get the hell outta there. Plus, you can be more helpful to me out here than in there if any thing rotten happens. Besides, I can't put you in any more danger."

"Because of what happened at the 'Golden Ticket'? That was just..."

"No, I can't" he interrupted with empathy.

Amanda paused for a moment, being surprised by the rare occasion of Wade's conscious rearing its head.

"Um, Mr.Smith..." Miranda butted in, "..you can let go of my boob now."

"Oh!? Are you sure?"

"I'm about to break your wrist." she warned.

Wade quickly removed his hand, "Well thank you, I appreicate the warning lieutenant."

"Do you also have your sword with you?"

"Yes, should I leave it?"

"No, it's probably best to bring it with you." she hypothesized.

Wade walked out of his mansion with the Vailstone soldiers while Amanda watched through the other side of a window. She had a negative feeling in her gut about the entire situation. Amanda was distracted for a slight moment of Pip Gordan's voice on the television mentioning a U.F.O. sighting over the Vailstone castle just before the king was murdered. She ignored the stupidity, turned off the T.V., and watched them drive away.

Else where, deep inside the woods bordering the kingdom, Fire starter stood with Grunt beside him. The entire surrounding area was scorched, even the soil on which they stood was burned to ash cinders. Large flaming footsteps lead one direction, heavy indentations in the ruined ground pointed off a seperate direction, leaving the fire weilding instigator in the center of many tracks. The fire elemental was determined to force the truth from Raziel and well on his threat.

"The'ya, wanna announce ta tha world where I'm at? Then we gotta make an example of'em Grunt!" the elemental angrily stated.

"..............................,...........!" Grunt added.

"Percisly."

28

GENEROSITY OF A GYPSY

Fire starter and Grunt began leaving the torched area after releasing the fire elemental's nine remaining summonings. As the two instigators began walking further into the forest Grunt heard a rustling in near by brush.

"..........." Grunt warned.

Fire starter stopped walking, "Hm? Think sumbody try'n ta get tha jump on us ah? Well, come on out'ya cowa'd!" the fire user threatened. He cluthed his staff in preparations for a fight.

Another shrub was disturbed as someone ran by it, kicking with their leg. The mystic and suit of armor both turned to see the spy, but saw no one. Both stood back to back ready and waiting for the intruder to expose themself. When suddenly an individual jumped through the greenery and landed before them both.

"SAMMY SAMMY SEVEN!" he yelled.

Fire starter and Grunt jumped in surprise, but were quickly annoyed. One of Fire starter's summonings, number seven, had been following them. A six foot tall mountain of muscle who's sadly lacking in the speach department. For Fire starter however, it wasn't the fact that Sammy sammy seven was stupid that annoyed him most, it was that he was incapable of not yelling everytime he spoke.

"Numb'a seven, what'r ya do'n he'ya?! Yer supposed'ta be out burn'n tha kingdom down with tha oth'a sum'nings." Fire starter scolded.

"SAMMY SAMMY!" Sammy sammy seven explained in a yelling boisterous voice.

"I don't need protection, I got Grunt."

"SEVEN SAMMY SEVEN!" he yelled.

"............................" Grunt defended.

"Ugh, screw it! Juss whateva! Let's go." the hot tempered elemental griped.

Fire starter, Grunt, and Sammy sammy seven disappeared as they marched deeper into the dark woods together.

Mean while, princess Alisha continued treversing through the darkening woods. The horrific day began to close, the blue sky began to transform into a heavy purple and fade into black. She eventually, after a fair amount of time traveling, sat down on a large tree root next to her shark dog friend. Vincent stood close by incase of danger while Wraith wondered off.

"Wraith seems to have been gone a long time, don't you think?" the princess asked.

"Yeah, hm. It is possible he's been eat'n I suppose." Bo thought out loud.

Alisha gasped, "You think so?"

"Possible, there's a lot of scary monsters in these magical woods ya know. Ogres, trolls, goblins, fairies, all sorts a stuff. Maybe we shouldn't have let the little tyke wonder off by himself." Bo figured.

Alisha began to worry, not only for herself, but Wraith and the others as well. "Vincent, do you think Wraith is okay?"

"Pft, I dunno. What? You care?" Vincent snipped back.

Alisha easily picked up on Vincent's negative attitude, "Yes as a matter of fact I do." she replied gaining Vincent's attention quickly. "I think there's been enough people,...." she stuttered a swallowed, "..getting hurt today. I can't deal with anymore." she teared up.

"Oh look what ya did there ya big jerk! Ya made her cry." Bo barked, "There, there princess I'm here for ya."

Vincent was shocked, he didn't give a damn about Wraith's saftey, but he certainly didn't like to make girls cry. Especailly a girl he found particularly interesting. "Wha?" his jaw dropped, "You're crying. Stop crying."

"I'm not crying!" she quipped back while crying softly.

"Ya big jerk! That's no way to stop somebody from crying." Bo complained.

"Is this really cause of Wraith or your dead parents?" he asked.

"You're such a jerk!" the princess yelled with watery eyes. She swung her arm in Vincent's direction hitting his braced arm to protect himself.

"Geez, just be thankful ya had parents will ya?"

"Hm?" she sniffled, "Your's are gone too?"

"Ha. Yeah, their gone alright. Cast me aside like a bag of trash." he explained reliving the burden.

"So? Their alive?" she sniffled.

"I dunno, who cares." he shrugged his shoulders. "They didn't want me and I don't want them."

"Why? What happened?"

"Ugh, would you drop it already? Damn. How did we get to talking about me anyways?"

The princess stopped for a moment, and looked away then scratched Bo's ear, "You don't like talking about yourself, do you?" she sniffled

Vincent sighed and ran his hand through his hair, "Ugh. No."

"Why is that?"

"Really?" he asked back looking towards her.

"Fine." she stopped for a brief moment. The silence however was soon broken yet again by another question. "Do you really think their both dead?"

"I don't know and I don't care, can we drop it already?"

"I meant mom and dad." she explained softly.

"What a jerk." Bo scorned.

Vincent actually felt a bit like a jerk, "Oh." he paused. "Yeah." He took a deep breath and walked over to the princess. As he sat down near her he looked away, "I'm sorry."

The princess toughened, "For what?"

"Ya know. You cried. I didn't mean to make you."

"I don't believe you." she accused.

"Huh? I didn't." he defended.

"Not that. I don't think you're really sorry."

"What?! Fine, whatever. Forget it then."

The princess gasped, "You're so rude."

"Me? I'm the one who apologized and YOU called me a lier."

"Well it certainly didn't sound sincere."

"Well I don't make a habit of apologizing to people. Damn, first time I do and I'm called a lier for it. Glad to see my words are meaningless, thanks." he replied with sarcasim.

Alisha had noticed she offeneded the silver haired teen. She placed her hands in her lap while looking down, "I'm the first person you've ever apologized to? So, you don't feel you've ever done anybody wrong before?"

"Didn't say that, just never cared to apologize to those people."

The princess blushed as she heard the messege through his strong words, "Then I'm sorry."

"Hm?"

"Thank you. It makes me feel kinda, special." she said looking away.

"Why?"

"Well, to be the first. I just didn't know you cared about me enough to apologize." she explained peering towards him.

Vincent swiftly looked her in the eyes and darted his head another direction to hide his blushing face, "I, um. Well, that's not exactly what I said." he recovered.

"What a dip." Bo said to himself.

"So, you care about Wraith huh?"

"Well, yeah. Right now I'll admit, I'm a little concerned for his well being. He has been gone a good while." she answered.

"Oh. Yeah." Vincent replied with a hinted lack of emotion due to hearing Alisha's concern for Wraith. "She cares about him?" he thought to himself.

The concerned princess continued disrupting the silence with further questions, "What about my brother?"

"Hm? What about him?"

"Do you think, he too is..." the lonely blonde couldn't bring herself to finishing her own question.

Vincent began to answer the girl's question, but stopped as he heard movement growing near. He jumped to his feet as did the others. He withdrew his dual blade katanas as he readied for what approached, but lowered his guard once he visibly identified it was in fact Wraith.

"On edge squirt?" Wraith mocked.

"Where you been this whole time?" Vincent inquired.

"I told you I'd look for some shelter stupid."

"Yeah, but I didn't know you were gonna take a nap first! Might as well of caught a movie while you were at it." Vincent returned.

The princess chimed in just in time to cut off Wraith's reply, "We were just worried that's all."

Wraith smirked and looked at Vincent, "Awe, wittle Vincent miss me?" he mocked as if talking to a baby.

"Screw off." Vincent stated.

"Hey! So? Did ya find anything?" Bo added in.

"Well, all I could find was a small bridge. We could sleep under that until morning. Should be pretty safe." Wraith answered.

"Under a bridge?" Alisha gasped.

"You expect a princess to sleep under a bridge like some hobo?" Vincent griped.

"Hey, we don't exactly have any hotel reservations out here. Unless you can pull a tent outta your ass that's the only option we've got." Wraith argued.

"You moth'a....." Vincent started.

"WAIT a second, wait a second!" Bo interrupted and sniffed the air, "I smell something. It smells like cooking meat." he informed licking his chops.

"Really? Where?" the blonde beauty wondered.

"It, it's coming from this direction." Bo pointed. "Come on, maybe there's a cabin we can sleep in?"

"Hold up, what if it's some Vailstone soldiers setting up camp out here looking for Alisha?" Wraith warned.

"Then we'll be careful." she said following Bo as he wondered off, "Come on."

The two swordsmen looked at each other with uncertainty before following after. The sun had long since set and darkness blanketed not only the sky, but the woods as well. Twinkling stars dangled over head as the three teenagers followed the sniffing sharkdog. Slight movement in the distance was heard around them from time to time. Sometimes from the ground and at other moments in the trees above making them more on edge. Finally, the glimmering shine of a small campfire was noticed several feet away.

"Hey, see that?" Bo asked happily.

"Shhhh, be quite." Vincent warned as they moved in closer.

The small group hid behind two trees, Alisha and Bo behind one while Wriath and Vincent hid behind the other. They peered around each tree to witness the owner of the campfire. As the four spied it was obvious it was only a single man traveling with a stage carriage who had set up camp for the night. Bo was drooling at the mouth as he became hypnotized by the delicious smell of the cooked sausage. The hungry shark dog leaned closer toward the odor, unfortunately in doing so he tripped an extremely thin wire with small bells tied to it causing them to jingle. The man turned in their direction once he was notified of their presence.

He was a man of average height with very baggy clothing. He wore a bandana on his head and around his neck, one peircing on the side of his nose, and multiple in his ears. On his shoulder, sitting with in his long black hair sat a small pet ferret. The tanned man had many belts one which contained a holster with a gun and another holding a sheath and sword.

"Who goes there?!" he yelled with concern.

"Please don't panic, we're coming out." Alisha warned. Despite Vincent and Wraith motioning for her to stay back the princess proceeded anyhow. "I am princess Alisha of Vailstone." she informed with her hands suspended in front of her.

Bo followed Alisha mimicing her with his paws in front of him as well, though his attention was soley on the cooking sausages.

"A princess, huh?" the man questioned.

"What're you crazy? You can't just announce to the world you're a princess." Wraith warned as he and Vincent stepped out from behind the trees.

"Oh? Um, how many more of you are hiding out there?" he wondered.

"Why?" Vincent returned.

"Well, I would like to simply rest easy tonight." he replied.

"It's just us four. I promise." the buxom girl declared.

"A princess' promise, well that's as good as gold." the man bowed slightly in the presence of the blonde beauty. "And what do I owe this pleasure?"

"We're hungry." Bo inturrupted.

"Oh? Certainly not for long, please sit down with me by the campfire. It's not much, but I can roast more if you like. It's not everday I am given the chance to dine with royalty."

"If it's not too much trouble." she asked softly.

"Certainly, um, pardon me for just a moment." the man stepped inside his stage carriage for a moment to collect more food.

"What makes you think we can trust this guy? He looks like he's dressed like a gypsy or something." Vincent pointed out.

"So? What's wrong with being a gypsy?"

"Have you ever stepped foot out of your comfy castle? Gypsy's are crooks and can't be trusted." Wraith added.

"Isn't that ironic." Vincent muttered glaring at Wraith.

"I'm starving and Bo too. We'll just be careful. Besides, I have my two body guards with me." she smiled.

Wraith and Vincent looked at each other, "Body guards?"

The man stepped out of his stage carriage with additional foods for roasting over the fire. "Please, sit. Sit."

The three teens and single shark dog walked over to the campfire and each sat down. Alisha sat on an upside down bucket while the two boys sat in the leaves with Bo.

"So what brings an angel like yourself this deep into creepy woods such as these?" he asked while placing more food in the fire.

Vincent and Wraith glared at the strange man with hate as he tried flattering Alisha. The two teens weren't fond of the idea of him moving in on 'their' girl. The princess smiled from the compliment before allowing it to fade away. "My kingdom was attacked early this morning. I fled with my two body guards for safety."

"That's awful. Any idea of who would do such a thing?" he asked.

"It was our own grand duke. He took possession of something that belonged to my father, the king."

"That's terrible."

"After doing so, he killed my mother and I'm fairly certain he's killed my father as well."

"Oh my God, you poor dear. You must be a strong young woman." he assumed.

"Oh, no. I've cried all day. My eyes hurt from all the tears actually." she woefully smirked.

"Well, a tear doesn't mean weakness. It's the truely weak that cannot cry."

A comment which caused Vinecent and Wraith to roll their eyes.

"Here ya go, eat up." he said handing her over a roasted sausage."

"Thank you." she thanked before taking a bite.

"You two seem a bit young for body guards." he continued while eating.

"So." Wraith replied as Vincent said nothing.

Everyone ate around the camp fire before the stranger broke the silence again, "So what's your course of action now? I mean, doesn't this make you a queen?"

Alisha was stunned for a slight moment, "I hadn't thought about it actually." she paused, "I suppose......I must avenge my parents. I couldn't live with myself knowing their murderer wandered freely."

"Pft, how are you going to stop Raziel?" Vincent inquired.

"I don't know, but we'll figure something out. I'm sure of it."

"'We'?" Wraith inturrupted, "What's this 'we'? I'm not getting involved."

"You're already involved." Bo stated.

"Not anymore. Fighting Raziel in that armor is a death sentence. Screw that."

"Wraith? I can't do this alone." she teared up. "I'm all by myself, I don't know what to do." she began crying.

"Smooth move jack-ass." Vincent whispered Wraith's direction.

"Well, maybe I can help." the man stated reaching into his deep pockets. Alisha was curious, 'what could this man do to help stop Raziel?'. He pulled out a bottle smaller than a finger, cupped the girl's hands, and handed it over.

"Hm?" she sniffled, "What's this?"

"It's a poison." he replied.

"WHAT!? SUICIDE'S NOT THE WAY YOU FREAK'N IDIOT!" Vincent yelled jumping to his feet.

"No, no. It's not that kind of poison. It's zamora."

"What's, zamora?" Alisha wondered.

"It's a poison that helps you forget. The story is that a great wizard was known around the north for his powerful potions, he was like the best or something. Anyway, he lost his one true love and couldn't bare the pain. He felt so lost that he created zamora. After he drank it, he forgot all about what hurt him most."

The princess looked at the tiny bottle, "How could he do that? How could he forget about what brought him so much happiness before?" she shook her head 'no' and handed the small bottle back to the oddly dressed man, "I'm sorry, but I couldn't. I couldn't bare the thought of forgetting about my family. I'm sorry, but thank you."

The man refused to take the bottle back, "No, no. You keep it. Think of it as a gift."

"Hey, we never got your name." Vincent announced with suspecion.

"Oh my God you're right. I am Enrique. It means 'lord of the manor'." he explained kissing Alisha's hand.

"You know what your name means?" Wraith questioned.

"Of course I do. Such as the lovely Alisha's here, 'protected by God'. You truely are an angel." he said making the princess blush.

"Well, well my name's Bo. What's it mean?" he asked excitedly.

"Bo? Hm, let see." he thought for a brief moment, "Ah yes, 'to live' or 'to dwell'."

Bo's enthusiasm suffered greatly, "Well that doesn't sound very awesome." he groaned folding his tiny arms.

"Hey silver, I don't remember catching your name." he smiled.

Vincent just looked towards Enrique with extreme dissatisfaction while chewing his food. "Vincent." Alisha stated, locking eyes with him for a long second before looking to their new friend for a response.

"Oh! Vincent, I remember that one well. It means 'conquering' or 'to win'."

Enrique then looked at Wraith last, "Wraith, right?"

"I know what Wraith means. I gave it to myself."

"What does it mean Wraith?" Bo wondered.

"A Wraith is kinda like a ghost, but shaped like a person even though it ain't. It appears before you, right before you die. It's the last thing you see." he explained.

"That's creepy. Why would you call yourself something like that for?" Bo asked further.

"Cause when I was with my crew and we ran into trouble," he paused as if recollecting moments in the past, "I was the last thing they saw."

"'Peanutbutter licker'."

Enrique's random statement gathered everyone's attention around the campfire.

"What?" Wraith asked.

"Or 'to lick nut butter'." Enrique smiled.

"What the hell are you talking about?"

"'Wraith', it means 'peanutbutter licker' or 'to lick nut butter'. I don't know where you got that other information from, but that's something else you're talking about there."

"That's not what it means." Wraith snapped back.

"Calm down 'nut licker'." Vincent smirked.

"Shut up!" Wraith warned.

"'Nut butter licker'." Bo corrected.

"Would you drop it!" Wraith yelled.

Enrique clapped his hands, "Very well, perhaps we should call it a night. Um, where will you all be sleeping tonight?"

"Oh, um, I don't know." Alisha wondered looking around noticing nothing but trees, leaf patches on the ground, and a few rocks.

"Well, in the dirt of a dark forest is no place for a princess to sleep." enrique motioned to his stage carriage, "You could sleep in the carriage with me if you like. It's much safer than the open wilderness, that's for sure." he smiled innocently.

"She stays with us." Wraith proclaimed.

Alisha noticed a certain determination in Wraith's eyes, "Yeah, we'll, we'll figure something out."

"Alright, suit yourselves." he began making his way to the carriage before stopping, "Actually, now that I think about it. I might have something. Hold on just a sec." he said stepping into the carriage.

Wraith walked over to Alisha, "You can't sleep in there with him. I don't trust this guy."

"I wasn't going to do that." she stated. "What's up with you two? Why are you guys always so negative? I swear you two probably hate everyone you meet."

Enrique started stepping out of the large carriage, but with resistance. In his hands was a large folded tent, which didn't pass through the carriage door very well.

"Come on Vincent, let's give'm a hand." Bo asked slapping on his arm. Vincent hesitated for minute before huffing and walking over to Enrique and Bo to help out.

Alisha and Wraith stood by the fire while the others pulled the large tent from the carriage. Small flickering embers floated from the campfire and drifted around the two while standing alone surrounded by darkness.

"You're wrong just so ya know." Wraith said easily.

"Hm?"

"About what you said a second ago. You were right, to say I hate a lot of people. But, I don't hate everybody." he continued softly.

Alisha looked at Wraith, he spoke softer than before. The tone of his voice had a level of comfort she hadn't heard before. The light of the campfire danced in his eyes as they were focused on hers.

"A part of the tent is caught right there, in the corner." Bo pointed out.

"Where? Can you get it silver?" Enrique asked.

"I've got it." Vincent groaned, "Just lose the nickname." Vincent moved around to the make an adjustment on the tent so the full object would fit through the doorway, but as he looked back at the campfire he noticed Wraith walk over to princess Alisha and softly grab her hand. He froze for a slight moment until further questioning from Enrique snapped him out of it. "Oh, uh yeah. Um, I got it." he said freeing the tent from the carriage.

Alisha saw Wraith move in close and removed her hand from his. She inhaled quickly and held her hands against her chest. Looking into Wraith's eyes, seeing a part of him she hadn't before.

"Tent's ready!" Bo happily yelled to them.

"That was fast." Wraith noticed.

"Yes, it was." Alisha agreed also refering to Wraith's actions.

"It was a pop-up tent." Bo said speedily wandering inside, "It's so big! I've never slept in one of these before." he said as his silhouette jumped up and down inside.

Vincent was upset and laid down inside the tent with some pillows and blankets given by Enrique.

"You two outta get inside there soon, there's no tell'n what's out here at night." Enrique warned with a smile, "Goodnight now." The long haired man climbed into his stage carriage and shut his door for the night.

Wraith walked over to the tent and stepped inside, "Come on Alisha, let's go ta sleep." Bo smiled largely.

The princess walked away from the weakening campfire and to the energetic shark dog.

The night sky was a comfortable black with twinkling stars scattered across the night sky. The forest was quiet and the terrible day finally came to a rest. The princess laid between her two new 'body guards' with a snuggly shark dog cuddling to her side. Before she drifted off to sleep she couldn't help but remember the tragedy that befell her parents and wondered, what was the condition of her older brother.

29

MENDING BONDS

Night had fallen over Vailstone kingdom and while the princess was sleeping under the roof of a tent the same couldn't be said for the lonely prince. It had been quite sometime since he had run away from the hospital and unfortunately eaten as well. Christian wandered under the night's blanket of stars. He was somewhat cold and his stomach constantly growled. The young prince held his belly while slowly entering a vast and empty park.

He walked a paved trail seeing playground equipment thanks to the stars twilight. A pond absent of any ducks harbored a park bench near the edge of the water. The brown haired teen walked over and sat down to rest his tired feet. His legs were sore from all the running and walking. Dodging into allyways so as not to be seen. He was uncertain of who he coud trust anymore. He looked up at the bright twinlking stars with exhaustion.

"What am I doing? All I wanted was to have an adventure of my own. Was that so much to ask for?" he questioned the sky. The boy began to muster tears, "Why did this happen? What DID I DO?!" he yelled. "What am I supposed to do now?"

Christian wiped the moisture from his eyes and sniffed for his runny nose. He tried to be strong but the pain was too much. The prince began crying again, tears fell from his cheeks onto his shirt and vest, but what distracted Christian from his misery was what happen once one of his tears dripped inside the spiral sea shell on the end of his necklace.

A tiny pink light shimmered from inside the sea shell for a small moment, but long enough for Christian to notice.

"Huh? Pink light?"

Christian grabbed the necklace and inspected it for a brief moment, but saw nothing unusual. "I could have sworn I just saw..." he stopped looking into the opening of the small shell.

As the boy peered inside again a small flicker of pink light flashed from deep with-in letting out a tiny bit of glitter into his face.

"Ah! Ptf, pft." he shook his face to scatter the pink glitter, "What tha heck was that? What's in there?"

"Excuse me?" a tiny voice asked.

"Huh? Who's there?" he questioned looking behind him and around the park bench.

"Oh, now I'm a 'who' and not a 'what'?"

"Hey? Is somebody inside there?" he inquired poking at the shell.

"Hey, stop it. Cut it out." the voice ordered.

"What's going on here?" he asked as his tears began to dry up. Christian blew inside the shell to try forcing what or who was inside out.

At that time a burst of pink light flew out of the sea shell and into Christian's face. A small pixie flew before him surrounded by pink glitter and shining light. Her tiny body had long wings attached to her back which allowed her to fly about. The small pixie was no larger than a small cup, her eyes were black, and her hair a ruby red.

"What's your problem tapping on people's houses and blowing inside, huh? You think you're some kind of big bad wolf?"

Christian gasped with amazment, "I've never seen a fairy before."

"Excuse me?! A FAIRY?! I'm a pixie you stupid jerk!"

"Hey, sorry. Geez, I've never met a fairy OR a pixie before."

"Well congratulations to you." The pixie flew back just an inch or two taking notice of the clothes the prince was wearing, "What are you doing wearing my master's clothes?"

"Oh, I got these from that preacher back at the..." then Christian realized the fate of the pixie's late master. "Oh, um, I'm not really sure how to tell you this but, your master passed away. His parent's handed over these clothes."

"Duh stupid. I know he's dead. Just because I don't blubber about dead people like you do doesn't mean I don't know. What I'm saying is WHY are YOU wearing his clothes."

"Hey! Like I said they were given to me. And you're a mean little bug."

"BUG!? Ugh, you don't deserve to wear my master's clothes."

"Well, I'm not walking around naked so deal with it."

"Urgh!" the little pixie was certainly upset Christian was wearing her late master's property. She looked around, "Why are you in a park in the middle of the night? Are you going to sleep on that bench? Are you homeless?"

"Gosh, for somebody so tiny you're sure full of questions. And no I'm not....." he paused, ".....homeless."

"Well it sure looks like it to me." the small pixie looked around at the empty park again, "I don't think you know anything."

"Just shut-up already." Christian weakly replied. He slowly laid down on the bench in a sleeping position. His eyes were vacant and his face void, he realized he hadn't any were to call home. He could'nt go back to the castle now and there was no where else to turn.

The small pixie drifted in mid-air in the same spot for a minute before flying to the prince's face. She saw the depression and void in his eyes. "I thought you said you weren't homeless? Caaauuse you sleeping on a park bench is kind of a homeless thing to do."

Christian laid silent allowing the pixie to say what ever she desired.

"You don't deserve my master's clothes." she stated once more before returning inside the small sea shell.

The park was empty but not silent. Christian looked up into a near by tree as a few black birds cawed and ruffled their feathers. 'It must be so easy to be a bird.' he thought to himself. 'Carefree, set up home where ever you feel. Once you grow up, you fly out on your own, never knowing if your family is dead or alive. Never having to feel that hurt.' Then he thought further, 'I'd hate eating bugs though.'

'I wonder where Alisha is.' he contemplated as he drifted off to sleep. 'I hope she's okay.'

Hours had passed and the moon had disappeared from the night sky allowing the sun to bring in a new dawn. The time was a bit passed noon and the pond was active. The sound of birds were so loud Christian couldn't sleep any longer. He slowly opened his eyes and was surprised by the awakening sight. The ground was nearly covered in black birds. The teen sat up smiling, it was such a nice surprise. Then he noticed the birds standing on the back of the bench and flying above him.

"I don't have any food. I'm sorry." he informed, as if the birds could understand him. The price slowly moved his pointer finger towards one of the birds to attempt petting it gently. His finger slowly inched closer and closer while the bird appeared distracted. As he was an inch away from petting the black bird it truned its head watching his finger move in closer. Christian smiled, he thought it was so cool getting to pet a wild black bird until suddenly the black birds began riling up and cawing incessantly.

Christian was taken aback by the sudden burts of panic by the feathered creatures. Swarms of black birds began flying over the head of the young prince and from behind. Christian ducked his head low for safety as the birds panicked above him. The excitement began making the brown haired teenager uneasy. He looked about the surrounding area for an escape from the nervous birds, but noticed an unexpected intruder closing in on him quickly.

"Grechov!" he shouted in a startle.

The general hurried through the birds crushing a few under his feet while trying to move around them, which slowed him down.

"Hold still Christian." Grechov warned.

The prince gasped and stood from the park bench to run until he was pecked in the head by swooping black birds. The birds began swarming his head to prevent his movements. In the panic one of the black birds scratched the side of Christian's face causing him to fall to his knees and block with his forearms. As the chaos ensued he noticed the general reaching closer.

The prince had to move, even if it meant getting blinded by crazy birds. Quite possibly with his life at stake Christian leapt up from off the ground and smacked some of the flying hazards away before darting off in the direction opposite from the general.

"STOP!" Grechov hurried. "Damn it." he muttered as he pushed through the airborne birds.

Christian ran as fast he could as the black birds followed in close persuit. He flung his arms about swatting at the birds as he ran across the park. As if ignoring him a massive swarm of black birds began forming a cyclone before his very eyes. As the feathered cyclone became its darkest a masculine man in a dark feathered dressed quickly approached the prince and forcefully grabbed his wrist.

Christian was in shock and tried jerking his arm free of the mysterious man.

"Who are you?! Let me go! Let go of me!" he wrestled.

The man in the black dress leaned towards the frightened prince, "I'm your new royal mystic." he smirked.

The prince swung his free arm to hit Crow, but was instantly stopped by Crow's free hand.

"You better freak'n clam yourself down you little punk." he quietly threatened drawing the prince in closer.

The prince paused for a second while at the mercy of this new supposed royal mystic.

Grechov finally caught up and wiped the sweat from his brow, "Gotch'cha." he stated grabbing hold of Christian. "No running this time." Grechov declared with a wicked grin.

The prince was forced into a Vailstone military vehicle and rushed back to the castle. Christian sat between general Grechov and a soldier while Crow sat across from them. The prince looked at the man in the black dress with anger as they josseled around in the large jeep.

"And when did this become official?" Christian asked.

"Hm?" Grechov wondered.

"When did he become Vailstone's new mystic advisor?"

Crow looked at the inquizative teen, "After I saved Raziel. He was under a nasty spell from that Fire starter fellow, haven't you heard?" he replied overdramatically with a smirk.

"That's enough Crow." Grechov ordered.

"Crow, huh?" Christian repeated. "That's right, I remember seeing you on the T.V.. Why didn't you use your magic to stop Fire starter yesterday?"

Without so much as a response Crow just managed to glare at the prince, then looked out the window with the scenery passing by.

"I know he killed mom and dad. What about Alisha? Is she okay?" Christian asked.

"Shhh. Not now." Grechov replied putting his pointer finger to his lips.

"Tell me Grechov, I want to know. What happened to Alisha?"

"Shh, shh, shh." Grechov seemed determined not to answer any of Christian's questions.

Finally after nearly an hour of silence the military jeep arrived to the Vailstone castle. Outside the castle walls were a massive swarm of protesters. Civilians of the kingdom slapped, vandalized, and rocked the military jeep while it slowly pushed through before being allowed entry. Soldiers at the front gate maintained the crowd to deter a riot. The vehicle reached the main entrance and finally came to a complete stop. Grechov stepped out of the jeep and waited for the prince to step out as well. Christian peered through the open vehicle door a gazed at the castle. The boy had a sickening feeling just looking at home. Memories came flooding back into his mind, he leaned out of the jeep weakly before throwing up in front on Grechov.

"Awe, shit!" he said as vomit collected on his boots.

"That's flattering." Crow stated sarcastically in a monotone voice.

With inside the castle ambassador Hikaru was sitting behind a large wooden desk that rest inside the late king's study. He stressed beyond his limits as all ties to the kingdom were slowly cut.

"I assure you your majesty, the situation is under control. It was a spell from our own mystic, he betrayed us. Raziel is innocent I swear to you. Yes we're having a bit of an issue with our citizen's understanding the truth at the moment, but it's just a slight bump in the road. A little hiccup like this shouldn't affect our proffessional relations. I hope it's safe to say we can muster through this affair together. I'll have my people contact your people monday morning. What do you say? That way we can carry on buisness as usual?" Hikaru awaited the response on the other line of the phone, anticipating the royalty's answer nervously.

"Hikaru...."

"Yes?"

"Do you know why everyone is withdrawing their connections with Vailstone? The king and queen were murdered by their own people. You may have a silver tounge, but you can't talk your way out of this one. I myself had warned Dorian of the people he surrounded himself with. First and foremost that general Raziel insisted upon. His horrific background should have been enough of a red flag. And now his grand duke and royal mystic slaughter him and his beloved. Yet you're telling me how everything is under control."

"I merely was saying....."

"Don't interrupt me Hikaru."

"Sorry, um." he replied nervously.

"My 'people' will not be meeting with 'your people' Hikaru. You have no 'people' Hikaru, are just an amassador. You've obviously set yourself in the position of authority rather quickly. You've already appointed Vailstone a new royal mystic. Either you were aware this moment was coming or you stupidly hired the first person who showed up at the front door without even so much as a background check. My informants, however, did run a background check on Vailstone's new mystic. So were you aware he's forbidden in nine different sections of the continent or is that information irrelevent?"

"Well, I certa...."

"Hikaru."

"Sorry." he apologized catching himself inturrupting the neighboring king once again.

"The bottom line is, you are not royalty. You are not a regent. You have no authority. None of the other kingdoms will listen to what you have to say because what you have to say is meaningless. As far as myself and everyone else is concerned, the true authority in Vailstone kingdom is the next eldest blood relative. And unless the princess has been wed as of recently that makes prince Christian your new king. Good day Hikaru." the king on the other side of the phone hung up before Hikaru could reply.

The kingdom's ambassador sat with the dial tone sounding off in his ear. He slowly hung up the phone and rest his forehead in his hands as he sat. All the kingdom's allys have removed themselves in light of what's happened. It was clear the kingdom could not properly function without the presence of the prince or princess. Hikaru's cheshire cat magically appeared on the desk beside him.

"Syrius, what am I supposed to do?" he paused. "Dorian and Natalia are dead, Christian and Alisha aren't capable of running this kingdom themselves." Hikaru reasoned with himself out loud to Syrius. "We need Raziel so we'll be safe, but he can't be in charge either. The people don't fully trust him like they did before. What other choice do I have here? This kingdom needs me, these people need a king." The ambassador looked at his reflection in a massive mirror hanging on the wall. "A new king....." he said having an epiphany.

A knock at the door disturbed Hikaru's train of thought, "Come in." he answered.

Grechov opened the large door and stepped inside, "I got'em." he smiled.

Christian was all alone in another one of the castle's many study's. He walked over to the window and looked out at the protesting civilian's around the castle.

"What's with all the anrgy people out there?" the tiny pixie asked fluttering beside Christian.

"Ugh!" he gasped, "When did you get out? I didn't summon you."

"Really? Summon me? Come on kid I'm not a genie. Now what's with all those ticked off people?"

"They're...protesting." he answered solomly.

"Duh, genius, but whyyyyy?" she asked fluttering about not really caring about the answer.

"Because somebody here killed the king and queen."

"Sucks to be them. That's the death penalty." the pixie stated without a care in the world. She poked at a large painting until the door to the room started to open. Hesitant on allowing her presence to be known, she instantly vanished back inside her shell around Christian's neck leaving only a tiny trail of pink glitter behind.

Christian turned from the window to witness Hikaru enter the room.

"That will be all general, thank you." Hikaru excused.

General Grechov watched Christian while he closed the door, leaving only the prince and ambassador alone together. Hikaru walked over to a large comfortable chair slightly adjacent to another chair identical to his.

"Please, be seated. We have much to discuss." he asked kindly.

Christian was hesitant at first, but eventually walked over to the empty seat and sat down. Hikaru unbuttoned his coat before seating himself.

The ambassador shrugged his shoulders, "You have no idea how relieved I am to see you. After what had happened and all, I wasn't even sure of you or your sister's safety."

"Alisha's okay?" he asked hopefully.

"Yes. We're tracking her down as well, like we found you."

"How did you find me?"

"Well, that was with the help of our new mystic advisor."

"Crow?"

"Yes. He can use birds for scouting and spying and such. One bird noticed you in the park so we rushed in to get you immediately. Out there isn't safe for someone of your royal blood. You belong here, with us, with me." he smiled.

"That Crow guy said he helped Raziel somehow."

Hikaru took a deep breath, the presentation of his next words were obviously formulating in his head. "Christian, as touchy as this subject is for you. For us. Raziel had been cast under a spell somehow during your adventure to obtain the Kamisama armor. How can I put this nicely? Fire starter is a tricky individual. Heck, he fooled us all for at least twenty years. Crow's bird's noticed this at some point and witnessed the spell used on Raziel, so he knew how to reverse it. Otherwise I would have kept him locked up in our dungeon."

"Raziel is free?!"

"Yes, Crow vouched for him. I witnessed him free Raziel from the spell myself. I wouldn't have believed it otherwise." he explained with assurance.

"Is he here?!" Christian panicked.

Hikaru reached out and placed his hand over Christian's, "Christian it's fine. Trust me. Raziel feels terrible for what has happened. He's beating himself up over this more than anyone else could. I need for you to calm down........He's in the library."

"What?!"

"Breath Christian, breath." Hikaru helped coach the prince into taking deep breaths to calm down. "He wants to speak with you. Think you're up to that?"

The prince shook his head answering 'NO' frantically.

Hikaru held both sides of Christian's face, "Now Christian look at me. Look at me!" he raised his voice gaining the teen's attention. "Now look, I need you. This kingdom needs you. Everything your mother and father have built here will crumble and fall to shambles unless you can keep it together. I know this is rushed upon you, but with your parents gone YOU are now in charge. None of the other kingdoms want anything to do with us unless they see you and your sister back here safe, sound, and happy. You know why you REALLY wanted to go out and have your own adventure Christian?"

The prince starred into the ambassador's eyes deeply, "Huh?"

"I'll tell you why. Because you wanted to have a purpose. Don't you get it? Can't you see you never came back from your adventure that day! Your still in it Christian." he explained theatrically. "And you've found your purpose, just like your father did. To come back and lead these lost people. To be a leader, hell, to be a KING!"

"Um, I dunno."

"You can't quite your adventure now. Adventurer's don't quite. Your father never quite. You wouldn't want to disappoint your father. Would you?" he prodded.

Christian's watery eyes had begun to overflow with the fear of being a disappointment to his late mother and father, "No."

"There, there Christian. Everything is going to be just fine. With you back home where you belong and me by your side, everything will be just fine." Hikaru explained while consoling the broken hearted boy. "You're doing the right thing staying here Christian. Dorian and Natasha would be proud of how strong you've become." The ambassador leaned away from the prince looking him in the face, "Christian," he stated with a stern voice, "now comes the hardest part. I know you can do this." Hikaru gripped the boy's shoulders tightly as Christian looked to the door.

Outside the library Christian and general Grechov waited. Hikaru cracked open the door and stepped outside into the hallway.

"Okay," he said taking a deep breath, "he's ready to see you now. Are you sure you're ready for this?" Christian nodded his head preparing himself to face Raziel after what he had done. "Good, I knew you were strong. Remember general Grechov and I will be right outside if you need us, alright?" The boy nodded his head once more, Hikaru patted him on the back and cracked open the door for him, "Good, good. Alright then."

Christian was gently nudged inside the dimly lit library. He peered back as the door closed behind. A flame danced in the fireplace. The burning wood crackled and snapped. A broken chair laid crushed on the floor near an elegant coffee table. On the table was placed a glass of cold milk, a plate with chocolate cake, a fork, and an extremely sharp knife. The brown haired teen walked over to the dessert sitting alone on the table. A figure sat on the opposite side of the room. Once Christian was in view the figure lifted its head and raised from the shadows.

"Christian?" he asked enthusiastically, which startled the prince. "You've come back."

"Raziel!?" he spouted in fear.

The grand duke began walking over, but stopped immediately after witnessing the boy's fear. He reached outward pleading to the youth, "Christian. It's been killing me inside not seeing you and Alisha after what happened. You have no idea how terrible I feel about all of this."

"I have no idea?! How terrible YOU feel?! YOU KILLED MOM AND DAD! I don't care how you feel!" he teared up.

"You don't mean that." Raziel responded sympathetically.

"I'm never going to see them again because of YOU! Momma's birthday was next month! She didn't even...get..to....." he struggled. "You ruined my life! You ruined everybody's life." Christian had a difficult time trying to maintain some composure. "What am I supposed to do now? Alisha? How can we stay here after what you did! Nobody wants you here anymore." he declared referring to the protesters outside the castle.

"Christian....." he began walking to him.

"Stay away from me." he ordered. Raziel stopped once again, "You're a monster. You are, a monster. You make us, believe in you. Trust you. Love," he paused, "you. And then attack?!"

"Christian," Raziel hesitated wanting nothing more than to tell him the truth, but telling him his father wasn't strong enough to bare the armor would only exacerbate his dilemma, "Fire starter, I trusted him and when I was most vulnerable he...cast some sort of magic spell on me. It was like mind control, except I could see everything happening, but was still powerless to stop it." Raziel teared up while pleading with the boy, "I wanted so badly to undo what was happening. What had been done."

Raziel began stepping closer over to Christian. The prince slowly took small steps back until he bumped into the coffee table. He looked back quickly to see what had stopped him and noticed the fire reflecting off the sharp knife. The prince looked back to the grand duke as he approached.

"With all my strength, I was still helpless to stop what had begun into motion. I messed up. You know I loved your mom and dad, Alisha, and you. I've put my life on the line for all of you time and time again. You know me. You know I would never intentionally hurt you or your family. I was family too, they were my family too Christian." Raziel stopped once he realized Christian was holding the knife behind his back.

Knowing he was holding that knife to protect himself from Raziel was even more painful. The powerful warrior had murdered his friends, betrayed the children he had helped raise, and realized what the situation had become.

"Is that for me?" he asked painfully.

Christian moved his hands around revealing the knife. Tears dripped onto the blade from his eyes, "I know what I gotta do now. I have to make things right." he whimpered.

Raziel smiled with hurt, "Is that it? Is that what needs to be done?" He dropped his hands to his sides, "Is that the only way to make everything right?"

Christian starred at Raziel, both with tears in their eyes and nodded. Raziel nodded, emotionally scarred. He grabbed a hold of part of his armor and struggled to remove the protection.

"What are you doing?" Christian asked.

"What needs to be done." Raziel answered back.

The armor fought to protect Raziel from danger, but ultimately the desire of the one wearing the armor decides if the armor stays on or not. Raziel kneeled before Christian with his exposed muscle bound chest and torso. The grand duke cast the chest plate, shirt, and coat to the floor. The prince was beside himself. Raziel shut his eyes, raised his head, and opened his arms to welcome death by Christian's hand.

"What are you doing?" Christian pleaded.

"I'm doing what's right." the grand duke took a deep breath, "Do what you feel need be done Christian. Just remember that no matter what you decide.......I love you."

Christian stood less then a foot away from the vulnerable grand duke as he raised the blade of the knife. The fire flickered, yet, the room grew cold. Raziel took one final deep breath, eyes shut tight, and listened to the sounds of the fireplace. Christian shook nervously, looking directly at the man who killed his parents, yet, helped protect and raise him. Teach him. His hand began shaking worse until eventually the knife flew through the air. Raziel slightly shuddered as the blade landed on the ground beside him and the warmth of the prince fell upon his chest with his arms around his neck. The young prince sobbed uncontrollably while embracing Raziel tightly.

"I can't, I can't. I can't do it. I love you too much. I couldn't do it. I couldn't, I couldn't do it." he blubbered.

Raziel wrapped his arms around the broken boy and returned the affection of his embrace.

30

LAYERS

Police cars parked outside a fresh crime scene kept civilians at bay to prevent anyone from disturbing evidence. An old rusted car pulled in front of the home police were guarding. The engine sounded awful, it seemed a car part was capable of falling off at any given point. A three hundred and eighty pound lieutenant detective removed the keys from the ignition and stepped out of his car. The car raised from the ground considerably upon his exit. The man pulled out a lighter with a fancy design on the outside, lit his cigarette, and flipped the lighter in the air, catching it with his free hand and placed it back into his pocket before proceeding to view the crime scene.

As the lieutenant detective approached an officer walked over to fill him in on all the details.

"Detective."

"Officer."

"Sorry to tear you away from the kingdom crisis, but it appears to be another of those bizarre suicides. Wife comes home sees husband laying on his back, bullet to the chest, exit wound from the back, but the bullet hit the wall on the opposite side of the room. Ballistics has matched the bullet to the victim's gun, but the gunpowder residue is on the victim's hand. No signs of a struggle, but there was clearly another suspect present." the officer informed.

"And why do you think that?"

"Forced entry. Window broken from the outside to unlock the backdoor. And this was personal. Nothing has been reported stolen, just like all the other bizarre suicides."

Lieutenant detective Hobbs looked at the evidence provided, "So, the ascalent breaks the back window here. Proceeds to the living room, sits down in this chair here. Waits for this schmuck to get home, but somehow gets the guy to kill his self."

"This ones got us confused. The positioning just doesn't add up. He couldn't have shot himself with this evidence." the officer scratched his temple, "There's not even any sign of tampering. I've never seen anything like this."

The detective squatted down looking at the chair and put on a latex glove, "Here, take this in for testing." he ordered while picking up a long black hair. After he put the hair in a zip bag and handed it over to the officer he ordered them to dust the chair for finger prints.

"Who ever's causing these string of bizarre suicides, he isn't very smart. Big mistake leaving behind hard evidence like this." the officer assumed.

"If this is the same guy that knocked off all the others then he's too smart to make mistakes like these. He doesn't care if he's caught. It doesn't matter to him if he's sloppy. Makes him more dangerous."

"How can you be sure? Maybe he just finally slipped up."

"The only thing all of these 'suicide' victims have in common is the detective that investigated them at some point in the past." Hobbs pointed out while taking another draw off his cigarette.

"What detective?"

"My old partner, Notch." Hobbs remained pondering about the supposed suicides wondering just how Seth was pulling them off.

Back in the forest at the gypsy's camp Bo helped Wraith fold up the tent to give back to Enrique. Alisha walked over to the gypsy's travel carriage and knocked on the door to return some mouth wash he had given her due to the fact that she didn't have a toothbrush.

"Ah, finished already?" he answered.

"Yes, thank you." she replied politely. Alisha took a quick glance at the camp area before asking, "Enrique, have you seen Vincent?"

"Yes I have actually. He wandered out that direction early this morning." he pointed.

"Why?"

"Dunno, maybe he needed to answer nature's call, know what I mean? Only reason I knew though is cause he triggered my string of cans there when he wandered off."

"I think I'll go look for him." Alisha stated.

"Princess, may I ask you a personal question?"

Alisha was weary, but allowed the questioning anyhow. "Sure."

"Which one of the two is your boyfriend?"

Alisha was stunned, "My, my boyfriend?! Neither, I'm not seeing anyone. Now is hardly the time to be searching for love."

"Oh? Alright then. My apologies." Enrique began to return inside his travel carriage until he was stopped by the princess.

"Enrique! Why do you ask?" she wondered.

The gypsy laughed slightly, "I just thought I picked up on a vibe last night. It appears to me that they both fancy you, but as you stated, now isn't the time to go searching for love, right?" he smiled before returning inside this carriage.

"Right." the princess replied questioning herself. "Both?" she thought out loud. She then turned and began walking off in search for Vincent. Alisha stepped over the string with cans tied to the trees as not to sound off that alarm. Alisha noticed foot prints on the soft soil and followed the trail. After fifteen minutes or following his tracks she began to hear huffing and grunting sounds. The princess slowly approached a litte slope which lead to a small brook of flowing clear water with healthy greenery all around.

The fair skinned beauty stood watching the silver haired teen swinging both his katana blades. Alisha was flustered by the sight of the shirtless young man practicing with his new weapons. She took notice of his muscled back and biceps. Sweat trickled down Vincent's tight pecks as he practiced more offensive manuvers. With in an instant one of Vincent's swords burst into scattered sharp metallic blades and flew around in the air at his control. The teen controlled his broken sword pieces like a swarm of bees then forced them all to stop and begin circulating around him in a large circle.

"That's amazing." Alisha complimented with a face of sheer astonishment.

Vincent was so focused that he hadn't noticed her watching him train, "Princess?!" Vincent returned the bits of katana back into an actual sword and connected the two back as one to return to its sheath.

"Oh, you don't have to stop on my account." she explained walking down the slope towards Vincent. "How long have you been training with that sword of yours?"

"I dunno. A while." he said wiping the sweat from his forehead.

Alisha noticed the circular pattern of scars on Vincent's chest once he faced her direction, "What's that? On your chest there?"

"Oh,..." he replied touching the scars, "...when the seven of us all removed the swords from a rock we all got scarred the same way some how."

"Why?" she asked walking up to him.

"I don't know. Probably cause we weren't supposed to swipe these swords."

Alisha hesitantly reached forward and gentally ran her fingers on Vincent's naked chest, feeling of the mysterious scars. "Does it hurt?"

"Not anymore." he answered uncomfortably. Vincent put his shirt back on and walked over to the brook to splash a bit of water on his face. "How did you find me out here?"

"Enrique noticed you leave this way earlier this morning."

"He told you I wandered off did he?"

"No, I asked him if he knew where you were."

"Oh? You noticed I was gone, hm?" he quipped.

"What is that supposed to mean?" she asked.

"Nothing, nevermind. Let's....go back to the camp." he replied wandering by her.

Alisha stepped in Vincent's way and looked him face to face, "Is something bothering you? Are you mad at me or something?"

"No. Let's just, go back." he answered in an aggrivated tone.

"Well it sure feels like you're mad about something. Did Wraith do something I don't know about?"

"You know."

"Know what?"

"Your boyfriend."

"My what?! Boyfriend? Wraith isn't my boyfriend. What made you think he was my boyfriend?" she asked with irritation.

"I saw you holding his hand last night at the camp fire."

"So! He made a pass at me and I denied him. I just met him. Not to mention Raziel just went all psycho and killed my family." she explained as she began to cry, "So I'm not exactly looking for a boyfriend at the moment thank you very much." The princess began sniffling and wiping tears from her eyes.

"Ugh, why are you crying." Vincent complained.

"Um, let's see, maybe because I'm all alone now. Family friend takes out my whole family, I'm left hiding in the woods with a gypse and two guys that couldn't care less about my life or what happened to my mom, dad, and brother. Bo's the only one that seems to care my whole life is ruined now. It's obvious to anyone that meets you and Wraith that you don't care about anyone but yourselves." she rambled.

Vincent felt awkward standing before her as she broke down yet again. The boy sighed before opening his arms and stepping forward.

"Wha, what are you doing?" she sobbed.

"Something I remembered that stupid shark-dog said." he explained before embracing her.

Alisha was stunned by Vincent's actions, but willingly accepted his offering of affection. The broken girl paused in the warmth of his arms and chest before wrapping her arms around him and placing her face on his clothed pecks to cry upon. Vincent's first intentions were to shut her up from crying, but in that moment of embrace he began to feel sturrings with in his heart. Something about witnessing Alisha cry brought him pain from with-in. It's the first time in his life someone else's emotions weighted on him.

The princess leaned her head back up right and chuckled, "I'd gotten make-up on your shirt."

Vincent sighed, "It's fine. Don't worry about it."

Alisha looked straight into Vincent's eyes while he held her in his strong arms. A calm breeze blew through the trees. Autumn leaves danced in the air while falling to the ground. The cool waters flowed through the brook ever so smoothly. The teen hearts pounded in sync. Their faces so close and moist lips closer. In the first moment since her world fell apart, she felt safe. Alisha's firm chest pressed against Vincent's tighter as she moved closer. Lost in the moment she placed her lips only a centimeter away from contact with Vincent's.

The silver haired teen's face blushed a bright red, he moved his head back and away from the would be kiss, "Really. It's, it's fine. Really."

The princess swallowed and took a deep breath as she stepped away from the orphaned boy. She had been swept away in the moment, but had returned back to her senses.

"Maybe we should head back." Vincent suggested.

"Yeah, yeah. Maybe we should head back. That's a, that's a good idea." she agreed returning from the passed moment.

"I'm gonna, get my swords." he explained. Vincent walked over and strapped his sheathed katanas to his side. He looked at the princess. She appeared dazed, "I'll lead the way."

"Yeah, you do that." she gasped.

Alisha followed closely behind Vincent as he retraced his steps back to camp. Alisha continued replaying the moment by the brook inside her head. She began wondering more about the silver haired teen while blocking branches from her face and watching her footing.

"Hm?"

Vincent didn't bother paying any mind to Alisha's sounds.

"HM!?" she announced more vocally.

"Ugh." Vincent rolled his eyes as he lead the way back, "What is it?"

"I was just wondering, can I ask you a personal question."

"Why?"

"I don't know. I'm curious I guess."

"What?"

"Why don't you talk about yourself? Like when we talked the other day. Are you shy? You don't have to be shy around me."

"No I'm not shy! Geez. I'm just, ugh. I'm just not that interesting. That's all." he defended, offended by the 'shy' remark.

"Well, like before. You said you didn't have parents, or you didn't really know them before. Why is that? What happened there?" she inquired.

Vincent stopped and looked up at the sky, "Ugh. What is it with you? Why do you wanna know about them? What do you care?"

"I don't know. I guess maybe I'd just like to know you better. Is that such a terrible thing? To know you better?"

"It just seems dumb."

"It's dumb to know you more?"

"No, it seems dumb to ask about them. Who cares about them? They don't define me."

"Well, I was curious. You said they got rid of you, right? Why did they do something like that?"

"Ugh, because I was born. There, are you happy now?" he stopped and turned back to look at Alisha. "I was born with this stupid hair color and it freaked'em out. It was a bad omen or something and they gave me away. They wiped me and flushed me away. I ended up at an orphanage after that."

"You were just a baby?"

"Yeah. My mistake was birth. Can we drop this now?"

"You don't like to talk about it do you?"

"No."

"Because of the strong hurt feelings?"

"No, because I get more pissed off everytime I think of those losers. I hate'em."

"You can't hate them." she condescended.

"Look, not everybody cry's about their mommy and daddies, okay?" he snapped back. "Now let's just move on." he said continuing on his way.

Alisha stood motionless by his insensitive remark. Vincent continued, but noticed her staying put.

"What are you doing? Come on." he could tell she was hurt and probably about to cry again. Vincent sighed and walked over to her to hug her again.

Alisha was upset and brushed his arms away from her, "Get away. I don't want a hug from you! Is that why you're so mean to me? So you can hurt my feelings and hug me 'to make it all better'?" she accused.

"What? No. Jus' seems like hugs stop you from blubber'n."

Alisha gasped, "What! Is that the only reason you've been hugging me? To shut me up?" Vincent stood in front of her without a single clue of what to tell her. The young blonde gasped again, "IT IS! You're just being nice so I'll stop talking."

"No, no, no, that's not it. You just, I mean I..." Vincent was confused and hadn't a clue where to go from this point. So he walked forward for another hug which she wrestled away from.

"What's wrong with you?" she replied.

"Well what do you want me to do?! I don't know? All this talk crap and hugs and emotional stuff! It's not me! I don't know what I'm doing! What do you want from me?!" he shouted back in a sheer misunderstanding of the entire situation.

"Vincent, all I want is to be able to talk with you." she answered in a more calm tone.

Vincent was huffing and feeling like a complete fool, "You need to understand, I'm not used to this whole 'talking about myself' and my parents and stuff. I've never done this before." The silver haired asian took in a deep breath of relief, "Look, I'll help you get to where you wanna go and then you won't have to deal with me anymore and you can find new people to ask all sorts of annoying personal questions."

"Is that what you want to do? Drop me off somewhere and then just leave?"

"What would I stick around for?"

A pause in the conversation crept in, "Let's just go." she replied with disappointment.

Alisha removed another protective layer from Vincent's emotional shell, but wasn't entirely ready for the revealed truths. Regardless, she continued close behind him once again.

Twenty minutes into walking back to the camp Vincent noticed some smoke off to his right. It seemed odd and out of place in the middle of a forest. Was someone else camping nearby? "Stay here." he warned Alisha before wandering slowly over to the smoke to investigate. A foul unpleasent odor began to become stronger as he creeped closer to the smoke emitting from behind the bushes. To Vincent's surprise he discovered a fully grown deer entangled in thick spider webs, but even more shocking were the burned holes from the deer's neck. The deer revealed holes burned through it's nostril's, mouth, and neck as if something it had breathed in burned through it's flesh.

"Oh my God, what happened to that poor deer?" Alisha inquired behind Vincent.

"What are you doing creeping up on me like that? You startled me half to death. I could have cut you down. What if I thought you were an enemy?" he snapped.

"Oh shut up, you're not going to cut me. So what happened to that poor deer?"

"I don't know, but let's just go back to camp before someone sees us. I don't think we're alone." Vincent led Alisha away from the tortured animal, still curious about who else was near.

31

DEEPER OBSERVATIONS

Inside the Vailstone castle walls locked away inside an interrogation room Wade Smith sat waiting patiently, but a tad uneasy given the circumstances. He began to tap his foot nervously as he started regretting his decision to willfully leave with the lieutenant.

Major Collins stood outside Rufus' interrogation room while waiting for general Grechov. After a moment the general opened the door and walked out into the hallway locking the door behind him.

"So? Did he have anything interesting to say? Anything about the princess, sir?" Collins inquired.

"No, but that one's not going to be a problem for us. He's, persuadable." Grechov guaranteed.

"And the entertainer?"

Grechov adjusted his coat, "I know his type. He won't be a problem. I'll handle him myself."

General Grechov unlocked Wade's room and walked inside. Wade was excited to finally see someone he could talk to and reason with. He stood up immediately as the general walked in.

"Oh thank goodness. I've been in here for like two hours or something. It's been driving me crazy." he chuckled.

"Three hours, actually. Please, sit down." Grechov asked politely. "I've seen you before, but we haven't been properly introduced. My name is Grechov, I'm the general to the grand duke of the kingdom of Vailstone." he informed extending his hand in greetings.

Wade happily shook the general's hand, "Thank you for your time. It's a pleasure to meet you. I'm Wade Smith by the way."

The two men sat down at a small interrogation table sitting on opposite sides of each other.

"Oh, I know who you are Mr. Smith. You're a big celebrity." Grechov complimented with sarcasim.

Wade started feeling a bad vibe from the general instantly.

"You 'Big' celebrity types usually have it pretty good right?"

"Yeah, I, I guess?" Wade answered not understanding what Grechov wanted to hear.

"Ya know, a lot of times I find that you big celebrity types don't see the big picture."

"Big picture?"

"Yeah. You see, we've got an ugly situation here. Raziel, he's having an image problem right now. You ever had an image problem?" the general asked in a coy manner.

"No." Wade answered almost in the form of a question.

"Of course not, you're a likable fellow right?" Grechov smiled. "You never really had to get down and dirty for your spotlight."

"Well, actually......"Wade began until being inturrupted by the General.

"You know sometimes when you're right in the thick of a problem you don't sometimes seem to really notice all of the details. Understand?"

".....What?"

"Like say for instance, when you and those other 'six chosen' were out in that forest of darkness with Fire starter and Raziel. You probably didn't notice that crutial moment when the mystic placed Raziel under a spell, did you?"

"No. There was a lot going on at the time and..."

"Right!" Grechov silenced Wade, "There WAS a lot going on at the time. So just because you didn't see something happen doesn't mean it didn't happen, right?"

"Yeah, but thinking about it, that fire mystic just wanted the armor. After Raziel had it, why didn't they just leave together? It doesn't really make sense to me that he'd have Raziel kill the king for no reason. See what I'm saying?" Wade pieced together.

"Yeah, that is wierd, but ya know what? Our new mystic advisor removed the spell that Fire starter put on the grand duke. So it DID happen, no matter what you think." Grechov returned with a much more serious tone. Before Wade could respond Grechov continued yet again, "Would you like to hear a funny observation?"

"Huh?"

"Let me tell you a funny observation. I don't know if I'm just more in tune with the world or what, but, I've come to notice that in life that celebrity types, like yourself of course, always seem to have the most to lose." he announced as he sat back with a wicked smile.

"What?"

"Oh yeah, I mean, you've got your big fancy houses, your shiny cars, your reputation, career, friends, family, all that cash." Grechov stopped, "I mean the list really goes on when you think about it."

"What's your point general?"

"Oh? Nothing, just making conversation, but you know, sometimes if a celebrity gets on the bad side of somebody in a place of power..."

Wade sat silently looking into Grechov's eyes and obvious threats.

"Well, they usually lose things. That's all. Did you know one time an organization set up somebody to kill a celebrity as a 'crazed fan'?"

"I don't think I'm actually comfortable with this subject matter." Wade said adjusting his seat.

"Oh, of course, of course." Grechov responded staring at Wade.

The two men sat in silence for two minutes before Grechov spoke up again, "Would you happen to know where we could find princess Alisha?"

"What? She's missing? No, I don't know. I didn't even know she was gone." Wade explained.

Grechov nodded, "Alright, because I'd hate to find out she'd been taken away and forced into some of those smut films you spit out."

"What?! NO!"

"Because I've got a search party looking through your places right now, and let me tell you something sex boy. If I find that she's been tied up and kept prisoner in one of your little sick fetish rooms you're gonna lose a hell of a lot more than material possessions! I can guarantee you that!" Grechov threatened while raising his voice.

"No, there's nothing like that honest. I mean, yeah she's really attractive and all and I wouldn't mind some one on one time with her if ya know what I mean." Wade rambled.

"Wha?" Grechov listened to the horny adult actor continue on.

"And yeah, a movie with me a her would be great. 'Princess gets the poper' or 'The royal treatment' something like that. Yeah, I suppose I could ask her. I mean this would really speak out to a certain crowd ya know? Wow, that's a great idea you had there. Hey, maybe something with your lieutenant there too, like 'Up in ranks' or 'Full salute'? We could even get..."

"SHUT UP! SHUT UP! SHUT UP! Quit talking about stupid shit and focus!!!" Grechov yelled losing his temper.

Major Collins knocked on the interrogation room door and peeked inside, "General Grechov sir, we have an issue.

"What is it? I'm right in the middle of something here."

"It's the royal mystic. We have reason to believe he's unleashed one of his summonings upon the kingdom." Collins informed.

Grechov grined his teeth before standing up and looking down on Smith, "We'll finish this up later." he announced before walking away from the table. Before leaving he turned and looked back at the worried celebrity, "You know, prosecution never goes further than the 'crazed fan'." he smirked.

"Hey, wait! When am I free to go?" Wade wondered.

"I haven't decided yet." Grechov stated as Collins shut and locked the door behind him.

Grechov marched down the hallway meeting up with lieutenant Brookes, "What's the situation?"

"Fire creatures attacking civilians and setting wildfires in rural areas."

"And where's Raziel on the matter?"

"Hikaru made the call not to inform the grand duke on account of his tarnished status."

"I see. Get me three jeeps of men, I'll handle this one myself. Major stay here and watch the prisoners and keep Raziel here." the general ordered.

"Prisoners? One of them is just a boy." Collins questioned. He was confused about their status. Once seeing Rufus and Wade foul play appeared quite the long shot.

"Yeah, PR-IS-ON-ERS! Think you can manage that without everybody ending up dead when I come back this time?" Grechov insulted.

"Yes, sir." Collins replied and stopped in his march, allowing the gerenal and lieutenant to leave him behind.

Lieutenant Brookes sped away from the castle with the general in the passenger seat followed by two jeeps. The vehicles made way through the crowd of protesters to respond to the threat.

Meanwhile, downtown, Seth approached the last criminal on his list. A low life thug responsible for the death of three innocent victims. Murdered in cold blood, innocent youths who were in the wrong place at the wrong time. The detective parked his car down the block and walked to the apartment complex. Seth was drowsy from his poor sleep on the backseat of his car, but relied on his cold cup of coffee to keep him awake. The day began to grow old, but he was determined to avenge the lives of the lost innocence and right his wrongs. Seth walked up to the thug's door, but noticed something was off. This time, something was different. The door was cracked open, not locked or shut.

Seth slowly opened the door with his black sword in hand. He glanced around the apartment looking for signs of a struggle, but only noticed a filthy home. The black haired detective crept into the kitchen slowly looking for a reason the door was a jar. His suspicions were validated once he noticed a bloody note folded and sitting in the middle of the floor.

Seth looked around before walking over and picking it up. He opened the note which read:

'Had a long day, going to bed.'

The detective tossed the note to his side and peered down a dark hallway. Seth slowly crept down the hallway eventually noticing blood stained walls on each side of him. In the small apartment Seth walked by a bathroom that he stuck his head inside for a slight moment so as not to fall into any traps. After seeing it was clear he slowly and quietly closed the door. He proceeded to the bedroom door at the very end of the hall. He reach out and pushed the door open with his sword. To Seth's disgust he witnessed the criminal he had come to kill already murdered. The man was ripped apart with body parts and organs strone about. The detective covered his mouth and nose once the horrific smell hit him in the face.

Seth slowly walked further inside to investigate, "Who in the hell...?" he wondered before his thought was rudely interrupted.

"Me!" Cain growled leaping from the shadows and striking Seth's exposed katana.

Seth quickly defended himself in surprise, "You?! But why?"

"I knew you'd be here." the assassin grumbled striking at the detective's sword wildly.

"While you've been making friends," he explained while clashing swords with Seth and knocking over lamps and cracking mirrors in thier duel, "I looked through your last case file in your car."

"You've been stalking me?!" he realized.

Cain noticed his sword's ability failed to activate by making him move at a much faster rate. He also took note that Seth's movement's were not hindered. For some reason the detective wasn't slowing down like he should have been.

"So you waited for me here, huh? Waiting for that perfect moment to strike, is that it?"

"Out of all of the murders you've committed, not one of them were with your sword. Why is that?" Cain asked frighteningly.

"So you HAVE been doing your homework I see!" Seth replied taking a stab at the masked murderer.

Cain dodged and grabbed Seth's sword arm while the black haired detective did like wise. Seth was close enough to look Cain in his cold eyes, "Don't be afraid. We're identical you and me."

"I'm nothing like you!" Seth argued during the stand off.

"I've done my research on you Notch. You're a killer at heart."

"You're wrong." he disputed pushing Cain away.

"Your hands are soaked with blood now. Don't be a fool. I see what you truely are."

"NO! These men were monsters. They raped and murdered and ruined some many innocent lives. And then, they just walked away. They walked away because I didn't notice a finger print before it was too late, or an eyewitness was threatened into changing their testimony. I didn't do enough then, but I'm serving justice now. I'm righting my wrongs and now I'll finish what was started!" Seth charged straight towards Cain.

Cain jumped away and began cutting the remains of his slain victim which caused him to move faster and faster. Seth pulled out his firearm and started shooting at the masked individual. Cain had begun to move so quickly that he had become a blur in Seth's sight. The masked assassin's speed had increased exponentionally.

"Hold still damn you!" Seth ordered while firing off his gun.

Cain swooped over to the detective in less than a second and grabbed both of his arms. "Now why would you try and kill me with your gun if your sword is so special?"

Seth gasped, Cain had moved so quickly that he hadn't realized what had happened.

"Unless your sword can't hurt me." Cain paused taking note of Seth's reaction to his question, "I see...your sword doesn't kill."

"You're wrong." Seth disputed.

"Am I now?" Cain growled in his demonic voice. A small trail of blood began to leak down Cain's arm and drip between the two swordmen. "Ah, the injuries you endure are passed on to your enemies. That explains everything. Back in the cave, the bodies."

"What?! How could you possibly tell?" Seth wondered.

"I made sure to slightly strike your arm right before restraining you. And sure enough my arm began to cut open and bleed in that very same spot. I had wondered how you cut me in that cave. But now, I understand your sword."

Seth grimaced at Cain's revelation when suddenly the moment was disturbed by a third party.

"Danny?!" a shocked teen noticed his older brother's remains all over the bedroom from down the hallway. The teen saw Seth and Cain and pulled out a small pistol, "Burn in hell assholes!" he shouted before opening fire on them.

One bullet struck Seth in the arm causing the teen to bleed and drop his gun. He turned and ran away afterwards. Cain lept away from the detective once the teen began shooting and stayed on the other side of the room until the shooting had stopped.

"You didn't kill the brother?" Seth asked in surprise. Cain stood staring at Seth in silence. "Fine. Shall we finish this then?"

"Seth, I could have killed you at anytime, but I didn't." Cain warned.

"Well aren't you considerate." he expressed with sarcasim.

"I'm purposing an offer."

"An offer?"

"An alliance."

Seth laughed, "Ha! You've got to be joking?!"

"Do I look like a joker? I need to know the source that leaked information about me to the grand duke."

"I heard what had happened. The informant was murdered in his cell."

"He was a loose end, but it didn't end with him. My trails run cold and I need the absolute truth. Someone else knew about my existance, name, and how to get in touch with me. I need to know the one who knows too much."

"You're out of your mind. There's no way in hell I'd help you find out anything."

"Seth, you murdered the men who raped and murdered your daughter, but you never punished the one who put them up to it."

"What did you say?"

"I will find the person who gave the drug dealers your daughter, in exchange, you will find the second informant."

Seth stood staring at Cain from across the room, both swords still drawn. The detective had been blinded with rage and revenge, despare and regret, it never crossed his mind the drug dealers were someone else's puppets.

32

UNTRUSTWORTHY ALLIES

A timid knock rung through a wooden door inside the Vailstone castle.

Chase opened the door allowing prince Christian entry, "You wanted to see me?" Christian asked.

"Yes. Um, that will be all for now soldier." Hikaru stated.

Chase closed the door behind the young king and stood on the opposite side until needed again. Christian slowly walked over to the ambassador who happened to be sitting at his deceased father's desk with-in his study. Hikaru sat comfortably petting his chesire cat, resting in his lap at the time. Christian approached the desk noticing a few organized stacks of papers.

"Welcome young king, I know this is so soon, but I really need your signature on these documents."

Christian looked down at the titled documents and skimmed over one. "Increased tax hikes?" he glanced at another, "Dorian Act? What are these?"

"I really thought it necessary that I handled the work load until you were capable of preforming your royal duties." The ambassador stood from the soft chair and walked around the large desk to the new king's side. "Look, Christian..." he paused resting his hand on the boy's shoulder, "the world doesn't stop when you do. I want you to grieve as long as you need. Because I know all of this can be overwhelming. I mean, Dorian and Natalia both dead and all of these responsibilities. They must be done so other people's lives aren't ruined as well." Christian quickly looked up at Hikaru in the face with watery eyes, "Oh my goodness, I'm so sorry Christian. I should have known this conversation was too soon. My most sincerest apologies. But you know what I meant, right? Look, why not just sign these right quick and just be done with them."

The nineteen year old king grabbed a pen which was conveniently with-in Hikaru's hand and began signing the documents as a single tear began to roll down Christian's cheek. Sitting in the chair across the other side of the desk the cheshire cat began to grin widely.

Back inside the wooded area with the gypse Vincent and Alisha finally returned to camp.

"Hey, look! They're back!" Bo stated excitedly while wagging his shark tail. He hurried over to Alisha, "I was getting worried. What took so long?"

Alisha glanced at Vincent, "Oh, um. Nothing, it was just a long walk, that's all." she smiled.

"Hey, I wanted to show you something I found! It's so cool!"

"Okay, what did you want to show me?" she asked.

Bo tugged on the princess' dress and walked her over to a big stone, "Check this out." Bo lifted the stone and revealed a stash of beetles. "I've been finding a lot of these little guys." he stated squatting down and poking at them.

"Oh, uh. Very nice Bo." she struggled to compliment.

Wraith walked over to Vincent with a curious look, "Why did you two take so long?"

"You heard her, it was a long walk." Vincent returned.

Wraith suspiciously nodded his head, his eyes zeroed in on something of interest, "What is that on your shirt?"

"Nothing."

"It looks like her make-up."

"Well, you're a dumb ass cause it ain't." Vincent insulted.

"Well I think you're a lier!"

"So what if it is, huh? What's it matter to you?"

"Look you little white haired freak of nature, she's my territory so you better back off."

"She's your territory huh?" Vincent asked.

"Yeah, maybe after I'm done with her then you can have her."

"Is that right?"

"Yeah, that's right. You look like the kinda guy that could only get sloppy seconds anyways."

"YOU BITCH!" Vincent shouted punching Wraith in the mouth.

Wraith feel back and reached his hand to his mouth. Upon looking at his hand he noticed blood, "You stupid F@#*!"

Wraith leapt off the ground and jumped into Vincent. The two began punching each other in the face and stomach as hard as they each could. Alisha screamed at the sight of the two fighting. The princess and little shark dog rushed over. Enrique stepped out of his travel trailer and hurried over to the fighting teens as well.

Alisha pulled Wraith away from Vincent, "What is wrong with you two?! Why do you two always have to be at each other's necks?!"

"This prick sucker punched me." Wraith defended.

"You forgot who you were talking to." Vincent replied as he wiped blood from his cheek.

"Why don't you two just seperate and leave each other alone? Look, you're both upsetting Alisha more then what she already is. It's already enough on her mind about her parents and that Kamisama armor, but for you two to be acting so reckless is unforgivable." Enrique shouted.

Vincent and Wraith made eye contact with no one while the gypse scolded them. Vincent tossed some dirt away from off the ground and walked away pissed.

"What was that all about?" Alisha questioned.

"That guy's messed up in the head." Wriath claimed.

"Hey look, your dress!" Bo pointed out a blood stain from one of the fighting swordsmen.

"Your dress is getting so filthy and now this? Here, come with me. I have some outfits you can wear in my carriage." Enrique offered.

"That's not necessary."

"Blood stains and dirt are unbefitting of a princess' gown. Please, I insist." he offered yet again.

"Well, alright. Thank you."

Enrique and Alisha walked away and into Enrique's trailer. Bo looked over at Wraith and growled to scold him. Wraith growled back and startled Bo who hurried after Alisha.

Alisha walked inside the trailer noticing all of the gypse's clutter. Boxes, chests, hanging clothes, pots and pans, and boxes of food everywhere.

"Please excuse the mess," he smiled, "but you're more then welcome to wear anything you find to your liking."

"You have women's clothes?" she noticed.

"A few long stories, really. Just wear whatever you like." he welcomed and stepped out of the carriage.

The princess glanced around over trinkets and charms, perfumes and all sorts of accessories. Alisha removed the white bow from around her neck and placed it on a narrow shelf. After she saw some clothing to patch together for an outfit she reached behind her back and started pulling a zipper down her back. She began to breath easier once the tight dress allowed her body to relax.

"What are you gonna wear?" Bo asked innocently.

Alisha was startled and totally forgot about the little shark dog being present.

"Bo! Why are you still in here? I'm changing."

"So?"

"Well, I don't want you to see me naked." she explained.

"Why? What's wrong? I used to walk around naked all the time until somebody made me wear these pants. They REALLY wanted me to wear these for some reason. I should've bit'em." he figured.

"It's just not appropriate for you to see me undress, because, I'm a girl and you're a boy."

"I thought we were friends?" Bo asked sadly.

"We are, it's just," Alisha sighed, "it's just something I'm not used to, that's all. I just have a hang up about undressing with other people around."

Bo's eyes began to water, "Bo, I'm sorry. I don't mean to hurt your feelings. I'm just weird that way."

Bo removed the tear from his eye and smiled up at Alisha, "It's not that. You called me 'people'. You're the first person to ever call me that."

"Really?"

"Yeah......I'm used to hearing monster or freak, but never a people. Thank you. That means a lot to me." he smiled happily with a sniffle.

"Well, you're welcome." she smiled.

Bo walked to the door of the carriage, "I'll wait outside until your done, okay?"

"Alright." she answered back.

After Bo closed the door Alisha dropped her dress to the floor and picked up an article of her new attire. After a few tugs, tied strings, and dashes of sparkling glitter she stepped in front of a filthy mirror. She looked at herself from front to back.

"I like it." she smiled.

She picked up her old dress and looked at the stains. As she folded her old dress the zamora poison fell out of one of her pockets and onto the floor. Alisha placed her dress down and picked up the tiny bottle.

"You're a terrible gift," she sighed "but a gift none-the-less." she stated. The princess stuffed the tiny bottle in her clevage and turned to leave the cluttered carriage.

After twenty five minutes of changing the princess stepped out of the carriage in her new gypse outfit.

Bo welcomed her new dress, "Wow! That looks really good on you. You're so pretty."

"Thank you, fine sir." she blushed.

"Oh, by the God's you look heavenly." Enrique complimented. "You have excellent taste. Excellent taste indeed."

"Well, thank you for the change of clothes Enrique. I appreciate it very much."

"Well, you are very welcome my dear." he paused for a moment admiring how her body filled the new outfit. "Well, are you hungry yet?"

"Yes, actually. Do you have something else to eat?"

"Don't worry, I'll prepare something for you." he offered.

As Enrique walked away to start a new fire Bo stood a tad puzzled, "Alisha? What's camasawa?" he asked a tad embarrassed.

"I'm not sure." she admitted. "Where did you hear that from?"

"Well, Enrique said something about camasawa armor earlier. I was just wondering what kinda armor it was, that's all."

Alisha began to recall their conversations the night before and couldn't recall ever mentioning the armor around the gypse. It seemed a tad suspicious to her, but she figured it best to ask Vincent and Wraith about it before bringing it up around Enrique.

Alisha walked over to Wraith who was sitting outide the string of cans.

"Wraith can I ask you something?"

"What?" he snapped.

Alisha was a bit taken back from his rude reply, "What, you mad at me too?"

"Whatever."

"No, no whatever. What did I do?"

"Nothi'n."

"Then you're just being a jerk?"

"Look, why don't you just leave me alone and ask your lover boy over there." he replied indicating Vincent.

"Lover?" she blushed looking in Vincent's direction.

"Yeah, I noticed your make up on his shirt earlier. I know you two did more then just talk obviously."

"I was crying and he hugged me, why is that such a bad thing?"

"Yeah, well he sure doesn't seem like the hugging type."

"He's not I assure you, but why is this an issue? He gave me a hug because I'm having the worst week of my life. He just wanted me to feel better."

"I bet he did."

"What is THAT supposed to mean?"

"Nothing, forget about it."

"No, really. What is that supposed to mean? You said it. Explain."

"He's just trying to make a move on you. He's a little weasel."

"Vincent? I don't think so." she disregarded.

"Come on, don't act like you're blind. It's obvious."

Alisha glanced over to Vincent off in the distance while he sat near Enrique preparing another meal.

"You really think he likes me?"

"No! He's just hungry for your sex." Wraith said to Alisha's surprise.

"What?!"

"Yeah, earlier he offered you to me as his sloppy seconds. I lost it so I punched him to the ground and started beating his ass. It pissed me off hearing him talk about you that way."

Alisha was beside herself, she didn't know what to think.

"I'm sorry, I wouldn't have brought it up, but you asked me, so..."

"Yeah,..." she replied somewhat confused.

"I'm sorry, what is it you wanted to ask me?" he wondered.

"Sorry?"

"You said you wanted to ask me something."

"Ask you something? Oh, right. Yeah, um, earlier when you and Vincent were fighting Enrique mentioned the Kamisama armor."

"So?"

"Did you ask him about it?"

"No, why?"

"Cause Bo and I didn't mention the armor and you didn't mention it either. I'm positive Vincent hadn't had the time to talk to him about it either."

"I don't get it, what's your point?"

"Well, how did he not know about mom or dad, but he knew about the armor? That doesn't make sense to me."

"Yeah. Yeah, you're right." Wraith agreed standing up and walking over to Enrique. "HEY! GYPSE!" he yelled.

"What are you doing?" she asked nervously following after him.

Wraith gained the attention of everyone by the fresh campfire.

"Is something wrong?" he asked?

"Yeah, how'd you know about the armor? None of us mentioned it before." Wraith asked with attitude.

Vincent listened in watching for Enrique's answer.

"It's all over the radio. I heard it in my carriage." he scoffed.

"But I didn't see a radio in your trailer." Alisha chimmed in.

"So then why didn't you know about her folks?"

Enrique stood trying to think of a good answer, but was helplessly drawing a blank. "Okay, fair enough." The gypse pulled a gun out the holster on his belt and pointed it at the three youths. "I would have rather drugged you all if you just would have waited and given me the opportunity to fix this meal up, cause I mean having to pull out a gun....it's just not my style."

"So you tried to posion me last night with that zamora juice?" Alisha asked.

"No, no. That really does what I said it did, but I also figured you'd have been more complacent. Oh well."

"What are you doing?" Vincent asked on guard.

"Well, I had hoped for the chance to kidnap her away from you morons. A princess randsom is a great payoff. Also figured I'd make some good cash off the dress, but now that we're here I might at well take the fancy swords you two have there."

"You, you...." she struggled for the insult.

"Gypse." Enrique grinned.

"I knew we couldn't trust a gypse." Wraith stated.

"Yeah, yeah, yeah. Now toss the swords this way, and no funny buisness." he demanded with the gun in hand.

Vincent glared at the gypse, "Choke on it." he stated tossing his sheathed weapon away.

Something near by tripped off the string of cans around the border of the campsite. It only managed to gain slight attention for only a brief second before everyone's attention returned back to the situation at hand. Bo's attention, however, was focused less on the gypse and rather something else very near.

"Alright, now you." Enrique ordered Wraith.

Wraith slowly removed his sword from the sheath on his side. Enrique began to laugh upon noticing the bladeless sword.

"What the hell happened to your sword?" he laughed. "Your blade snapped right out of your hilt! Man, what a joke. Never mind, keep it. That cheap garbage is useless to me." Enrique added salt to injury.

"Na, you know what. Take it, you deserve this." he replied as he tossed his sword in the air over to the gypse.

As Wraith's sword hilt whirled in the air Wraith made sure to take his weapon's ability into effect. The sword of void cut Enrique mulitple times while being tossed over to him forcing him to drop the gun in shock. The gun fired off as it landed on the ground, but luckily the bullet hit no one. The gypse fell to the ground bleeding badly.

"What was that?!" he asked in a state of shock.

"Just the beginning." Wraith answered.

"No, Wraith. That's enough." Alisha intervened stepping in front of Wraith and placing her hands on his chest to prevent him from moving forward.

Vincent made sure to stand up and retrieved his swords. Bo on the other hand began barking as his fur started standing on end.

"What are you barking about?" Vincent asked. "The douche is down." he informed referring to Enrique.

"No! There's something watching us! I can sense it. I smell it too, it's in those trees!" Bo pointed over to the hovering trees above.

"Well I don't see anything." Vincent stated.

"AAAAAHHHHHHHH!!!!!!!!!!!!!" Alisha screamed as a massive spider creeped down while attached to a thick string of burning thread.

"Whoa, never seen a spider like that before." Wraith noticed.

Enrique made a desperate attempt to grab the gun, but Bo was on guard and near the gun and snapped at his hand. Enrique in that instant chose to abondon his entire plot of thievery and flee. He managed to get to his feet and slowly run hobble to his travel carriage.

"No you don't."Wraith declared and ran lungging for his weapon. The gypse hopped inside this carriage and whipped his horses to get away as quickly as possible. Wraith grabbed hold of his sword and tried slicing the wheels of the carriage to prevent his escape, but it failed. The gypse fled the scene trying to gain as much distance between him and the group as fast he could.

"What tha? Why didn't it work?" he wondered.

"Wraith!" Bo yelled.

The tattooed twenty two year old turned around and witnessed the large spider glarring at them all. Vincent gripped both his blades tightly and prepared for combat while Bo stood guard of Alisha and growled at the large creature to protect her. Wraith tightened his grip of his sword and readied to slay the beast.

33

Arachnid of flame!

As the gypse fled for his life the remaining four were left at the mercy of the giant fiery spider. The massive eight legged beast was equal to the size of a small car. The large arachnid had huge horns around its large body and a mane of fire that circle its neck and down the center of its back.

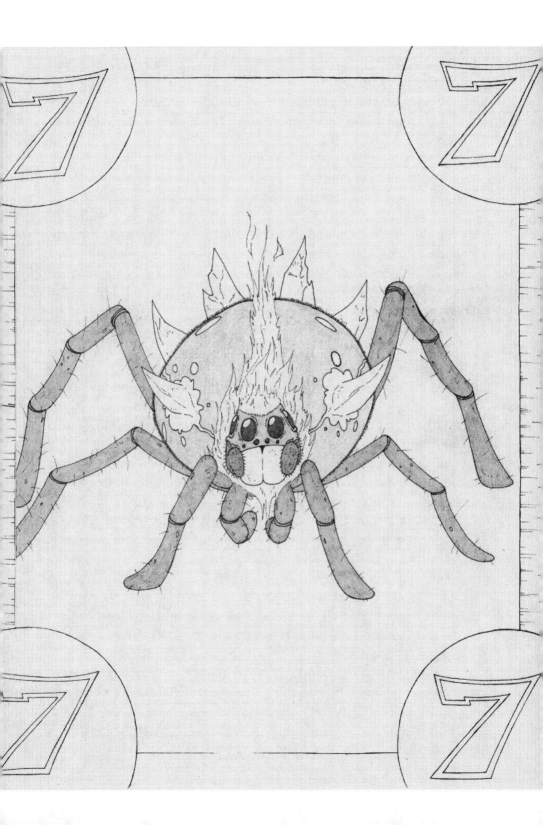

Before Wraith could lift his arm for a vital strike the arachnid scurried up its burning thread and back into the trees.

"Everybody stay close together!" Wraith shouted.

"You don't have to tell me twice!" Bo agreed as he rushed to Wraith with Alisha by his side.

"Vincent, come over here!" Alisha called out.

Vincent kept his eyes open looking for the location of the massive spider hiding behind the thick wall of leaves. Finally the monster's location was given away by the burning leaves. Vincent cast one of his katanas aside and forced it to burst into multiple metallic shards. The bits of metal danced in the air around him in a circular motion. Vincent had been practicing his swords abilities to prepare for such threats. The silver haired teen directed the shards with his free hand while the other clutched the other twin blade.

"NOOOOWWWW!" Vincent ordered in anger.

The swarm of metal shred into the burning trees striking the spider in a flurry of cuts and slices. The mammoth beast surprisingly spewed burning webs from its mouth hitting the ground and close trees.

"AAHHHH! Look out!" Bo cried out while covering his large head with his tiny paws.

The burning creature lept to the ground below and tried shooting Vincent with a thread of burning web. He narrowly jump out of the direction of the attack. The asian boy used his shards to hover around the massive target, but noticed less shards then before. He was shocked to see a fair amount of his scattered katanas shards stuck in sticky burning spider webs.

"Damn you ugly beast." Vincent readied a near by blade shard to stab through the spider's skull, but was forced to abandon the plan once a near by tree began falling over in his direction. Vincent turned and jumped over a burning thread to reach a safer location.

Alisha began coughing, "There's so much smoke." she cried.

"I know!" Wraith agreed, "It's the only thing stopping me from getting a clear strike on this thing." he muttered.

"RUN, DAMN IT! RUN!!" Vincent ordered.

Bo's fin upon his head began to tingle, "Oh boy, something's coming this way fast and I bet it's got eight legs!" The tiny shark dog pulled on Alisha's gypse dress in a safer direction. "Come on, follow me!"

Wraith felt the vibration from the beast's many footsteps on the ground and didn't hesitate to follow after. Vincent witnessed the great beast scurry their direction from behind the fallen tree. The heat from the flames were quite intense. The teen was already sweating profusely. He climbed on top of the fallen tree to get a visual on his missing blades. It was truely amazing how much smoke had been created in such little time, however, the young man had still managed to catch a shining reflection of the fire in his shards.

"There you are." he stated before coughing from the smoke.

Vincent used more scattered shards to slice at thick fiery web, but only managed to free some while getting more stuck.

"Ugh!" his judgment was getting clouded as his aggrivation grew. He looked around at anything to throw to jar some shards loose, but only found cans and pine cones. Then suddenly it hit him, "Wait a sec!"

Vincent used one of his remaining shards to hover in front of him while another floated in front of one of the entangling webs threads. He aimed with his katana and stabbed through the shard before him having the end of his blade appear through the other shard floating in the tress near the burning web. Vincent started hacking away at the web in the trees while standing on the ground surrounded by thick smoke.

"Come on." he tried rushing.

Meanwhile, Bo fled from the massive arachnid while leading Alisha and Wraith to safety as well. Alisha was becoming short of breath, but was certainly determined not to stop. Wraith managed to catch up to the pair and looked behind. Nothing appeared to be following aside from burning trees and thick smoke.

"Hey! I think we lost it." Wraith mentioned.

"Huh?" Alisha asked slowing down.

"What's going on? Why are you guys stopping? Come on Vincent's probably fighting that thing for us to run, now let's go!" he stated wagging his shark tail in distress.

"Vincent!? You're right. We have to go back." Alisha stated.

"What? Hell no. You crazy?" Wraith disagreed.

"But Vincent is still back there. What if he's in trouble?"

"Then screw'em. I'm not die'n for him." Wraith admitted.

"God Wraith can't you think of somebody other than yourself for once?!"

"Nope." he answered rudely.

"You might be too scared to go, but I'm not." she insulted. The princess began marching back in the direction they ran away from to assist Vincent.

Bo watched with terrified big round eyes.

Wraith reached out and grabbed the princess by the wrist, "Where tha hell do you think you're go'n?"

"How dare you talk to me like that. Let go of me!" she ordered trying to jerk her arm away from the purple haired youth.

"I'm not letting you go back to that thing." Wraith replied while struggling to keep his grip on her thin wrist.

"Hey, you two stop it!" Bo cried out.

"Let go of me!" Alisha shouted. Unable to break free of Wraith's resistance Alisha reared back and slapped Wraith in the face.

The moment was a surprise to all, especially Wraith who jerked her wrist free and reared back a fist of his own. Bo and Alisha were stunned to witness Wraith readying a punch for the princess. Suddenly a large crackle sounded off near by catching everyone's attention. Bo's fin upon his head began to tingle again warning him of more in coming danger.

"MOVE!" Bo yelled leeping into Alisha and knocking her to the ground.

A thick strand of web darted right where she stood. Wraith glanced quickly for the other end of the web, but saw nothing but more burning trees and smoke.

"COME ON!" he yelled attempting to sever the fiery spider thread. "Huh? Come on, cut damn it!" Wraith was surprised his weapon refused to cut the spider's thread. "I cut that bug guy and that fallen tree before, so why not now? What gives?"

The large spider rushed from one tree top to another.

"Can't you do something Wraith?" Bo wondered. "It's not broke is it?"

Wraith grimaced, looking at his perplexing weapon. He returned his attention to the threat at large now with uncertainty in his sword's ability. As the creature darted from one tree top to another it tried sniping the three with burning web.

"AAAHHHH!!!" Bo screached.

Alisha stood back up and picked Bo off the ground to hold him tightly, "Don't worry Bo, I'll think of something. I'll think of something." she repeated trying to figure a way out of such danger.

"I've got this." Wraith muttered. He tried watching the large spider as closely as he could through the chaos and smoke. "Enough running." he stated before slicing down a large oak tree. "Whoa. Look out!" he warned carelessly cutting the tree to tip over in their direction.

"HEY! Who are you try'n ta get with that thing, huh?!" Bo barked.

"Shut-up will ya?" he said regaining his attention to the scurrying spider. "Got'cha!" he declared swinging his blade to cut yet another tree it hid with in, but the blade refused to cut yet again. " W h y is this stupid thing not cutting?" Wraith attempted cutting the previously sliced tree and was successful, but once his attention returned to the tree at hand his attempts failed. "Damn! I don't know what's wrong."

Alisha glanced around for a large blunt object hoping to find a broken branch to protect herself with, but was given no such luck.

"Ah, screw it." Wraith began running away from the danger.

The spider was distracted with Wraith more so than Alisha and Bo and began following after.

"Look! He's drawing its attention away to save us." the shark dog excitedly announced, however, Alisha witnessed the reality of the situation and saw the young man abandon them to save himself.

Wraith looked behind and saw large amounts of burning leaves falling from the trees, a clear sign he failed to avoid the beast. Wraith was getting short winded and turned around quick for a view of an open shot. He was watching closely at the approaching danger's movements hiding with in the trees and spotted a large hairy leg. In that moment Wraith reacted and swung his blade successfully severing half of one of the creature's many legs.

"YES! Got it!" he realized happily. "Alright, it's all work'n again. Just show yourself. I dare ya." he smiled wickedly.

"I SEE IT!" Vincent shouted.

"Vincent?!"

A large flurry of Vincent's blades swept in the trees chopping down large quantities of burning leaves, branches, and two massive spider legs causing the creature to tumble and slam to the ground.

"I've got it now!" Wraith announced and swung his blade cutting the thick hide of the monster.

In a defensive manuver the spider sprayed small hairs, which appeared as burning embers, all around the area. Vincent was breathing heavily as the small burning hairs drifted in the wind. Suddenly a thought occurred to him about the small burned holes through the deceased deer from before.

"The drifting burning hairs and the deer's death, they have to be related." Vincent figured. "Don't breath in those hairs!" he warned.

"Huh?" Wraith heard quickly covering his mouth and nose with his free hand. Wraith was determined to end this now and struck the spider once more which cut its back wide open.

More burning hairs fluttered around the area endangering the two even more.

"Idiot." Vincent said to himself. He used a floating shard to drift in front of the spider's head while using another to float in front of himself. In one strike Vincent stabbed the spider directly in the brain from over thirty feet away.

The massive spider wiggled and squirmed before ceasing to move.

"Get away from there." Vincent told Wraith.

Wraith slowly jogged away and back over to Vincent before something grabbed both their attention. As the two looked back at the dead beast swarms of tiny baby fire spiders began crawling from the gapping wounds in its back.

"Oh shit!" Wraith said rushing over to Vincent faster.

Rather than freaking out over the worsening situation Vincent used the hovering blade shards to fly about cutting apart the football sized baby arachnids. Alisha and Bo finally caught up to the two swordsmen just in time to witness Wraith join in on cutting down the swarm of offspring with his blade as well.

Once every creepy crawler was killed Wraith decided to take out some revenge.

"Time to have a little fun." he smirked. The purple haired youth swung his sword at the dead spider to slice and dice the monster to bits, but failed embarrassingly. "Ugh! This stupid thing just works when ever it damn well feels like it."

"Hey, wait a second. That tree you were trying to cut before and couldn't was an old dead tree just like tha spider. Maybe you can only cut stuff that ain't dead." Bo thought and shared with all.

"Huh?" Wraith finally realized and stared at his weapon, "Only on the living?"

"What do ya think?" Bo inquired.

"Makes sense I guess." Wraith confessed.

The killed spider suddenly burst into intense flame and burned completely into cinder and ash.

"Let's get away from here." Alisha asked.

"Yeah, good idea. Especially since that stupid thing probably drew in a lot of unwanted attention." Vincent added. "Come on, I noticed a road before. It's gotta be safer than dealing with things like this in the woods.

Alisha, Bo, and Wraith trailed behind while Vincent recalled how to get back to the road he discovered running through the woods. It was certainly a quiet and uncomfortable walk between the purple haired youth and princess until Wraith finally broke the silence.

"So how did Vincent know where to find me?" he asked.

Alisha was silent for a moment as if pondering to answer his question, "He finally caught up to Bo and me. Bo told him that you were sacrificing yourself to save us."

"Oh, so you told him to come and help me?"

"No, I'm not his boss. I didn't tell him to do anything. He just ran off after you to help. I've discovered Vincent has a really tough outer shell, but is a great guy deep inside."

"Oh." Wraith paused, "So, is that ALL you two told him?"

"Hmm." Alisha huffed, "Do you mean did I actually explain that you abandoned us to save yourself and left us to die. Or that you were about to punch me in the face?"

Wraith just walked with her without anything to say in return.

"No, I didn't tell him. It would only cause you two to fight again and there isn't any need in that."

"Thanks."

"Don't thank me. I don't want your 'blessings' nor 'gratitude'. Let's just get out of here." Alisha hurried to catch up with Vincent and began keeping closer to him.

After a long twenty-five minutes the group finally reached the road.

"Hey, tha road! I see it!" Bo announced excitedly.

"Bout time, thought we were lost." Wraith added.

"Alright, so now what's the plan?" Alisha questioned.

"Hm, I guess follow the road back into the kingdom?" Vincent said, taking a shot in the dark.

"Yeah, but then what?" Alisha wondered.

"Look, let's just take the road back into to town. I've got a friend I know we can crash with until we figure out what's going on and what we're do'n. Alright?" Wraith informed.

"Fine. Anything sounds good right now, cause I missed breakfast and I'm starving." Vincent admitted.

"Can I come to Alisha?" Bo questioned.

"Well, of course you can. I sure wouldn't feel right leaving you here with fire monster spiders." she smiled. "Why do you feel like I didn't want you to come with me?" she asked kneeling down to look him in the eyes.

"It's not that, it's just, I'm a shark dog. I'm not gonna be welcome there."

"Hey, you're with me now and you're welcome to come with me anywhere I go, okay?" she charmed.

"Okay!" Bo joyfully agreed giving her a big hug. "Then what're we waiting for? Lead tha way good sir." he instructed Wraith who began leading the way.

While Wraith and Bo walked in front Alisha used the oppurtinity to set things straight with Vincent, "Hey."

"You're not going to ask me about my parent's now, are you?"

"No. I was just going to say that you were actually pretty heroic back there."

Vincent quickly glanced at the blushing beauty, "Heroic huh? I'm not a hero, I was just fighting a big monster to live."

"Stop it. You rescued us all back there. You're a hero whether you like it or not."

Alisha wasn't too sure, but for a slight moment it almost appeared as if Vincent may have blushed. If even for a second.

"You've got some big walls built up, but I think it's because you've got an even bigger heart behind them." she confessed touching his chest softly.

"Ugh." Vincent scoffed.

Alisha smiled for a moment before continuing, "I also wanted to talk to you about something else."

"Hm?" Vincent asked regretting another deep personal question.

"So I was talking with Wraith earlier, ya know, before the spider thing."

"Oh? What about?" he genuinely wondered.

"Wraith told me about that whole 'sloppy seconds' remark."

"I don't know where you're going with this, but I'm not going to apologize to him if that's what you're after. He deserved it."

"Wait, what?"

"You said he confessed, right?"

"Oh? Oh, yeah." she recovered.

"Look, I know you're probably going to keep asking me about it so look." Vincent stopped walking and looked Alisha straight in the eyes, "Something about somebody talking about you that way just really pissed me off, okay? I don't know why, but it just doesn't sit well with me and I'm not gonna take it, alright?" he confessed in sheer honesty.

Alisha was captivated in his eyes and completely blind sided by the actual truth. She slighty began nodding her head until finally answering, "Okay."

"Hey, hurry up back there!" Bo called behind.

Wraith, Bo, Vincent, and Alisha all continued on their way together back into the kingdom while another individual wandered the forest. A lone hiker followed the burning brush and smoke to the ashy remains of the deceased spider summoning. Beside the ash stood a small albino child entirely in white clothing holding a small lantern.

"Hey, kid. What happened here? Are you lost?" the hiker asked.

The small child turned and looked at the man without saying a word.

"I saw all of this smoke for miles. Did you cause all this?" he asked looking at the boy's lantern.

The small child remained silent which began giving the man an uneasy feeling.

"You should go." the small child eventually answered in a low whisper.

"Huh?" the man asked.

"You should go. He's hungry."

"What are you talking about?" the hiker wondered.

While the strange man kept his attention on the albino child a long slender tounge stretched out and wrapped around the hiker's torso. The man was startled and immediately tried freeing himself before he was swept off his feet and ripped to shreds in the death trap mouth of another one of Fire starter's summonings.

"I warned you." the child muttered quietly.

34

ON THE CORNER OF THIRTY SEVENTH AND FORTY FIRST STREET

While Seth exacts his revenge on criminals who've managed to cheat the system it would appear he's made an unlikely ally. Rufus and Wade have been taken into custody and held at the Vaistone castle. Vincent and Wraith have been protecting princess Alisha from danger while hiding in the woods and Christian has been kept in the castle with Raziel and Hikaru. Fire starter has unleashed his monsterous summonings upon the innocent of the kingdom and Kaz, he's been sitting down in a fast food joint eating a burger while looking through a phone book.

An employee of the establishment walked over to Kaz's table, "Um, Honey? I'm sorry, but we need to use the phone book. The manager needs to call maintenance."

"Fine, go ahead and take it. Didn't help me at all." Kaz confessed.

"Oh? What is it you're trying to find?" she asked nicely.

"Well, there's this detective guy with long black hair that really sucks at his job. I mean, he didn't notice his name card at the table. No wonder he wasn't a detective anymore, right? Any way know where I could find him?"

"Uh, I see a lot of guys with long black hair, so I doubt it. Do you know his name?"

"Simon or Seth, it's one of them."

"What about his last name?"

"I don't think it was ever brought up." Kaz tried recalling.

The employee smiled, "I know exactly what you mean. There's been a time or two I wish I had gotten more then a first name. I could use the child support." she admitted. "Well, I hope you find your guy."

Kaz didn't realize her assumption and took a bite of a few more fries. As he remained seated he began noticing a few people running by the windows of the building in a panic. Patrons of the resturant who started getting up and looking through the window became frightened and evacuated. Kaz stood up and walked over to the soda machine to refill his drink. After taking another swig he passed through the glass entrance and stepped out into the street. The large man was suddenly a needle in a haystack. Swarms of civilians ran in terror from a familiar looking snake monster down the street. Kaz slowly walked through the crowd of panicing people. Once the large beast turned the corner Kaz sipped more of his soda and followed after at his own leisurely pace.

In the center of the street Kaz spotted Fire starter and Grunt slowly walking with his summoning Basoomamba accompanied by a new musclely individual. Basoomamba whipped its tail sending cars flying over the heads of innocent people and spit streams of intense fire upon the buildings surrounding it.

"Hey, is this your turf or what?" Kaz asked loudly.

Fire starter turned to acknowledge Kaz, even gaining the attention of Grunt, Basoomamba, and Sammy sammy seven. The Fire elemental smiled from underneath his wicker hat, "Yeah, somethi'n like that. Carl right?"

"It's Kaz."

"Kaz, so what'cha do'n he'ya? Ya got'cha sword, what'cha still around for?"

"I've got some undesired attention I wanna lose. You?"

"Same he'ya. Looks like Raziel blame'n me for Dorian's death. That lie's not do'n me any fav'as."

"........" Grunt added.

"I've been curious about something I wanted ta ask you." Kaz admitted, "If you knew where that armor was the whole time, why didn't you just get it when ever you wanted? Why bring all this attention?"

"Ha! Wasn't that simple, tha ruler of tha north placed that spell ov'a tha arm'a. Seven random swordsmen were requi'ya ta free it from tha spell. You and those oth'a six. Tha barri'a around tha arm'a nev'a would'a feel unless tha seven of ya removed tha swords. But you didn't come all this way ta ask me about that did ya?" Fire starter asked suspiciously.

"Na." Kaz answered pulling out his broad sword, "I was gonna kick your ass too."

Fire starter cackled, "You're out numb'ad. Grunt, Sammy sammy sev'n, get'em." he ordered.

Grunt slowly started making his way over, but Sammy sammy seven smiled and ran over to engage in combat with Kaz right away.

"This should be a good workout." Kaz muttered.

Basoomamba spit a huge fireball over the heads of everyone sending it right towards Kaz. Kaz didn't hesitate to jump back from the bursting sphere of flame. As it connected with the ground Sammy sammy seven lunged through the fiery attack and swung his fist at full force. Kaz used his sword to block the physical attack surrounded by a huge wave of fire. Kaz managed to avoid the punch directly, but still was burned and sent flying back with great force.

"Damn! That shit's strong." he quietly announced while kneeling off the ground.

As he looked up he noticed Sammy sammy seven relentlessly attacking again, but this time from above. Kaz quickly jumped over to the side and avoided the summonings powerful flame kick that left a crater in the cement.

"Not do'n so well are ya?" Fire starter taunted with a chuckle.

Grunt lunged over to Kaz trying to smack him with one of his ball-and-chain arm swings. Luckily Kaz heard the rattling metal and moved in time, but just barely.

"Now I've got ya!" Kaz shouted striking Grunt with his blade.

Lightening struck Grunt and sent him flying backward into a parked car.

"SAMMY!" Sammy sammy seven yelled during his attack.

Kaz was punched and launched hurling several feet away once more. Kaz took a huge burning blow to the ribs, he'd never felt a hit like that before.

"Cheap shot." Kaz complained.

"Sammy seven." Sammy sammy seven smiled.

"What're you, retarded? Can't you say something else?" Kaz mocked.

Sammy sammy seven's vocabulary was severely limited and he didn't appreciate mockery at his expense much at all. The summoning yelled his name once more and clapped both of his fists together and slammed them on the ground at the same time causing a massive fiery wave of destruction directed solely at Kaz. Kaz accepted the challenge and buckled down to prepare for the attack. Once the flaming wave was in range Kaz slashed his sword into the ground causing a large burst of lightening which clashed with the summonings attack, however, the attack launched by Kaz didn't stop upon colliding with Sammy sammy seven's. Instead the lightening appeared to bounce and leep upon the ground sparatically in the summoning's direction.

"Sammy seven!?" he worried.

The attack smashed into Sammy sammy seven and sent him soaring through the air quiet an impressive distance. The summoning was launch passed Fire starter and Basoomamba, nearly hitting them.

"What tha hell was that?" Fire starter argued.

Kaz held his sword high in the air with great confidence and admiration, "Now THAT, was a legendary attack."

"Legend?! What ev'a, Basoomamb'a kill'em." the fire sorcerer ordered.

The hovering bizarre structure on Basoomamba's back began to spin rapidly which appeared to make the indentions in it's two orbiting spheres glow an unbelievable bright white.

"Feel tha heat of tha sun ya idiot!" Fire starter laughed.

Kaz was thankful for the accidental warning from Fire starter and ran while watching the massive snake's aim. Suddenly streams of unbearable heat shot from the spheres instantly slicing through the road, cars, and buildings. Kaz desperately lunged beside an eighteen wheeler in an attempt to sheild him from the crumbling buildings, collapsing streets, and exploding cars and fire hydrants. Fire starter gazed forward noticing nothing but rubble and dust.

"Good werk mamba." he appreciated.

"Sammy sammy seven." Sammy sammy seven complained rotating his sore arm.

"...........!" Grunt compared to Sammy sammy seven's injury. "..........."

"Oh? More company?" Fire starter asked intrigued.

Three Vailstone military jeeps speedily came to a hault a small distance away. The soldiers, including general Grechov and lieutenant Brookes immediately emptied out of the vehicles and aimed their weapons at Fire starter and his minions.

"It's over mystic! Drop your weapons and surrender now." Grechov ordered.

"A TRAP!" Fire starter defended instantly upon seeing the quick response of the Vailstone military and stabbed his fire staff on the ground forcing Basoomamba, Sammy sammy seven, Grunt, and himself away from danger.

"Damn it! He just disappeared into fire!" Grechov regrettably cursed.

"We need an E.M.S. team to scope the streets of thirty seventh and forty first street." Brookes informed over her radio. "Possible injured and trapped civilains under large debris."

"Roger that lieutenant." the voice on the other side confirmed. "Two other sightings of monsters with in the kingdom's city reported attacking people. Closest to your location is twelve blocks away."

"Good, send me the coordinants to my G.P.S., General another attack near by." Brookes informed without hesitation.

"If we could have gotten him it would have stopped already. I should have just shot him in the back of the head." Grechov thought out load.

"Sir! Another attack." she repeated.

"What? Oh right, let's go." he replied returning to his senses.

"Follow me!" Brookes yelled to the troops before seating. Grechov followed and sat in the passenger seat, "Killing Fire starter wouldn't have stopped the summonings, you know that. It's why we needed him alive." she stated while starting the engine and driving towards the next spotted fire summoning.

"Yeah, but he's as good as dead already anyways. I should have just ended him and killed his monsters one by one." Grechov complained.

Grechov and Brookes had driven away with the other two jeeps full of soldiers and Kaz was left pinned underneath the rubble to suffocate. The large damaged eigtheen wheeler did provide some guard from the fallen rubble, but didn't leave him in a position to walk away.

Kaz coughed from under the slabs of cement blocking him. In the chaos of the attack the burly swordman dropped his sword. He tried looking around and shifting from underneath the debris, but his foot was wedged tight leaving him unable to move about. It was like laying in a coffin of stone and thick dust.

"My sword?" he thought wondering of its location.

He struggled to see in the poorly illuminated darkness. He swept his hands along the ground trying to feel about for his weapon. As the dust began to settle it just so happened that a burning flame from Fire starter's monster was in the distance and just enough to shine upon Kaz's weapons blade.

"That shine! It's gotta be!" he concluded.

The man desperately attempted reaching over to his companion. His arm fully extended was barely enough to touch the tip of the sword's handle.

"Come on!" he struggled.

He reached with all his might getting closer and closer until finally he was able to grab the handle of the weapon, but sadly it also was pinned underneath rubble.

"No." he said to himself trying to jerk the weapon free.

Kaz continued shifting his body in a jerking motion as his breaths began to decrease in quantity.

"Come on." he ordered, "Come ON!"

In a bout of sheer frustration Kaz shouted at the top of his lungs, "Come OOOOONNNNN!!! AAAAAAAHHHHHHHHHHHHHHH!!!!!!!!!" In his determination for survival he summoned the power of his sword forcing a blinding burst of lightening from the blade of the broad sword which obliterated the rubble that kept him trapped underneath into tiny pebbles of debris.

To Kaz's amazment he was freed from his tomb of stone. He looked at his weapon with excitement and admiration once more, "Oh yeah baby. I like this." he grinned.

35

CITY A CINDER

Seth had been driving his car to a known hangout of the brother that got away, hoping to find him there and finish his list of unpunished criminals. He sat alone however, he may have an odd alliance with Cain, but he certainly doesn't trust him much at all. Traffic began to pile up forcing Seth to come to a complete stop. He looked through his window at the roof tops of the buildings near by and the sidewalks.

"Just how IS that assassin keeping up?" he wondered.

Seth also began to ponder what the problem was holding up all of the traffic from flowing. The detective eventually decided to flip on the radio for a bit of music while he waited.

"...all they can to try and reduce the casualties, but the monsters appear to be attacking without reason nor direction all across the kingdom. The fact that these beings are using fire to attack leaves many to believe they are the creatures the previous royal mystic threatened the current temporary ruler of Vailstone with. Hikaru Yotameshii has yet to have made a public announcement. Fire fighter's and law enforcement are doing all they can, but are leaving many to believe perhaps a kingdom evacuation is in order." the radio announcer broadcasted.

"What?" Seth was stunned, he had been so involved with exacting his vigilante justice that he was entirely oblivious to information regarding attacks on the Vailstone kingdom.

He looked forward seeing a panicking swarm of families running for their lives with children in arms. People of all ages getting out of their cars and running in terror. The detective's curiosity had peaked. He wondered what was causing so much fear in these people that would force them to abandon their cars. He tried opening his door to exit the vehicle and investigate, but there were too many civilian's running by his car and the ones parked beside him. Seth quickly looked inside his glove compartment and pulled out a box of bullets and loaded his gun. He tucked the gun inside his coat and grabbed hold of his sword. In all the panic opening the door was not an option so the black haired man rolled down his window and started crawling out of his car, even though he was still forced to push up against strangers running by.

From on top a not too distant building Cain was watching the detective leave his old car, "What are you doing now?" he muttered.

A massive shadow suddenly covered Cain and multiple buildings during all the chaos. The masked assassin looked upward and was taken back by the massive beast at which he saw.

Seth stood on the ground by his car and began to traverse his way through the crowd of people until he saw the giant beast land from the sky above. Several car alarms started sounding off once the great beast landed on the street. Towering over the buildings around it stood a huge dragon of intense heat. Instead of scales the dragon had a body of brittle cooling magma with lava dripping from the cracks in his supposed skin. The monster had enormous horns and it's wing span was the length of a city block. The dragon watched everyone run from it in terror, but the dragon was not sent to scare. It was sent for another purpose, so it forced up a great deal of energy and breathed fire of unbearable heat upon the running innocent people. Lava poured from his mouth as the fire scorched everyone down the block. Cars began exploding and bursting into flame as people were turned to ash or clumps of burning meat. Cain watched from a far as Seth was engulfed in the hot doom.

Meanwhile, at the Vailstone kingdom Christian remained locked in his room for his own protection. He sat on his bed bored, but not feeling the energy to do anything. He recalled being brought back and his discussions with Hikaru and Raziel. Then his hatred for Fire starter began to grow, recalling the events of his adventure and imagining the moment the mystic placed his spell over Raziel. At that moment the shell on Christian's necklace began to shake. The pixie appeared from inside and flew in front of the young king's face.

"What are you doing? Why is it so quiet out here?" she asked.

"Ugh! Come to pester me some more?" Christian accused.

"No!" she replied spraying pink glitter in his face.

"Awk!" he coughed and shook the dust from his face.

"So?"

"So what?"

"So when are you getting out of here?"

"I'm not, I live here." he answered with a bit of attitude.

"You live here? Am I wrong or did these people murder your parents? Maybe it sounded differently in my shell."

"No, Raziel did, but he was under an evil spell by some guy named Fire starter. It wasn't really his fault."

"And you believe that? Man you're really quick to forgive a guy that murdered your parents."

"Stop saying it like that!"

"What? The truth?"

"No! I mean, yes! I mean, you know what I'm saying."

"Kiddo, I don't think even you know what you're saying."

"That Raziel..." he stopped.

The tiny pixie fluttered her wings and eventually realized what Christian's real problem was. "Oh my, you....you can't accept reality can you? You don't want to believe what happened? How sad. How really really sad that is."

"I know, I know. It's so hard though and I don't know what to do. I don't even know what I'm doing here."

"You're so weak you can't even accept the truth?" she insulted.

"What?! I thought you understood where I was coming from?"

"Ha. NO, I'm not weak, and neither was my master. He's nothing like you are. There's no doubt in my mind that if he was in your shoes that he would get justice for his murdered parents. He certainly wouldn't be in his room pouting and crying like a little girl human."

"Your master this, your master that. YOU'RE one to talk. You can't accept reality either. That's all I've heard from you since we met. Your old master is dead so let it go."

The pixie's eyes began to tear up which forced Christian to regret snapping back at the tiny pink girl.

"Yeah, well I loved my master and I'll never let go! I'll never forget! But I'll tell you this, if he was murdered I would at least avenge his death and not hide in my shell the rest of my life. You're still not fit to wear his clothes and you never will be! NEVER!" she cried back before zipping back into her shell.

Christian looked down at the shell around his neck, "Hey, I wasn't saying to forget about him." He waited for a respond of some kind before continuing, "Hello in there? Ugh, come on. Don't cry."

"I'm not crying." she stated as she cried inside her shell.

"I'm sorry. I didn't mean to hurt your feelings." he sighed. "I'm just really upset and confused and I took it out on you and that was wrong of me and I'm sorry. Now will you please come out?"

"Why?"

"Just come out. Please?"

Christian waited for the pixie to come forth. After a minute the tiny pixie popped out of the shell and landed on the bed in front of Christian. She stood with her head held low and not saying a word. The young king looked at the tiny pixie with curiosity and compassion.

"What's your name?"

"Huh?"

"I said what's your name?" he repeated with a soft smile.

"Why do you want to know my name?"

"Because," he chuckled, "it's polite to know someone's name if your going to continue to carry on conversations with them."

The tiny girl smiled slightly, "Oyova."

"Oh-yova?"

"No, Oyova." she corrected.

"Oh, Oyova. Okay. That's a pretty name. I've never heard of it before."

"You really think so?"

"What?"

"What you said, that it's a pretty name?"

"Oh, yeah. I like it."

It was very difficult to tell, but the small pixie girl blushed, "Well thank you."

The two shared a warm moment until someone at the door began frantically unlocking the door to barge in.

"Someone's coming!" Christian stated.

Oyova gasped and hurried back into her shell just as the door opened. Crow marched inside and began looking around his room.

"Who's in here?" he demand.

"Nobody."

"Don't lie to me, the guard told me you were talking with someone in here. And I heard it too, now where are they."

"Nobody is in here, now get out!" Christian ordered.

Two soldiers entered with Crow into the young king's room. Crow ordered them to search his closet and bathroom.

"I said get outta here!"

Crow hurried over to Christian and pulled him off the bed by his wrist. "Look here ya little snot. I know you're lying to me, I heard the talking on the other side of the door.

"Let go of me!" the young king shouted.

Hikaru and Raziel had immediately been informed of someone else inside Christian's room and hurried to investigate without haste.

"What's going on in here?" Raziel asked as he arrived.

Crow released Christian's wrist once the grand duke walked through the door. "Somebody is in here with him. I heard the voices." Crow informed.

"Christian is this true?" Raziel asked.

"No. Nobody is in here."

"You wouldn't be lying to me now would you?" he asked condescendingly.

"No. Would you?" Christian replied.

"What is that supposed to mean?" Raziel asked.

Hikaru finally walked in while holding his cane, "What happened? What seems to be the problem."

"Um, there..." Raziel stuttered from being caught off guard by Christian's question, "....there's apparently someone else in the room so we're searching it through."

"Is there someone in here with you Christian?" Hikaru inquired.

"No, nobody else is in here with me. Now I want you all out of my room right now!" the young king ordered.

"Certainly, right after everyone's done searching the room." Hikaru humored.

"No! Right now! Everyone out at once!" Christian demanded.

Crow smirked looking down at Christian, "Just calm down Christian their almost done." Raziel tried pacifying.

"Look I'm the king now because of you and I demand you all leave my room at once!" he shouted getting red in the face.

"Calm down will you?" Raziel asked.

"No I will not calm down. Now you will listen to me and get out of here!"

Hikaru smiled and waved his hand toward Christian, "Look Christian, you might be the new king in town, but you're certainly not calling the shots around here."

"What?!" the young king asked in shock.

"Hikaru?" Raziel was stunned.

"Oh don't act so surprised Raziel. You and I know damn well the boy's not ready for the thrown yet. Especially with the current condition that it's in. Maybe, in time, but not now."

"It's all clear sir." a soldier informed

"Thank you, back to you're post soldier." Hikaru ordered.

Christian stood in awe of the awakening truth as Hikaru, Crow, and Raziel walked out of the room.

"RAZIEL!?" Christian pleaded, asking for support.

Raziel looked back, but continued on his way out the door.

The young prince's door room was closed and guarded for safety. The ambassador started walking down the hall until Raziel stopped him.

"Hikaru what was that back there?! He IS the new king now."

"Raziel please, get a hold of yourself. You know deep down in your heart that boy's not ready yet for the responsibilities of being king. And with his judgement clouded as it is he's certainly in no position to start making choices that change people's lives. Now look, telling him the truth may hurt his feelings and ours as well, but its a small price to pay for putting the people of this kingdom first."

The grand duke sighed, "You're right, it's just that look on his face."

"SIR! SIR!" major Collins interrupted, "We have a problem!"

"What's wrong soldier?" Raziel wondered.

"The general and lieutenant went off to remove a threat in the kingdom, but now there is an out break. It's Fire starter, he's unleashed his summonings!" Collins informed. "We're losing this battle, sir."

"Damn it! Why wasn't I informed about this at the start!?" Raziel questioned.

Raziel started to make his way to assist in the matter before Hikaru jumped in front of him.

"Whoa, whoa, whoa! Where do you think you're going? You still have a terrible image problem my friend. The public is NOT ready to see you just yet." The ambassador made an adjustment to his jacket, "Perhaps this little fiasco is just what we needed. Maybe now the people of this kingdom will remember who truly kept it safe."

"Out of my way Hikaru."

"I'm sorry Raziel, but I can't let you go out there just yet. It's not in our best interest."

Raziel leaned towards Hikaru with serious overwhelming intimidation, "Stop me."

Hikaru cowarded off to the grand duke's side and allowed him to pass him by. Raziel began running through the castle, but careful not to accidentally kill anyone who may turn the corner and step in his way. As common knowledge, if someone begins to run quickly one begins to apply more force with each fast step, unfortunately this is usless information to everyone unless one's force cannot be stopped. So as Raziel ran faster he unfortuately broke through the ceiling of the floor below and fell through, luckily without crushing anyone underneath.

Hikaru and the others carefully hurried over to look down the hole in the floor to see if he was alright. Raziel stood up without a scratch and charged out into the courtyard. Christian was curious what all the loud commotion was and opened his door just a crack to peek outside into the hallway. The young boy was uncertain what everyone was looking at, but couldn't care less. Now was a golden oppurtunity to sneak out of his room since the soldiers were distracted. Christian quietly closed his door and silently crept down the hall.

Raziel started running by a soldier leaving a military jeep, "KEYS!" he shouted.

The soldier obeyed his grand duke and tossed the keys toward Raziel. He managed to catch the keys flying through the air and stopped at the vehicle. Sadly, the simple force of clutching the keys in mid-air was too much and disfigured the shape of the keys. It was certainly an annoying set back, but Raziel didn't have time to waste. He started running to the gated entrance full of protesting citizens. With the city under attack there was no time to spare, Raziel picked up speed and lept into the air. The grand duke accidentally excerpted too much force in his jump and was sky born miles into the air. He soared over the gate and all its protesters with ease. Without much effort Raziel jumped a distance of fifty three miles in a single bound.

But, luckliy for Raziel he hadn't jumped with all his might and began plumitting down back to earth. He had gained a great deal of speed falling back down without resistance. His human instincts kicked in forcing him to worry about the landing. While airborn it was obvious by the large amounts of smoke from the kingdom that Vailstone's people were truly in need of his aid.

Raziel eventually hit the ground causing a huge crater which only destroyed trees and a gravel road near by. He stood up inside the creater and slowly walked out. He was greatly relieved nobody was around to be hurt.

"I didn't think I was jumping that hard?" he thought to himself. "I need to try and get used to being weaker before I really hurt someone."

Raziel slightly hopped up a bit gaining significant height. He struggled a tad finding the right amount of force to use in order to prevent over shooting his bounds. Little by little he began gaining distance and gaining a better understanding of the right amount of force to use in the armor for running.

Raziel looked forward towards the kingdom, "I'm coming."

Back inside the kingdom the ground quaked with each step of the frightening dragon of boiling magma. The devestation it caused left everything behind to burn and melt from its extreme heat. Seth's car had melted halfway and burned with all the other cars surrounding it. The air was a toxic cocktail of burning metals, fumes, and corpses. Cain looked down from the roof top, but couldn't see Seth's remains. Suddenly, the assassin witnessed movement on the ground. The black haird swordsman emerged from cooling liquid rock and metals with his sheath in one hand and his withdrawn sword in the other.

Seth squinted his eyes looking where the monster stood. Noticing it had moved on as he spoke to himself, "Guess it's immune to lava."

Even though Seth's clothing was on fire and he was sweating terribly he was still unharmed soely for the fact of the ability of his sword. Seth hurried out of the debris of the dragon and into the intersection it walked away from. He saw the large beast trampling smaller objects and damaging buildings in its path down the road. The assassin swiftly lept to the ground with a safe distance away from the incredibly hot detective.

"We can't." he spoke in his demonic voice.

"We have to. I have to try and stop that thing. It can't hurt me."

"But you can't stop it either. You'll just piss it off."

Seth turned around to see Cain when suddenly bolts of lightening started crackling down the road a few blocks away.

"So much lightening in one spot. Another monster?" Seth wondered loudly.

"The burly guy with the lightening sword. It must be him." Cain reminded.

At the realization Cain was right Seth ran off in the direction of the striking lightening bolts.

"He's not important!" Cain growled. The assassin was ignored and groaned before darting off behind Seth.

36

MAGMA MONSTER

Many of the soldiers attention were drawn to the rampaging grand duke as he fled the castle to aid the kingdom's people.

"He wasn't supposed to know." Hikaru scolded.

Hikaru removed a hand radio from major Collins side and gave the order, "Troops dispatch! All available personel, follow Raziel to the city. Neutralize the threat. I repeat dispatch. Assist the grand duke NOW!"

Hikaru glared at Tydus before walking down the hallway in the opposite direction.

Christian hurried down the spiral stair case and croutched behind large furniture. Oyova fluttered out of her shell from around Christian's neck.

"What are you doing hiding behind this sofa?"

Christian quickly grabbed her and kept her out of sight for others. He then placed one finger to his lips, "Shhhhhhhh." The young prince glanced over the sofa with speed, "I getting out of here."

"Huh? Why now?"

"You were right. I don't think I can trust them here. Hikaru just wants me here so he can run my dad's kingdom. He told me himself. He said he's the one calling all the shots now."

"But I thought you were a king now cause your parents are gone."

"I'm supposed to be and Raziel just stood there and didn't stick up for me at all." Christian quieted down as soldiers ran passed. "Look hide in here until it's safe, okay?"

"Do you actually think you're in danger?" the pixie wondered.

"I don't know really, but I don't want to find out. Just hide in your shell until the coast is clear, okay? Please?"

The little pixie girl noticed the sincerity and fear in the prince's eyes and nodded her small head. The pink girl flew back into the shell until notified otherwise. Christian slowly stood from behind the sofa and turned down a hallway for a quick get away. A few castle guards entered down the hall and began running his way. The prince panicked and darted through a near by door. He stood in the library until the soldiers finished running by.

"Did they not see me?" he wondered.

The prince slowly looked out from the library entrance and started sneaking down the hallway again. A startling sound spooked him and he decided to hide in the next closest room. Christian jump inside and popped Chase with the door causing him to fall to the floor and drop his tray of food. The prince ran into Lee causing him to spill his soda on Chase.

"Hey! Why don't'cha watch where you're...Prince Christian?!" Chase realized.

"Are you alright Prince Dalton?" Lee asked.

"Yeah, I'm fine I suppose." he answered nervously.

"Ya look a little shook up there." Lee noticed.

"Probably because there's spaghetti all over the floor." Chase figured.

"What? Why would he be shook up because of spaghetti being on the floor?"

"Cause it sometime looks like long, thin, bloody organs and that can creep people out."

"First of all, he's probably shook up cause he thinks one of those prisoners with the swords are busting loose from all the commotion. And second, it doesn't look like bloody organs." Lee argued.

"Sure it does, look at the squished meat ball there and those noodles."

Lee looked from Chase's point of view, "Oh yeah, at this angle. Huh, that IS creepy." he shuttered.

"Wait! Prisoners with swords?" Christian inturrupted.

"Oh yeah, like the one that had you at the hospital, but we have him locked away now so you're safe." Chase shrugged off.

"Rufus?"

"I don't remember his name." Lee admitted looking at Chase who agreed.

"I didn't know he was being kept prisoner here. Take me to him." Christian ordered.

"We should probably get Grechov's permission before.."

"NO! I am Grechov's boss. I am in charge now. I am king. Now take me to this prisoner at once or you're both outta here!" he threatened knowing full well Grechov would object.

Chase and Lee both saluted Christian and obeyed without haste, "Yes, sir!"

Christian followed the two soldiers down to the holding cells of Rufus and Wade.

"They're both in seperate rooms."

"They?" the prince asked.

"Yeah, the one from the hospital is on the right and the one from the masion is on the left."

"Wade?" Christian hurried to the two rooms and looked through the small windows to peer inside. He noticed Wade resting his head on the table and knocked on the glass. The blond man looked up and gladly witnessed the prince waving to him.

"Christian! Christian you gotta get me outta here! That general is psycho!" Wade pleaded.

"Yeah!" he agreed trying to open the locked door. He glanced back up at Wade, "It won't open. It's locked!"

"Get the key! Find the key!" he asked at the door. Wade had certainly had enough of Grechov's warnings and threats and was ready to leave as soon as possible.

Christian glanced around then looked at Chase and Lee, "You, guards. Open the door."

"Whoa, I'm pretty sure we can't do that." Lee chuckled nervously.

"If you disobey an order I'll have you fired and locked away for treason against the kingdom of Vailstone RIGHT NOW!" Christian shouted.

Chase instantly walked over shifting through the keys in his hand.

"What are you doing?!" Lee asked.

"I'm obeying a direct order. I'm not get'n in trouble." Chase explained.

Lee witnessed Chase unlocking the door and hurried to unlock Rufus' door to stay of the prince's good side.

Wade jumped out hugging the small prince, lifting him off the ground happily.

"YEAH! Christian! Thank you so much! Ha, ha, ha, ha, ha!" he excitedly hugged Christian.

"What's going on?" Rufus asked walking out of his room.

"I'll explain everything, but for now we gotta go. Trust me." Christian stated.

"I couldn't agree more." Wade agreed.

"Come on let's go."

"Without our swords?" Rufus asked.

"Your swords? Where are they?" he asked looking at the two confused guards.

"We'll get'em." they said in sync.

"What's been going on? I heard a loud noise earlier." Wade asked.

"I'm not sure, but it's the distraction we needed to get away from here." Christian informed.

Rufus looked about the room.

"What are you looking for?" Christian asked.

"I don't see it. It has to be here somewhere. It has to."

"What?"

Rufus pilfered inside some of the desks around the room until a smile came over his face. He turned around facing the others with his cell phone. "Damn, thirty seven missed messages."

Christian and Wade dropped their heads in shame for Rufus' love for his cell phone.

"Here ya go." Chase and Lee announced to the swordsmen presenting them with they're blades once more.

"Oh I've missed you!" Rufus chuckled happily while holding his sword as Wade did the same replying, "Welcome back baby."

"Now, how are we getting out of here? We'll need a quick get a way." Wade said.

"We could get one of the military jeeps, but where would we get the keys from?" Christian pondered.

At that moment Rufus, Wade, and Christian all slowly turned their sights on Chase and Lee who dropped their heads and extended their arms each holding a key to a military vehicle. Eight minutes later the two soldiers were standing behind the castle watching the three drive away at high speed.

"Ya know, I'm pretty sure we're gonna be in BIIIIG trouble." Lee stated.

"Oh yeah." Chase replied immediately after Lee made his comment.

As the Prince escaped the Vailstone castle with two swordsmen another two swordsmen in the chaos of the kingdom's city rushed into battle. Seth ran as fast he could to the striking lightening bolts certain it would lead to Kaz in danger. However, while the detective ran to Kaz's aid he surprisingly ran into another threat.

Standing before Seth was another of Fire starter's summonings, a molten hot, dripping, lava monster. An actual creature composed entirely of hot lava.

Cain caught up to Seth and stood by his side, "Screw that. I'm not fighting a lava monster."

Gun fire sounded off heading in their direction. Cain swiftly darted behind obsticles from the bullets. Seth peered around the eight foot lava monster to see general Grechov and lieutenant Brookes attacking with armed forces on the other side.

"You go. See if it's Kaz. Help him out if you can." Seth shouted.

"He's of no use to us." Cain stated in a growl.

"No! We need him. He's one of the seven like us," Seth pointed to his heart where the seven cuts are marked on each of their chests, "he's involved. Go help him or the deal is off."

"You can't do that!" Cain roared.

"I don't owe you anything." Seth stated.

"DAMN!" Cain shouted and lept up easily scaling a building to avoid contact with the monster and army.

"Alright ugly, let's dance." Seth muttered holding his sword tightly.

The detective looked around the block careful not to catch any of the soldiers bullets to avoid harming them. Seth noticed a parked car off to the side of the street and rushed over to quickly break the window. The car alarm sounded off grabbing the monster's attention.

"Blargh." was the only sound emitted from the creature.

"Duck and cover!" Grechov shouted throwing a grenade at the monster.

The idea was to blast the monster apart, but the sheer heat coming from off the monster forced the grenade to explode before even getting close enough to have any effect. However, the blast did distract the monster back to watching the general and his men. The monster pointed its arm in their direction and began firing off intensely hot parts of itself from with-in. Lava smacked against the jeeps and splattered killing off some of the soldiers. Men's faces were entirely burned off, torso's were burned hollow, and one shot even hit a gas tank making the vehicle explode completely.

Seth finally rigged the car and got it to start up.

"Alright molten man." he mumbled as he shifted the car into gear.

The black haired detecive stomped on the gas to get the car going as fast as it could go as quick as he could. He steered the car directly into the distracted monster seperating it from its legs and crashing it and the car into a building close by. Hitting the monster with the car was certainly a solid hit, but luckily the car continued moving.

Seth stepped out of the vehicle feeling a bit woozy from the crash.

"I had the sword out, but I wasn't immune to the dangers of the crash. Was it because I did it to myself? Someone else wasn't inflicting the pain?" he asked in his head while looking at his shiny black blade.

Suddenly Seth heard a crackle around his wrist. He quickly looked and noticed a handcuff upon his right wrist.

"What are you doing?" Seth asked a wickedly smiling Grechov.

"Rounding you boys up. You make three."

"Take this off I'm not the enemy here." the detective ordered.

Grechov pulled him closer, "Tell me, just how long you been running around with that assassin? And don't you lie to me, I know what my eyes saw." he informed pointing to his right eye.

"What?! No, you've got it all wrong Grechov." Seth defended.

"Drop your weapon." Grechov threatened while pointing a gun at Seth's chest.

"NO! STOP!" Seth noticed the gun and clutched onto his sword, but also began wrestling with Grechov to drop the gun before he fired at Seth and hurt himself. "You're gonna get hurt."

"You threatening me, huh?" Grechov laughed off while the two attempted to overpower each other.

"No, I'm trying to help save you ya dick!" Seth explained. The detective head butt the general in their struggle which didn't appear to phase the brute much.

Grechov muscled out of Seth's grip and punched him in the face with his free hand which only resulted in hurting the general's face.

"Dagh!" he spouted in surprise.

As the two adults wrestled for seperate reasons the liquid rock monster reattacthed his body completely and removed itself from the melting buring car. It began gurgling and groaning frighteningly once again.

Seth looked back in surprise, "Oh yeah, you."

Grechov reopened his eyes after feeling the effect of his own punch to the face. The creature launched a blob of molten lava towards Seth and Grechov without warning.

"Look out!" Seth shouted and hunched his back to brace for the blow knowing he could shield the attack and protect them both. Grechov tried to lunge out of the way, but since he was cuffed to Seth he was incapable. Grechov looked at Seth in shock as the swordsman refused to move.

"Stay in front.." but before Seth could finish his warning the lava splattered against his back and head. In doing so, a small quantity splashed against Grechov's face and instantly began burning away his skin and face.

Seth used the handcuff to flick some of the lava from Grechov's face, but his body was going into shock from the attack. Lieutenant Brookes rushed over and witnessed the injured general.

"GRECHOV!"

The bit of lava melted the handcuffs enough for Seth to break free, "Get him to a hospital fast. He's going into shock." Seth stood to face the lava monster until hearing the click of a gun readying to fire.

He turned his head seeing lieutenant Brookes aiming her gun directly at him.

"Save him or waste time." he stated before running at the monster and drawing its attention away from the injured general.

Miranda decided to take the opportunity and attempt rescuing Grechov. She struggled, but hoisted his body over her shoulder and placed him in one of the damaged jeeps. She sped away as the confused and scared soldiers retreated with her.

"Good call. Now it's just you and me asshole."

"Blargh!" it called out tossing more amounts of lava aimed toward Seth.

He began running and jumping about to dodge the attacks. Light posts started bending and falling into the streets. The buildings around them where engulfed with flame. Even the monster's foot steps left dangerous burning spot of melting cement.

"Ugh! I thought the more lava it threw at me the smaller it would become, but it doesn't seem to be changing in size at all. What gives?" he pondered.

To the black haired man's surprise the lava monster rushed at him and body slammed into Seth. The detective was completely smothered by the foe.

"The monster's not burning itself. No surprise there." he thought before forcing his way through the thick monster and standing out of it.

"AAAHHHHHHH!!!!!!!!!" he shouted striking, stabbing, and slashing about the lava creature's body. "There's nothing here?! Nothing to stab! No weakness!" the detective panicked in frustration.

In the heat of the battle Seth had forgotten his sword was incapable of bringing harm to another. The monster's face began surfacing from it's supposed back, which Seth happened to be standing directly inside.

For a glimmering moment Seth caught his reflection in the black sword, "Why am I stabbing with this again?" he realized.

Suddenly a loud pop sounded off startling the swordsman.

"What tha?!" he began wondering.

Crackling sounds began snapping left and right. Seth looked around and noticed the road they had been fighting on had been severely weakened by all of the hot lava. And the clumped body of the lava creature was proving to be the last straw. Seth looked away and noticed the remaining, but damaged military jeeps.

"Oh I've got you now." he stated forcing through the thick lava of the monster even while it swung at him.

Seth managed to free himself and run over to the jeeps. He removed his burning coat and placed his sword on the ground. In a mad dash he glanced inside each jeep to see what it could offer him.

"This will do." he smiled.

The detective threw all the grenades, bullets, and explosives into one jeep and pointed the vehicle directly at the monster. He started the engine and released the unmanned jeep right into the creature. He watched with anticipation as the jeep drove into the monster. The vehicle exploded upon contact. Seth ducked to miss flying lava and debris. In the mass explosion however, the weakned road finally gave way and crumbled to bits underneath the lava monster forcing it to fall into the rushing waters of the sewer below.

Seth smiled in relief, picked up his sword, and put out the fire on his coat.

Looking back at the burning rubble and destroyed road he simply wore a satisfied grin, "And that's how it's done."

37

UNDERSTAND

Kaz sat on his motorcycle in the city park with his broad sword extended off to his side. His left hand to steer and his right hand to sever with his sights set on the fire summoning of Fire starter's. On the opposite side of Kaz hovered a giant japanese lantern with an eye symbol on the front. Just bellow the symbol was a huge tear in the lantern providing a mouth for the fire using monster. Inside that mouth, however, a smaller being rest using the protection of the lantern monster. With two ghoulish severed rotting hands levitating by it's sides the creature was truly other worldly in appearance.

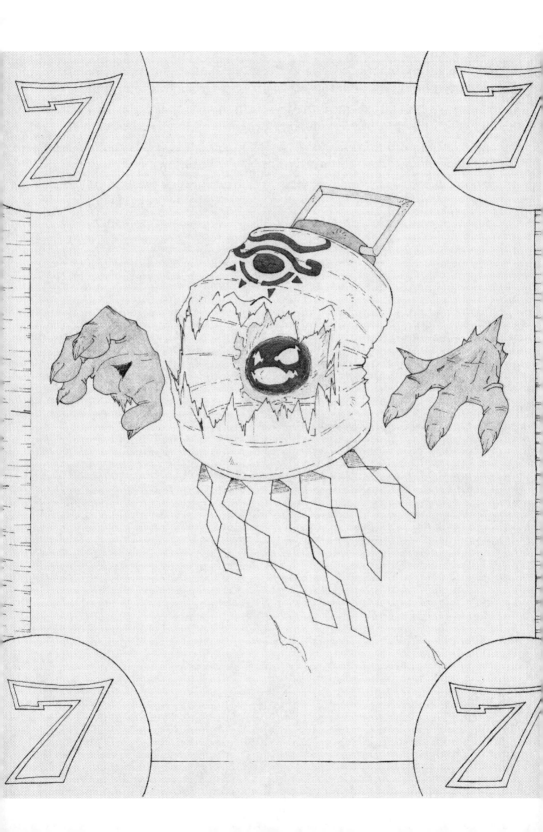

Kaz revved the engine of his motorcycle before pressing the gas and charging at the monster at full speed. The lantern summoning opened its mouth shreeking out a frightful noise before spraying large fire balls towards the swordsman. Kaz zipped past each one, nearly being struck a time or two. Kaz knew defeating Fire starter's summonings would draw him a step closer to facing off against the fire elemental once more, giving him a chance to redeem himself after his defeat by Basoomamba.

"AAAHHHH!" he shouted as he drew near the creature.

The monster spat yet another fire ball as Kaz connected it with his sword. Lightening struck the monster causing it to scream an unworldly sound, but its fire attack dealt its damage and struck Kaz's motorcycle. Kaz was flung from the bike as it flipped about until smashing into a tree.

The biker stood from off the ground with determonation, "You're gonna pay for that."

Kaz strengthened the clutch on his sword and swung his sword above his head in a few circular motions before striking the ground in a vicious yell, "LEGEND!"

Lightening crashed against the ground instantly and bolted to the hovering summoning. The monster in return created fire balls from his floating hands to throw at the powerful attack. As the fire and lightening clashed an explosion ignited. Through the smoke Kaz saw the monster crack its back opening the mouth enormously wide and sending a barrage of raining fire balls into the air. Kaz began a foot dodging left and right as spheres of flame exploded on the ground all around him. The man evaded the sparatic attacks as best he could before eventually resulting to a lunging tuck and roll for survival.

"RAWRRR!" the creature angrily roared.

Its hand danced about summoning a small army of two foot tall fire monsters with poor speed, however, their ability to self destruct and spew fire made them dangerous enough.

"What the hell are those things?" Kaz asked aloud.

Suddenly a small fire creature shot fire out of its mouth at Kaz which he blocked with his broad sword.

"You're first!" Kaz announced running at the small monster and with a single sweep of his sword the fire monster evaporated into extinguished flame.

More small monsters started moving as fast as they could to attack while the real threat shot more raining fire balls into the air. The distracted swordsman was nearly hit by the falling fire and was thrown away. Kaz endured the pain, but noticed another small fire creature nearing. Before Kaz could attack the little monster self destructed and snarred Kaz in its fire throwing him further away.

"Uggghhhh. I could use some armor." Kaz grumbled holding his chest and noticing a blood stain.

Perched in a burning tree the masked assassin looked down at the hurt biker safely.

"Having trouble?" he spoke demonicly.

Kaz's eyes widened, "YOU!"

He quickly stood to his feet with his sword ready for further combat despite the summoning and its monsters drawing closer on him.

"Come for round two?" Kaz asked reffering to their first fight in the chamber of which they retrieved their swords.

Cain looked away from Kaz and back at the threat he had been watching him fight since locating him.

"Came to help." Cain grumbled before blindingly darting from out of the tree, landing to the ground, and dashing at the small monsters.

The murderer took aim, readied his sword, and expertly moved around the small monsters with presicion. Each little monster was turned into dwindling flame as the assassin moved in and out of them. Cain finally came to a halt as the last one was slain.

"I don't believe you." Kaz confessed pointing his blade at Cain.

"Your death is meaningless to me, but the detective wants you to survive." Cain informed.

"Simon? You know where to find him?" Kaz asked.

"Seth." Cain corrected.

"You know where to find Seth?"

"................Yes, follow me and I'll take you to him."

"Humph." Kaz cockly chuckled. "Right after I take care of buisness."

As Kaz charged at the fire summoning Cain shrugged, "Fool." and darted into the fight as well.

Kaz swung his massive broad sword attempting to strike the monster directly in the face. However, with great reflexes, the fire summoning clapped the sword still between it's morbid rotting hands. Lightening electricuted the monster's detached hands most of all, but the summoning did take minor damage. Kaz forced his sword down and out of the summonings grip and slashed against the magical monster several times until blowing it away into a patch of burning grass.

Cain ran passed Kaz for further attacks.

"It's over." Kaz laughed.

"Not yet." Cain stated making Kaz realize the creature was still fighting fit.

The monster began getting off the ground to fight further. The masked swordsman zipped over to the creature and began slicing his sword into it multiple times. The monster screeched and bellowed as the assassin's sword forced the summoning to move at a far more hindered pace than usual.

"I'll finish this!" Kaz shouted.

Cain noticed Kaz readying another attack and swooped out of the way of the unpredictable electric attack he secretly observed before.

"LEGEND!" Kaz shouted.

With a strike to the ground the powerful electric attack was launched at the foe. Blasting against the fire summoning of Fire starter's the creature began receiving extensive damage. A huge explosion ignited after a moment offically killing off the fire summoning.

Cain sheathed his sword giving Kaz the chance to sheath his, which he did reluctantly.

"I could've handled that alone ya know."

"Sure you could've." Cain replied.

"So is that your regular voice or are you just putting one on?" Kaz questioned.

Cain stood silently standing before Kaz without an answer, "Come, the detective could be dying."

"What? What'd you do? I need him." Kaz inquired.

"Hm? What's this connection between you two?"

"What? I need him to get the Vailstone army off my back. He's a cop, they'll listen to him." Kaz explained.

"Hm, don't you understand? The Vailstone police work for the Vailstone army. They will only obey what they are told. The detective is wanted as well." Cain informed.

"Huh? Well, I didn't kidnap no kids like the news is say'n. I'll be dammned if I'm taking the blame for that." Kaz paused for a moment, "Wait a sec, what're you help'n for? You've certainly done far worse than kidnap, why didn't you just run?"

Cain stood silently before walking further, "Come."

"Hold up. What's your story, huh? Why are you even around? Nobody knows who you really are so why didn't you just vanish?"

"The detective knows enough. Let's go." Cain growled.

Kaz walked a slower pace a small distance behind Cain for he did not trust him. The two strolled through the burning park until a figure with a long burned coat began walking their direction.

Kaz stopped for a moment while Cain continued walking, "Who's that?" he asked squinting to see beyond the heat waves and smoke.

"He survived." Cain stated.

As the figure walked closer Kaz recognized the man, "Seth."

"So you're both alright, that's good I suppose." Seth acknowledged.

"How did you two know where to find me?" Kaz wondered.

"The bolts of lightening were a dead give away for starters." Seth replied.

"Oh, well, I've been look'n for you. The news been say'n we kidnapped them royal kids and now I got police and soldiers barrel'n down my neck."

"What do you want me to do about it?"

"Fix it. You're a cop."

"I can't."

"What?! Why tha hell not?" Kaz stepped forward grabbing Seth's coat.

"I just can't. It's too late for me now." Seth answered looking down and away.

"TOO LATE! What are you talk'n about? Why's it too late?! What'd you do?" he asked angrily shaking Seth.

"He did worse." Cain softly growled.

Kaz released Seth, "To those kids?"

"No! Never. I.....I just..had to," Seth began muscling through his confession, but was inturrupted by the police sirens from three cars rushing into the scorching park followed by two large fire trucks.

"Cops." Kaz noticed.

"We don't hurt the innocent, are we clear?" Seth stated.

Seth didn't get a reply from either Kaz nor Cain and looked behind himself, but to his surprise only one fellow swordsman remained.

"Where's Cain?"

"He was just here." Kaz answered with confusion of his disappearance.

"How does he do that?" Seth wondered.

"Well, I be dammned." one of the drivers cursed.

The cop cars stopped several feet away from the swordsman. The officers jumped out of their cars immediately with guns aimmed.

"Drop your weapons!" an officer ordered.

"What? No, no, no, no, we're helping. We just killed one of those... those monster things. We're good guys." Seth answered.

"Sure you are. I know that to be a fact." a familiar voice returned.

The old voice rang a bell in Seth's head. His mind was at full attention, an old friend? "Hobbs? Hobbs is that you?"

"Yeah, it's me Notch." Hobbs answered back walking before the officers and lighting a cigarette. "How are ya Notch? You, been okay?"

"Huh? Aside from the kingdom going to shit and all safety out tha window I suppose I've been just fine." Seth smiled sadly.

"You know this guy?" Kaz asked.

"He's my old partner. Don't worry, he's a friend." Seth informed his fellow swordsman with relief.

"What do you know about the kingdom going to shit, huh? You know anything about that?" he asked before drawing off his cigarette.

"Some fire guy, I think it was 'Fire starter' he's doing a real number here. He's the guy you want." Seth yelled out over the burning park.

"No Notch, I don't think he's the guy I want." Hobbs replied taking another draw off his cigarette. "What about that princess Notch? I heard the prince is back at the castle, but what about that princess? Know where she might be?"

"Hobbs? What're ya do'n?" he asked in innocent confusion.

"Where's that princess Notch?"

"I don't know. I haven't seen princess Alisha since the night before the ceremonies." Seth confessed.

"Yeah, that's right." he puffed. "I got a few statements says you were out of control the night before at dinner. Said you had to be removed from the castle entirely." Hobbs paused, "What was that about Notch?"

"You know my history Hobbs. You know damn well how I felt about Dorian."

"Yeah I do. You're right there...............I do. So? You saying it was one of the other sword wielding friends of yours that took her? You weren't in that part of the plans then? Is that what you're say'n to me?"

"He doesn't sound like a friend right now." Kaz muttered softly loud enough for Seth to hear.

Seth slightly turned his head as he listened to Kaz, "Hobbs what are you doing to me here? You know me."

"I used to know you Notch. I used to." Hobbs paused for another draw on his cigarette. "Then you went Rambo on some thugs. It looks to me, that you're at it again."

Seth stood a safe distance away from his old friend and listened as he crucified him before all.

"I have a whole stack of old case files in my car Notch. You're old case files. You know how many of those suspects are dead now?......I bet you do......See, what's so bizzare is that they all died with-in a two today span. It LOOKS like they committed suicide, but C.S.I. can't figure out how it happened. It just doesn't add up." Hobbs puffed further on his cigarette. "Figured you could help me figure this one out old buddy. So, how'd you do it, hm? How'd you kill those people?"

"Hobbs, I, I can expl.." Seth began walking over but stopped as Hobbs drew a gun on his old parnter.

"That's close enough Notch. Now why don't you, me, and your tall friend there take a ride back to the precinct, huh?" Hobbs asked holding a pair of cuffs in his hand.

"I, I can't." Notch struggled to reply as a tear built up in his eye.

"And why is that Notch?"

"I have to finish what I've started. Just one more."

"What have you started Notch? What is the one thing you have left to do?" Hobbs prodded for the confession.

"I, I have to..." but suddenly before Seth could finish his sentence random smoke bombs fired off amoungst the cop cars hindering visibility.

Gun fire sounded off in the smoke behind Hobbs. The old partner was distracted in the chaos behind him.

"CAIN NO!" Seth called out moving forward.

Hobbs took aim and fired off his pistol shooting Seth right in the left shoulder. Seth fell back and down with the force of the shot.

"Aahhh!" Seth gasped in surprise.

He laid on the grass bleeding from the shoulder and looking at his sword on the ground. His sword was unsheathed and didn't protect him from danger this time.

"What!? Why now?" he wondered to himself. "Why didn't the sword keep him safe like all the other times before?

Hobbs crept closer, but pointed the gun at Kaz.

"Go ahead. Drop the weapon big fella." Hobbs ordered.

Kaz was pissed that he was helpless to do anything to help assist out of the situation. He tossed his sword forward, but not too far if needed.

"Yep, I need armor." he stated to himself with the gun aimmed at him by Hobbs.

Hobbs stood before Notch, "Was that it Notch? Was I the last 'something' to finish?"

"No! Nothing like that I swear." Notch answered.

"How did you do it Notch? How did you kill those people?"

Seth huffed to endure his pain of being shot. Hobbs kept the gun pointed at Kaz, but stepped on Seth's injured shoulder.

"AARRAAGGHHHH!!!!!" Seth yelled in sheer pain.

"Tell me how you did it Notch." he ordered pressing down with his foot, "I want to know how you did those murders." he slowly threatened.

In an instant a white blade swung around and stopped against the skin of Hobbs' neck.

"Drop the gun." Cain ordered in his demonic voice.

"If you do anything I'll shot your friend over there." Hobbs warned reffering to Kaz.

"He's not my friend." Cain responded honestly. "Shot him."

As Cain's blade got closer to the detective's neck it started to draw blood. Hobbs quickly decided to take Cain seriously and dropped his gun.

"You've got some interesting friends here Notch."

"At least I still have some." Seth replied as he tenderly held his wound.

The black haired detective stood from the ground slowly and picked up his black sword. Kaz walked over with his sword sheathed on his back.

"Car keys. Where are they?" Cain questioned.

"They're all still in the ignition." Hobbs informed.

Seth picked up Hobb's pistol from off the ground and placed it in his coat, "See ya round old friend." he said in a sarcastic tone.

Kaz ran over to one of the police cars and drove it beside the other two swordsmen.

"Get in." Kaz ordered.

Seth walked around to the passenger side and got in the car.

"If you turn around. You're dead." Cain warned.

Hobbs continued facing away while Cain climbed in the car with the others. Kaz began speeding off away from the other vechiles. Hobbs waited five minutes before turning around, just to be on the safe side. The detective hurried to the other cop cars to radio in a stolen police car, but as soon as he grabbed the radio he felt a sticky liquid on his fingers. Hobbs released the radio and noticed blood on his fingers. He was stunned for a moment before treading through the smoke further and calling out for the other officers. Hobbs was horrified to see the bloody requiem Cain had left behind as the smoke cleared away.

As Kaz speed away the car bounced and shook on the fractured road.

"Ugh! Could you try to not hit EVERY bump and pot hole out here?" Seth griped as he tried attending to his bleeding shoulder.

"Hey, I'm just getting us the hell away from your psycho friend back there."

"I don't even understand. Why didn't my sword protect me this time? When Hobbs shot at me. Why didn't the sword's ability work for me?" Seth asked out loud.

"The first thing you do when you retrieve something you don't fully understand is start understanding it. You've had your sword out of it's sheath for too long. After that, the powers it hold wear off." Cain informed.

Kaz sat silently driving the car while listening intently.

"That doesn't make any sense. My sword's only been used since...."

"The dragon." Cain reminded.

"But.....that's only been a few hours at best." he realized. "And how did you come to know this?" Seth inquired.

"I started understanding."

"And it never occured to you to share this information earlier?" Seth groaned.

"I didn't tell you in case I needed to kill you." Cain factually stated. Seth looked back at the masked murderer with anger, "You should have stabbed the detective once your sword's power stopped." Cain informed.

"He's a friend." Seth replied.

"Not anymore." Cain returned.

"Well then why didn't you when you had the chance, huh?" Seth asked.

Cain sat silent for a moment before answering, "Because you're confused and I still need your cooperation."

"And when you don't need me?" Seth asked further looking back at Cain in the backseat.

Cain sat without an answer hiding behind his cold blood stained mask.

38

THE TERRIBLE EUROASHIEN'S DEVASTATION

Raziel had finally arrived at the burning city and made his way into the streets. Civilains still ran up to Raziel for aid and support, despite all of the hate the news had been spinning about him and the attack on the castle.

"Quickly now! Run away. Get out of here. Go. Run." he ordered to those seeking his help.

The golden hero made certain to move fiery obsticales and clear pathways for those in need. Raziel crushed fire hydrants to create rushing water to counteract the fire and heat. He made his way helping citizens evacuate until the situation grew a tad more compliacated.

"Grand duke, HELP! Please! Help me!" a man called out standing before a burning apartment complex.

Raziel hurried over to aid the man in distress. The golden hero was careful not to use too much force in heading his direction. He noticed an entire crowd of people watching their homes burn down.

"Raziel?!" a firefighter realized in surprise.

"What's wrong?" the grand duke asked.

"It's my son. He's still in there, but the firemen can't get to him!" the father panicked.

"Which one?"

"Twenty-five seventy-two." the man answer quickly.

"Anyone else that we know of trapped in there?" Raziel asked the fire chief.

"No, but it's much too dangerous. You can't go in there." he warned.

"I'll be right back. Get these other people out of here." Raziel ordered.

"But you can't. You won't make it." he warned again.

"Get these people out of here." Raziel demanded.

As the grand duke hurried inside the burning apartment complex the fire chief started ordering for the people standing by to evactuate to a safer area.

Raziel had only just entered the buliding and the fire was horrific, yet as he stood looking around he was immune to the heat. Raziel placed his hand in some fire for a brief moment and turned it around before pulling it out.

"Nothing." he stated to himself.

The fire made the building creek and crack, beams from the ceiling began to fall from over head. He noticed darkening and melting metal in areas of what appeared to be intense heat. The fire raged on. Without the protection of the armor of Kamisama Raziel's life would've be in extreme danger. The grand duke tried locating the right apartment to rescue the boy, but the numbers were entirely burned away in some cases.

Raziel continued walking on the weakening floor until it eventually gave way and dropped him to the bottom floor. Without injury he hurried back up to his feet and jumped to land back on the floor above, but the force of lunging onto an object would prove usless for he could never be stopped. The grand duke crashed through the floor yet again. He lightly hopped up to grab the edge of the broken floor above, but only ripped off what he grabbed.

"Damn this won't work."

He looked around for another stair case down the hall. In time he found another stair case and slowly made each step up the stairs to the second floor. Raziel made sure to pace himself in a speed fast enough to try and rescue the boy, but also slow enough not to destroy his flooring.

Raziel happily found the apartment he was looking for and reached out to open the door. On accident, however, he broke the door apart ripping it off the wall.

"That'll do." he said in surprise. "Hello? Some one in here?" Raziel asked calling out.

"Daddy?" a feint voice coughed.

Raziel slowly moved to what used to have appeared to be a bedroom. In the room Raziel heard flowing water. He thought it peculiar and moved further to investigate. As he carefully opened a bathroom door he saw a small boy curled up in a shower with the water running on him in a desperate attempt for protection.

The boy looked over at Raziel in the shiny golden armor and immediately felt a presence of saftey. Raziel moved in to pick up the wet child, but was uncertain just how much pressure to apply when picking the boy up so as not to crush him.

"It's okay, I'm here to help you." he smiled happy to see the boy was still alive.

Despite Raziel's words the child was still nervous, afraid, and longing for his parent's. The grand duke reached out to lift the child, but was reluctant.

"Um, hey. I've got an idea." Raziel told the boy, "You just sit tight, okay?"

The boy nodded his head and remained in a fetal position. The firefighters watched the building burn with the boy's father nervously. To everyone's surprise the brick side wall was blown away suddenly with a man in golden armor walking through the newly created hole in the wall. The man was worried because he didn't see his son.

"My son? My little boy?" he man fell to his knees in tears.

"Don't worry, he's right here." Raziel reassured.

What the other's didn't see was the bathtub Raziel was dragging behind him the entire time. The bathtub was blanketed by the grand duke's cape protecting the boy which rest inside the entire time. The royal soldier removed his cape freeing the boy to run to his father. It was a heart warming moment as the two hugged, rejoicing in their good fortune.

"Now, quickly. The rest of you must get out of here as fast you can." Raziel warned.

As the grand duke walked away from the burning apartment complex he noticed a strange eerie green light. It appeared to be an opening to another place. The bizzare thing was the opening wasn't attached to a wall or floor, instead it was just on the ground as if created from thin air. The door instantly closed and left all traces of its ever being there. Off to the side Raziel noticed a young man with a cigarette in his mouth and a hoodie hiding his face.

"Did you make that?" he asked.

The mysterious man just smiled a skin crawling smile and simply replied, "We'll talk later." and flicked his lit cigarette away.

A monsterously loud stomp was created blocks away from where they stood. Raziel turned to see what could have created the sound then quickly looked back to see the mysterious man, but it was too late, he vanished without a trace. Raziel looked left and right, but only saw burning buildings and people in need of rescuing. He hadn't any time to waste wondering about an odd young man.

Titanic bursts of flame resonated far away from Raziel's location. Buildings began to crumble from the devestation. The ground quaked in the pattern of foot steps. The grand duke knew an enormous threat awaited him. After rescuing several other trapped people he chose to lightly thrust off the ground giving himself an airborn view. A large fierce dragon lay before him crushing buildings and setting fire to all in it's path. Raziel flew through a burned hollowed out building and crashed onto the pavement.

He stood from his landing and remained in his crater.

"Finally get'n used ta tha arm'a?" a familiar crackly voice cackled.

Raziel looked about, "Fire starter where are you?! Show yourself!" he yelled threateningly.

Suddenly a burst of fire appeared fifty feet away from the grand duke. Fire starter stepped forth with Grunt and Sammy sammy seven by his side.

"You've gone too far mystic."

"Fa tha last time it's fi'ya stat'a! An NO! It is you who has gone to fa. You had ya chance ta make things right an ya blew it! I gave ya more than enough chances, but ya just refused ta listen ta reason."

"This is no longer between you and me. You've killed countless innocent lives. You must pay for these crimes Fire starter. Can't you see this is wrong?!"

"Tha only thing I've done wrong he'ya is put my trust'n you! That obviously was a BIG mistake! I lied ta HELP ya. An ya lied to screw me ov'a! Now anybody that's ever need'ed me dead knows where ta find me. Ya just had ta broadcast it ov'a tha news there didn't ya?!" Fire starter raged.

"You lied to me to HELP me? What are you talking about? What lie of yours has helped me out in any way?"

Fire starter chuckled, "Well, guess there's no ha'rm 'n tell'n ya now. Rememb'a that whole thing about only a true warri'a could wear tha ar'ma or they'd die? Ya,..........that weren't true." he stated with a sniker.

"Wha? What did you say?" Raziel asked in disbelief.

"Ya, so ya betrayed Dorian fa no reason. Boo hoo. Ya stab me in tha back an still got tha ar'ma!"

"You lied to me. You tricked me into betraying my best friend and he's dead now because of you!" Raziel fumed.

"No, he's dead cause he was an asshole. Don't ignore wat he tried ta do." Fire starter shouted.

"I'm going to get you for this Fire starter. You, will, pay." Raziel promised as he began walking toward Fire starter to attack.

"Look's ta me yur tha only one pay'n round he'ya. And Euroashien'll take ov'a from he'ya." Fire starter cackled wickedly as he and his two body guards disappeared into a burst of flame as Raziel lunged toward them.

"NNOOO!! Get back here you coward."

Raziel yelled out of sheer frustration from all of the lies and betrayal. He turned around looking at all of the burning scenery and fell to his knees. Raziel lowered his head in the sea of drifting cinders in the wind.

"This is all.........my fault. I let him get in my head." he muttered shaking his head in defeat.

A tremendous roar blew through out the smoldering city block. Suddenly the quaking ground became more prominent. The massive britle cooling magma skinned dragon stood its ground across the block from Raziel. It released another great terrifying bellow. As it roared unbearably hot magma spewwed from its maw creating new fires to punish the innocent.

The 'wounded' hero slowly lifted himself up from the pavement and turned to face the frightening beast. Raziel had an expression of pure rage as he charged into the large fiery dragon. The grand duke jumped into the air and tackled through the dragon's neck puncturing a lagre hole from front to back. As he entered and exit it, parts of its crust snapped and flung hot stone about causing more lava to drip everywhere.

Euroashien had flame burst out of it's neck holes as a massive fire blast engulfed Raziel and the entire city block. All was immersed in intense fire. The grand duke forged through the deadly flame and straight into the dragon's mouth. His punch alone was enough to destroy and entirely remove its lower jaw.

A waterfall of lava drained from the removed jaw all over Raziel. The grand duke lunged in the air and penetrated the skull of the magical flying serpent. The dragon, however, backed away from Raziel as it regrew a new lower jaw from the ever flowing amount of lava inside its body. Once the grand duke landed back on the ground the dragon quickly lunged its head outward eating Raziel whole.

The warrior fell to the bottom of the dragon's gut instantly.

"Time to do some damage." he thought to himself during the battle.

Raziel started puncturing holes from inside the beast's stomach. Eventually Raziel stomped completely out of the dragon creating a hole under its entire underbelly. Somehow the being seemed incapable of running out of lava to expose.

As the dragon's lava started repairing the damage it whipped it's tail about crashing buildings to the ground having them fall on top of the grand duke. Raziel emerged from the rubble holding enormous boulders of cement and threw them at the dragon.

"How am I supposed to beat this thing? It doesn't even have internal organs." Raziel wondered.

The dragon was outraged at the damage being dealt to it. It couldn't understand why Raziel was still alive. Nothing has ever been able to survive the attacks its been dealing before. Euroashien flapped it's wings creating raining fire in the process. As it flew above it gained the aerial advanage over its worthy foe. Rivers of lava pooled from the mouth of the dragon as it flew down the city block. Everything in the surrounding area was melting or turned to ash.

"No you don't." Raziel muttered as he followed in pursuit of the summoning.

He lept into the air and grabbed hold of the airborne reptiles tail. As Raziel fell back to the ground he managed to rip apart the grabbed portion of the drangon's tail. Once the severed tail collided with the ground it caused a burst of fire and magma to burn the area. The monster countinued flying allowing the pouring lava from its wound to form a new tail of cooling magma.

"I'll get your attention." he declared.

Raziel picked up a truck from off the street and threw it into the dragon forcing it to crash into a building near by. The building collapsed as the summoning collided against it's surface. Magma and rock went everywhere. The grand duke, however, was a cautious man and waited to see further movement before calling in a victory.

Sure enough the dragon emerged in liquid lava form and instantly began cooling off and creating a new outter shell of rock. Amazingly, the dragon instantly turned the rubble it was crushed under into an explosion of ash and dust as it's body was fully exposed.

"The heat from its body must be more intense without that rocky shell." he figured.

Euroashien was completely angry now and dead set on finishing off Raziel. It charged after Raziel tackling him with its head, which only snapped its skull apart. As the dragon's head reformed it desperatly attempted grabbing Raziel with it's claws and tearing into him. Raziel on the other hand was standing his ground ripping of the fingers, claws, and even feet of the magical monster all while being drenched in lava.

Eventually the monster realized it couldn't knock Raziel away, so it did the next best thing and lifted him off the ground and threw him across the kingdom. The grand duke was sent flying into buildings and breaking through each one of them until stopping inside an office building. The dragon wasted no time following after Raziel.

Euroashien flew to the grand duke's location chipping away cooling magma from the movement of its body and spraying fire down with every flap of it's wings. People started screaming on the streets informing Raziel not all have evacuated. He rushed out of the building he crashed in all while being careful not to step too forcfully.

Citizens ran for their lives when suddenly Pip Gordan burst on the scene with his camera man Carl.

"Hurry Carl, you getting this?" Pip asked reffering to the attacking lava dragon.

The news anchor stood in place once Carl gave him the signal, "Pip Gordan reporting here as the kingdom of Vailstone is under attack by a loch ness monster made of burning rock. The death doll has been rising as the royal mystic unleashed his pets across the city."

Raziel flew through the sky as he jumped into the dragon and hooked its horns on it's neck pulling it down with him. The two collided into a building which fell on top of them. The dragon reared it's ugly head of pure lava spraying the liquid rock everywhere. Lava flew towards Pip Gordan, but luckily Carl pushed him aside and saved his life.

"Hey, watch where your," Pip Gordan stopped as he saw the horrific chared remains.

Carl blocked the spary of deadly liquid with the video camera saving both of their lives.

"Damn it Carl! There goes our footage! You've had so many strikes I've lost count. You're lucky you just saved my life or I would've fired you on the spot for a stunt like that." Pip complained.

As the lava dragon reformed its body the reporter figured there was no longer any sense in staying now that they couldn't record the events taking place any further.

"Um, maybe we should get back in tha car." Pip reasoned.

Raziel charged from out of the broken brick and snapped the dragon's healing legs while the news van speed away. It started flying again to try avoiding the grand duke more easily. Streams of intense fire poured from the lava spewing mouth of Euroashien.

"What does it take?!" Raziel asked furiously.

He carefully ran to a fire hydrant and snapped it apart, throwing the metal at the dragon and aiming the water towards the flying fiend. The water steamed and evaporated almost instantly upon contact with the monster. Though the water was cooling the monster down, it was not enough to stop it for good.

"Wasting yur time Raziel." Fire starter's voice chimmed in taunting.

"Fire starter? Where are you?" Raziel demand to know.

"No where ya can get me. I'm speaking to ya through my Euroashien's fi'ya."

"You coward!"

"Cowa'd 'n sma't r two differ'nt things."

Raziel began picking up near by cars and vans and hurling them at the flying monster.

"Ya seem frus'trated." Fire starter mocked.

"All I can see is you. Every time I break this thing, all I see is you ya little worm." Raziel raged.

Fire starter mearly cackled, "Where's tha love old frien?"

"You want love?! How about I rip this monster's heart out and shove it down your throat, you heartless wretch."

"You fool, not even you could endure the exposed heat of Euoashien's heart." Fire starter laughed.

Raziel stopped his onslaught upon the dragon for a brief moment, "What? It actually has a heart?"

"Wait? What? No!" Fire starter recanted.

"New strategy." Raziel told himself.

"Wait! No! Stop whateva yur think'n Raziel! It ain't gunna work! Razieeellll!!!!!!" the elemental shouted.

The grand duke ripped light posts from out of the ground and tried piercing the chest cavity of the summoning. It wasn't long before the tools were burned beyond use.

"Raziel stop. I'm warn'n you! Euroashien's heart is five times hotta than tha sun. Yu'll be incin'arated instantly. Everyone'll die! Raziel!!" the elemental yelled.

"Now you're concerned for everyone?" Raziel mocked.

The grand duke began removing large quantities of the pavement and hurling them into the dragon which broke away massive parts of its body. Euroashien flew above Raziel and started blasting fire attacks upon him yet again. Raziel began to sink in the ground underneath him. The flying dragon stopped its attack and noticed Raziel was no longer below it.

Without warning Raziel tossed the entire side of a building into the air and removed the neck of Euroashien causing it to plummet to the ground. Raziel jumped back onto the scene and rushed into the chest cavity of the dragon as it instantly began regenorating a new head out of lava. The creature was left on its back as Raziel continued breaking away parts of its body to try and prevent it from having a solid form.

As Raziel snapped away another chunck of chest the lava flowed lower and exposed a blinding object. Luckily for Raziel he was able to perfectly see the heart without fail, but upon its exposure all around them was instantly burst into flame and turned to burned cinder. Only in a matter of seconds everything in a ten mile radius was suddenly obliterated.

Raziel stood waist deep in hot magma, depsite Euroashien clawing at him in its chest cavity. He reached out and crushed the intensly hot massive heart of the legendary fire dragon with both hands. At that moment a pure white explosion created a massive blast radius and a deep crater was forged from underneath them. Lava went everywhere about the burning kingdom.

Inside the enormous pit of the crater Raziel laid on his back in utter amazmant. A creature like that would have been impossible to slay without the armor of Kamisama. He sat up and looked around to verify Euroashien would not return. Charred earth, drifting ash, and smoke were all that could be seen. Raziel climbed out of the devestating hole in the ground and lay witness to all of the destruction the poor kingdom has recieved.

The night sky had fallen during the course of his battle, but the wild fires and dancing cinders in the air still lit the sky.

"What's the matter Fire starter? Finished taunting?" Raziel asked out loud.

The golden armor glittered with the flickering flames all about. Raziel was not exhausted, not once felt heat from Euroashien, and suffered no injuries, however, with a victory at such a great cost he felt as though he still suffered a defeat. Raziel continued walking on to find other people in danger. Perhaps more summonings at large or to simply aid in the recovery process of this tragedy.

39

A place to stay, something to eat, and someone to hold

Bo's little puppy feet were sore from all of the walking.

"My feet are barking." he cried.

"I think you mean, 'your dogs are barking'." Alisha corrected.

"But I'm talking about my feet." he answered back.

"Um, yeah. That's right, I must have been thinking of something else." she smiled. "It's a wierd saying anyhow."

"There's some more." Wraith pointed out, "Off the trail over there."

Vincent, Alisha, and Bo looked a small ways off to the side of the trail back to Vailstone.

"More of those huge foot prints. What tha heck is that big with feet like that?" Vincent asked.

"I've lived in these woods for a long years, but I've never seen something that would leave footsteps in the ground like those before." Bo informed his group.

"Think it might be another sort of spider monster thing?" Alisha asked.

"It looks like a two or four legged whatever, obviously not a spider." Wraith quipped.

"I'm not saying another spider. I mean like, another monster sort of thing? Cause spiders like that we saw back there, that's not normal by any means." she defended.

"And it had fire." Bo stated the obvious.

"I dunno, so let's stop talking and start walking again." Vincent suggested.

"But my feet really hurt." Bo whined.

"Come here Bo. I'll carry you." Alisha offered.

The little shark-dog hurried over to rest in her arms. He smiled, being off of his feet instantly started to make them feel better.

"Thank you Alisha. If your feet hurt later let me know and I'll carry you for a bit, okay?"

"Sure." she chuckled lightly.

"Finally." Wraith spouted.

"Huh?" Vincent asked.

"We've made it back into town."

"Yeah, but what kinda town?" Vincent wondered noticing all of the smoke off in the distance.

"What happened?" Alisha worried.

As the four looked forward towards the punished kingdom they all witnessed a tremendous exploison of epic proportion.

"Oh my God......" Alisha covered her mouth as she gasped in horror.

"What's happening?" Bo asked lowering his ears.

Vincent turned to Alisha and noticed the terror in her eyes. Powerful emotions stirred inside the teenager seeing Alisha in such a state.

"I don't know, but we need to keep moving." Wraith answered.

"Into that?!" Vincent responded.

"What? You wanna go back to spider valley?" Wraith replied.

Wraith continued walking away. Vincent stood in place and watched the princess slowly begin to follow. Uncertain of what to do Vincent simply followed as well.

The group reached a small house right before entering the kingdom and immediately could tell something was wrong. Windows were shattered, the door left open, and burn damage to the roof.

"Let's see if anybody's in there." Wraith suggested.

"Why?" Vincent asked rudely.

"Um, cause it's freak'n late and we don't have a place to sleep."

"So we ask some weirdos if we can jus' spend tha night?" Vincent asked sarcastically.

"A sleep over?" Bo asked wagging his shark tail.

"Something like that." Wraith answer, "I doubt anybody's home. Look's like the people here left in a hurry."

"Why do you think that?" Alisha asked.

"Cause I see a bunch of crap all over the floor in there." Wraith observed.

Bo was shocked, "There's POOP all over tha floor?!"

Wraith sighed, "No. There's stuff everywhere. I mean, like picture frames and paper'n stuff."

"Oh! Thank goodness. I don't wanna walk on a poo-poo floor." Bo smiled. "I'm sure they use a corner like everybody else."

"Check it out quick silver." Wraith taunted.

"What? Hell no, I'm not getting shot for trespassing on some crazy person's property." Vincent figured.

"Dude, there's nobody even home. Don't be such a freak'n wuss."

"If there's nobody home, then why don't you go inside and prove it to me?"

Alisha rolled her eyes from the two bickering yet again and walked over to the broken window. She looked through the window and into the house. The royal decided to knock on the side loudly to see if anyone surfaced.

"Hello? Is anyone home?" she asked out loud.

"Whoa, whoa, whoa! What're you doing?!" Wraith and Vincent asked.

"I'm seeing if anyone is home like a normal person would do."

A moment passed and only hot air answered the call.

Bo sniffed the air, "I'm pretty sure nobody's home."

"Ugh, fine. I'll go and check since I'm the only one here with balls." Vincent insulted.

"What the hell is that supposed to mean?" Wraith challenged.

"Oh, I figured you were smart enough to crack that riddle." Vincent smirked.

Bo laughed, "He said you don't have a hangy bag!" he chuckled hysterically.

"Oh, I've got balls runt. Step aside, I'll check it out."

"No screw it. It's too late I'm already checking it out first." Vincent declared walking to the doorway.

"Move squirt." Wraith walked by pushing Vincent away.

"Screw you!" Vincent returned moving Wraith out of his way.

Alisha waited holding little Bo while the two boys were pinned in the doorway with each other, pushing and grappling.

"Move you idiot!"

"No! I was here first."

"You're just trying to prove a point. Just let me do it!"

"Yeah! Yeah, that's right. Cause I've got balls!"

"No! No you don't. You don't have balls."

"Yes I do! Yes I do!"

"No you don't! No you don't!"

"Shut-up! Stop it! Yes I do! I do to"

"Do not!"

"Do to!"

"Do not!'

"Do to!"

Lightening dashed across the night sky followed by a booming thunder.

Bo shivvered, "It's gonna rain pretty hard tonight."

Alisha dropped her head, "Of course it is." she figured with the string of terrible luck she's been having. Alisha, however, did notice how unnaturally fast the strom began to form, "Although, it sure looks like its rolling in pretty quickly.

The two boys finally pushed on and entered the house at the same time. The dark house smelled of burned wood with a stale air about it. Shattered glass, trash, and broken furniture were obvious eye sores with in the rooms. Vincent unsheathed his sword as one while Wraith copied. The two creeped deeper into the house, eventually seperating into different rooms.

Wraith slowly opened a door into a master bedroom.

"Hey, come out." he ordered in a monotone voice. "Ya know I'm not afraid'a you."

He opened the closet with his arm fully extened after he looked under the bed. The purple haired youth shifted through the clothing in the closet to assure no one was hiding inside. He peered into the bathroom and saw nobody around in there either.

"Pft."

Wraith shifted his eyes around at first, then proceeded to the dresser and jewlery box.

"Jackpot." he declared as he loaded his pockets with expensive stones and metals. "A cross?" he noticed. "Looks like real silver." he stated dropping it into his pocket.

Meanwhile, Vincent searched a spare room that looked to be a hobby room. Small figures and torn clothes were scattered on the floor.

"What tha hell happened in this place?"

The orphan looked through the room coming across a family photo. A father, mother, and daughter all smiling happily together. The family appeared to be at some sort of contest show with a puppet in the girls arms.

"Well that explains a lot." he said until hearing a small rustle in a closet.

He turned immediately pointing his double sword in the direction. He squinted his eyes as he prepared himself for someone or something behind the two door closet. Vincent reached forward slowly, touched the nob, and swung one door open as he jumped back. At that moment boxes and puppet parts came pouring out almost hitting him.

"Really?"

He asked looking down at an ugly puppet. He opened the other door receiving the same outcome.

"Stupid doll." Vincent scoffed as he smacked the puppet on the side of the head.

Wraith walked back to tell the others he found no one inside, but before he could he realized Alisha and Bo were both in the kitchen. Bo sat eating a bowl of cereal while Alisha stood by the counter making a sandwich.

"What'd you think you're doing?"

"What does it look like I'm doing? I'm hungry so I'm making a sandwich."

"No, I mean why are you in the house?"

"Cause it's scary out there and it's about to rain." Bo answered with cereal in his mouth.

"Plus if you two found anything it would have already been made clear by now." she assumed.

Vincent walked into the kitchen and noticed Alisha making a sandwich, "Keep it out will ya? I'll make me one to."

"It's okay. I can make you a sandwich." Alisha offered with a soft grin.

"Really?"

"Sure, it's okay."

"Thanks."

"Can I have one?" Wraith asked.

"Sure, all the stuff is over here. You can use this knife when I'm done with it." she pointed to him. "That is, if you done mind using our sloppy seconds."

"Wait what?" Wraith asked stunned.

Vincent found Alisha's choice of words a tad odd. "Hey wait, I checked those two rooms in the hallway, two kids rooms, and a bathroom. Where did you look?" Vincent inquired.

"I looked in the master bedroom and the bathroom." Wraith answered.

"That's it?"

"It was a big room." Wraith snapped.

"Food is ready." Alisha said setting Vincent's sandwich on the table with some tea from the refrigerator.

"This is delicious!" Bo excitedly ate. "I like the marshmallows."

Wraith walked over and prepared his own meal, but instead of sitting at the table with the others he chose to eat in the living room. He turned on the television and ate all alone.

"I've never had this before." Bo informed.

"A sandwich?" Alisha asked.

"No. I mean, sitting down at a table and eating with friends."

"Oh, well I got to quite often but it was just my family. I didn't really have friends back at the castle. Thinking about it, I think you're my first real friend I've had." she explained to Bo.

Bo looked at Vincent, "But you knew Vincent first, I thought you two were friends to."

Vincent and Alisha locked eyes for a moment, "You're right. I guess that makes Vincent my first real friend."

Vincent looked away slightly blushing, "What about you Vincent?" Bo prodded.

"No. Or yes......whatever. She's a friend." he brushed off.

"Oh, well did you eat with your family a lot too?" Bo asked innocently.

Alisha noticed the conversation taking a turn to upset Vincent so quickly changed the subject.

"Speaking of family, I remember you mentioned your mom and dad before. What are they like?" Alisha asked.

"Oh! They were super great. Momma showed me how to swim really fast and poppa showed me how to doggy paddle. Momma's way is faster though." he smiled pathetically

"Were?" she asked regretfully.

Bo's ears lowered a bit while he crammed cereal into his large mouth, "Anthro's don't like cross breeding."

"So?" Alisha prodded.

"You're just not supposed to. I think momma and poppa would have been better off if they didn't have me and my brother."

Vincent looked over at Bo with strong relation to his feelings.

"I didn't know you had a brother. I have one also. Does your brother live around here to?"

"I dunno. I haven't seen my brother in a really long time." he confessed. "What about your brother? Where's he at?"

"I'm not sure either to be honest."

"Oh. I'm sorry."

"There's no need to apologize. Besides, it helps to talk about yourself." she stated scratching Bo's head. "Especially with those that really care about you a lot." she continued looking directly at Vincent. The silver haired teen locked eyes with the beautiful princess once more and swallowed nervously, "Excuse me." she asked as she stood and left the room.

Vincent sat still with a mouth full of sandwich.

Bo continued chomping on his cereal, "Wanna try some of my marshmallows?" he offered reaching his spoon towards Vincent.

Alisha walked into the livingroom where Wraith sat alone watching television.

"I'm going to bed now. I'm going sleep in the master bedroom you found." Alisha informed.

"Alright, I'll be in there in a minute." Wraith mocked.

"Oh, no Wraith. I'm sleeping with just Bo by my side tonight."

"So you wanted to come and rub it in my face that we're not all sleeping together like we did at gypse camp now?"

"No, I just wanted you to understand how it was."

"Well you didn't hurt me if that was your goal. So, good night."

"Trying to hurt you?"

"Yeah. You're obviously pissed at me for some stupid reason. Which reminds me, thanks for the sandwich. I'm sure Vincent loved his."

Alisha walked closer to Wraith keeping mind of the volume of her voice not to get everyone involved.

"You're darn right I'm ticked off at you. That sloppy seconds remark. I know what that means. I'm not stupid Wraith."

"Yeah, what was that all about in the kitchen in there?"

"Because I know it was you. Vincent didn't say that about me Wraith, you did. And then you lie to me? Trying to make me mad at Vincent? So, so that I think that's all he sees when he looks at me?"

"Whatever."

"Vincent was right earlier about you." she accused gaining Wraith's attention. "You don't have any balls."

"Let's go into the bedroom there and I'll prove you wrong right now." Wraith insulted.

Alisha was stunned at Wraith's rude manner, "That's never going to happen Wraith."

"Oh, and I guess Vincent does?"

"Well, he certainly didn't leave me and Bo out there to die by that, that spider thing. Not like you did." she started walking out of the room, but commented once more before leaving. "And I know he sees more then just a body to use. Until you can think about someone other than yourself, that's the only body you'll be touching."

Wraith stood from the chair he sat in and looked at the princess in the gypse attire, "I really do have feelings for you."

"I'm sure you do Wraith, too bad all the feelings between your legs and not your heart."

"Hold up!" he called out. "Check this out." he asked changing the channel to the news station.

Alisha saw the pictures and images of the kingdom under attack by the fire summonings and the ensuing chaos.

"If I didn't care then why would I stick around, huh? That's what we're going into. You need me and that's why I'm still here. For you."

The princess had no more to say, she simply turned and walked into the master bedroom. The blonde readied the bed for herself and Bo. She walked over to the window noticing the rain starting to fall against the glass. She closed the curtains and sat on the bed thinking of everything.

Her mother, her father, Christian, little Bo and his family, Vincent, and Wraith. So many memories and thoughts started rushing through her mind. Vincent inturrupted her chain of concentration though once he knocked on the door frame from in the hall. Bo walked in and hopped on the bed laying in the very center of the comfy bed.

"Oh wow this is amazing soft." Bo informed.

"We're going to sleep. Wraith said his friend's place isn't too far from here so we should make it there sorta quick tomorrow." he informed turning away.

"Um, Vincent?" she called bringing him back. "Where're you going?"

"Sleep in other bedrooms. Why?"

"You're not going to sleep in here with me? I mean...together.... with us? Bo and me of course."

"I thought Wraith said it was just you and Bo in here tonight?"

Alisha walked over to the door frame, "Well, I was thinking about a lot of stuff and I think I would feel safer if we had some protection in here. In case another spider came around."

"Or those footsteps. What if that was a monster and it attacked us in our sleep?" Bo asked scaring himself under the covers.

"Ugh, I'll tell Wraith." Vincent turned.

Alisha reached out and stopped Vincent by grabbing his forearm, "No! I just want you. I mean, I'll feel safer with you around. That's what I'm trying to say." She blushed from her difficulty explaining, "Oh my gosh, I must be super tired. I can't even speak correctly." she chuckled.

"Well, I..." Vincent hesitated.

"Please Vincent?" she asked softly touching his arm.

Vincent couldn't help but agree to her desires after looking her in the eyes and seeing her face.

"Yeah, sure. Okay, um, yeah. That's fine." he agreed walking into the room while Alisha closed the door behind him and locked it from the inside.

Vincent walked around and laid on the side of the bed next to Bo. The small shark-dog smiled and wagged his shark tail just a bit.

"This bed is so comfy!" he happily growled and snuggled against Vincent.

"What are you doing?" the teenager asked.

"You're super warm." Bo explained as if Vincent asked a stupid question.

Alisha walked around and laid down on the opposite side of the bed facing the other direction.

"What are you do'n?" Bo asked the princess.

"Going to sleep silly. I'm exhausted."

"No, I mean why are you over there? It doesn't make any sense. Scoot over here and snuggle with us. Vincent is super warm."

"Oh Bo, I don't know about that." she answered looking at Vincent.

"Come on, or my back will get cold. Please!"

Alisha bit her bottom lip and scooted over to the center of the bed snuggling against little Bo and placing her arm around him, except that her arm reached passed his small body and rest on top of Vincent's chest. She felt Vincent take a deep breath as she touched his body and quickly removed her hand.

"I'm sorry."

"It's okay.......it's whatever." he corrected.

Alisha rest her head back down on the soft pillow and snuggled beside Bo while her arm reached around resting on top of Vincent's clothed chest once more. She could feel that Vincent's heart rate was increasing, however, she did not let it known that her's was doing the same.

40

DEATH

In the fall of night a down pour of rain blanketed the city aiding in the extinguishment of fires scattered about. Seth was looking out of a hotel room window examining the sudden rain.

"It's really coming down out there." he commented before moving away from the window allowing the curtain to close.

Kaz sat on one of the two beds in the room with his shoes off watching the television. All that was on were emergency broadcasts about the death of the royal king and queen and the fire summoning attacks of the kingdom.

"Ya know, I ran into that Fire starter out there today during all that." Kaz pointed to the T.V..

"Oh?" Seth replied.

"Yeah, I fought that damn giant snake thing of his."

"Did you kill it?" Seth asked sitting on his bed.

"It's tougher than it looks." Kaz simply replied.

Seth nodded understanding his answer. He removed his coat, sandals, and socks.

"Looks like my sword helped provide a bit of resistance for my clothes to, not as much, but some. Luckily I didn't turn out naked, or dead. Anyways, before we head out tomorrow I'll need to pick up some more clothes."

"You're going to go shopping?" Kaz asked emphasizing how stupid it sounded.

"Well, I can't go around in these burned holey clothes."

"Whatever." Kaz paused for a moment before continuing. "Hey, where's that Cain guy?"

"He's getting rid of the police car. Said he was covering our tracks."

"Well, I don't trust him."

"Neither do I." Seth agreed.

"Then why are you working with him?"

"Because, he's going to give me information I need to know."

"Like what?"

"It's just really personal."

"I thought you were a detective? You can't find out what ever it is by yourself?"

"I killed them all. Anybody that could have given me information, they're dead." Seth stopped, "It's why I'm not a detective anymore. Lifes over."

"What?"

"I said that lifes over."

"No, you said lifes over."

"Did I?" Seth asked curiously.

Kaz remembered detective Hobbs in the park and Seth's past job position, "You wanted to get caught didn't you?"

Seth sat on his bed without even a reply. His face was unresponsive.

"Be'n a detective you should have known how to cover your own tracks. Look, if you're trying to get yourelf killed or something then that's fine with me, but don't go taking me down with you."

"Fair enough." Seth answered back.

"Ya know, I came look'n for you cause I figured you could help me outta of this mess." Kaz said with disgust.

"Alright. We'll stick with the plan. First, we find my guy then we figure out a way to get the kingdom off all our backs.

"Good. So how you gonna find your guy if he's on the run like you said?" Kaz wondered.

"He's in a gang so they're not that smart. He's most likely retreated to their hang-out. He probably thinks they give a damn about him." Seth chuckled, "They never do ya know."

Kaz was a bit offended by the stupid gang members comment seeing as how he's in a biker gang, but he chose not to address it and continued on.

"And you know where his gang hangs out?"

"Yep. There's an abandonded train station not far from here, if anywhere, that's where he'll be."

A massive clap of thunder rang from outside with lightening dancing in the night sky. The rain poured far enough to reach the kingdom's castle where Raziel finally arrived after assisting the fire fighters and police force settle down the chaos due to Fire starter.

The gate to the Vailstone castle opened slowly revealing a large figure on the other side. He walked into the courtyard with his head held low. The grand duke looked up into the skys above wishing for the feeling of fresh cold rain, but was denied the pleasure. The dark haired hero was met at the door by one of the maids with a towel to help dry him off. She was confused due to the fact that he was completely dry once stepping foot inside.

"That won't be neccessary." he asured.

Raziel returned to his room and carefully sat down on his bed and laid down. He lay listening to the sound of the powerful rain. Unable to still fall asleep he decided to get up and watch the news for updating information. All that was reported were horror stories of what had happened. Monsters that appeared and attacked, people questioning if the crisis could have been avoided by the authorities of Vailstone, and who was truly to blame?

Finally Raziel turned the station and witnessed a broadcast of a man praising the grand duke for appearing and saving his son from a burning building. Others were pleased for his heroic acts. Fighting the frightening dragon of lava appeared to have caused most of the danger to vanish. Raziel heard stories of people he wasn't even aware he had rescued. All of these tails caused the grand duke to relive his fight with the powerful dragon. He smiled thinking perhaps he could start bonding with Christian again over the tail.

He got up and left his quarters and made his way to the young prince's room. After approaching the cracked door he realized something was wrong.

"What's going on? Where's the prince? Where's Christian?" Raziel questioned the guard outside his door.

"I'm, I'm not sure, sir. The king has asked to see you upon your return." the soldier informed.

"The KING?"

"Um, ambassador Hikaru Yotameshii's orders, sir. He's to be referred to as king."

Raziel was surprised and highly upset to hear the ambassador being reffered to as king. He immediately made his way to Hikaru's room, but failed to find him. The grand duke searched the castle for the self proclaimed king until walking by the library and noticing someone sitting in one of the chairs.

"Hikaru? Is that you?" Raziel asked.

The ambassador removed a pair of reading glasses and placed a book down in his lap, "Raziel? You've returned at last. Thank goodness."

"Where's Christian? And what's this I hear about the soldier's calling you king now?"

"Raziel, we need to talk. Please, sit down."

"Answer me Hikaru."

"I shall, now will you PLEASE sit down? You're making me nervous."

The grand duke huffed, but abided to the ambassador's wishes.

"Now, what exactly is going on here? Why are the men referring to you as king and WHERE is Christian?"

"Like we talked before Raziel, Christian is not yet ready to be king. We both agreed on this matter, he is not prepared emotionally nor mentally. The death of his poor parents and knowing that you carried out,.......well his trust has been tested to say the least. Look at the facts Raziel, you and I are left in the turmoil and it is up to US, you and I, me and you alone to rebuild this shattered kingdom. Now, certainly I would have preferred you take on such a leadership roll. It's in your blood, it's who you are. People trust you and listen to you, your a hero, but in light of what's happened your image has been dragged through the mud. The people are nervous perhaps even afraid of you at the moment.

So, who else to accept this position with you unable to take on the responsibility? Grechov? His background alone would send the people running for the hills. So....with no one else capable, I took it upon myself to accept the burden and don the crown until you and I see fit for Christian to take his rightful place on the thrown. Walk in his father's footsteps and all. Would you disagree?" the well groomed man explained while petting his chesire cat.

"Well, no. I don't suppose. But no one outside of the kingdom will take us seriously. Nobody's going to listen to you as a king." Raziel reasoned.

"Well, that might not be so true." Hikaru shook his head slightly, "You see while here, Christian agreed with the both of us actually. And, of his own free will signed this legally binding document, which has now moved into effect as law, states that in said crisis that yourself, or I, be held as king until Christian or Alisha are seen fit to serve as king or queen."

"What law is that?" Raziel wondered.

"We both agreed to call it the 'Dorian act' in honor of his father and our dear late friend. Unfortunately, as fate would have it the possability of Alisha ever becoming queen are no more."

"What?! Why is that?" Raziel asked standing up.

"As our troops were out they happened across a wounded gypsy. The gypsy was in possession of the princess' dress. The dress contained blood that did not belong to the gypsy. From the story he had provided, it would seem he abandoned her at the mercy of one of Fire starter's summonings. A large spider of sorts."

Raziel slowly sat down and held his head in shame, "I couldn't protect her. Even in this armor, I can't protect the ones I love." He looked up at the ambassador, "Does Christian know of this?"

"Interesting that you should ask seeing as how the prince is no longer with us."

"WHAT?!" Raziel asked in fear.

"NO, no. Nothing like that. He's just isn't in the castle any longer."

"But, why? Why did you allow him to leave the castle at such a terrible time?"

"Actually, he left under major Tydus Collins watch. Video cameras show that the prince somehow escaped his room and tricked two soldiers into allowing him and two prisoners to escape."

"Two prisoners?"

"Rufus Navarro Jr. and Wade Smith, the swordsmen you both traveled with."

"Smith? I wasn't aware he was even in our custody. And Rufus, why wasn't he released by now?"

"Raziel we needed to be certain that the children were not kidnapped. The fat fellow was seen leaving with the prince..."

"In an ambulance!" Raziel interrupted.

"And the other a sex crazed pervert, who knows what might have happened if he kidnapped the Dalton's little girl?" he explained as he sipped warm tea from a fancy cup while holding the saucer underneath. "Besides, those seven swords they all posses, what is the purpose of them? What is it that they do?"

"Well, from what I understood they each provide a unique ability."

"Can these abilities be combined to over power the armor of Kamisama? Can they stop you?"

"I don't know. I don't think so."

"Then why were they in the forest with the armor? There must be some significance behind them."

"I seriously doubt they would try and all attack me."

"One of them were an assassin, am I right? If this assassin kills them and obtains all seven swords, then he may very well try and kill you as well. Heaven knows the trouble if an assassin gained that armor of yours."

Raziel sighed, "Well, first thing is first. I'll notify the major to send out a search party for the prince and then we can worry about those swords afterwards."

"The major? Um, he actually doesn't hold that title anymore."

"Now what?"

"Major Tydus Collins has been terminated."

"What?! When did this happen?"

"As soon as he allowed the prince to escape with two prisoners. Not to mention the fact that it was under his supervision the king and queen were killed AND he disobeyed a direct order to keep you from the events in the kingdom and keep you here in the castle."

"That's right, I certainly didn't appreciate being kept out of the loop. And it seems a lot more has been going on that I hadn't been aware of." He stood from his chair.

"It was much too soon for you to be seen back in the public eye and fighting monsters again."

"People were dying out there. I put a stop to it."

"Very well Raziel, have it your way. We'll call the shots together." Yotameshii softly agreed.

"I suppose Grechov supported this decision as well?"

"Oh Grechov, yes. He's actually down in the intensive care unit here at the castle."

"Intensive care?! What happened to him?" the grand duke asked in surprise.

"I was told he went into shock after having half of his face burned off. I believe he may or may not have also suffered from a light heart attack, if that's even possible. The doctor's aren't very optimistic about his condition, you know."

Raziel began walking out of the room.

"Raziel? Where are you going?" king yotameshii asked.

"I need to........clear my head." he muttered just loud enough for Hikaru to hear.

Hikaru smiled while he sat in the library petting the back of the cheshire cat. Lightening flashed on the other side of the windows as thunder clapped outside booming through out the sky.

"A friendly smile and an understanding voice will get you far in this world Syrius."

Raziel was blind sided by all of the new information. He wandered the castle halls aimlessly. Thinking of Grechov clinging to life, the death of the princess, the death of Dorian and Natalia, the devestation of Fire starter's summonings, and the where abouts of Christian. So much was weighing on the grand duke's mind.

"Carmon." he realized.

Perhaps she might have an idea where the prince would go. They were close friends. The father made his way to his daughter's room and knocked on the door accidentally knocking it down. Carmon was startled as he unintentionally exposed her room.

"DAD! What're you doing?!" she scolded.

"Sorry, I was just, knocking on the door is all." he explain as he bent over to pick up the door.

Carmon watched her door crumble into wooden shards in her father's hands. His grip wasn't weak enough to prevent destroying the door. He looked up at her with an expression on his face as if asking for her forgivness.

"What do you want dad?" she asked already annoyed.

"Well, I wanted to come and see how you were doing."

"I'm fine." she answered sitting back down on her bed and watching DVDs of her favorite shows.

"I mean, there's been a lot going on around here lately. Don't you want to talk about it? I'm sure you have a ton of questions for me."

"Nope." she snubbed.

The grand duke sighed, he knew she was upset with him about something, but she obviously refused to explain herself.

"I can tell when something is bothering you."

"You're not as good at it as you think you are." she confessed.

"Come on Bud. Don't be mad at me, please? I've had a really long day." he tried sympathizing.

"Urgh! I hate that stupid nickname." she fussed.

"Come on." he smirked.

"I'm fine dad, really. Can I get back to my shows now?" she asked with attitude.

"Well, I also wanted to ask you something else." he admitted.

Carmon looked at him for his true purpose in coming to her room, "Christian has disappeared and I was wondering if maybe you might know..."

"THAT'S IT!" I knew it!" she shouted cutting him off.

"Huh?" he asked in confusion.

"You didn't come up here to see me or see if I'm okay. No, you came up here cause of Christian. Ugh, I knew it. You're more concerned about him than me." she ranted.

"Hey, now that's not true."

"I don't know where your son is, sorry sir." she mouthed off walking towards the bathroom.

"Hey, now cut that out. You know I love you. Your my little Bud."

Carmon screamed hearing her nickname from him again after slamming the bathroom door shut.

"Carmon come on. Come talk to me. Please?" he pleaded.

Raziel prepared to knock on the door until hearing her warning, "And ya better not knock on the door unless you want to see me naked!" she yelled out of frustration while starting a shower.

Raziel was shocked and heeded her warning leaving her room immediately.

Raziel watched the rain pour down on the kingdom and its castle. After thirty minutes of standing alone and thinking to himself he decided to go to the intensive care unit and check in on general Grechov's current state. He walked into the nursing facility and nodded to a soldier on duty with a nurse behind a desk.

"Grand Duke, sir." the two saluted.

"At ease. How's the general?"

"His pulse is weak, but he appears to be stablizing." the nurse answered.

"This way?" he pointed.

"Yes, sir."

Raziel walked passed a curtain to see the general's face heavily bandaged, hooked up to the machinery, and laying unconscious. Beside the bed were two chairs on each side. The grand duke walked over and gazed down at the injured general.

"This wouldn't have happened to you if I were there Grechov. I'm sorry." he reasoned before sitting down with his back to the wall.

He motioned to touch the bed, but decided not to out of safety for the already injured man. Raziel carefully leaned back trying to make sure not to snap the chair. He stopped leaning as he heard the chair creeking. He just sat watching his friend making sure his condition didn't worsen.

Lightening lit up the room several times. The lights in the room where dim due to the late hours. Raziel heard an unfamiliar click on the other side of the room and looked up. He noticed a small flame in the darkness.

"Fire starter?" he asked.

The flame lit up the end of a cigarette before going out. A figure in the darkness took a draw off the stick of tabacco before laughing at the grand duke's guess.

"Fire starter? No, no, no, no, no. He's not here." the voice simply answered.

"Who goes there?" Raziel questioned.

"'Who goes there?' Who talks like that anymore?" the man asked mocking Raziel.

A body stepped forward showing only a wicked smile and vague silhouette. The individual was a pale skinned white male wearing a hoodie and baggy pants. The person had dark orange hair with blond streaks and a unique pair of shades. If anything, it were the eyes that were most unsettling about the young man.

"Get the hell out of here. How'd you get in anyways?" Raziel questioned. He paused for a moment after finally getting a look at the young man's face, "You. From before. You were by that burning apartment complex. What are you doing here?"

"I'm came in with him." the man pointed to Grechov.

"You saw what happened?"

The young man in the hoodie laughed with a wicked smile, "I know more than just that friend."

"Am I supposed to know you or something?" Raziel wondered.

"You should," he paused puffing off of his cigarette, "but ch'a don't." He answered sloutching sideways in the chair opposite from Raziel with his leg over the arm rest.

"You better start answering me before I remove you from this room myself." Raziel warned standing up from his seat.

The man with the shades smiled, "Calm down, I'll tell you who I am. Not only that, I'll tell you why I'm here."

Raziel glared at the pale skinned man, but slowly sat back down.

"To be honest, I have many names. Death, Grim reaper, La Muerte, Malach HaMavet, the list goes on really. But when I think about it, I like Grim. It just seems to have that sort of uniqueness to it, but I don't know, maybe it's just me."

"Do you think I'm some kind of idiot? You expect me to believe you're the Grim reaper?" Raziel chuckled. "Aren't you supposed to be a skeleton in a black robe?"

"Oh, come on. You mean like this?" he asked.

Right before Raziel's eyes the flesh, meat, and eyes disintegrated from the pale youth leaving nothing behind other than dry bone. The clothing drooped on the skeletal being, "See I could walk around like the stereotype everybody thinks of me, but it really makes it hard to enjoy my cigarettes. Beside, I like the other look." it confessed. "Although, if it makes it easier for you I guess I could look like you're old wife. Rose, wasn't that her name?" Death asked looking exactly like Raziel's deceased wife.

"Stop it. Stop it NOW!" Raziel yelled out of pain preparing to strike the intruder.

A soldier and nurse ran into the room, "Sir, are you alright?"

"Who are you talking to?"

Raziel looked at Death, "They can't see me." he informed smoking his tabacco, "Cause I don't want them to."

Raziel looked back at the two, "Um, nobody. Back to your stations."

"Yes, sir."

"As you wish, sir."

The grand duke sat back down and rubbed his hand through his hair.

"You had better change your face or I'll do it for you." the grand duke threatened.

The mysterious being morphed it's face back into the young man's once again.

"So is this what you really look like?" Raziel asked. "I'm supposed to believe you're the true face of death itself?"

The pale being smiled, "No." he chuckled thinking to himself. "Anyone who sees my true form will die instantly. This form is a little safer."

Raziel watched the shape shifter with seriousness.

"You still don't believe me. I can tell." Grim scratched his neck, "You think I'm using magic or something, huh?"

"Now you're going to tell me you're a mind reader to?"

"Na, nothing like that. That would take all the fun out of watching."

"Watching? Watching who?"

"The human race. It's like the greatest show ever. It's got it all. Drama, violence, action, romance, betryal all that good stuff. Plus, I've got all my favorite characters I can route for. It may sound a little queer, but your one of'em."

"One of what?"

"My favorite characters. You're like the hero always saving people. You always got the girl, killed the monsters, saved the day. There were a few times where it seemed like I was gonna finally get ya, but you still managed to pull out a victory." Grim nodded fanboying over Raziel. "You human beings make one hell of an entertaining story book."

"Yeah, okay. So, if you're Death like you say you are then wouldn't that mean that nobody around the world is dying right now because you're here with me?"

"I've got a system. Don't fix what ain't broke." it grinned. " Besides I could explain it all to you, but you wouldn't understand."

"Riiiight." Raziel grinned. "You just have an answer for everything don't you?"

"Look, I came to talk with you not screw with your head."

"I don't know who you really are, but we're done here. It's time for you to go."

The grand duke stood to remove the individual until Grechov's monitor began showing him flat line. Raziel panicked as the nurse came running in to aid the general.

"Convinced now?" Grim asked allowing the pulse to return.

Raziel watched the nurse checking his vitals, "It was just a scare, he's back as he was before, but I'll inform the doctor." she explained before leaving. "It's so cold over there, I'll turn the heat up too."

"Want me to kill her? There's that guard over there, he could die. You're call." Grim asked throwing his hands in the air.

"No, that won't be neccessary. Let's just calm down, alright?"

Grim smiled it's unsettling smile, "It's fine, I wasn't going to kill them anyways. It's not their time just yet. But I feel you're starting to finally catch on."

"Are you saying you can't kill?"

"Unless attacked of course, then people forfeit their right to live. People have," it paused, "'jobs' to do, if you will, so I can't just go around claiming people as I please. Although," it chuckled, "it's funny. There are exceptions a time or two. Ya know, there are people out there that try hunting me down who think they can fight me and steal my scythe." Death laughed hard. "How could they possibly kill me? I mean, It's me!" he laughed.

Raziel started considering the individual's claims and glanced over at the general as he laid in the bed hooked up to the medical equipment. "Are you here for Grechov?"

Grim finally took control of his laughter, "Who this guy? Na, he'll be fine. I got a general in Syberia due for a heartattack in like five minutes though, but this general still has a while. I'm not supposed to really tell you, but you and I are going to be real close, so it's not that big a deal."

"I don't intend on seeing you often." Raziel stated bluntly.

"Raziel, I'm around more often than you think. Let's not be stupid, okay? Besides, We're so alike you and me. Two immortals unfazed by this world, destined to last til the end of time." Death revealed. "You and me, peas in a pod."

"So then, it's true? I really can't die while in the armor of Kamisama?"

"Right. You're so suspicous of everything, but then again that's also kept you alive all this time. Anyways, as long as you wear that suit you can't die. You're safe."

"So you're saying if someone can remove me from the suit then I can be killed."

"What? No, nobody can take you out of the armor. Where are you getting this from? Look, you wear the armor, you cannot die or be killed. Nobody can take you out of the armor. It's GOD'S armor, nobody can remove any piece of the armor. Okay?"

"That's what's hard for me to process here. God's armor, why would God need a suit of armor?" Raziel questioned.

"He doesn't. It's for..." Grim paused as if catching itself revealing too much, "......look. It's God's armor, okay." it grinned yet again.

"What about psychics and mind control?" Raziel continued. "That's the only way around it's power, right? Make me remove the armor myself with mind control?"

"Where aren't you getting?! Nobody can make you do anything. Okay, you seem to have a hard time understanding something really simple. You wear the armor of Kamisama you can't die, you can't be stopped, you can't be injured, you cannot be opposed in anyway, ya don't eat, sleep, poop or pee okay? Oh, oh, oh I got it! Think of it like you've stopped in time, but everything else hasn't kind of thing." Death explained becoming frustrated.

"So that's why everything I touch breaks or is ripped apart? Nothing can stop my actions?" he asked a loud recalling every instance that he's ruined by applying normal human effort for daily life.

"Right, now you've got it." Death agreed. "You apply any force to something and something loses."

Raziel sat thinking for a moment, "But when I jump and land, why don't a keep going? Why do I stop?"

"Well, first off let's start by saying don't jump as high as you can. Second, your normal center of gravity is you plus the weight of the armor. Now, you can apply force and jump super high and you'll fall like you normally would, but if you stomped when you hit the ground, you'd probably keep going. So, don't do that." Death removed the hoodie from resting a top it's head. "Ya know, usually when ever people meet me they tend to ask questions about myself." Grim pointed out.

"I'm sorry, it's just I've had so many questions about this armor and no one to ask. I know I have more questions, but they're just not coming to me at the moment."

"It's fine, we literally have all the time in the world, and passed that." it grinned.

"So, Death is a man then? I never considered your gender."

"Oh, na. I'm merely part of the life cycle. I don't have a gender, but I can be whatever I want though. It's sort of cool." Death lit up another cigarette and began smoking another.

"Wait, I have another question. Back when I saw you in the kingdom, there was a flash of light. What was that?"

"Hm? Oh yeah, well when ever there's requiem I just open a gateway. Sucks in all the wandering souls for me. I have my own method of doing things." Grim thought for a moment before continuing, "Now it's my turn. There's a little something I've wanted to ask you for some time now. Why this guy?" he motioned towards Grechov. "You'd stuck your neck out for him to get him into this army. I mean, you two are like night and day. Did you know his own mother disowned him cause of the things he did to his prisoners of war due to her religious beliefs? Yet....there you were...sticking up for the guy to get him in your army. It just puzzled me."

Raziel sat for a moment looking at Grechov's bandaged face, "There are times I wonder if what I do is justifyable. Grechov's actions were in the name of the ruler he served. My actions were for the saftey of others and now for this kingdom, but does that obsolve me for the acts I commit? Sometimes I'm torn apart inside, but I put on a strong face and keep on. Because, others need for me to. Giving Grechov a second chance felt like I was giving myself a second chance. He's not the monster everyone thought he was, so maybe I'm not a monster." he confessed. After seeing Grim's lame expression he shrugged off his speech, "I don't know."

"Sorry I asked." Death admitted.

"Hey!" Raziel defended.

"Oh well, looks like everythings worked out for the best in the end anyways, right?"

"What do you mean?" the grand duke wondered.

"You know, cause of your fear there." it pointed at the center of it's own head referring to Raziel's silver hair patch.

"I don't know what you're talking about."

Grim laughed from Raziel's response, "Don't lie to me. As much danger as you've faced in your lifetime I always felt it was kind of lame that your biggest fear was death. I don't know, a big hero and all, I guess I would have guessed something more dramatic or unique."

"It's not death." Raziel corrected.

"Oh really now?" it played along. "Then do tell, cause that's what it appears to me."

Death leaned forward for Raziel's answer. Raziel swallowed and paused for a moment, discussing his secrets wasn't normal for him, but he was convinced the being he was talking to was beyond man kind and made the exception.

"Well......." Raziel paused struggling to confess, "my father...he was...I looked up to him. I aspired to be what he was. My dad.." Raziel chuckled, "the stories he had. I mean, I've always felt shadowed by him. The things he had accomplished in his lifetime. And he was tough. Tough as nails. I remember a story about him and mom at a party. This one guy comes up, very disrespectful to mother. Man.... dad got up and knocked that guys teeth right out of his head." Raziel smiled recalling the events, "The guy was three times dad's size, but it didn't matter."

Raziel nodded his head slightly, "But, as I got older, so did he. I remember visiting after traveling here and there and, I came home to tell him what I've been up to. When I saw him, he'd lost so much weight." Raziel struggled as he remembered more of the story taking a troubling turn. "Months later.....like maybe seven, eight maybe? Mom had to put him in a home. That last time I went to visit him, he was so frail. He, he was stuck in a wheel chair. He couldn't use the bathroom on his own, he had to be feed. It....it scared the living hell out of me." he confessed looking Death in the face.

"Everything I do, all these evils I face, the monsters I come across. I've thought about it for a long time now. I'm good at what I do but, I've always sort of hoped to find that someone better. Ya know? I've lived the life of a warrior, I am a warrior. I want to die the life I've lived. I want to die a warrior not........not an old man with a lung disease stuck in a wheel chair put away in some old folks home. My daughter coming to see me a broken shell of what I once was. Fighting for what's right, being a hero in a glorified battle to save the day. Making the ultimate sacrifice, that's how I want to be remembered. Not pooping on myself hooked up to breathing machines."

Death gazed deeply into Raziel upon this new revolation.

"Not like that. Falling to you......no. That's not my fear........growing old." he answered staring off in the distance.

"Well, that's all the time we have for today. You can pay the woman at the front desk on your way out." it joked standing up and walking away from it's comfy spot.

"Hm? Where are you going?" Raziel wondered.

"Look, I've got to run, but we'll chat another time. Trust me." Grim informed.

"Wait, I remebered some of the other questions I wanted to ask you." Raziel recalled.

"Sorry pal, next time. I've got an appointment to keep." it stated. " And I HATE to miss an appointment." flicking it's cigarette to the side Death faded into a shadows in the room.

Raziel sat wondering if what just happened had truly transpired. Did he hallucinate? Was the being actually Death in carnate or a magical creature? A summoning perhaps? The grand duke started thinking to himself that maybe he was to quick to assume that Grim fellow was telling the truth. But, he was convincing none the less. Regardless, Raziel was hopful the being was telling the truth and that Grechov would eventually pull through.

Despite being protected by the armor of Kamisama Raziel still preferred the entity gone.

41

WADE'S ALTRUISM

Deep inside a cave at the base of a cliff not too far away from the kingdom of Vailstone Fire starter used the remnants left behind at the castle by the animal people to summon the sacred saber-tooth. The clever elder remembered the chants used to correctly call forth the old cat. Grunt and Sammy sammy seven stood near as the feline appeared before the fire elemental. The cave darkened eerily with a strong wind starting to flow through. The cat spector appeared before Fire starter with displeasure.

"You are not of anthro-kind. You are forbidden to summon me." the mystical cat warned.

"Ya, whateve'a. Look, I know ya can foresee int'a tha futu'a n' I need some answa's. Now first thing's first......." Fire starter was inturrupted by the aged spirit cat.

"You are not of anthro-kind, therefore, I shall not assist you."

Fire starter twitched slightly at the uncooperative feline's remark, "Okay, I get it. I don't have fleas, but this ain't a request."

"You have wasted my time foolish one. I shall not help you."

"Alright! Now look he'ya ya stupid CAT! Ya'r gonna help me wheth'a ya like it 'r not. Now don't test me or I won't hav'a use for ya. N' I will kill ya if I don't need ya." the elemental warned.

The spirital cat raised it's head, "Fool, I am of the spirit world and cannot be killed. Now be gone with you."

The sacred saber-tooth vanished before Fire starter and his lackies. The fire user however was sorely displeased and gripped his fire staff tightly as he muttered, "Challenge accepted."

Meanwhile, Kaz and Seth both waited for Cain at the dirty slum hotel. Seth finished washing his hands after "taking care of buisness" in the restroom. He stepped out into the double bedroom and noticed Kaz wearing S.W.A.T. team gear.

"What tha hell? Why are you wearing S.W.A.T. gear?" Seth asked.

"Cause I'm getting ready to fight. After fighting those fire monsters and having guns pointed at me I feel it's a pretty good idea to be prepared." Kaz explained.

"Where did you even get that?"

"From the cop car."

"Tha cop ca..? Ya mean the one Cain got rid of to avoid getting us noticed?" Seth pointed out.

"Yeah."

"Think about that for a second." he asked holding his temples, "Don't ya think it's gonna be a little obvious walking around in that S.W.A.T. gear? Drawing a lot of unwanted attention? Kind of defeating the whole purpose of losing the car?"

Kaz shrugged his shoulders, "I don't care. You've got instant protect sword over there and ninja boy becomes a shadow when ever he wants to get lost. I've got nothin, so I'm using this as armor." Kaz glanced over at Seth while tightening his gear, "We don't all wanna die."

Seth sighed, before capable of responding there was a swift knock at the door.

"Who's that?" the black haired detective asked.

Kaz immediately grabbed his broad sword and stood near the door ready for an attack. Seth unsheathed his sword and looked at Kaz who gave him a small nod. Seth walked over to the door and reached his hand to the door nob.

"Hello?" he asked before opening the door, but received no answer. "Who is it?"

He looked at Kaz once more and nodded back as he slowly opened the door. To his surprise there was no one on the other side of the door. He stuck his head out and looked both directions from the room.

"Nobody there." he explained to Kaz.

At that brief moment Cain appeared at the door and entered without wasting anytime.

"What tha?! Where the heck were you? I just looked outside?!"

"You should be more cautious. It could have been a trap." Cain grumbled.

"That's what I told him." Kaz lied.

Seth looked at Kaz swiftly with displeasure.

"Here." Cain said before tossing a bag to Seth.

The detective caught the bag and looked inside, "What's this?"

"What'd you do to the car?" Kaz asked.

"Lost it." Cain simply replied.

"What the hell is this?" Seth asked looking at the clothing.

"Change of clothes. As not to draw attention." the assassin stated slowly looking at Kaz in the S.W.A.T. gear.

"I'm not wearing this crap."

"Why?" Cain questioned.

Seth pulled out a teenage girl's shirt with a music band's faces on the front, "The Naughty Boys?" he stated as if asking.

"It's a shirt."

"It's a GIRL'S shirt!" Seth emphasized.

"It's unisex."

"It's PINK."

"Men wear pink." Cain claimed.

"Not REAL men." Kaz quipped.

"Thank you." Seth agreed with Kaz for once. "Me walking around in THIS will draw more attention then Kaz in the cop suit. Uh uh, this isn't gonna happen. Nope." he said dropping the shirt back in the bag.

"You're clothes are badly burned, your final target is getting away, and we are all running out of time. There are no other clothes." Cain reminded.

Kaz looked at Seth wondering what he would do. The black haired detective glared at the assassin with a look of death.

"FINE dammit! Fine." he said stomping into the bathroom to change.

"Once he's out, we go to the station." Cain demand receiving a nod of agreement from Kaz.

On the outskirts of Vailstone the princess and two youthful swordsmen prepared to move on from the house they slept. Alisha bent over the kitchen table writing down a sincere thank you note to the owner's of the home and wished them well. She placed a salt shaker on top of the note and stepped away from the table. With a big breath she left the house and walked outside to look for Wraith and Vincent. As she walked around to the side of the house she noticed Wraith with his head underneath the steering wheel. After a volt the abandoned mini van was started and operational.

"What's up?" she asked curiously.

"Oh, Wraith hot wired the van so we can use it to meet up with his friend." Vincent answered.

"Where did you say he was again?"

"He's held up at a train station. If anywhere, that place we'll be safe." Wraith answered back. Wraith sat in the driver's seat and shut the door, "Well, let's go before more spiders show up."

"Wait, where's the dog?" Vincent asked.

"Bo must still be in the restroom." Alisha informed.

"Ugh, I'll get'em." Vincent volunteered running back into the house.

Alisha stood outside for a moment before Wraith started talking, "You riding along? I won't bite ya know?" he joked.

Alisha looked at the vehicle and sighed before sitting in the passenger backseat.

"Being a princess I'd of figured you'd be sitting in the front seat."

"I'd rather not thank you." she replied looking out the window.

"I meant it just so you know."

"Meant what?"

"What I said last night. I really DO like you a lot." Wraith confessed again.

"Thanks." she snipped.

"No really, I mean it. You're not like other chicks. I don't know how to explain, but I can tell you're special." he admitted looking down at the steering wheel and in the rearview mirror frequently. "It bugs the hell outta me talking to you like this. But, I know I can't get your attention like I used to with other girls. I see that now. So, what I'm say'n is, can we start over?" he asked turning around and looking at her in the backseat.

Alisha smiled beautifully and blushed, "I'll think about it." she smirked.

Wraith smiled back, "Thanks."

In the awkward silence Wraith decided to lighten the mood with a joke, "Guess I ended up with a 'sloppy second chance'."

Alisha's face quickly grew cold, "Don't push it."

Wraith panicked, "Yeah, you're right! Too soon. Not funny. It was a stupid joke. Wasn't even a joke. Well I was joking, but it wasn't funny so I don't even know why I said it. It, I, I'm just gonna shut-up now. Yeah, I'm unna shut-up." he stated recovering from bad humor. "Gee, where's Vincent already, huh?"

Vincent walked up to the bathroom door and knocked, "Hey, pup! You almost done in there?"

"Yeah, just a minute." Bo answered back on the other side of the door."

Vincent waited a moment until Bo unlocked the door and stepped into the hallway.

"Ready." Bo stated.

"You didn't even flush." Vincent pointed out.

"Flush? What are you talking about?" Bo giggled and walked outside.

Vincent caught a whiff of a foul odor and peered inside. The teen's face fell once he realized Bo relieved himself in the corner of the bathroom rather than the toilet. Both left the home locked and hurried to the van. The silver haired teen sat in the front passenger seat while Bo sat in the back with Alisha.

Vincent shut his side door, "Ready."

"Finally." Wraith said pulling out of the drive way, "Let's go."

In an empty ally in the Vailstone kingdom prince Christian wakes up from a short sleep in the military jeep. Wade made the decision that with the gas tank nearly on empty that the ally was their best bet for staying the night.

"Huh? Oh yeah...that's right. I keep waking back up in this bad dream." Christian announced with depression.

Oyova shook inside Christian's shell hanging from his neck and popped out.

"Huh?! This doesn't look like the dream world. Are you okay?" she asked.

The young prince smiled, "Yeah, I'm fine. Sleep well?"

"Yep, it's cozy in there." she smiled back. "Where are we? Are you homeless again?"

The prince sighed, "Yes and no. Somebody else is just living in my house."

"Well? You gonna take it back?"

Christian thought for a moment before looking directly at Oyova, "Yeah."

"Who you talk'n to?" Rufus asked poking his head into the jeep.

"Ah!" Oyova panicked and retreated back inside her shell.

"Huh! What was that?!" Rufus asked in surprise.

"Oh! Oyova, it's okay. That's just Rufus." Christian assured happily.

Wade walked over to the jeep curious of the commotion, "What're you so excited over?"

"Christian has a little fairy!" Rufus explained.

"It's okay, Rufus and Wade are my friends. They're good guys."

"A fairy?" Wade wondered. "Where?"

Oyova popped out of her shell once more and fluttered in Wade's face, "HEY! I'm NOT a fairy! I'm a PIXIE! Got that!"

"Whoa, well give you a look. A pixie. Sorry."

Oyova huffed.

"You're awfully pretty for such a small thing." Wade thought for a second, "Hm.....I'm pretty sure I could make it work."

"Make WHAT work?" Rufus asked scrupulously.

Rufus glanced over to Wade immediately. Wade shook his head and merely smiled embarrassingly while waving off Rufus' glare.

"Huh?! Oh, um. Nothing." Wade smirked nervously.

Oyova flew to Christian, "You can't go around telling people about me. Got it."

"But why?"

"Cause, I have magic. Some people would want to use me for very bad purposes." she explained.

"I didn't know."

"Well now you do. So remember that, okay?" she asked poking the tip of his nose.

"Okay. I will."

"Promise?"

"I promise."

"Where did you find the pixie?" Wade asked.

"My name is Oyova."

"Ogava?"

"Oh-yo-va."

"Oh, Ofubu." Wade muttered under his breath to mask the fact that he couldn't clearly make out the tiny syllables from her tiny voice.

Oyova looked at Wade sternly with suspicion.

"We met at the hospital."

"The hospital?" Rufus asked.

"Yeah, in the chapel." he explained looking at Oyova happily. "That's when our friendship started. Right?"

"No, I hated you a lot when I met you then." she admitted embarrassing the young prince. "Now I just find you weak and annoying."

"Well, that's a conflicting story." Wade announced, "So, let's ditch this gasless jeep and head to one of my clubs. There's one not to far from here. It'll be safe and I'll call Amanda, see if she know's about what's been going on."

"Sound's good." Christian agreed exiting the jeep.

After the pink pixie retreated back into her shell around Christian's neck, the prince and two swordsmen continued on their way. The streets were dead due to the horriffic attack on the kingdom from Fire starter's monsters.

"Whoa, it's sort a creepy." Rufus announced.

"Hm?" Wade inquired.

"The neighborhood and these buildings. All empty and burned out. It's just kind a creepy, ya know? Kind a like a ghost town or something."

"Yeah." Wade agreed looking around at the devesation.

The playboy became lost in thought reflecting on what he had stated in the past when talking to Raziel. "I'm not a hero." Wade thought about his selfishness. Wade stopped walking with the other two as he noticed a burned pacifire laying on the sidewalk at his feet. His mind raced with situations that could have occured that would result in a baby's burned pacifier and every scenario turned grim in his head.

Wade looked around and remembered slaying the forest of darkness creature and wondered what would've happened had he have stayed behind and not fought. Wade picked up the pacifier thinking about the innocence and future stolen from its owner.

"Fire starter is just like the forest darkness monster." Wade stated with frustration as he balled up a fist.

Christian and Rufus looked back realizing they had left him behind, "What do mean?"

"He's dangerous. He's powerful, he's tricky, and heartless and that makes him dangerous. And I'm gonna stop him." the entertainer vowed.

"How are you gonna do that?" Rufus asked.

"I don't know." He thought for a moment then grabbed the hilt of his sword, "With this sword."

"You'll never get close enough to use it on him."

"Maybe I don't have to. He doesn't know what it can do. If I can change the ground underneath him into water."

"Extinguish the fire!" Christian finished Wade's thought with excitment.

"Yeah!"

"Hm," Rufus smiled, "that just might work. But, why the sudde......" the large young man was silenced by the screams of a woman in the distance the next block over.

"What's that?" the young prince panicked.

"Hurry! It sounded like someone need'n help." Wade replied leading the way as he ran to the aid of a stranger.

To the group's surprise they noticed a very small group of people standing outside a five story building engulfed in a green flame, however, it appeared not to emmit any heat nor did it burn the building.

"Green fire?" Wade said to himself in amazment.

"What's going on here?" Rufus asked the small crowd as they approached.

A man answered, "There're children inside there with one of them monsters, but the fire department and police are too busy elsewhere."

"Prince Christian?" a woman acknowledged.

"We're here to help." he answered.

"But you can't pass through the fire." a stranger confirmed.

"Then what are we supposed to do?" the orange haired swordsman questioned.

Wade stood trying to figure out a plan while Christian heard a tiny voice from the sea shell around his neck.

"Christian. Christian, its a protection spell. I can get you in, but not with all of these people around. I don't want them to see me."

"Huh? Ya, okay. Um,..." the youthful prince looked around trying to figure out what to do. "Hey, Wade, Rufus lets try looking around the back or something."

"We've already walked around the whole building. There's no way in or out." a man confirmed.

"Well, let's give it another look." Christian suggested.

"Christian they've already tried. We need a new idea." Rufus added.

"I've got a really good feeling about this. Come on. Everyone else stay here!" Christian darted off around the other side of the building.

Wade and Rufus quickly followed after wondering just what was up his sleeve. The young prince waited until the two swordsmen showed up around the back.

"What's going on now? Did you see an opening or something?" Rufus inquired.

"From on the other side of the building?" Wade pointed out. "Why did you run off back here?" he asked looking around, "There's still no way inside."

"Oyova said she can get us inside. Go on Oyova, come out. It's safe." Christian assured.

The tiny pink pixie emerged from the sea shell and looked around to verify the truth. "Okay. I told Christian to come back this way because I can get you inside, but not in front of others."

"You can get us in?" Rufus repeated.

"What'd I just say?" she asked rudely throwing off Rufus.

"The fire is green. It's a protective fire to keep danger out." Oyova informed.

"A protective fire? Fire starter might be hiding in there with those children as hostages." Wade concluded.

"Stay close to me." she ordered.

The three circled around Oyova closely. She closed her eyes and formed a small light in her hands which slowly began to expand. Eventually the four were engulfed in the orb of shining light.

"Stay close." she reminded as she slowly flew forward towards the intense green fire.

"Couldn't help but notice we're walking right to the fire." Rufus nervously mentioned.

"Don't wuss out now. You'll be safe as long as you're in my light."

The three boys hung close to the pixie as they slowly entered the green flame. Christian watched in bewilderment as he was surrounded in the intense flame, yet completely unharmed. Wade opened the door while inside the pixie's light and assisted in getting them all inside the building. However, once inside they were surprised to see that the green fire was not burning through out the entire building, but yet only on the outside.

"Whoa, this is pretty trippy." Rufus expressed.

"Hey, be ready." Wade told the orange haired youth.

As the blond man exposed his sword cool icy mist poured from the empty sheath. Rufus mimicked and removed the large cloth that proved as his sword's sheath. Both swordsmen were ready and prepared for danger with their weapons drawn.

"Spread out and look around?" Christian asked.

"Spread out?! Hell no, stick close together. Ain't nothing killing us off one by one in this dump." Wade disagreed.

"Killing us off?!" Rufus asked nervously.

"Oh come'on. Nothing in here can be any scarier then that forest monster thing, right?" the prince thought.

Rufus swallowed and slightly nodded his head, "Yeah." he agreed with uncertainty.

"Alright, I got you three inside so you can save some kids, I'm outta here." Oyova declared.

The small pixie disappeared back inside the sea shell for her own safety while the rest hunted inside the building.

"Alright, where do we start?" Rufus asked.

Wade looked to a door close by and shrugged his shoulders, "Well, I guess here's as good as any."

The entertainer shook the door nob, but was unable to enter.

"How are we gonna check out this whole building if the doors are locked?" Christian wondered.

The three stood perplexed for a moment until Wade shrugged his shoulders once more, "Ah, screw it." Wade poked the door with his sword turning the locked door into a puddle of water on the ground. "Door's open."

Slowly Wade and Rufus walked inside the room, hesitantly poking their heads around corners and into other rooms while Christian waited keeping an eye for any movement in the hallway.

"How many of these rooms are we going to look through?" Rufus cried.

"All of'em. All of'em until we can save these kids. Where ever they are."

Rufus sighed, "We just looked at the whole first floor and nothing. Maybe those people are confused or something."

"Look, if you don't want to help out then just leave or stay back then, alright."

"I didn't say that."

"Well then act like a man alright?"

"Are you mad?" Christian asked.

"What? No, I'm not, I'm not mad." Wade sighed.

"Then what's wrong?"

Wade's face revealed exhaustion as he took a deep breath, "Back at 'The Golden Ticket' I almost lost my closest friend because of Fire starter. When Raziel came looking for me to help out I told him 'No'. I told him I wasn't a hero. Then when the place started burning down to the ground Amanda stepped up to protect everybody. Myself incuded....and it took it's toll on her. I almost lost her cause I didn't care to get involved. Then your parents and what all's happened to Vailstone. And now these kids! I can't anymore, I can't NOT get involved anymore." Wade confessed.

Christian walked over to Wade and placed his hand on the man's arm, "Hey, I'm involved. You're not alone."

"Yeah, I'm here to man. I can't let anything happen to my grandad, ya know?" Rufus added.

Wade grew a small smile as a faint noise was heard from upstairs alerting the three of near by danger.

"The second floor." Rufus announced stating the obvious.

"Stay close together." Wade warned.

"Together." Christian assured.

The trio slowly and carefully crept up the staircase making sure not to warn their enemies of their arrival. Wade took each step cautiously. He began to sweat from his temple. As he lead the other two down the hallway it was clear which of the rooms to enter due to the faint sounds of the children on the other side. His mind feared the condition of the innocent children, the safety for himself and new friends, and the dangerous evils that awaited to face off against them.

Wade raised his finger to quietly remind Christian and Rufus to be quiet as he prepared to enter the correct room. He motioned for them to be ready on the count of three. Wade started the countdown with his fingers. Three, two, one, he took another deep breath before turning the door into water and charging in.

Wade barged in with his sword ready for battle as Rufus and Christian followed close behind him. As they ran inside the trio stopped almost immediately in sheer befuddlement. Before them stood a pretty girl with wings of shining flame. She appeared as if a large fairy with fiery hair and tattered clothing. But even more curious was the small group of happy children playing with her.

Upon their entering the startled children ran and hid behind the fire girl, surprisingly enough her wings of glittering fire did not burn them.

"Leave them alone!" she warned using herself as a shield between the children and the swordsmen.

The fiery girl fluttered her wings projecting wide bursts of flame to shoot her intruders.

"Look out!" Wade shouted.

Rufus managed to jump to the left and out of the line of fire while Wade moved right, however, Christian stood petrified.

"Christian!" Rufus shouted.

Wade quickly looked back and struck the ground with his sword creating the floor underneath the prince to transform into water. The young prince fell to the first floor apartment below with intense wing shaped fire barely missing him overhead. He landed hard and painfully, but thankfully not severely burned half to death.

"Christian! Christian are you okay?!" Wade called out.

The brown haired teen was dazed and confused for a moment until realizing what had happened. He held his sore head, "Yeah. I'm okay." he assured with tears in his eyes from the pain.

"Leave us be! Turn back now!" the fire girl shouted to the swordsmen hiding behind a recliner and a sofa.

"Go away!"

"Leave us alone."

"Don't let'em get us Fyra."

"Abud derp!" one random kid added.

Wade and Rufus had the strange feeling that they were suddenly the monsters. The children looked to the fiery girl for safety and protection.

"Hold on there. We're here for the kids. We're the rescue team." Wade declared.

"These children don't need your help. They're safe here with me." the girl answered back.

Wade and Rufus looked at each other from their distances. Wade remained crouched reevaluating the situation for a moment before slowly standing up and sheathing his sword despite Rufus' disapproval.

"Okay, I'm coming out now and I'm putting my sword away." he announced doing just that. His hands were empty with his palms facing the fiery girl. "Hi there........I'm a little confused here. There's some really worried parents outside that asked us to come save their kids, but I don't see any danger." he stated in a charming puzzled manner.

The girl stood wiery of the handsome blond man, "You can leave, these kids are safe here with me."

"Yeah, I can see that, but their moms and dads are worried sick about'em though."

"Well, if they wouldn't have left them to die then I wouldn't have had to rescue them from Euroashien." she informed.

"I know a lot of scary stuff has been happening lately that we're ALL not used to around here and sometimes people panick. So.... you saved these kids?"

"Yes. I did."

"Then you did a great job cause their all safe. That makes you a hero, but now it's time to finish the job and give them back to their families downstairs. They're worried sick and I don't blame them. There's been a lot of crazy stuff, they just want their families back. That's all."

Rufus slowly stood up in a less than aggressive posture watching the situation unfold.

The fiery girl's eyes glanced around wondering what course of action to take. She wearly turned her back on Wade and Rufus and kneeled down before the children. She smiled happily yet saddened as she gave them a group hug.

"It's time to go see your families again, okay? Remember what I said, you can't hide from fire, you can only run." The girl stood from the kids and looked at Wade. "Go on kids. Be careful now."

The children slowly moved away from the girl and to Rufus and Wade.

"Rufus, can you take the kids downstairs to Christian please."

"Yeah, sure. Come on, everybody follow me. Be careful around the hole in the floor over here."

"I'm not a hero the girl declared. I followed my orders."

"You're with Fire starter then?"

"Yes."

"He ordered you to protect little kids?"

"Of course not."

"Then you have a heart. You're the hero that saved those kids from Europasaun."

"Euroashien." she corrected

"Whatever."

"I attacked this kingdom like he wanted me to."

"Why?"

"Because he was framed."

"Look sister, Fire starter isn't an innocent guy."

"No, he is. Fire starter didn't put the grand duke under a spell. They lied and set him up and now all of his enemies know where to find him. It won't be long now."

"Until what?"

"They come looking for him. It's not safe here anymore, especailly with him close by now. Fire starter will retreat soon."

"They? He? Who's he?"

"He doesn't have a name."

Wade was puzzled, but listening intently. "Who are you?"

"I'm Fyra. Why?"

"I wanted to know the name of the woman who saves children from burning buildings and scary monsters."

"I'm one of those monsters."

"No, you're not."

"Yes, I am."

"You don't have to be. Come with me."

"I can't."

"Why not?"

"Because he'll never let me go." she expressed emotionally.

"Then let me help you."

"Why would you want to go out of your way to help me?"

"Well......I usually make a habit out of helping beautiful fire babes with sparkly wings such as yours. Your lucky, cause if they didn't sparkle like that then I would seriously have to reconsider." he joked charmingly causing her to laugh.

"Your sweet 'guy who turns doors to water'."

"So you know my REAL name, but my friends call me Wade for short."

"You're sweet Wade. You have a good heart too."

"Take my hand, let me help you." he offered extending his hand outward.

"I can't, I wish I could, but I just can't. He'll never let me go." she confessed hopelessly. "I'm his soldier. Take the kids to their parents make sure they leave soon."

"Why what's happening soon?"

"This place is too close to the old northern central station. My brother's through Fire starter are going. We're meeting up there, it won't be safe. Please, go. Run from fire." she warned creating a purple fire behind her and walking through.

In an instant Wade was left alone. He turned to walked down stairs thinking about everything said. As he walked down the first floor hallway a near by room opened. Wade stopped with hesitation, but was relieved to see Christian slowly emerge.

"Sorry about earlier. Are you oka...." he asked before getting inturrupted.

"Is it true?" Christian asked.

"Huh? Is what true?" Wade asked.

"What she said? Raziel is lying about the spell? If he didn't kill mom and dad because of a spell then he just..." the young prince failed to finish the sentence.

"I don't know." Wade confessed.

"Do you think she was lying?" he asked looking away.

Wade paused not knowing what to say.

"You don't think she was lying do you?" Christian bluntly asked.

"No." Wade answered softly and honestly.

Christian's emotions began tearing him apart inside all over again. He began tearing up while trying to remain strong, "Then why? Why'd he do it? Why he...?" the young prince began ruining his sentences due to his distraught nature.

Wade walked over and placed his hand on the prince's shoulder, "Hey, come on now." To Wade's surprise the prince hugged on to him tighly for emotional support. In return Wade supportingly hugged him back.

Eventually Wade and Christian walked out of the building to a happy crowd of blessed families rejoicing. Rufus turned to see his friends exiting the building.

"Everything okay?" Rufus asked.

"Yeah, everything's fine." Wade assured.

"Did you kill the monster?" a man shouted.

All of the children looked at Wade with worry, "Look everything is fine now, but it's no longer safe here. You all need to move towards the eastern part of the kingdom as fast as possible."

"Why?"

"There's no time for explanations now. Just get your stuff and leave quickly." Wade ordered before walking down the steps of the entrance and walking away.

Rufus and Christian rushed over to the side with Wade.

"I thought you said go east, so why are you going west?" Rufus asked.

"I've got to go save her now." Wade informed.

"The fire girl?" Rufus asked.

"Yes."

"Why?"

"She's trapped in Fire starter's hell and I have to save her."

"But she's with him."

"No, that's just it, she's not and she'll never be free unless somebody gives a damn." Wade announced before continuing to walk away.

"I'm coming too." Christian said.

"What? It's going to be too dangerous. There's going to be other monsters there." Wade argued.

"Wade, I have to know the truth." Christian stated.

"Okay," Rufus agreed throwing his sword over his shoulder, "then let's go."

"You too?"

"You two are gonna need all the help you can get. Luckily for you I'm all that you'll need." Rufus smirked.

"Okay then, let's go." Wade grinned.

"Together." Christian reminded.

Back in the cave outside of Vailstone the sacred sabertooth was summoned once again, but this time was much different then any other time before. He opened his eyes from inside the body of a tiny canary trapped in a bird cage. Fire starter stood peering directly at him from the outside of the birdcage. The sacred sabertooth panicked due to being summoned into a physical and vulnerable form.

"Memb'a last time we had a little con'vasation bout wast'n people's time. Memb'a that, huh?"

Fire starter angrily and aggressivly reached into the birdcage as the sacred sabertooth panicked while being concealed in the tiny canary's body. He fluttered around inside the cage trying to avoid the old elemental's hand. Eventually Fire starter snatched the possessed canary from out of the cage in a firm death grip. The sacred sabertooth pecked and bit the elemental's hand trying to force him to lossen his grip, but only succeeded in pissing off Fire starter even further.

"You little shit!" Fire starter insulted squeezing the bird harder and snapping its neck with his thumb.

"Sammy sammy seven!" Sammy sammy seven announced.

Fire starter turned around witnessing his lava monster, summoning number three, entering the cave.

"Welcome back numb'a three. This is fa you!" he stated throwing the dead bird into number three's lava body.

42

THE UGLY SIDE OF LUSCIOUS LUCIOUS

Carmon slowly walked down the hallway passing up medical staff and military personel without acknowledging them at all. The grand duke's daughter remembered seeing general Grechov being rushed by nurses panicking for his life. But, what happened to his face? She couldn't see passed all the staff as he was taken in to the emergency unit.

The teenager poked her head into the room looking at him from a distance, yet still unable to see what had become of his face. The room was kept dimly lit as not to disturb him. The brunette took small steps closer and closer to his bed. She recalled over hearing rumors of his disfigurement, but her curiosity had gotten the better of her. She needed to see what had become of him.

She raised her head to try seeing the left side of his face from where she stood far on his right side. Carmon approached closer until a small light flickered on a side table beside his bed. It was the general's cell phone, he had received a text message. Carmon reached over and picked up his phone to read the text. She was surprised to read the message intended for the general and more importantly, who it was from.

Suddenly a hand firmly grabbed her hand from the hospital bed. General Grechov raised from his bed and leaned closely to Carmon.

"That's not for you." he warned.

The air was stolen from her lungs as she saw the gruesome side of his face. She covered her mouth with her free hand to try preventing from vomiting. Carmon tried averting her eyes and not looking at the man.

"Oh my God. Oh my God." she struggled.

Carmon broke free of Grechov's grasp and turned running. The general smash the lamp on his bed side table with his forearm in rage letting out a growling yell of anger.

The mini van Wraith had been driving finally pulled up to the train station.

"Welp, here we are. It'll be safe here." Wraith assured.

"This place doesn't look very safe." Bo confessed. "It makes my fur stand on end."

Vincent glared at the station, "Looks like a dump."

"If Wraith says we'll be safe here then let's at least give it a try." Alisha added.

Vincent noticed a quick glance and smile between Alisha and Wraith, but remained silent. Vincent was last to exit the mini van, he made sure to look around due to the uneasy feeling in his stomach. All attention was turned to a receiving door being raised in the distance. A group of thugs with baseball bats and guns started walking out slowly.

"Okay, maybe we should go." Alisha stated quickly changing her mind.

Wraith raised his hand motioning for Alisha and the rest to calm down. He began walking towards the unsettling group.

"Put that shit up." Wraith ordered to the tattooed gang members.

"Who you think yo punk ass is talking to us like dat?" a dirty gang member replied.

"Oppose me, and as you collapse your last vision upon this world will be the Wraith." Wraith quoted.

Upon Wraith's quote the thugs slowly lowered their weapons.

"Wraith?!" a voice responded in the crowd.

A handsome youth wandered from the group of gang members in very baggy clothing. The young man had deep yellow eyes and golden messy, yet styled hair.

"Wraith you son-of-a-bitch! You're out!" the man replied happily.
"Lucious!" Wraith smiled.

The two walked over to each other and greeted with a unique hand shake.

"You get out while one of them monsters tore up tha prison or what?" Lucious inquired.

"Yeah, something like that." Wraith lied.

The fact that Wraith was already starting off untruthful with his friend made Alisha and Vincent on edge even more.

"Damn, dude!" Lucious laughed clapping his hands once approaching Vincent, "That's some wicked ass hair color you've got go'n on there." Rather than words Lucious only received a glare off death from Vincent. "Asian boy here don't speak english or what?"

"I know english." Vincent corrected.

Lucious slapped Vincent's arm near his shoulder, "Then loosen that tight ass asian boy." The young man then set his sights on princess Alisha standing not to far from Vincent. "Damn, gurl." Lucious tilted and looked back at Wraith before approaching Alisha with a suave walk. "You have my most sincerest apologies. Where have my manners gone? I was unaware I was in the presence of such sheer beauty." he announced holding Alisha's hand and kissing it lightly.

Wraith and Vincent were both annoyed by Lucious' flirtatious nature towards Alisha.

"Allow me proper intro, everyone calls me "Luscious Lucious", but you can call me 'Yum'." he smiled. It was hard to describe, but somehow there was a weird charming quality to Lucious Alisha couldn't quite figure out. "And miss dream come true, please bless me with your name."

Alisha blushed from Lucious' extreme flattery, "My name is Alisha. Pleased to meet you Lucious."

"Yum." he corrected.

"Yum." Alisha chuckled.

Both swordsmen sighed at the stupid humor.

"You all must be here cause ya'll need some refuge cause there ain't no other reason this bastard would be here." Lucious joked pointing at Wraith. "Come on! Come inside to my palace." he invited holding the princess' hand delicately leading her and the others inside.

"He sure cusses a lot." Bo stated.

"Ya think?" Vincent remarked.

Inside the train station gang members of all ages sat around watching Alisha and her group intently. Lucious lured the four into a smoky seating area with huge couches, drugs and needles on the tables, and open containers of alcohol sitting everywhere. Lucious jumped into the air crashing onto one of the couches.

"You guys hungry? Want something to drink?" Lucious offered.

"I'm starving." Bo cried.

Lucious chuckled in amazmnt, "That dog just talked. What tha f.."

"His name is Bo." Vincent inturrupted.

Lucious looked at Vincent with lazy eyes and a funny smile.

"Hey, Jose! Burgers for our special guests." Lucious called out. The gang member froze for a moment before listening to his leaders instructions. "And what would you like to drink my dear?" he asked Alisha.

"Just some water would be nice."

"You can't have a 'fun' time jus drink'n water." Lucious replied.

"She's not looking for a 'fun' time." Vincent snapped back.

"Then she's hanging out with the right people." Lucious snapped his fingers, "How bout some water fu these ladies." Lucious grinned, "So what's go'n on Wraith? Why you at my crib?" he asked lighting a blunt.

"My company here just needs a place to crash for a few days, til they can figure out what to do." Wraith informed.

"What's there to figure?"

"Her folks kicked it. She needs to lay low for a bit."

Lucious looked at Alisha's long smooth legs and firm breasts, "She's gonna need to lay REAL low." he smiled blowing smoke from his mouth. Lucious walked over to Alisha and sat very close beside her with his arm over her shoulders. "I'm sorry to hear that about yur folk's ya know? If you need to lay low then consider yourself laid babydoll." he smiled. "A friend of Wraith's is a friend of mine." he tried comforting while trying to look down Alisha's top.

"You see a ghost or somethin' bro?" a thug laughed. "Hair all white like ya seen a ghost." the gold toothed simplton mocked towards Vincent.

Vincent was instantly getting pissed off at the mockery.

"Hey, homey. You know you not in china town no more." another thug added.

"Hey little asian boy, show me some karate kicks." another bully chimed in. "You japanese boy, huh? You know kung-fu?" the bully laughed.

"I know f@*#-yu." Vincent announced surprising the thugs. The silver haired teen spun around and punched the laughing gang member right in metal mouth.

The other two jumped in attacking Vincent while their friend was dazed and bleeding. Both punching and kicking him on the ground.

"STOP!" Alisha screamed.

Lucious noticed Alisha getting upset and intervened by getting up and getting between the thugs and Vincent.

"Come on boys. Break it up. He don't get jokes like you'n me." Lucious smirked looking down at Vincent's bleeding lower lip.

Alisha ran over to Vincent and tried to look at his injuries, but he shoved her away.

"I don't need your help." Vincent snapped.

"Ugh! Stop being a jerk and let me help you." she argued.

"I get jumped by two assholes and I'M the one being a jerk?"

"Shut up." she replied. The princess removed a tissue from one of her pockets and used it to soak up the blood from his lip.

Bo leaned over towards the thugs and whispered, "That one has an attitude. Sometimes I have to put him down to." he winked.

"What'd you say tuna-pup?!" he shouted startling Bo and causing him to hide behind the couch pillows.

At that moment a ghetto looking girl walked out with a tray of burgers and drinks for all. She placed them on the table and walked away.

"Yeah! Food!" Bo responded excitedly jumping to the burgers.

"Sorry, the boys juss don't take kindly to being punched in the mouth." Lucious informed Vincent while offering him a hand from off the ground.

Vincent slapped his hand away and got up himself.

"Vincent be nice." Alisha scolded. Vincent looked at her with an annoyed expression. "Just come sit with me and eat, okay?" she asked pulling his hand over to the couch.

Wraith rolled his eyes at Vincent's special attention with the princess. Lucious sat down on the opposite side of Vincent and Alisha and relaxed while Wraith and the others ate.

"So you think'n bout getting the old crew together?" the pretty boy asked.

"Yeah. I'm back now. Why not?" Wraith answered.

"You know Chewy got shot?" Lucious informed.

"What?"

"He didn't make it. We think it was the south side, but we don't know fur sure yet."

"How's Sly?" Wraith asked while taking a huge bite.

"He's been try'n to get out, but he ain't keep'n that gold digger if he stops sell'n."

"Awe, he's still got that hoe? She's gotta be milk'n him dry by now." Wraith figured.

"She better for as much money he gives her." Lucious added turning Wraith's comment into a dirty joke making them both laugh. "You turn fag in prison or you gotta girl?" Lucious joked further.

"Screw you." Wraith replied smiling. "I'm working some stuff out.... it's complicated."

"What's his name?" Lucious carried further.

"Piss off douche." Wraith chuckled.

"How is it complicated?" Lucious asked chummy.

"She's gotta a lot of stuff go'n on right now, that's all."

"So how's that complicated?"

"She want's me, but she's just too stubborn to see it yet." Wraith stated having himself and Alisha lock eyes for a moment.

Lucious picked up on Wraith's comment immediately while Vincent was a little late due to the fact that he was pretty much ignoring everyone other than Alisha.

Lucious picked up a silver spoon and adjusted his hair and looked at his reflection. "Better hope she doesn't know a good thing when she sees it."

Outside the train station Rufus, Wade, and Christian approached slowly and cautiously from the wooded area.

"These tracks will lead us straight to the old train station. So if we just keep on'em we'll be fine." Wade informed.

"Why doesn't anybody use the train station anymore?" Rufus asked.

"Um. Well,.." Wade tried recalling why it failed, but honestly didn't have a clue. The entertainer was too involved with his own life and the party scene that he was completely unaware.

"Economics." Christian bluntly answered.

"Economics?" Rufus replied.

"There ya go, economics." Wade smiled brushing off the question.

"It was a tax issue. Dad couldn't keep up with the charity orginazations AND afford to keep the train station running without increasing taxes. There just wasn't enough revenue coming in at that time so he chose to cut the funds to the station. Besides, this train station had seen better days." Christian continued. "It was in need of some extensive repairs."

The three continued walking until they heard a rustling in the leaves off the side of the tracks.

"What was that?" Rufus asked nervously.

"Looks like your worse nightmare tubby." a saggy clothed youth replied walking out of the woods with a gun pointed at them.

"Is that a fat joke?" Rufus asked.

Three other hoodlums followed after, all carrying weapons of some sort.

"So what should we do?" one asked in a terribly nasally voice.

"Hey, they gots swords like those guys with Lucious." one thug realized.

"Looks like we spoiled ya'll's little surprise for Luscious don't it." the guy said keeping his gun pointed at the three as they pointed hands outward in surrender.

Alisha, Vincent, and Bo sat alone on the couches while Wraith and Lucious played some billiards several feet away. Vincent sat in silence looking off into the distance. He was trying to calm down by relaxing and taking deep breaths, but failing miserably. He sat staring away trying to resist the feeling of someone just sitting by and watching him. It started annoying him further and further until he eventually broke.

"What?! Why do you keep looking at me with those judging eyes!" he asked turning to face Alisha who had actually been staring him down the entire time.

"Why can't you just try to get along with people?" she asked.

"Because he's mean." Bo replied.

Vincent looked and Bo and growled startling the little pup and causing a whimper.

"Did you expect me to just sit by while those pukes were making fun of me?"

"I'm just saying not to take everything to heart. This obviously isn't a friendly group we're here with so let's try to keep from lashing out at them. Okay?"

"Is that it? Or you just don't want me to knock the teeth out of your friend Mr. Romance there?"

"Ugh! Get real Vincent. He's not exactly what I would call my type."

"And Wraith?" he asked.

"What about Wraith?"

"Is he your type?"

"Hardly. And why do you care?"

"I don't." he answered defensively.

"Sure doesn't seem that way to me." Alisha admitted.

"Then how's it seem to you?"

"Ya know, it seems to me that Wraith was right." she stated surprising Vincent, "I DO want a certain someone for myself, but I'm not the one that's being stubborn in accepting that."

Alisha stood up to walk away, but stopped once Vincent questioned her further, "Wait! Who are you talking about?" he asked anxiously.

The princess sighed, "Figure it out Vincent. Let your guard down every once and a while." she expressed exhaustingly.

"Wait, where are you going?"

"To the bathroom." she answered drained.

"Hey, use the one down the hall. Somebody pooped in the corner in that one." a ghetto chick warned.

Alisha used a different bathroom while Vincent quickly leered at Bo.

"What? How was I supposed to know they poop in a water bowl here?" Bo quietly defended.

Lucious leaned over the pool table and struck a striped ball into the hole he was aiming for, "Nice." he complimented himself. He walked around the table stopping in front of a mirror to catch a view of himself before continuing. "So how'd you meet that gypse babe and the two freaks?" he asked Wraith.

"Oh, well....after I got out I just sort of bumped into'em."

"So they're a couple with a little dog mutant?"

"No, they're not together. In fact, he's gay. Super gay even."

"Really?"

"Oh yeah."

"I didn't pick that up. What about her? She like's the 'D', right?"

"Yeah, she's into guys."

"Good, cause I'm thinking of mov'n in on her." Lucious confessed. "Alisha?"

"Yeah, the babe is smok'n. You've had to have noticed that body. You weren't in prison THAT long, man." the pretty boy mocked with a smile.

"Yeah, but.." Wraith stumbled.

"What? You want it?"

"Yeah, I saw her first."

Lucious laughed, "Dude if you wanted it first then you know you should've gotten it before bring'n her to me. Now you'll end up getting my leftovers. Again." Lucious chuckled striking another ball.

"Lucious! Somethin's up!" a gang member shouted pulling the two away from their billiard's game.

The leader pulled a gun from underneath his waistband and rushed over to the group coming inside.

"We found these three wander'n the tracks."

"So why didn't you beat the shit out of'em or shot'em?" Lucious questioned.

"We would've, but we think they were getting ready to set up a little surprise for us. They've got swords just like Wraith and his friend over there."

"We weren't gonna do anything I swear." Rufus added.

"We're looking for a summoning actually." Wade confessed.

"Shhshhshhhsh, shut-it. Wraith, this true? You know these guys?" Lucious asked as Wraith walked closer.

Wraith stood before them with hesitation.

"Wraith?" Christian pleaded.

Lucious looked at the intrusive three and back at Wraith, "Wraith?"

Vincent stood from the couch looking off into the distance trying to make out the faces.

Bo stood up on the sofa to look with Vincent, "Vincent what is it? What is it Vincent?"

"Christian?" Vincent questioned.

"Your new asian friend there seems to know'em." Lucious pointed out to Wraith. "Ain't that sum'thin?"

"I didn't say I didn't know'em." Wraith defended.

"Did you have somethin planned here tonight buddy?" Lucious prodded.

"No man. Nothing like that."

"Cause they've all got swords and, if I remember correctly, which I think I do, swords were kind of your signature thing." Lucious prodded further, "You sure you don't wanna just come clean about somethin' here?"

"Chri...? Christian?" a girl's voice asked in the distance.

The young prince looked further passed Vincent at the oddly dressing blonde girl behind him, "Alisha?"

The sister's eyes began to quickly water up as she began slowly walking closer to her brother. Christian had completely forgotten about the danger he was in and began walking towards Alisha. Some of the gang members pointed their guns on the prince, but Lucious waved them down to lower their guns. Eventually the brother and sister started running to each other colliding into a hug of joyful tears. In that moment a wave of emotions washed over them. They each suddenly relived the horrors and deaths of their parents, the fears of abandonment, realizing the fact that all they have now was each other, the joy that their sibling survived their new reality hell.

"I thought you were....I didn't think you made it. I, I,.." Alisha stuttered.

"I didn't know what to think. I was so worried. There's just been so much going on, I don't even know where to being." Chirstian cried.

The brother and sister were lost for words.

"Remember now?" Lucious asked his purple haired friend.

"Yeah." Wraith answered reluctantly.

Lucious walked over to Christian and Alisha, "SO. You two know each other?" he asked suspicously.

"Christian's my brother!" Alisha sobbed. "I thought I'd never see you again." she stated holding her brother closely.

"Wow, what were the odds, huh? All the way out here outta no where. And you juss so happened to find each other AND you brought friends with weapons to. Cause of all da scawy monshturs, huh?" he taunted in a kiddy voice.

"Lucious what's wrong?" Alisha asked.

"I'll tell you what's wrong here! This pimple over here's full a shit!" he shouted pointing his gun against Wraith's face. "I knew you didn't escape from prison ya worm. Danny's brother is still locked up, he saw you talk with some Vailstone cops and leave a free turd. And now all of a sudden you come here with this pathetic group all wielding swords like a group of freak'n ninjas like yur gonna cut us down? Huh? Take over my turf?"

"Nothin like that Lucious. I swear." Wraith tried conviencing.

"Bullshit! That's why the other half of your team just starts coming along after we let our guard down, huh? Bullshit." he angrily accused. "Jose told me his brother was killed by a prick with a sword, but he didn't recognize your little asian friend there. So we waited, and sure nough, here come more dips with swords. I knew you were behind it Wraith. You were the only idiot I ever knew to bring a sword to a gun fight. I was just giving you a chance to come clean cause I'm your friend. I was giving you a way out, but you missed your shot......I won't." he promised taking aim.

"Lucious...." Wraith started.

Lucious pressed the gun roughly against Wraith's neck, "SHUT-UP! You don't get to talk now." he said nodding to his own words. It was obvious he was plotting what to do on the fly. "How about I blow your damn throat off, huh? Make sure you don't ever talk again. Huh? How bout that?.......Now you may talk."

"Lucious stop! Why are you acting like this? Nobody was trying anything, please." Alisha pleaded.

Lucious glared at Alisha then Wraith then Alisha again, "Oh. Oh, I get it now. I see what ya did there. You bring in this babe for me to bang then stab me in the back while I'm distracted."

"What are you talking about? How dare you." Alisha gasped.

"Hey! Watch your mouth you jerk. Your talking to royalty." Christian threatened.

Wade and Rufus slapped their foreheads with their open palms from Christian's stupidity.

Lucious focused his eyes on Alisha and Christian and walked away from Wraith. He got right in each of their faces. He brushed some hair away from Alisha's face for a closer inspection. "Well, I'll be dammed. The freak'n prince and princess, here at my crib. No wonder you look so tempting. You've got that royal stuff." Lucious teased.

He went in to steal a kiss from Alisha, but she resisted and tried pushing away. Vincent jumped over the other couch and began to run over until Lucious stopped and pointed the gun at him.

"You better not take one more damn step fool cause if you do I'll cap her in the stomach right now." he threatened.

"Now why don't you and me put on a little show for everybody, huh?" he suggested as he firmly grabbed hold of one of her breasts. "It'll be fun cause you hot as hell and, damn baby, I am too." he smiled unzipping his pants.

"You leave her alone!" Christian shouted pushing into Lucious and knocking the gun out of his hand, which accidentally fired off a shot when hitting the ground.

Lucious grabbed hold of the young prince's clothing and jerked him around. Christian was so full of rage from how he was treating his sister. He balled up a fist and punched Lucious in the face. Lucious completely froze from shock. He stopped and looked Christian in the eyes seeing the fear in the prince's face.

"My face. You struck me in the face. You lil' bitch. Nobody hits the face." Lucious informed.

The thug plowed punches into Christian's stomach and kicked him in the ribs once he had fallen to the ground. Alisha jumped on Lucious' back to stop the attack, but was thrown aside instead. He then pulled Christian up by the hair on his head.

"Ya know what I'm gonna do. I'm gonna teach you a valuable lesson. To the pit boys!" Lucious ordered.

Lucious dragged Christian by his hair kicking and screaming while the rest of the gang forced the remainder of the group to follow by gun point. In a seperate room Lucious stopped beside a locked metal door on the ground.

"Jose, open tha pit." Lucious ordered.

Everyone watched with uncertainty of what horrors where hidden in the cement pit covered by the metallic grate. Jose obeyed, unlocked, and removed the grate. Lucious dragged Christian beside the open pit against his will.

"Goblins." Christian stated quietly. As the young prince peered inside he saw a pit full of helpless goblins of all ages.

"That's right, goblins." he said with disgust. "I feel like I'm making my throat ugly just say'n the word. Such an ugly word. The perfect word to discribe ugliness." he expressed. "Get one." the handsome bully ordered in a cold tone.

Jose walked down a few stairs leading below and returned with both arms pulling out a defenseless goblin. Crazy thoughts began forming in everyone's minds of what terrors he had in store for them.

Lucious yanked on Christian's hair and forced him to look while he cried in fear, "You see this fugly thing? HUH!?"

Christian nodded his head as he cried fearfully.

Lucious jerked free of his grip on Christian's scalp and walked away. The goblin and prince nervously watched as the handsome thug lifted a dented bloody metallic baseball bat leaning against the far wall. As he comfortably approached the frightened two he began explaining himself, "THIS is 'ugly stick'." he informed dragging the cold stained metal against the cement. "This world has so much ugliness, it sickens me. But, I do understand not everything can look as great as me." he announced in an unsettling charming manner. "So it's important that I realize I'm a one-of-a-kind and nothing will meet this level of beauty." he informed directing attention to his face. "So I've developed a small tolerance of ugly that can be allowed to live, but THESE things," he stated pointing the bat at the goblin quickly forcing it to shiver defensively, "Ugh, ha ha. Plauges against the world. And you," he pointed the bat at Christian, "striking perfection. Now you think about that. God makes a beautiful masterpiece that is 'me' and you spit on his work by slapping me with your little baby fists there. Now don't that just seem rude, huh? Dudn't that just seem flat out wrong to you?" he paused, "Well it does me."

At that very moment Lucious swug the metallic bat hitting the goblin right in the face as if trying to hit a 'home run'. Everyone was terrified by the sudden act of utter violence against the innocent goblin. Alisha screamed and teared up while her brother, who was next, cried further. The goblin stumbled in a daze trying to block the onslaught, but the gang member broke its arm and continued smashing the bat into its face relentlessly until its face was nothing more than a pool of blood in a cracked skull. The slight enjoyment the young leader showed off was almost as distrubing as the rage he displayed.

Lucious giggled as he pulled out a sanitation wipe from his pocket "Even their blood is ugly." he joked. He sighed from the exercise of the brutal beating, "Now see? This is what we do to God's ugly mistakes. Understand now?" he asked the crying prince. Without an answer he slapped the prince in the face and repeated himself, "Understand!" he yelled grabbing his chin.

"Uh...hu." he prince mustered.

"Leave him alone." Wade shouted.

Lucious pointed at Wade, "Don't worry, you'll get your turn. You'll all get your turn. Except you babydoll, me and the boys are gonna appreciate your beauty differently." he smiled winking at Alisha. The smug brute pulled on Christian's hair again and jerked his head around making him look at his face. "Now look at me. Huh, look at my face. I had to make sure you truely understood the process and the crime you committed against perfection." Lucious smiled and patted the prince on the shoulder, "Now it's time to finish the lesson." he stood up rearing back and readying to strike the boy's face like the goblin's.

Christian whimpered helplessly on his knees when suddenly a humongous flash of lightening and clap of thunder rang from outside. Gun fire began sounding off as if without direction or purpose. More pounding bursts of lightening crackled outside until the sound of the front entrance could be heard exploding open.

"What the heck's going on out there? Go check it out." Lucious ordered his fellow gang members. "More forgotten friends of yours?" he asked looking at Wraith.

In a flash Cain fell from the ceiling slicing Lucious' back causing him to drop 'Ugly stick'. As the gang leader yelled out in pain the assassin darted over to the gang members holding the others hostage. Shots were fired at the masked murder, but all far to slow to connect to the assassin's current rate of speed.

"Cain?!" Wade announced in utter surprise.

The masked ally sliced the remaining thugs down except for Jose who watched frozen where he stood.

"What da f*%# is that?!" Lucious yelled freaking out and cluthing his bleeding back.

"LUSCIOUS!" Wraith yelled withdrawing his sword and slashing the vain youth in his face.

Lucious freaked out from suddenly having his face cut and bleeding down his chin. Christian panicked and took advantage of the distracted youth by pushing him into the goblin pit.

"JOSE!" Seth called out gaining the thugs attention as he burst through the only entrance. Once the gang member saw Seth he remembered him from before over his dead brother's body. Seth fired his gun shooting the thug in the chest killing him instantly.

The very moment Lucious hit the ground the goblins began circling around him chanting and muttering amoungst themselves. The injured teen was helpless and paralyzed with fear. One goblin smiled wickedly and stated something in their language which caused them all to grin mischievously. Suddenly they all moved in on the cowering frightened blond. Terrifying screams of pain were all that were heard from down below in the pit.

Seth's body was catching bullets while his sword was withdrawn and slaying his attackers in the process without effort.

"Everybody get down!" Seth shouted. "Kaz is coming. Cain can you find us a safe way outta here?" Seth asked.

Cain darted away in a blur to scout for a safe exit.

"Is that a 'Naughty Boys' shirt you're wearing?" Wade questioned as Alisha ran over to aid her injured brother.

"Is that really important right now?" Seth asked.

"I'm just say'n ya bust into a hide out full of gang members kick'n ass in a 'Naughty Boys' shirt." Wade complained.

"I like the 'Naughty Boys'." Rufus added.

"And we promise not to judge you." Seth spouted.

Kaz came running in still wearing his police riot uniform, "They're all starting to freak out and run away." he reported.

"That's good." Seth stated. "Look who we found."

"What the heck?" Kaz couldn't believe his eyes.

Random gun shouts and Lucious' continuous screams reminded everyone that the reunion was to be short lived. Cain slithered from the shadows and motioned for all to follow.

"Quickly, everyone follow Cain!" Seth ordered.

"You mean follow and trust the murder with our lives?" Vincent asked with sarcasim while running to assist the princess and her brother.

"Follow the assissin that just saved your asses." Seth pointed out.

Without many options otherwise, the group carefully followed the lead of the assassin down a dark hallway with many side rooms and slain gang members. Alisha helped her brother up from off the floor and tried to help him run. Vincent, however, took him over his back and carried him away while grabbing Alisha's hand and keeping her close. Seth stayed at the rear of the line in case gun fire came from behind. Cain opened a door outside and took out three gang members as quickly as they were spotted. He then motioned for the rest to follow after. It was suddenly a mad dash away from the gangs hide out and back into the woods.

43

MIRANDA'S STAND

While behind the Vaistone castle walls Raziel paced in front of Hikaru as he sat petting his cheshire cat.

"I still think I should have gone with them." Raziel expressed.

"I've already told you. With you out there on the field we're vulnerable. We'd be sitting ducks for another one of those, those fiery monster things. It's best you stay here and let the lieutenant do her job." Hikaru reasoned.

"I'm just not used to sitting on the side lines. I need to be doing something."

"Then why not go check on Carmon? It seemed unlike her to want to go with lieutenant Brookes on a mission. She seemed pretty casual about you telling her 'no'."

"Yeah, maybe I'll do that. I'll go check on her, see how she's doing with all that's been going on." Raziel agreed as he made up his mind and left the room.

Hikaru held the cheshire cats face in his hands, "See? I make a good daddy." he spoke in a cutesy voice. "Cause you're my little man. Yes you are. Yes you are." he played, touching noses with the cat.

Raziel lifted his hand to knock on the door before realizing he would tear it apart. So, instead he called out to her from the hallway until she answered the door.

"Carmon? Are you in there? I wanted to talk with you for a minute." he shouted through the door. "Carm.." he stopped as she answered her door.

"What?" she asked innocently.

"I just wanted to check and see how you were doing."

"I'm fine."

"Oh...okay." the two stood with their eyes wandering from an ackward silence. "Cause I know you wanted to go with lieutenant Brookes."

"Yeah and you said no, so I didn't."

"Yeah."

"You wanted to rub it in my face or...?"

"No, I was just, ya know."

"What?"

"I don't know." he confessed. "Hikaru figured I should check up on you. See if you were okay."

260

"You took parenting advice, from a guy who thinks he's parenting a cat? Dad, Hikaru chose not to have any kids because he couldn't decide which ethnic group of maids he would prefer raising them." Carmon explained.

Raziel laughed after realizing the silliness of the situation.

"What was I thinking." he smiled. "Hikaru probably thinks he birthed that cat." Raziel joked. The father and daughter shared a few laughs together for a short moment, "So you're okay?"

"Dad, I'm fine. I'm a big girl. If you didn't want me to go then that's fine, I'm sure you had your reasons." Carmon assured.

Raziel's face revealed great surprise, "Wow, I'm impressed. You're showing such maturity for yourself."

"Thank you sir." she answered playfully.

"Good day mad'am." Raziel played back. "Just so ya know, lunch will be ready in an hour Bud." he reminded while walking away from her room down the hall.

"Dad!" she complained due to the nickname.

"Sorry."

Meanwhile, lieutenant Brookes speed down the road next to the train tracks.

"I'm surprised the grand duke allowed you to come along while he stayed back." she said looking at the real Carmon sitting in the passenger seat beside her.

"Yeah, me to." she grinned innocently.

"That text the general had gotten said to meet up at the old central train station, so if we stick to the tracks we'll be there in no time."

Carmon looked in the rearview mirror seeing the other military jeeps rushing behind them and following the lieutenant's lead. Without warning the jeep swerved to avoid multiple large potholes in the gravel road. Carmon's attention was suddenly on the road and braced herself once the lieutenant veared off the gravel road and slammed on the brakes. The following jeeps slowly parked behind her and exit their vehicles.

"What the hell is that?" she asked herself, unbuckling, and stepping out of the car.

Carmon did the same and met Brookes around her side of the jeep. The lieutenant walked onto the gravel road and took a closer look at the potholes with the other soldiers.

"Footprints." Brookes realized.

"Footprints? You mean those holes in the ground?" Carmon asked.

"Yeah, they're footprints, but to what?"

"Looks like the size of an elephant." a random soldier added.

The lieutenant scratched her head in mystery, "Everyone stick close. I want tight formation. You see, hear anything, radio it. Move out!" she ordered.

Everyone filed back into their jeeps and began following the lieutenant's lead once more, except this time much closer than before.

"What do you think left those foot steps?" Carmon asked.

"I don't know, but we need to be ready for what ever it is."

Carmon sat quiet for a moment thinking to herself, "Brookes, what do you think about everything that's happened?"

"What do mean? With the mystic?"

"More like with dad and Christian's parents."

Miranda sat for a second focusing on her steering before answering, "I think it sucks."

"You think dad was right to do what he did or Dorian?"

The lieutenant paused before answering again, "I think it sucks." she answered again.

Carmon nodded and turned her attention outside the window.

"Why do we need a prince or princess when Hikaru has that new bill?"

"New bill? Miranda asked puzzled.

"Yeah, dad said the new bill places Hikaru in full power of the kingdom. Christian signed it before he ran off."

It was obvious this was new information to the lieutenant. "Probably because Hikaru and your dad, I mean, the grand duke will look bad with Christian and Alisha running away from their own kingdom telling everyone how bad they are."

"So everyone probably would have been better off if they died with their mom and dad." Carmon figured.

Miranda looked at Carmon shocked, "No. That's a terrible thing to say. We need to avoid as much blood shed out of this as possible. It's a blessing they're alive."

"But if they weren't." Carmon muttered under her breath watching out the window.

The military jeep began slowing down as a large moving mass began setting in the lieutenant's visibility.

"I think we found our elephant." she declared. Brookes lifted her radio and communicated with the other jeeps, "Closing in on possible enemy target. Circle formation!" she ordered.

The gutsy lieutenant slammed down on the pedal and speed up to cut off the large mysterious being. As she circled around it she noticed it wasn't traveling alone. The jeep haulted roughly in front of the strange trio. Brookes jumped out of her vehicle with her firearm aimed with her target in sight.

"Stop where you are!" she ordered.

Carmon jumped out of the passenger side door with her sword drawn. She gazed at the three odd beings. One, a large four legged creature with a large mouth containing several sharp rows of teeth, covered in horns every which way, and a human-esk torso pertruding from the top. The monster attached looked smug and confident in itself with it's fire like hair. The second, a small frail albino child dressed entirely in white carrying an odd looking lantern. And third, unknowingly to Carmon, was Fyra, the very summoning Wade had set out to rescue.

"Wings of fire and a lanturn. Are you associated with the fire mystic?" Brookes asked.

"Fire mystic? I don't know any fire mystic's. Do you number nine?" the large summoning asked the pale child which simply shook his head. "What about you eight? You know any fire mystics?" Fyra simply answered 'no'. "Gee, sorry lady, we don't know any fire mystics round here." the massive summoning answered in a coy manner.

"You're going to need to come with us." Brookes informed.

The largest summoning stomped one fat leg forward, "Make me!" he laughed opening his mouth and blasting a large ball of fire towards the lieutenant and Carmon.

"Move!" Brookes shouted.

Without delay Carmon obeyed and dodged the attack with Brookes. The monster laughed until the soldiers opened fire once their superior was out of the line of fire. The summoning blocked his face while bullets were clogged in the mounds of his fat skin. Bullets passed through the spirit child while Fyra cast a pillar of green flame around herself.

"My turn!" the massive summoning declared and fired off horns from its body.

The projectiles of the summoning pierced the jeeps, soldiers, and near by trees. The child raised his lanturn and allowed spheres of fire to drift out and over to his targets. The flames exploded near the soldiers as they tried blocking the fire. Fyra, on the other hand, flapped her wings sending out large wing shaped fire strikes.

The soldiers used their jeeps to block most of the attacks and opened fire once again on the trio. The largest summoning had enough and charged into the vehicles knocking them out of his way easily. A few men ran up trying to stab the fatty monster or get close shots towards his head. The summoning, however, had a defense for such strategy and sucked his torso inside the top of his fat body.

One Vailstone soldier drove his jeep into the summoning getting off a great hit and knocking the beast down. In a moment the summoning recovered and lashed out multiple extended tounges from its second mouth which ripped the jeep door off, snarred the soldier, and pulled him inside it's mouth ripping him apart limb from limb with ease. Carmon witnessed the incident and was horrifed by the sight.

Carmon created a doppleganger to assist in fighting the fearsome foe and charged into battle. She ran up stabbing it's fatty leg while the doppleganger climbed on top trying to force the torso out by stabbing where it sank in retreat. The creature bucked about pushing the teenager away and launching the double back to the ground.

Fyra defended herself against the attacking soldiers and forced them back lest they get burned. She watched number nine burning others to death and absorbing their souls into his lantern to help it burn stronger. Then she cast her attention over to number twelve who was clashing against Carmon.

"She's just a girl." she said to herself.

The massive summoning charged after Carmon. Miranda ran by helping Carmon to her feet and out of the way of the monsters stampede. The lieutenant lunged forward into the monster kicking it with her foot glowing a blue light. The attack seemed to deal great damage to the monster, but not enough.

The massive summoning exposed himself from its fatty body once more and sprayed horns everywhere trying to pierce the two women. Carmon's double was poofed way after taking a hit while the real duke's daughter ducked behind a near by jeep. The lieutenant was quick on her feet and dodged the deadly barrage.

Once the attack finished she opened fire on the creature once more successfully shoting him in the eye.

"AAAAARRRRGGHHHHAAA!!!!!!!" the creature flailed about rampaging wildly while holding his fresh wound.

Miranda ran away from the unpredictable stampede, but was stopped by the white child.

"You must be punished. Fire starter would like you killed." he stated.

"I...I can't move." Brookes tried muttering.

The lieutenant was instantly paralyzed and engulf in a blue flame. The fire in the child's lantern began glowing a bright blue. Miranda tossed and turned in great agony. Her very soul was burning and she was helpless to stop it.

Carmon ran up on the ghoulish boy with a new doppleganger and slashed at him with her swords. She was shocked to see her swords pass right through the boy's ghostly body. He vanished and appeared further away launching more spheres of flame towards the girls. Both Carmon's dodged the exploding balls of fire and rushed in on the boy once more. Forcing him the vanish and reappear else where.

"I don't have to hit you to kill you." he informed.

In that instant the soul burning attack ceased burning lieutenant Brookes and began burning the real Carmon. The doppleganger vanished while the original was surrounded in blue fire. She screamed from the unimaginable pain of having her soul burn.

Miranda was still a bit shocked from the experiance, but managed to pull herself together. She sat up from off the ground and noticed Carmon suffering the very same fate she given. Her legs were weak, but she stood aiming her pistol at the strange child.

"No you don't." the lieutenant stated firing off at the small pale boy.

"You can't kill me." the boy informed void of emotion.

Gun fire sounded off as the remaining guards fought after the large angry summoning.

"Nine, she's just a child!" Fyra pleaded off from the side.

Miranda was taken back from the plea of an enemy on the battle field. Number nine, however, merely looked off to Frya on the side and looked back at Miranda as he continued killing Carmon. The Lieutenant noticed the lantern's fire burning blue and brighter as Carmon suffered. She took aim and fired off another shot passing a bullet through the ghostly boys face.

"I told you. You can't kill me."

"Damn." she said taking aim again.

"The lantern!" Fyra shouted.

Nine turned his head and looked towards Fyra, "You would sacrifice a child to save a child?" The young summoning glared at his sister through Fire starter, "Traitor."

This time Miranda took a deep breath, ignored Carmon's screams of pain, and all other distractions around her and fired hitting Nine's rope he used to hold his lantern. The rope had torn from the bullet and fell apart as it crashed against the ground.

The boy sighed as he vanished into thin air and the blue fire was removed from Carmon's body. She was still in a weakened state from the long period of time she endured the attack.

"Thank you." Miranda appreciated.

"She's just an innocent little girl. Not a murdering slave like Nine was." Fyra stated.

Miranda ran over to Carmon trying to aid her in her state of dismay.

"I need to get her out of here." Miranda stated.

"Please allow me to help." Fyra asked.

She kneeled beside Carmon and began using an orange fire over her.

"What are you doing!?" she panicked.

"She's injured. I'm trying to heal her wounds."

"Damn you, Eight! What is it with you and kids?" the large summoning asked stomping forward. "Here, let me help eleminate the problem!" he said blasting a ball of fire at the three.

Fyra grabbed Carmon and flew up into the air narrowly dodging the attack. Miranda leapt off to the side with a new clip in her gun. She immediately opened fire on the gluttonous summoning. Fyra flew away and continued to the train station.

"She can't stay here! It's not safe." she exclaimed as she flew away with the grand duke's daughter.

"No! Wait! Come back here! Carmon!" Miranda called out.

"Focus on me idiot! I'll kill that girl after your death then teach Eight a lesson." he claimed.

The monsterously sized summoning charged towards Miranda once more. She quickly moved into full sprint to try out running the beast. The summoning opened his mouth once again and tried snarring the lieutenant.

"Watch out!" fellow military personal shouted.

The lieutenant looked back in time to jump out of the way of the tounge aiming for her legs. One soldier busted open a crate from one of the jeeps and pulled out a rocket launcher.

"Heads up!" he shouted firing the weapon.

The rocket exploded upon contact with the massive fire summoning and knocked him off balance. The lieutenant noticed and turned around leaping into the air and delivering and impressive powerful kick to the ferocious monster.

"AAAAHHHH!!!!!!!" Twelve yelled out firing off another spray of horns.

Brookes was forced to back away from the wall of danger. The summoning muscled up to it's feet and started inhailing anything and everything into it's gaping mouth. It was equivalent to a windtunnel pulling everything inside while the creature's tounges assissted in the opponent's demise.

Brookes held onto the other side of a military jeep for dear life until the attack was finished. Once she heard more stomping she got up and moved. Blasts of fire slammed against the jeeps catching them on fire.

The lieutenant was worried fighting against the fiery threat, but keep her head on her shoulders. She looked around while the remaining soldiers attacked the monster. She opened a crate and picked up another rocket launcher as the soldier did before her. She took aim and fired, sending the rocket directly at the summoning. Had number Twelve not been in motion the rocket would have connected with his torso. The summoning noticed the attempt and was enraged further.

"That's it! I'm just going straight for you now girly!" he stated.

The summoning opened his mouth wide again and began inhailing all around once more pulling in soldiers and objects to be ripped apart in his disgusting rows of jagged teeth. Miranda braced herself against another jeep, but started to worry once the jeep was starting to pull towards the summoning. She saw a fallen comrade with a penetrating horn wound to the chest inching closer beside her from the summoning's suction.

"Forgive me." she asked as she removed his dog tags and placed them in her pocket.

Twelve started slowly stomping forward closer to Miranda while he inhailed and inihilated everything before him. After the summoning was nearly ten feet away the lieutenant tossed the deceased soldier into the open mouth of the summoning. Twelve ate the man and swallowed him up.

He began laughing, "You're strategy is to feed people to me?"

"Hardly." she replied.

"I'm going to make you pay for this!" he promised pointing to his wounded eye.

Lieutenant Brookes raised her hand with grenade rings on each finger. She then dove behind the jeep again for protection.

"Oh shit!" the summoning panicked feeling his stomach.

Like clock work the grenades went off inside the summoning of Fire starter's blowing him apart in every direction. Brookes crept from behind the jeep to view the remains of the monster. Soldiers who fought bravely and kept their distance walked out from their safety zones with their leader.

"Find our wounded. We need to recover from this." she ordered.

As the soldiers obeyed one called out for the lieutenant, "Lieutenant, sir! Over here!" he waved.

Miranda marched over to the soldier curious of what was next. To her surprise the upper torso of Twelve was intact, but severely injured.

"Fire starter holds grudges." he chuckled in pain. "You'll all burn."

Miranda Brookes lifted her leg with her foot glowing blue once more. She scissor kicked the summoning finishing him off for good. Once completely defeated Twelve's remains began to disappear into ash.

"Think it's dead?" the soldier questioned.

"If it comes back we'll kill it again. Find our wounded. I'll radio in." she ordered.

"Yes, sir!"

Meanwhile, back at the Vailstone castle Carmon's copy began to worry. With the real Carmon injured and unconscious lieutenant Brookes was liable to call Raziel and reveal her trick. Carmon picked up her cell phone and called the lieutenant right away.

"Come on. Pick up, pick up, pick up, pick up." she waited anxiously.

Miranda felt her phone buzz in her pocket and looked at who was calling, "Carmon?...Hello?" she answered.

"Miranda! Please don't be mad." Carmon pleaded.

"Carmon are you okay? Where are you?" she asked worriedly.

"I'm fine." she lied. "I never left the castle."

"Never left tha......" she huffed. "Your father never gave you permission to come along did he?"

"No. But I knew if I sent a fake that...."Carmon stopped from the lieutenant's interruption.

"You had me risking my life and the life of my soldiers for a fake YOU? Not to mention being worried sick with some fire mutant running off with you." Miranda closed her eyes and took a deep breath. "Look, a stunt like this could have cost me my job, not to mention my life." she paused. "I'm not reporting this to Raziel, but you have to earn back my trust before I can believing you again."

"Thank you, Miranda. Really. Thank you. And I'm so, so sorry." Carmon apologized gracefully hanging up the phone.

The Carmon copy fell on her bed with her eyes closed resting one hand on her stomach and the other hand against her forehead. She closed her eyes as she began to feel weak.

Back in the woods Fyra flew further and further away from the battle between Twelve and the army. She had to try and save Carmon. It pained Eight to see kids wounded in the crossfire. She placed Carmon back onto the ground and started healing her wounded soul with the orange fire again.

"Please, stay strong little girl. You'll be fine. You have to be."

Fyra's healing process was inturrupted once more by the approaching sound of yet another individual. She stopped and lifted her head to see Cain standing before her with his sword drawn and ready to attack.

44

MI CASA ES SU CASA

Fyra stood from assisting Carmon and faced Cain, "You're one of those swordsmen aren't you. The one's Fire starter found?"

Cain watched the fire summoning without answering her question. The masked murderer made Fyra feel highly uncomfortable. The anticipation was rising. The woman made her butterfly wings of fire vanish.

"You can go." she tried convincing,"We don't have to fight. Fire starter will never know." The motionless and speachless masked mystery continued making Fyra more nervous for not only her safety, but Carmon's as well. "This girl, she's dying." she pleaded. "I'm her only chance right now."

Cain slowly began to approach Fyra with his sword ready. His grip tightened as he prepared a strike for the kill, throwing away Carmon's life as a result.

"WAIT! Stop! Cain stop!" Wade shouted running up behind Cain as the rest of the group finally caught up with the scouting assassin. "I know her, she's..." he stopped noticing Carmon on the ground, "What happened here?" he asked looking at Cain and Fyra. "That's the grand duke's daughter."

"Carmon?!" Christian asked while still being held by Vincent.

"She's been attacked. Please, let me save her." the summoning pleaded further.

With the nod from the spikey haired blond Fyra kneeled down beside Carmon and once again began using her healing flame on Raziel's daughter. After several minutes Carmon suddenly took a deep breath and opened her eyes.

"What happened?" she asked sitting up slowly. "I feel so light headed."

"Number Nine was burning your soul with his lantern. I had to get you to safety to repair what he had done before it was too late." Fyra explained.

"But why? I saw what you were doing to those soldiers. Why help me?"

"You're only a child." she stated brushing the back of Carmon's head lightly.

"You said she was attacked?" Kaz asked, "Is Fire starter or that big snake around?"

"No, but number Twelve is and he's fighting an army all by himself now." number Eight answered.

"We need to go. We can't just remain sitting ducks and get caught in this crossfire. Any minute those gang members are going to rally back up and come looking for us from behind and apparently an army or this, number Twelve, is going to come marching before us." Seth reasoned.

"Fyra, can you get us out of here like you did before?" Wade asked seeing confusion in Fyra's face. "When you made that purple looking fire and left the building earlier today by walking through."

The fire woman looked at Cain and the rest of the group, "It's okay. You can trust us." Wade assured.

Fyra stood watching Cain then summoned her purple fire against a tree and created a safe get away for the group.

"Everyone hurry, it's okay. Trust me." Wade explained.

One by one each member of the group passed through the fiery door way. Cain was hesitant, but eventually darted passed as well. Eventually all that remained was Fyra and Wade.

"Hurry, leave while you can." Frya warned.

"Just as long as you're coming with me." Wade informed.

"I can't. I've already explained before. You are nice, but Fire starter, he'll never let me go."

Wade extended his hand towards Fyra, "The only reason we met up again is because I'm destined to rescue you. You deserve your freedom." he explained surprising Fyra, "I promise to free you from Fire starter, but I can only do that if you allow me to stand between you two."

"No Wade, I've done terrible things." she shuttered. "The only thing I deserve is..."

"A second chance." Wade interrupted extending his hand further.

Fyra thought for a moment, no one has ever cared to try and rescue her from Fire starter. Could it actually be done? She made up her mind and grabbed hold of Wade's hand and exit through the doorway of purple fire together.

"Where are we?" Rufus asked looking around a quiet neighborhood.

Seth noticed the street signs down the road, "Wedge Way and Chestnut. We're only a few blocks away from my house." he realized.

"Can we eat there, cause I'm hungry again." Bo wondered.

"Um, sure. Everyone follow me." Seth instructed.

The seven swordsmen, royal siblings, shark-dog, and fire summoning traversed through the neighborhood blocks until eventually reaching Seth's house.

"Living room's to the left there." Seth informed as everyone entered.

"Oh wow, this place is a mess." Alisha said quietly to herself.

"Why am I still carrying you?" Vincent asked Christian before dumping him on the couch.

Cain stood silently in the corner of the room looking around at all of the filth and dirty clothes laying around.

Seth looked around at the room full of odd strangers, "Um, anybody want some sandwiches or microwave dinners?"

"What kind of sandwiches you got?" Rufus asked.

"I'll have a sandwich!" Christian answered out loud.

Seth looked in his refridgerator, "Okay, scratch that on the sandwiches."

"Ugh, no meat?" the prince wondered.

"No, just has mold on it." the detective answered removing the old meat from his fridge. He looked in his freezer seeing only frozen dinners, "Frozen meals it is."

Seth walked back into the living room while he microwaved one of the meals, "It'll just be a minute." he informed scrathing behind his ear.

"Alright, so I'm just curious here. How is it that everybody showed up at the train station?" Wraith inquired.

"Rufus, Christian, and me were there to find Fyra and fight Fire starter." Wade answered.

"Fire starter was there?" Kaz asked thinking he missed his chance for his rematch.

"No, he's not in the kingdom." Fyra answered.

"You know where he is?" Kaz asked.

"No." she answered lowering her head.

"Now why is it that we're cool with this one?" Vincent asked refering to Fyra.

"Her name is Fyra thank you." Wade snapped, "And she's our friend." he answered resting his hand on her leg smiling.

"Yeah, she saved a whole bunch of kids from Fire starter's monsters." Christian informed.

"So Fire starter is okay with you going around saving children?" Seth prodded.

"No, I carry out his orders. But,..." she stopped.

"Go on, we're listening." Seth assured.

"Well, when I was a human, I was a mother of four and I died protecting my children from number Twelve. For some reason Fire starter thought it was a good idea to transform my remains into a summoning to carry out his bidding. I do as I'm told. He knows I can't attack children and that I'll save them if I can, but he doesn't seem to mind as much as long as I obey his commands."

"He brought you back to life?" Wraith inquired.

"Well, not exactly. I was reborn through his mastery of fire and some magic. Sometimes, however, I can recall faint memories of my past life. I wish I could return to my children, but it would only bring them danger while under Fire starter's control."

"Don't worry Fyra." Wade comforted, "We'll get'em."

"So what were..." Seth stopped as the microwave sounded off, "Hold on." he said going to the kitchen and putting in a new meal to heat up. He returned with a meal and fork for Christian before continuing, "What were all of you doing at the train station with those thugs?"

"Lucious was an associate of mine." Wraith answered.

"The lunatic with the goblin pit?" Cain muttered.

"Yeah. In hindsight, maybe it wasn't such a hot idea going there." he admitted.

"Or maybe it would have been fine if you would have just been honest with him from the get go." Vincent chimed in.

"I was trying to avoid the hell he was going to put you all through."

"Or avoid your hell." Alisha added looking at Wraith.

Wraith looked at Alisha's eyes of disappointment and lowered his head as he looked away in silence.

"Well, we were hunting down one of those punks that hung out there." Seth informed.

"You got'em?" Kaz asked with uncertainty.

"Yeah." the detective nodded, followed by a bit of silence.

Christian chewed with his mouth full of microwaved broccoli, "I have a question." he stated raising his hand, "Why is he here? I thought he tried to kill us." he announced pointing at Cain.

"If I was going to kill you, you would already be dead." Cain growled.

"Yeah, why IS that guy here?" Bo asked noticing his lack of concern for everyone else.

"Cain and Seth have a little deal going on the side." Kaz exposed.

"A deal?" Wade asked.

"What kind of side deal?" Wraith pressed.

"It's personal, but rest assured as long as Cain is here you're all..." he was cut off by the microwave timer yet again leaving everyone in suspense of the ending for that sentence. He returned with another meal and fork handing it over to Bo, "What?" he asked noticing everyone's bizarre expressions.

"We're all?" Carmon asked.

"Safe, safe, you're all safe." he expressed.

A noticible moment of relief came over them.

"Yum! This is really good." Bo said with macaroni on the side of his face.

"Who's dog and why's it got fish parts?" Kaz pondered.

"I'm nobody's dog. I'm Bo, I'm a shark-dog." he announced.

"We ran into Bo in the woods a few days ago. He's my big helper." Alisha claimed.

The remark made Bo happy, he wagged his tail before continuing to chow down on the mac and cheese. Vincent and Wraith both sent dagger eyes to the innocent shark-dog for taking credit.

"Yeah right." Kaz scoffed.

"How'd you come in to all this?" Rufus asked Carmon.

"Oh, lieutenant Brookes was heading out to the train station with some of the troops and she let me join her."

"Why the train station of all places? Did they know our location?" Seth asked.

"No, I don't think so." Carmon disputed.

"That's one hell of a coincidence." Seth thought to himself.

"So what's the game plan? What do we do from here?" Kaz asked all.

"We? What'd you mean 'we'? I'm get'n the hell outta here now thanks to all of you. I can't stick around here now cause some of Lucious' boys'll find me and gun me down." Wraith bitched.

"Sorry your friends are psycho murdering assholes." Vincent barked.

"I'm just going back to gran-dad's." Rufus answered.

"You can't, Grechov will get you." Wade reminded.

"Grechov?" Alisha asked.

"Yeah, that guy's out of his mind. He had me and Rufus here arrested and then locked away in some rooms for some one on one time. He sat across the table threatening my life. I can't go back home or to see Amanda now. He basically told me he'd hurt the people close to me if I wasn't cooperative." Wade informed.

Bo scooted a bit away from Wade due to his warning.

"Grechov is dead. He was burned." Seth declared.

"No, he's alive." Carmon claimed.

"What?"

"Yeah, but his face was burned pretty bad."

"At least he's alive I guess." Seth figured.

"Grechov suggested you and me make a movie together ya know." Wade suggested to Alisha under his breath.

"Well the news is telling everybody around here that I kidnapped you two kids." Kaz pointed out Alisha and Christian.

"Huh? Kidnapped? How did that come about?" the prince wondered.

"I don't know, but the army and some crazy cop friends of Seth's seem to think so."

"Hobbs is just confused with what all that's been happening I'm sure." Seth reasoned touching his bullet wound.

"We have to take back the castle. I'm the king now and Hikaru's trying to cut me out. He told me that he was calling the shots now."

"Hikaru told you that?" Alisha asked in shock.

"Well with an army and a guy in super armor it ain't happen'n kid." Wraith spoiled.

"Stop it okay? Just stop it. You've been saying it's impossible from the very beginning, but you're wrong okay? You're wrong." The royal daughter jumped from her seat, "That's our army and we will punish Hikaru and Raziel both for their betrayl." Alisha declared. The princess looked down at Carmon, "I'm sorry Carmon, but you must understand."

"I understand. I do. I don't agree with what dad has done. And I'm sorry for all that he's put you all through." Carmon apologized.

"So we all have randsoms on our heads cause we're labeled kidnappers and the only way to clear our names will be to stop a skilled warrior in some legendary armor. Greeaaat." Vincent repeated in sarcasim.

Seth handed over a microwaved dinner to Rufus, "Well, we certainly have a hell of a lot to think about. Why don't we all just sleep on it and figure something out in the morning?"

"Sounds like a good plan to me." Wade agreed.

Cain started walking for the door, "Where you going?" Seth asked.

Cain stopped at the door without turning to face anyone in the living room, "Out." he said before leaving the house.

"Actually I'm pretty sure I'm gonna sleep better with him out of the house." Wade admitted.

"Alright, everybody. Um, there's blankets in the closet here and you can use the couch pillows I guess." Seth tried figuring it all out on the fly. "Girls you can all sleep in Lilith's room I suppose."

"Who's Lilith?" Alisha asked.

"She's my daughter."

"I hope she won't mind."

"Are you kidding? If she knew a princess was sleeping in her bed she'd be thrilled. It's upstairs, I'll show you."

Seth started up the staircase with Carmon behind him. Wraith stepped close to Alisha for a side conversation as she tried to go upstairs.

"Hey, about what happened before at the station..." Wraith started.

"Wraith don't. Just don't, okay? I'm tired."

"But, I wanted to explain myself."

"Wraith you don't have to explain yourself. I already know the truth. It's okay, really."

"The truth?"

The princess sighed, "You're incapable of thinking about others."

"No."

"You've had a life of being alone and looking out for only yourself. I understand why you don't care."

"I DO care."

"No Wraith. You left me to be eaten by a big spider monster and when your friend wanted to rape me in front of everyone and kill my brother you said nothing. There goes that second chance." she finished and walked upstairs.

Wraith turned away looking at Vincent with hatred.

"You're not going upstairs with the girls?" Wade asked Fyra.

"No. I figured I'd stay close with you."

"Oh yeah?" he smiled.

"Yeah, I think I feel safest around you Mr.Wade." she smiled laying beside Wade on some blankets on the floor.

Seth opened the door to Lilith's room, "Here's Lilith's room. Just try not to make a mess, okay?"

Alisha and Carmon walked into the deceased daughter's bedroom. It was spotless. Everything was folded neatly and tucked away. Not a spec of dust in sight and all of her small collectable figurines and plush dolls were sitting in an organized manner.

"Wow, this room......certainly isn't like the rest of the house." Carmon admitted.

"Yeah, I have to clean it up a lot for her."

"Um, Mr.Seth? Is there somewhere I can wash off? After what Lucious did..I just feel....dirty." Alisha confessed.

"Oh, sure. There's a shower in my bedroom."

Carmon's curiousity got the best of her, "What'd this Lucious guy do?"

Alisha took a deep breath to admit the truth before answering, "He tried to take advantage of me."

"So?"

"So?" the princess laughed at Carmon's lack of concern. "It's quiet an ordeal, okay? When some gross slease ball starts gropping on me, it leaves me feeling unclean."

"Just cause somebody rapes you doesn't mean you're unclean." Carmon snapped.

"I wasn't raped." Alisha defended.

"Then what're you cry'n about?"

"It's a hard thing to deal with Carmon. Heaven forbidden you ever have to understand."

"You don't know what it's like."

"And you do?" Alisha snapped back with a question.

Carmon was very upset and grew silent, "Go take your shower."

"Ugh!" Alisha scoffed and turned away storming off to find Seth's room to start her shower.

Seth was amazed by the surprise argument, "Carmon....is everything okay?"

"Some creepy kid tried to kill me with fire today, yeah I'm fine."

"You sure there's not something you want to talk about? Cause if you change your mind I'll be right down the hall, okay?"

"Just leave me alone."

Seth walked down the hall and into his bedroom. Carmon looked back and removed a tear from her eye. She started breathing slower to calm herself down while she looked around the room. She was not impressed by the plush dolls and trinkets around the room. The brunette walked over to Lilith's desk and slowly started looking through her drawers.

Stationary and personal notes were all see found until she peered into the girl's top middle drawer. She looked back to make sure nobody was watching before pulling out a gold necklace.

"Hello, pretty thing you."

The necklace had a golden heart that opened up with a picture inside. She looked at the picture inside, but thought it was strange.

"Who keeps their own picture in their necklace? That's dumb." she stated slipping the golden necklace in one of her pockets.

Once Alisha had finished her shower she retired to Lilith's bed with Carmon, Seth laid alone in his own bed, while the remaining members of the group slept downstairs. Cain was tucked away in a secure area, easily overlooked by anyone searching for him. He made sure he was deep in the shadows, but still capable of keeping an eye on Seth's home from a distance. As the night grew older, even he too finally fell asleep.

Seth tossed and turned reflecting on recent events of the past few days. The detective rolled on his side facing a picture frame with his late daughter and wife, "What am I doing?"

Resting against his bed side table was his sheathed sword. After starring at it for thirty seconds he turned over and rolled out of bed. The detective threw on a rob and crept downstairs, traversed around his sleeping guests, and recovered a bottle of water from his refrigerator.

The black haired man sat at his small dinner table drinking his cold bottle of water and stared off into the distance. The moment he closed his eyes he visioned flashes of blood shed. The screams, deaths, and guilt of what he's done weighed on his conscience. He wiped his forehead and took a deep breath. Seth sighed and stood up placing the bottle of water in the pocket of his pajama pants. The tormented soul walked over to his microwave and reached behind it to pull out a hidden flask of alcohol.

"Looks like it's you and me again tonight old friend."

Seth placed the flask in his other pajama pocket and snuck upstairs. As he passed Lilith's room he noticed princess Alisha sitting outside the door with her head held low.

"Hm? Princess?" he called quietly.

She lifted her head and sniffled, "Huh? Oh...I thought everybody was sleeping."

"Having trouble sleeping I take it?" he asked.

She wiped the tears away from her eyes before standing up, "It's just...all this. It's all so, overwhelming. Raziel....mom and dad.........Lucious." she recalled crossing her arms and looking down and to the side.

Seth noticed her eyes beginning to water, "Hey, hey come on now." he comforted.

He reached out pulling her in for a hug and allowing her to cry in his chest.

"This takes me back." he stated subtly.

Alisha looked up asking, "Huh?"

"Just....with Lilith...is all." he smiled.

"Then she's lucky. Having a father she can confide in like you." Alisha wiped her tears, "Do you have any dad tricks for when she's having trouble sleeping." she chuckled sadly.

"Well...Yes, but..it's been such a long time." Seth admitted.

"Oh yeah? What did you do?"

Seth half smiled, "I'd sing her a small little lullaby."

Alisha chuckled further, "That might actually do me a bit of good at the moment."

Seth shook his, "I don't know......it's been"

"Oh no, it's fine. I'll be alright." she inturrupted pulling some dangling hair behind her ear. An awkward silence became present, "Well, I should go lay down." she explained walking back into the bedroom and closing the door behind her.

Seth wiped a small tear from his eye and began walking to his bedroom before stopping at the door. He reached out for his door knob, but hesitated to open the door.

Alisha laid beside Carmon in Lilith's bed trying to relax when she noticed the door knob slowy turn and the door open. To her surprise Seth walked in and around to her side of the bed.

"Seth?" she asked softly.

The detective set half his butt on the bed, "Like I said,.....it's been a while." he replied quietly.

The princess snuggled comfortably in the bed while Seth moved a stray hair across her forehead. He coughed slightly to clear his throat without waking Carmon.

"Bear with me now." he pleaded before continuing further. "Alright,..hmm..hm..hhmmhm..." he hummed remembering the tune and the beginning of the song. "Okay."

"Somewhere....over tha rainbow,.....Way up high, And the dreams that you dreamed of........, Once in a lullaby."

"Oh, somewhere over tha rainbow,.....blue birds fly, And the dream that you dreamed of,......Dreams really do come true." he sang poorly in a low near whimpering voice.

"Someday I'll wish upon a star, And wake up where the clouds are far behind.....me, Where troubles........melt........." he paused looking down and noticing Alisha was fast asleep.

He slowly removed his hand from her shoulder and lifted himself off the bed and crept out of the bedroom. He made sure to close their bedroom door as he went back to his bedroom. Seth entered and shut his door, but instead off walking further he chose to lean his back against the door.

The long haired detective took a very deep breath fighting the tears from the memeories of singing his late daughter to sleep. He moved on and sat on his bed next to the bedside table. He reached in his pajama pocket and removed the flask from earlier. Seth looked at the picture of his wife and daughter before taking a drink. As he slowly lifted the flask his hand began to quiver. As the flask reached his lips he suddenly stopped. He thought for a moment and removed the flask away from his face and gave it a strong look.

After a moment the detective dropped the flask in a small trash can beside his bedside table and removed the bottle of water from his other pocket. He took a few gulps of the cold water and placed the bottle on the small table next to the picture and his sword. He kissed his fingers then touched the glass.

"Good night." he said softly before laying down to sleep for the night.

45

THE WEAKNESS TO THE ARMOR OF KAMISAMA

Seth laid comfortably in his own bed.

His eyes slowly opened up, "Damn. I woke up."

He struggled to force his legs to slide off the bed and touch the floor. He lazily sat upward and stretched. The tired detective shuffled into the restroom while he scratched his belly. The black haired man looked into the mirror with his head low trying to gain the energy for the day.

"About time you woke up." Cain growled as he appeared from behind the shower curtain.

Seth freaked out and leaped back falling on his butt and bumping the back of his head. "Daaahhhh!! What're you doing?!"

"What?" Cain asked standing in the shower looking down at Seth.

Seth stared back up at Cain from off the bathroom floor annoyed.

Downstairs Rufus texted and searched the internet on his cell phone while Christian and Bo bonded over watching cartoons. Vincent sat in the kitchen eating cereal as Kaz continued working out. He had been working up a good sweat all morning. Wraith sat in Seth's recliner listening in on Wade and Fyra's conversation.

"I've never seen these before." Bo stated wagging his shark tail.

"Yeah, they always go around solving mysteries and running into monsters. I've grown up watching this every Saturday morning." Christian admitted.

Bo started laughing, "HA, ha, ha, ha! A talking dog! Where do people get these ideas?" he snickered.

Wraith's attention was suddenly directed to Bo at the ironic observation.

"Remember that rain we got the other day? 'They' said if we didn't get that strong rain when we did that the death toll from Fire starter's summoning attacks would have doubled." Rufus informed out loud from reading internet 'news'.

"Oh, it wasn't just a fluke." Fyra added. "Someone used magic that night to put out most of the fires. Fire starter is furious no doubt."

"Magic is forbidden with in the Vailstone kingdom." Christian claimed.

"Then it's a good thing somebody took the risk." Wade added.

"Whoever it was, they had powerful magic." Fyra noticed.

Wraith stood from the recliner and headed up stairs without saying a word to anyone.

Carmon tossed and turned as she continued to dream. She lay resting in her bed as a man slowly snuck into the room and placed his hand over her mouth waking her up immediately.

"If you say anything..........I'll kill him." he warned.

Carmon jumped sitting up in bed next to Alisha sweating and breathing heavily. She held her temple and closed her eyes, "Stupid." She looked over to the princess with her messy hair and little bit of drool from her mouth, "You have no idea."

She layed back down in the bed and snuggled under the covers looking about the room. She remembered Seth mentioning he kept it clean. She couldn't help but think of how much he loved his daughter and how lucky she must be. She clutched the golden necklace she swiped from the desk. The purple haired young man crept in the hallway until finding Lilith's room. Carmon noticed the door cracking open and quickly pretended to sleep. Wraith slide into the room unnoticed and closed the door once more.

Carmon peeked from her barely open eye and watched him come to the bed. He reached over Carmon to touch Alisha's arm.

"Alisha, pst. Alisha, wake up." he request shaking her arm lightly.

The princess eventually opened her eyes and sat up slightly, "Huh? What is it? What's wrong?"

"I wanted to talk to you about last night."

"Huh? That again? Wraith, what time is it?"

"I dunno, a little after noon or something. Look, I wanted to clear things up between us."

"Wraith there's nothing left to be said. I meant what I said last night."

"But it's not true."

"Actions speak louder than words Wraith and your actions have been speaking loud and clear for you."

Wraith sighed from frustration, "Just give me a third chance."

"A third chance?"

"Come on, third times a charm."

"Are you talking about putting my life in danger a third time to see if you'll do the right thing? No thanks."

"Is this cause of Vincent?"

"Vincent? What are you talking about? He hasn't done anything."

"Nothing you know about."

"Wraith we are not going down this road again."

"You like him don't you?"

"What?"

"You like him more than me. Admit it."

"What? No, I'm not admitting anything. I don't have to confess my feelings to you."

"Then it's true. You do like him." he assumed getting a surprised look from Alisha. "I've seen how you look at him."

"What is wrong with you? Is this really why you came up here to wake me up and start a fight about Vincent? Just get out."

Carmon continued spying as Wraith grabbed Alisha's wrist, "I love you."
Alisha gasped and looked at Wraith with disbelief. Carmon was surprised by the sudden turn in the conversation also.

"Come on, admit it too. You're in love." Wraith prodded.

"Wraith, I..." she shook her head.

"Admit it Alisha." he pleaded tightening his hold on her.

"Wraith, I am falling in love..." but by fate, Alisha was interrupted by a scream from downstairs which snarred everyone's attention.

"What was that?!" Carmon sprang up.

Wraith and Alisha looked into each other's eyes before the princess broke free of his grip and ran downstairs with Carmon following after her. Wraith reached the bottom of the staircase with everyone in the living room almost circling Fyra. Her wings of fire were spread and shining brightly.

"He knows! He knows and he's angry." she panicked.

"What are you doing? Put those wings away!" Wade pleaded.

"I can't. Fire starter is doing it!"

To everyone's shock the image of Fire starter appeared in Fyra's wings.

"Well, well. Look at who all suvived tha forest a darkness. You all been a busy lil group haven't cha?!" Fire starter spoke out.

"What do you want Fire starter? We haven't done anything to you." Seth tried reasoning.

"Oh, haven't cha though." The elemental counted on his boney fingers, "Let's see na, numba Six, numba Two, numba Five, numba Elevin, numba Twelve, n' numba Nine." he ended looking towards Fyra. "Curious how yur jus hang'n out with'em ain't it Fyra!"

"Fire starter please, I can explain." Fyra pleaded.

"Fire starter! Let her go." Wade ordered.

"No." the fire user quickly answered.

"Why are you doing all of this?" Christian whined.

"Oh, little boy. Raziel was supposed ta help me out, but I was butrayed. Aft'a help'n ya all get yur swords and tha arm'a a Kamisama he butrayed meh!"

"We were betrayed to though. It's not just you." Christian pleaded.

"Yur right Christian! He betrayed ya fath'a cause he believed he couldn't handle tha arm'a an' more importan'nly me, tell'n everyone I put'em und'a a spell. His true arm'a is noth'n but lies!"

"You mean non of it's true?" Rufus asked.

"A course not!"

"He's lied about everything." Christian realized quietly to himself.

"I been framed, butrayed, and na all my enemies know exactly where ta find meh!" he announced angrily.

"You want him dead." Cain grumbled.

"Yes!" Fire starter agreed.

"NO! I won't let you!" Carmon vowed.

"He doesn't need to die, we just need to defeat that armor." Seth stated to all. "If we can beat him, will you leave? Stop these violent attacks?"

Fire starter's shifty red eyes darted at the swordsmen as he pondered, "Yes."

"And give Fyra her freedom! Or no deal." Wade added.

"Whoa! You can't make that call." Kaz jumped in.

"Bullshit! Deal or no deal. Your call Fire starter." Wade negotiated.

Fire starter hesitated, "Very well. I trust ya know how ta beat'em?"

The room was silent. None of the swordsmen had a single clue on how to stop Raziel with the Kamisama armor.

"Fools. Yur swords. Tha very seven legendary swords ya each possess this very moment. Alone tha swords'll fail, but, ta'geth'a they can supress tha pow'a of tha arm'a. Only then can ya all defeat Raziel." Fire starter informed.

291

Each one of the swordsmen looked at their swords and the mysterious mystical wonders they possess.

"Tommorr'a, you up hold yer end uh tha bargin'n I'll keep mine." the fire elemental promised as he vanished from the flame in Fyra's wings.

After Fire starter's disappearance Fyra quickly removed her wings of fire from the area.

"Can we trust him?" Kaz asked out loud.

"I don't know." Rufus figured.

"We DO all share a common enemy I suppose. It wouldn't do him any good to lie to us now. Not about this." Seth reasoned.

"If he's lying, I'll be the one to kill that giant snake of his." Kaz claimed.

"Basoomamba? It can't be slain with power or muscle." Fyra paused. "If you truly wish to defeat Basoomamba you'll need lost blood."

"Wha?"

"Lost blood. The two stone orbs that float around Basoomamba, each of them have an indention. Only once the fresh blood of someone who is truly lost has stained the inside of each of those orbs can Fire starter's Basoomamba be killed." Fyra warned.

"So that's why I couldn't kill it last time." Kaz lied trying to look strong in front of everyone.

Seth rolled his eyes remembering the truth about his fight. "Fyra, what exactly is 'lost blood'?"

"I'm not quite sure, but I know that's the only key for defeating it. I over heard a conversation before. I know I shouldn't have been ease dropping, but...." the summoning explained.

"Fyra, it's okay." Wade interrupted.

"So we're doing this then? Destroy the armor and take back the kingdom?" Alisha asked.

"Nobody kills my father, right?" Carmon asked worried.

"Right." Alisha agreed comforting Carmon and informing the swordsmen.

"Remember what Fire starter said, it will only work if ALL seven swords fight together. As one." Seth restated.

Cain nodded his head.

"You will be free Fyra, I promise." Wade guaranteed. "I'll fight."

"I'm fighting." Kaz declared.

"Yeah." Vincent assured.

"Only to destroy the armor." Rufus chimed in.

"Well, I'm in." Seth added.

Everyone looked at Wraith who stood by silently, "It will only work if we're a team." Wade reminded.

Wraith looked at Alisha with warm eyes, "I'll do it."

Seth took a deep sigh of relief, "Good. Then let's iron out some kind of plan and figure out what to do."

46

THE ARMOR OF KAMISAMA
V.S. THE SEVEN
BLADES OF LEGEND

At the northern central train station four gang members returned to reevaluate the damages from yesterday. The four searched through the rooms collecting weapons and drugs left behind.

"Hey! Dwyane, come look at this!"

The thug named Dwyane and the other two gang members hurried into the room to see what the commotion was about. As they entered the room they stummbled upon large amounts of blood and a metal baseball bat laying beside a large open pit.

"What is it?"

Upon looking down in the pit they saw a large deformed creature.

"Is that a goblin?"

"Na, fool. That's too big to be a goblin."

"Ah man, that looks like Lucious beanie."

"Whoa, I think it's still alive."

Inside the train station the four gang members began yelling in terror. The movement of a large beast could be heard viciously attacking them while gun fire sounded off. Silence fell over the train station once again in a matter of minutes.

At the Vailstone castle Raziel watched as general Grechov and lieutenant Brookes rallied troops to go back and investigate the train station.

"You sure you're up for this?" Raziel asked Grechov who wore bandages around his head concealing his burned face.

"Laying around in a stiff bed with tubes up my nose is a luxory I'll pass on." Gerchov replied.

Raziel watched as the general and lieutenant drove off with eight military jeeps following close behind. The grand duke turned around to re-enter the castle. He stopped at the door and tried lightly opening the door. He successfully used the handle without destroying it, but unfortunately it had started snapping at the henges when he tried opening door.

"Ah, I think I'm getting better at this 'holding back' thing." he self congratulated.

Raziel, however, now had a new problem of closing a door that leaned off the wall.

"Ugh! Stupid doors."

Carmon came running up to her father from behind, "Dad!"

"Carmon? What's tha matter?" he asked with fatherly concern.

"I got a message on my phone from Christian. He said he's scared and hiding at that detective guy's house."

"Seth's? What would he be doing there? I'm going, tell Hikaru to send help."

"He asked for you to come by yourself. He's embarassed about something, I think."

"Alone? He's been through so much." he stated running his hand through his hair, "I'll be right back Bud." He turned to leave, but stopped unexpectedly, "You sure you're alright pumpkin?" He thought it peculiar Carmon didn't oppose her childhood nickname for once.

"Yeah, fine." she assured, "Now hurry, he's scared."

The grand duke accidentally ripped the door off the wall due to the fact of being distracted about Christian's condition.

"Can you have someone fix this?" he asked taking off to rescue the scared lonely prince.

Carmon watched her father run to the prince's rescue, "Be careful." she spoke quietly.

Six of the seven swordsmen, excluding Cain, sat planning their strategy against Raziel in the detective's living room. Carmon sat in the kitchen biting her thumb nail nervous for the safety of her father.

Princess Alisha walked up behind her and placed her hand on her shoulder for comfort, "They've all agreed, just the armor."

Carmon nodded nervously, obviously overwhelmed with worry.

Christian sat in the living room with the swordsmen listening to their plan to stop Raziel and the armor of Kamisama, but his mind was entirely distracted elsewhere. The prince's mind was flooded with fond memories of his parents and Raziel alike. Birthdays and vacations with Natalia and Dorian. Sitting on his father's lap as a boy listening to his marvelous tales of epic adventure and death defying battles. The embrace of his mother when scared late at night. The fun they shared on family get away vacations.

Memories of holiday celebrations lead to fond memories of the grand duke. A thoughtful present on Christmas morning. Training in the mornings and afternoons to try and learn his skills and techniques. Moments of Raziel sitting with Natalia and Dorian laughing and joking with each other. Suddenly the young prince recalled the day in the library with Raziel. If what Fire starter said was true, about not being under a spell, then Raziel lied to Christian's face. Did he truely kill them just to keep the armor for himself? The inner turmoil was too much to bear for the young prince.

"Alright, sounds like a good plan to me." Seth assured. "Rufus, would you get off that damn cell phone of yours and listen. Do you even remember what you're supposed to do?"

"Yeah, I'm gonna wait at the end of the block by the brick house."

"Idiot. That's my spot. Freak'n pay attention." Vincent scolded.

"If I die out there cause you ain't pay'n attention I'm gonna come back and haunt your fat ass." Kaz threatened.

"Guys, nobody's dying today." Wade promised.

At that moment Cain came charging through the kitchen and into the living room, "Problem." he growled drawing out his sword.

The remaining six swordsmen stood clutching their hilts or swordhandles.

Seth walked over to the front window and looked passed his living room curtain, "Raziel." he stated.

"How did he know where to find us?" Wraith questioned.

"Let's end the madness." Wade calmly suggested.

Raziel walked down the middle of the street slowly approaching Seth's house with caution. "What was Christian scared or embarassed about." he wondered. The grand duke stopped walking as the front door opened up. It was a questionable sight as Kaz walked out of the house slowly.

"I remember you." Raziel realized.

After Kaz, Wade followed after. One by one six of the swordsmen exitted the detective's home and walked out into the middle of the street facing off against the grand duke.

"What is this?" Raziel asked suspiciously.

Raziel turned to look behind himself noticing Cain several feet away with his white bladed sword drawn. The remaining swordsmen walked around the grand duke until forming a circular formation. Surrounded by the seven swordsmen Raziel stood in the middle at full attention. Kaz pulled his broad sword from out of its sheath and made sure he had a firm strong grip with both hands. Vincent kept his eyes firmly on the grand duke while he removed both katanas, holding one in each hand. Wraith swiped his hilt from off his sheath and readied for attack. A cold frost poured from Wade's sheath, ice covered the steel blade, and the entertainer stood strong in his resolve. Rufus was hesitant, but did what must be done and unwrapped his large sword catching the reflection of the grand duke in his blade. Raziel glared forward at the last swordsman before him. Seth flung the side of his coat and revealed his sheath. The black haired detective pulled out the black bladed katana and positioned his feet for battle.

"A murderer,..." he looked at Cain, "a thug,...." referring to Kaz, "a mere boy,....." directing at Rufus, "a degenerate,......." insulting Wade, "a curse,....." mocking Vincent, "a criminal,......" addressing Wraith, "and broken man." he finished with Seth. "I didn't realize our little quest into the forest of darkness created this......little neighborhood watch of best friends." he mocked. "It was like pulling teeth convicing you all to join me for the good of the kingdom and now you're holding your swords to me? Now I understand what all of your true motives were. Did you orchestrate all this...Seth?" he asked pointing to everyone. "I'm warning, all of you. If you stand against me.....I WILL crush you."

"Like King Dorian? Was he standing against you too? Don't you think there's been enough senseless violence Raziel. Let it end today." Seth replied.

"Oh what? Now he's a king to you again? Pft. You didn't give a shit about the state of the kingdom until I bribed you to come along by giving you your old job back. With a promotion." he exposed to the remaining six surrounding him. "Now you're Captain Righteous? Please, don't put on this masquirade for justice now. I know exactly what you've done and who you are.....so don't stand before me in judgement. Righteousness is your mask, but your driven by evny and hatred."

"So the people should turn to you for righteousness? The kind of justice that allows the murderer of our leaders to wonder freely without consequence?" Seth replied.

"Oh, don't you even act high and mighty with me. Hell, you probably danced the night away the day Dorian died. I did you a personal favor."

Christian stood behind the door of Seth's house watching outside and listening in pain.

"I did what you couldn't do. That's what this is all about isn't it? You couldn't protect your own daughter and I killed Dorian and now you feel killing me will somehow be just as gratifying." Raziel looked at the expressions on the faces of the other swordsmen, "Oh, what's this? Surprisingly enough, you haven't told them your secrets? Yep, ol' buddy boy Seth here wanted Dorian dead in the first place. Bet you kept your daughter a secret too, didn't you?" Raziel mocked in pure anger.

"We knew." Wade stated getting attention from the other swordsmen, "I knew"

"Of course YOU did. By the way, what are you still doing around anyway? Don't you have some pathetic party to go to so you and some bimbo can get drunk, have sex, and shot a porno together? Please, you kill one monster in a forest and now all of a sudden you're some tough guy? I'm sorry, excuse my rudeness. I've forgotten what a valuable asset you are to society." Raziel mocked in sarcasim.

"My priorities have changed." Wade returned.

Raziel nodded and turned to looked at Rufus and saw the hesitation in his face, "Rufus? You're standing against me as well? If I recall correctly, you were the only one here that agreed to join for reasons other than personal gain. Am I right, or was I wrong about you to?"

"I just wanted to help." Rufus answered with conviction in his voice. "I....."

"Shut-up and stop listening. He's getting into your heads." Cain shouted demonically.

Inside the house Fyra and the young ones watched with anticipation.

"Wait?" Bo tugged on the tattered shirt of the fire summoning, "I just realized, what're we supposed to do if we have to run away?"

Fyra watched outside and looked down at the little shark-dog. She smiled and kneeled down to face him, "Here, take this." she said extending her hands together.

"What is it?" the pup asked.

"Let me see your paw little one."

Bo reached his open paw out to hold whatever she had in her hands. Fyra cupped the top and bottom of Bo's paw and pulled away. Resting in the center of Bo's paw was a purple flame.

"What's this?" he asked in amazment.

"Remember when we left the woods and walked through my fire of purple?" she asked.

"Uh-hu." he nodded.

"Now, whenever you feel like you or your friends here are in a really bad spot or danger of any kind, then all you have to do is think about holding the purple flame and it will appear in your hand. Then just throw it and run through the opening, okay?"

"Wow, thank you. Nobody's ever given me anything like this before."

Fyra smiled and looked into the innocence of the small boy's puppy eyes. She rubbed the top of his head and noticed Christian walking outside.

"Boy, wait!" Fyra called out.

"Christian what are you doing?!" Alisha shouted.

"Wait here." Fyra instructed as she rushed out after Christian.

The young prince slowly walked out and into the street watching Raziel. Fyra stopped at the door and watched not knowing exactly what to do. The grand duke eventually turned his attention away from the seven swordsmen and noticed Christian.

"Christian? It is you! Are you alright? Have they hurt you at all?" Raziel asked loudly. Noticing he wasn't getting an answer back made him grow more suspicous, "Christian?"

"I heard what you said. All of it." he confessed.

"Christian, I..." the grand duke started.

"How could you? I trusted in you. WE trusted in you. Mom and dad trusted you. You were their BEST friend." the prince started crying, but maintained the stregth to continue. "You lied, right to my face. I tried forgiving you because of a lie. Now I hate myself for even giving you the benefit of the doubt after what you did. Do you know how it tore me up inside standing in front of you trying to forgive you for mom and dad?"

"I can explain. Just come with me and I'll explain everything. Come Christian, you're all the kingdom has left and we can't afford to lose you too." Raziel shook his head trying to reason with the pained prince.

"I'm all that's left?"

Raziel realized he screwed up his timing, "This isn't the ideal situation to tell you this, but.....Alisha didn't make it Christian. I'm... so....very sorry."

"No! I don't want to hear anymore of your lies. I can't bear them. Fire starter told me. Told me everything. He told me it was a lie. He told me the truth," he paused, ".....why you..." he stopped again fighting the tears. The young prince tried his best to explain his knowledge about the lie of Fire starter putting Raziel under a spell.

"Christian, I'm sorry. I truly am. I should have been honest with you from the start, I see that now. I was only trying to protect everyone." Raziel admitted. "I confess. I lied, but I had to. If I didn't do what I did the kingdom would have been worse off than what it is now. I'm just asking you to open you're mind and look passed all this ugliness at the moment. It wasn't in my best judgement, but it was the right call at the time. I was only trying to protect everyone. Can't you see that it was for the best?"

Princess Alisha gasped in shock from the safety of Seth's home at what sounded as a heartless Raziel.

Unfortunately, Raziel misunderstood the lie Christian was referring to as the fake 'spell' Fire starter cast upon him and NOT the lie Fire starter tricked Raziel with into keeping the armor from Dorian. The misunderstanding lead to such great torn emotions with in the young prince, but ultimately the decision in Christian's mind was made. Raziel truly betrayed the royal family for the armor of Kamisama.

"For the best? HOW COULD YOU!" he screamed in tears.

Raziel took a step forward towards the young prince, "That's as close as you get!" Kaz warned running forward and striking Raziel with his broad sword.

The grand duke lifted his forearm to block the attack, however, he was struck by powerful lightening regardless. Raziel stood in a blocking position and entirely blanketed in electricity as Kaz struck the royal warrior multiple times. Kaz noticed an angered Raziel make a fist and lung forward to punch through the brute. Kaz moved out of the way of the powerful man's punch with great haste.

"Ha! What's the matter? I thought you wanted to fight?" Raziel boast.

Suddenly Raziel began backing up as fluttering metallic shards of Vincent's sword began circling his head and hitting his eyes. Despite the fact that Raziel was incapable of being injured by the flying metal he still was unable to resist human natural instict to shield objects from hitting ones eyes. He backed up slightly and closed his eyes blocking the sword shards with his arms. The other swordsmen happily took note of Vincent's amazing sword.

Cain moved in swiftly and darted about the area Raziel was in dashing by and attempting to slash his thighs, knees, ankles, or throat. After a moment Raziel started ignoring Vincent's attacks and began taking aim at Cain. The assassin dodged every swing the massive threat was hurling at him. Raziel quickly moved ahead and stomped on Cain's cape which tripped him up and caused him to fall to the ground.

Raziel smiled as he immobilized his prey and readied a fatal strick. Cain hurried and used his sword to rip his cape and narrowly miss the grand duke's strike. Seth stepped forward as a distracted Raziel watched his target dart away. The detective exposed his pistol and began shooting his firearm. Each bullet would ricochet off the armor of Kamisama so he tried hitting the grand duke's face and finally getting the center of his forehead as his enemy angrily marched towards him.

Once out of bullets Seth dropped his gun with his black sword in hand, "Let's see how you like the taste of your own medicine." he readied.

Raziel stood before Seth and swung his arm launching him threw neighboring houses and distant building walls until eventually he had smacked into enough random objects to stop his unexpected travel.

Seth leaned up from off the ground holding the back of his head, "Well that didn't go according to plan."

Back in front of the detective's house Wraith took aim and made many attempts to sever the grand duke in to several pieces. Cain hopped about smacking the grand duke with his sword and gaining more and more speed, yet for some reason his enemy refused to slow down.

"What? Why isn't this working? I thought it cut the living." Wraith complained not effecting the battle.

"Alright, my turn." Wade declared rushing up to the armored menace, "The madness ends now!" he shouted running up and striking Raziel with his ice covered sword.

Wade was stunned at the outcome, ice scattered everywhere yet Raziel stood before him perfectly fine.

Raziel turned his attention to Wade and grabbed him by the collar, "So NOW you want to be a 'hero'? You couldn't have chosen a worse opponent then I." he informed beginning to apply pressure to his throat.

Wade was entirely incapable of freeing himself from the grasp of Raziel no matter how hard he struggled to break free.

"No! Raziel STOP it, PLEASE!" Christian cried.

Raziel looked back at the prince and dropped Wade to the ground once he remembered he was being watched.

"Christian I..." Raziel started talking to the prince once again, but was suddenly hushed by the surprise of falling into a deep pit of water.

Wade lifted his sword from the ground where he kneeled, "Christian go. Back inside." he ordered in a hoarse voice. He noticed the prince's hesitation, "Now!"

Christian obeyed and rushed back inside with his sister and the others.

"Good job." Rufus complimented.

"It won't stop him." Wade warned, "It's just to stall."

"Our swords aren't working." Cain informed.

"Yeah, I can't cut him." Wraith complained.

Seth finally rejoined the battle after running back from where Raziel sent him, "What's going on? Did we win?"

"We're not effecting the armor like Fire starter said." Vincent revealed.

"Probably because Fire starter's the one who said it." Kaz assumed.

"Fire starter's trying to get us killed." Vincent realized.

"So what do we do now, then?" Rufus asked.

"Retreat." Cain ordered.

Rufus, Seth, Wade, and Vincent began running back to the house while Kaz, Cain, and Wraith took off in different directions. In a moment Raziel burst from underneath the ground cutting Rufus and the other three swordsmen off. The startling surprise caused Alisha to scream in fright.

Raziel turned back looking at the house, "Who's in there with Christian?" he asked glaring suspiciously at Seth.

The sound of Alisha's scream caused memories to fill in Wraith's mind, leaving her at the mercy of the fire spider, taking her to the dangers of Lucious, her words telling him he's incapable of love or looking out for anyone else, but himself. The purple haired swordsman stopped running away, mustered his courage, and ran into battle.

"No! Raziel leave them alone." Seth demand.

"So there IS someone else you're keeping from me."

"Um, he's coming in! We've gotta do something!" Bo panicked.

Fyra backed away from peeking behind the curtain with the others and worried for a moment before creating a solution. She used her purple fire to create an exit for them once more, "Quickly children, through here."

Bo grabbed hold of Alisha's hand, "Come on, let's get outta here."

Alisha followed through the purple fire with Bo leaving Christian and Carmon behind. Christian began escaping as well until stopping and noticing Carmon's hesitation.

"Carmon, aren't you coming?"

Carmon stood waiting for her father to burst inside the house, "Dad..."

Christian grabbed her wrist, "Carmon?"

"Run." she instructed and returned to her senses running through the purple fire door with the prince.

Rufus charged up on Raziel slamming his massive sword on his back. Raziel didn't even flinch and continued running to the house.

"Does he even know I attacked him?" Rufus questioned.

"Look out!" Vincent shouted warning Wade and Rufus to move.

Both swordsman barely dodged the 'Legend' blast of Kaz's lightening sword. Raziel turned out of curiousity since he noticed all of the bright flashing from behind. He was slammed by Kaz's blast setting fire to Seth's house and the yards.

"That didn't work the first time it's not going to work the next eighteen million times!" Raziel mocked.

Cain realized instead of retreating the other swordsman were returning back to the house for the prince and princess, "Idiots." he complained flashing by and jumping into the thick of battle. "Get back!" the masked man growled demonically.

The assassin smashed small orbs onto the ground which created thick clouds of smoke around the area.

"Ugh!" Raziel groaned, "Where the hell did you all sneak off to?" he asked swinging his arms wildly.

Rufus stood paralyzed not knowing what to do and unaware Raziel was walking forward to carelessly knock his head off. Rufus shouted in terror once Cain grabbed his arm and guided him and Vincent to the front door of Seth's house. The assassin kicked open the door startling Fyra.

"Ahh!" she gasped, "Oh, it's you. Quick, hurry through!" she pleaded.

"Where's Alisha?" Vincent asked sternfully.

"She's on the other side. Now hurry!" Fyra request.

Cain, Rufus, and Vincent all three ran through the fiery purple door.

"That's three." Fyra counted.

"Enough of this!" Kaz shouted smashing his sword into the ground and dissipating the clouds of smoke created by the assassin with his lightning.

Raziel lept forward trying to tackle Kaz, but Seth tackled him first and out of the way of the bulldozing grand duke. Wraith finally caught up and sliced a tree in Seth's yard forcing it to fall on top of Raziel.

"Timber!" Wraith yelled smugly.

The grand duke stood up from off the ground and lifted the large tree which fell on to him.

"I'll give you something to shout. How about home-run?! he asked swinging the massive lumber around in an attempt to strike one of the remaining swordsmen.

Raziel smashed the tree on the ground trying to crush Wraith as he made his way closer to the house entrance.

"Not so fast!" he surprised swinging the tree only inches away from Wraith's head as he ducked.

Kaz ran up trying to electricute the grand duke once again, but was struck by the large tree and sent flying.

The wind was knocked completely out of Kaz. He struggled to lift himself up and looked down at his chest thankful he was still wearing his padded riot gear.

"Come on dip." Seth insulted as he helped Kaz lift from off the ground.

"Leave'em alone Raziel!" Wade ordered.

The grand duke launched the broken tree over at Wade in an attempt to crush him. Wade turned running from the rolling lumber until it came to a complete stop, at which point he turned back around to witness Wraith taking on Raziel by his own.

"Wraith." Wade muttered.

Raziel had noticed Wraith still on the ground and at his mercy. Raziel lifted his leg to stomp the purple haired young man, but missed as his target rolled to the side.

"Ha! Like squashing a bug." he mocked.

Wraith tried using his sword on Raziel at the close range to see if the outcome had changed. Raziel reached down and grabbed Wraith's wrist accidentally snapping in the process. Wraith cursed in pain while Raziel pulled his sword away from him, crushed it with one hand, and tossed it to the side.

"Now what?" Raziel asked dropping Wraith back to the ground.

Wraith was riddled with pain of his broken wrist which flopped around like a fish out of water. Wraith, still on his back, lifted both legs and kicked both feet forward trying to kick the grand duke in his genitals with all his might. The kick only pushed Wraith back an inch or two and hurt his legs in the process.

"Awh!" Wraith shouted climbing to his feet.

"Pathetic." Raziel replied grabbing hold of both hands and swinging both arms into Wraith.

The hit sent Wraith flying threw the air and the large front widow of Seth's house and straight through the purple fire wall provided by Fyra.

"NNOOOO!!!" Wade shouted as he witnessed Wraith launched from the ground.

The entertainer grabbed his sword tightly creating a much thicker and more jagged barrier of ice around his sword. In his fit of desperation Wade stabbed the ground turning the spot from where he stood all the way underneath the grand duke into cold water. Raziel instantly fell sinking to the bottom of the pond created by Wade.

"Hurry!" Seth shouted after Wade while helping support Kaz to the burning house.

Kaz paused a moment and bent down.

"What are you doing?" Seth asked worriedly.

Kaz stood back up to his feet using Seth for support, "The purple haired kid's sword." Kaz explained holding the mangled remains of Wraith's crushed sword.

Wade ran around the large body of water meeting Seth and Kaz inside the door. Once inside they noticed Fyra's escape route.

"Where's Wraith?" Kaz asked.

"Everyone's inside." Fyra explained as the detective's house burned.

The foundation of Seth's home began creeking and cracking. As the ground support had been removed and with the outter exterior burning to ash the house wasn't given much time. Seth's suffering caused him to pause and look around at his rapidly burning home full of memories.

"Please........we must go." Fyra pleaded anxiously and softly touching the side of his arm.

Seth and Kaz listened to Fyra's plea and entered the magical doorway. Wade held Fyra's hand and led her beside him as they followed Seth into the purple fire and escaped safely on the other side with the rest. The ceiling began caving in and collapsing to the bottom floor. Raziel climbed back up to the ground's surface with half his body out of the water and braced himself as he looked up at the burning house that leaned over falling on top of him. As part of the home burned in the grass the rest of it sank to the bottom of the newly created pond with Raziel. Inside, a cracked picture frame on the floor burned a picture of Seth, Lilith, and his wife.

47

LOST BLOOD

Wade and Fyra both arrived safetly to the other side with their friends and fellow swordsmen. The purple fire which Fyra created vanished once she had passed through completely.

"What the hell was that back there? We were supposed to destroy that damn armor." Wade complained.

"Fire starter lied Wade." Seth answered, "He can't be trusted. We were stupid for thinking so in the first place."

"But why? What was the point in lying to us? What did he possibly have to gain?" Wade wondered.

"Our death." Cain bluntly replied.

"That's it, we've gotta track him down and kill'em. There's no other choice." Wade decided.

"Um, yeah. There is, how about resting for a minute." Vincent snapped.

"No, we can't. The longer we wait the farther he gets."

"Farther from where? Even if we did want to go fight him, we don't even know where to look." Rufus added.

Wade turned to Fyra, "Fyra you've got to know some of his hideout places, right? Where can we find him?"

"Wade I'm sorry. I don't know." she apologized. "He never stays in one place long after he's be found out."

Wade was exhausted, "We juss," he paused, "you mean we just nearly died out there," he breathed heavily, " and for nothing? We didn't accomplish anything." he stated regretfully.

Wraith stood leaning up against a tree away from everyone else and holding his torso. The purple haired young man coughed blood from his mouth, "Shit."

Due to Bo's great hearing and sence of smell he looked over at Wraith, "You're bleeding." he stated in surprise.

"I don't feel well." Wraith explained collapsing to the ground.

"Hey, Wraith!" Bo pointed out alerting everyone.

"Wraith?!" Alisha called out running over to his side.

"Wraith?" Christian asked softly.

Everyone approached Wraith while he coughed up more blood and bled internally.

Alisha kneeled beside him, "Wraith we have to get you to a doctor." she stated trying to move him, but only caused more pain.

Alisha stopped once she realized she was making things worse.

"Can you use your healing fire? Like you did with Carmon?" Wade asked Fyra.

"It wouldn't have any effect on physical injuries." the summoning regretfully informed.

"We have to do something." Alisha cried. "We can't just leave him like this. Seth call for an ambulance or something."

"There's no reception." Rufus informed.

Carmon stood back watching, terrified of what her father had done. What she had done. If she had not tipped her father off earlier, would Wraith have suffered such injuries?

"I'm feeling really," Wraith paused, "light headed. And kinda sleepy."

"Wraith I'm sorry, I'm so, so sorry." Alisha cried on him.

He leaned over and placed his head in her lap beside him, hurting himself in the process.

"Wraith don't move." Alisha pleaded.

Wraith looked up and into Alisha's eyes, "I love you." he expressed softly.

Vincent stood near watching in surprise of the confession.

Wraith reached up and touched the side of Alisha's face, "I'm sorry. For everything. For.." he coughed, "for leaving you and.." Alisha inturrupted his apology.

"No, it's okay Wraith. Really forget about all that now."

"No. Its..," he struggled swallowing, "it's not okay. I need to say I'm sorry for what happened." he spoke softly and slowly.

"I forgive you Wraith." she accepted brushing his hair with her hand.

Wraith coughed further, "You love me too? I mean, do you love me?" he asked with the most worried expression.

Alisha looked down at his pitiful watery eyes and lonely soul with-in. The young man deperately pleaded while bleeding from the mouth. Tears dripping down his face. Wraith held one of Alisha's hands as tightly as he could.

"Alisha?" he asked starting to fade off with a blank stare, taking short breaths, "You love me?"

Alisha looked down at Wraith with her teary eyes and his hopeful stare and nodded.

"Yes....I love you Wraith........I love you to." she cried.

Vincent has hurt to hear Alisha's "confession" and lowered his head looking away.

Wraith smiled a bloody smile and gazed upward blankly. Without a single breath more, he passed away in the arms of the princess he loved.

The princess sobbed heavily looking down at her friend now passed. Seth walked over and lifted the princess away from the swordsman's body. He walked with her a small distance and stopped. Alisha hugged Seth tightly crying deeply into his chest. Rufus and Bo began to cry. Kaz walked over and dropped Wraith's ruined sword beside his body with remorse on his face. Christian stood back remembering Wraith before the journey began and wishing now that he didn't join the quest at all.

Suddenly Kaz, Cain, Seth, Wade, Vincent, and Rufus all felt a sharp pain on their chests over their heart. Each swordsman looked at their own bare chest and witnessed one of the seven scars in the circular pattern on their chest heal away and vanish entirely as if never there. Each swordsman at that point knew, upon each one of their deaths another scar would heal away and vanish.

"We're connected." Kaz stated out loud.

Fyra looked over Wraith, "If only I could shed tears, I would." she explained to the passed youth. She closed his eyes.

Suddenly a large burst of fire appeared a distance from the group of swordsmen. Fire starter and Grunt stood safely away from danger.

"Well? I noticed from Fyra's flame ya retreated. Too much ta handle?" Fire starter ridiculed.

"Leave us alone Fire starter!" Christian shouted.

"Now's not a good time for this." Seth stated.

"No. It's the perfect time." Wade argued.

The spikey hair swordsman walked away from the group and faced Fire starter with his blade drawn.

"You lied to us you son of a bitch! You put us all through hell just now. Our friends, our families, time to answer for the suffering you've caused." Wade declared.

Rufus exposed his sword from the cloth on his back, "I'll fight with you Wade."

Seth softly brushed a tearful Alisha back with one arm and unsheathed his sword with the other, "A time of atonement Fire starter."

Vincent walked over with both katana's in his hands, but said nothing.

Cain leapt forward and slowly withdrew the white blade from his sheath.

Kaz walked up and readied his sword for attack, "Why don't you do me a favor and call out your litte snake monster so I can kick it's ass this time."

"Why certainly, if ya insist." Fire starter cackled.

Magically Basoomamba, Sammy sammy seven, and the lava monster appeared on Fire starter and Grunt's sides.

"............?" Grunt noticed.

"True. Thy'rs only six of ya. Wher'as tha seventh?" Fire starter asked.

Wade tilted his head for a quick glance at Wraith's body laying peacfully off beside the large tree.

"Ah. So my little fib did surv'a purpose." Fire starter congratulated.

"Damn you Fire starter!" Wade shouted charging towards him.

Fire starter vanished with Grunt into a burst of fire to escape any possible danger. Sammy sammy seven ran full speed in Wade's direction.

"Sammy seven!" he shouted.

"Shut-up!" Wade replied.

Sammy sammy seven used a sliding fire kick on the ground which somehow projected him forward faster and tripped up Wade sending him flying over the summoning's head. Vincent shattered one of his katana's and used the swarm of blades to assist to cut Sammy sammy seven. The summoning backed away trying to avoid the attacks until eventually taking enough damage that he decide to attack back. Wade ran in for an attack while he was distracted, but stopped once the summoning began punching wildly at Vincent's blades. The flurry of fists created huge bursts of fire that ignited upon contact with the mystical blade shards. Vincent's shards were scattered about, but not destroyed. Vincent ran up on Sammy

sammy seven and regained the shards to his broken katana and began sword fighting the weaponless summoning.

Wade was prepared to assisst, but felt an incredible heat from behind. The entertainer looked back and noticed the lava monster trying to tackle him. Wade ran away still sweating from the sheer presence of the intensely hot foe. Seth ran up and stabbed his sword into the moist burning ground.

"Wade, sink'em!" Seth shouted.

"Right." Wade stopped and used his sword to turn the ground into water and sank the heavy blob of liquid rock.

After doing so Wade was surprised to see Seth take a deep breath and dive in after the creature.

"Seth what are you doing?!" Wade panicked.

Basoomamba slithered over to the rampaging Kaz swiftly with its gapping maw wide open. Kaz smacked his broad sword against the outter surface of the great summonings mouth, preventing it from eating him up. At the point of contact Basoomamba was struck by powerful lightning forcing it to retract its attack against Kaz.

"Yeah! Didn't like that very much did'cha?" he mocked.

Rufus ran up and captured the reflection of Kaz's sword giving him the same abilities as his ally. The portly young man ran stabbing the beast with his massive sword electricuting it further. Basoomamba swung its tail around flinging Rufus off to the side and making him drop his sword. Cain dashed in striking the massive snake monster all over its body forcing it to move slower and slower as the assassin picked up speed.

Basoomamba's eyes shined a bright red creating a burst of fire to hit Cain instantly making it an attack incapable of dodging. The assassin landed on the ground, but quickly recovered. Basoomamba belched wide ranged fire attacks at the swordmen to burn them all alive. Cain covered himself with is cape which just so happened to be fire retardant, shielding him from fiery harm, Kaz and Rufus were hit and thrown further back however.

Deep at the bottom of the significantly sized pool Wade created Seth swam down through all of the steam and hesitated for a brief moment before making physical contact with the lava summoning.

The detective began attempting to dig away layers of the lava creature to expose the molten core of the monster. Each layer Seth removed slowly, but sure enough, began cooling into stone. The creature tried fighting back and hugging the man assuming he would instantly burn like everything else it touched.

Christian, Alisha, Bo, and Carmon stood safely behind Fyra and watched on as the fight continued. Suddenly a huge burst of fire was created behind the young teenagers. The fire elemental and suit of armor appeared from the flame and stood confidently. Carmon screamed out of surprise by the sudden appearance. The distant scream snarred Wade's attention causing him to run over to assist. Christian and the others hurried behind Fyra to shield from the evil danger.

Fire starter laughed in his weird way as if victorious, "Foolish children. Hiding behind my summon'n. Fyra burn'em to a crisp." he ordered.

She looked over her shoulder at the youths, "N..No, Fire starter."

"What did ya say ta me?!" he asked angrily.

"No. They are just children. You know I can't. They're no threat to you. Please, just leave them alone." Fyra pleaded.

"You little pest. Disobey me!?" he shouted.

Fire starter reached his wrinkled hand outward and created a magically sparkling flame like non-other. Fyra gasped and watched in awe knowing full well what fate was to befall her. Fire starter winced and crushed the fire in his hand eternally extinguishing it. Fyra suddenly was out of breath and fell to the ground.

"Fyra!" Christian called out.

"What'd you do?" Bo barked.

"I blew out a candle." Fire starter snipped.

Wade ran up watching his failed rescue, "Fyra!"

"You'll pay Fire starter. I swear it!" Carmon promised drawing out her sword and creating a single doppleganger to fight by herside.

"Grunt, teach this puke a lesson." the fire elemental ordered.

Grunt stepped forward and tromped over to the two Carmons. The hollow suit of armor began swinging its spiked ball and chains around trying to smash the brunette. Both Carmons jumped about dodging the ghastly suits advances.

Wade finally reached Fyra's blackening body. He kneeled beside the royal siblings and shark-dog.

"Fyra, I'm sorry. I tried, I really did." Wade apologized.

"Don't be sorry. I'm finally free Wade. Fire starter can't control me any longer." she smiled sadly.

Wade watched the summoning turn to charred ashy cinder before him, blowing in the wind piece by piece.

Seth continued tearing away at the lava summoning until pounds of stone rubble were underneath his feet and the creature was no larger than the palm of his hand. The detective waited until the summoning was composed entierly of stone before resurfacing. Seth climbed out of the water gasping for a deep breath. As the remains of the monster sank to the bottom he looked up noticing Vincent facing off against Sammy sammy seven alone. He stood up grabbed his sword and ran over to assist.

The silver haired teen kept the burly summoning at bay with his dual blades. Sammy sammy seven was growing agitated and jumped back from Vincent's barrage of attacks. The summoning lunged forward with a fiery kick forcing Vincent to break strategy and move out of the way.

Seth ran up beside Vincent, "Need a hand?" he smirked.

"No."

Sammy sammy seven saw the two swordsmen prepared to team up against him and decided to evade the unfair fight, "Sammy sammy seven!" he shouted sending a fire puch to the ground creating a huge mound of dirt and rubble to mask his escape.

Both swordsmen stepped back and shielded their eyes and allowed the dirt to subside.

"He's retreating!" Vincent noticed.

Both swordsmen followed suit as the muscular summoning ran back to Grunt and Fire starter. While running Seth pushed Vincent out of the way and took a hit from Basoomamba's floating orbs. The overwhelmingly powerful heat wasn't enough to injure Basoomamba however.

"Damn it. It's not effected by it's own attacks." Seth realized.

"Asshole." Vincent insulted.

"Hey, I just saved you from that attack." Seth reminded.

Kaz stood back launching another 'Legend' attack at the massive snake summoning making direct contact.

"It's moving so slow." Vincent stated.

"It's Cain. His sword's forcing that thing to move slower with each strike." Seth informed.

"Doesn't matter. Can't kill it without lost blood." Vincent reminded.

Seth watched Rufus and Kaz blasting the beast with electricity while evading its slow, but deadly attacks. The detective noticed a tiny bit of rock debris from the lava summoning on his coat.

"Lost. Lost blood! The blood of someone who you've lost!" Seth figured out.

"You're just saying the same thing over and over again like you're figuring something out." Vincent ridiculed.

"Wraith's blood, the blood of someone we've lost." Seth explained.

"Oh, dead people blood." Vincent realized, "You really think that's the answer?"

"It's a hunch worth going on. You get some of Wraith's blood while I help out the others." Seth planned. "I hope this works."

Wade stood from Fyra's remains and stepped forward, "You kids stay back." he instructed Christian, Alisha, and Bo.

Carmon continued striking against Grunt's metal plated armor, but was unsuccessful in delivering any damage to the silent suit. Wade interfered and swung his blade trying to transform the armor into water.

"Three against one ain't fair!" Fire starter complained.

"I'm done playing by your rules Fire starter." Wade declared.

"Guys, we've got an idea. We just need to keep big ugly distracted." Seth ran up explaining.

"No problem." Kaz assured sending another bolt of lightening at the serpent summoning.

"Up there!" Rufus warned pointing out the glowing orbs.

Basoomamba was moving to slow to evade any attacks or deal any physical damage so it had to resort to using its projectile moves. Massive solar flares fired out of its rotating orbs. Kaz ran away as the attacks had gotten closer to him. Basoomamba's eyes shined red instantly hitting the retreating Kaz with a burst of fire knocking him to the ground. Seth quickly stood in the way shielding the swordsman from the attack.

"Don't move." Seth warned.

Cain ran in stabbing the summoning violently hundreds of time in a matter of seconds. Basoomamba's eyes slowly glowed red instantly hitting the assassin once more. Rufus maintained a safe distance, but held his sword ready for attack. Vincent only ran half way and used his shattered katana to dip into Wraith's blood. The silver haired teen grimmaced at the reality then turned his sights on Basoomamba.

"SETH NOW!" Vincent shouted.

"Cain, Rufus a little help here." Seth called out.

Cain recovered to his feet and dashed upon the large snake summoning and stabbed its throat distracting it from its own attack. Finally the rotating orbs stopped blasting the solar fire at Seth and Kaz. Vincent lunged forward and directed his shattered katana blades to pierce the inside of the floating orbs. The two stone spheres began to crack and shine brightly from the inside until eventually exploding in the air.

"Now's my chance!" Kaz realized hurrying to his feet and rushing towards the screeching summoning.

Kaz readied his sword, "I win this time!" he announced stabbing his broad sword completely inside the massive summoning.

Continous blasting explosions of lightening relentlessly struck Basoomamba, who was too slow to retaliate. The giant summoning's scaley skin started to crack while it whined in agony.

"Kaz move!" Seth shouted.

Cain zipped over to Kaz in a flash and removed him from the danger of the dying serpent. Basoomamba's body began creating lines of red light all over its body until blowing up into a cloud of sparkling magical powders and dust. The large circular crest which hovered behind Basoomamba fell and stabbed the ground landing at a slant.

Fire starter noticed the death of one of his most formidable summonings and was outraged.

"Basa....mam" he stopped.

Sammy sammy seven stood away from the fighting and beside Wraith's body. He tried recovering from his fight with Vincent and catching his breath. The muscular summoning stepped back a bit further stepping on something hard.

"Sammy?" he wondered. The summoning picked up Wraith's crushed sword and looked at the deceased swordsman behind him, "Seven."

Carmon continued tripping up Grunt and distracting it while Wade moved it trying to finish off the armor once and for all. Grunt was on the defensive, but decided it was time to change it up and moved forward for a strike with its spiked ball. Wade noticed the move and countered the attack by striking the metal weighted ball and turning it to water. Grunt was stunned and stepped backward.

"Grunt!" Fire starter panicked and blasted the fighting team against Grunt with a wall of intense fire by swinging his staff.

Wade dodged the attack with Carmon by turning the ground to water, allowing them to both fall in safely.

"Grunt, let's go!" Fire starter ordered.

"Sammy sammy seven!" Sammy sammy seven shouted.

Fire starter glanced over realizing the opportunity.

Vincent, who was near by, rushed over with one katana ready for battle. Wade and Carmon swam up from the water and started climbing out of the steep puddle.

"An opa'tunity presents itself." Fire starter declared. "Let's go!"

"See you in hell Fire starter." Vincent threatened.

Fire starter smirked underneath his large wicker hat and glared his beady red glowing eyes, "Satan bett'a pray ta God I nev'a make it ta hell."

With-in a sudden burst of fire the Fire summoning vanished with his two comrades.

"Where is he? Where'd he go?" Wade asked running up to Vincent.

"He escaped." he replied returning the scattered shards to his katana and sheathing them both.

"You let him get away?" Wade accused.

"Let him? And how do you think I was gonna freak'n stop him, huh?" Vincent shouted. "Want me to apologize for not running up to him and getting burned while he runs away?"

Cain dashed over to Wade and Vincent for information, "What happened?" he grumbled.

"Fire starter bolted." Wade announced obviously upset.

"Everybody is okay though right? That's what really matters here." Seth chimed in.

"Fire starter killed Fyra. He turned her to ash." Christian informed.

Seth sighed regretfully.

The six remaining swordsmen were wounded, but alive, Christian and Alisha were both reunited together at last, and Carmon and Bo were unharmed.

"Alisha?" Bo asked tugging on her skirt, "Where is he?"

"I don't know Bo. Fire starter could be anywhere, but we'll be alright as long as we stick together." Alsiha reassured.

"No, not Fire starter." Bo explained, "Wraith. Where'd he go?"

Alisha glanced over where Wraith's body lay and Fire starter vanished.

The princess gasped, "He took him. Fire starter, he took Wraith."

Christian and the remainder of the group looked at the empty spot were the swordsman's body rest. An ominous feeling befell them as they realized what the elemental had taken from them.

48

Poto

Vailstone military vehicles were stationed all around the northern central train station creating a secure perimeter. Soldiers had scouted the area for any traces of Fire starter or his summonings, but nothing linked the fire elemental with the activity which occured at the train station.

The Vailstone army awaited the arrival of general Grechov and his lieutenant. Discussions of rumors spread through the ranks of the general's disfigurement. Lieutenant Brookes drove one of the jeeps with Grechov in the passenger seat. She slowed the jeep down once she approached the battle site where summoning Nine and Twelve died.

"Did you wish to inspect the area, sir?" she asked.

* soldiers at the train station; "I heard half of his face melted off."

Grechov's face was heavily badaged hiding his grotesque facial features. He barely shifted his head and glanced at the destruction.

* soldiers at the train station; "They said he refused his medication after a while. Heard he's different now."

Grechov solemnly shook his head, "No. There's nothing left to see here." he softly replied. The general nodded and pointed forward, "Continue."

* soldiers at the train station; "The other cadets are starting to call him Poto."

Lieutenant Brookes finally arrived at the train station and parked the jeep near the other military vehicles.

* soldiers at the train station; "Poto?"

General Grechov stepped out of the jeep and put on his cap before looking at the soldiers around him.

*soldiers at the train station; "Yeah, you know. Phantom of the opera." he explained covering half his face with his hand.

General Grechov began marching forward and instructed his lieutenant to follow. A guard at the entrance greeted his superiors with a salute before informing them of the situation.

"We believe the fire monsters lieutenant Brookes had encountered were headed to this destinantion for some sort of rendezvous, but rather than finding burned materials or anything that would give theory to fire attacks we found evidence of gun play." the guard informed.

Grechov looked over the area as they walked through the old gang members hideout.

"We ran background checks on these victims and discovered they were all in fact in relation to a gang that resided here."

"Who was your informant?" Brookes inquired.

"The lieutenant detective of the Vailstone police department." he replied opening a file in his hands and reading, "A detective by the name of Randell Hobbs."

"I don't care about shit that flushes each other." Grechov spoke honestly.

"Actually, the detective believes this was a hit job by a rouge ex-detective," he paused, "Seth Notch." which quickly gained the general's attention.

"Seth?" he asked wild eyed. Grechov touched his face and pondered, but stopped immediately after feeling of his injury. The general slightly nodded his head, "Good work."

Grechov turned to inspect another area before being stopped, "Wait, sir. There's something else. Something you need to see."

In a seperate room Grechov and the lieutenant entered with the high ranking soldier. Limbs of men were ripped apart, nearly everything in the room was stained with blood, an entire side of the wall was destroyed making a huge exit, and gun shot holes decorated the vast room. Grechov slowly walked around the area paying attention to all detail he could pick up.

"Sir, take a look at this." Brookes requested.

Grechov walked over peering into the openned pit in the center of the room. The members of military gazed down looking at parts of goblins and puddles of blood.

"What the hell happened here?" Brookes wondered.

Grechov kneeled down looking at the blood stains on the cement floor, "There're footprints in the puddles of blood. Small footprints."

"Goblins that survived?" Brookes figured.

"Survived what?" the soldier inquired.

"Whatever left those footprints." Grechov revealed.

To the surprise of Brookes, and the soldier with them at the time, many of the large puddles of blood were in actuality huge bloody footprints.

"A giant gorilla!?" the soldier claimed.

"Hardly, but whatever it was," Grechov paused standing up and pointing at the massive hole in the wall, "it let itself out." The general began marching out with his lieutenant and the soldier, "Take photographs of everything you see here. Fill out a report and have it on my desk before night fall."

"Yes, sir." the soldier agreed walking the general out.

Grechov stopped suddenly at the sound of a whisper and a snicker. He turned looking at two soldiers guarding the entrance to the room he had just walked away from. Grechov turned from Brookes and the soldier and slowly approached the guards. His eyes shifted between the two, which immediately straightened up.

"Who was laughing?" Grechov asked innocently.

"No one, sir." a soldier answered.

Grechov raised his hand to his ear, "Am I hearing things?" he turned looking at Brookes, "I must be stupid." Grechov turned back to the guards and tilted his head asking the soldiers, "Am I stupid?"

"Sir, no, sir." they replied.

"Then, somebody's lying. Am I a lier?" Grechov questioned.

"Sir, no, sir." they answered.

"Then, are one of you a lier?" he asked further.

The two soldiers began sweating nervously. The general noticed a quick glance of panick to the other soldier. Grechov walked over and was inches away from the soldiers face. The smell of burned flesh made the soldier nauseous.

"Now, would you like to tell me what was so funny?" Grechov asked.

"No, sir." he answered honestly.

"Tell me what was funny soldier." the general ordered seriously.

The soldier swallowed nervously as his forehead sweat heavily, "Poto, sir." he answerd timidly.

"What?"

"Poto, sir." he answered louder.

"And what is 'Poto'?" Grechov asked.

The soldier was very hesitant, "Phantom....Phantom of the opera, sir."

The exposed side of Grechov's face certainly expressed his displeasure as he made the connection. He closed his eyes and touched the unscorched side of his temple.

"Is that a nickname? Is that, my nickname?" Grechov asked calmly.

The soldier was terrified to answer.

"IS THAT! MY! NICKNAME!?" Grechov shouted.

Blood stains began seeping through the generals bandages. The soldier was afraid of the consequences, but slightly nodded his head to answer. Grechov was furious and the rage brewed with inside him, however, he turned away and said nothing.

"That's funny." he replied sarcastically, "I like it, it's clever." the general paused, "But what will they call you?"

"Sir?" the soldier asked.

Grechov in a pure rage turned around and punched the soldier in the face knocking him to the ground. The gerenal kicked the soldier's torso before sitting on top of him and slamming his fists into his face time and time again. Lieutenant Brookes and the high ranking soldier rushed over to pull Grechov off of the unconscius bloodied soldier.

"Sir!" Brookes shouted, "Sir, stop! You must stop."

Grechov struggled to continue punching the soldier. Brookes motioned for more troops to rush over and assist removing the general from the soldier. Six men including Brookes finally pulled the general off of the soldier.

"Let me go!" Grechov demanded.

Brookes nodded and the soldiers obeyed.

"Get him to our medical staff immediately." Brookes ordered.

"Sir, yes, sir." the soldiers obeyed.

Grechov took a deep breath as he regained his composure. He adjusted his coat and exit the building.

"Follow the general's instructions and finish that report tonight." Brookes reminded before marching outside and meeting up with Grechov who was sitting in the driver's seat of the jeep.

"You're not driving." Brookes demand.

"Excuse me?" Grechov replied.

"You're obviously in no condition to be driving in this state." Brookes stated.

"And what state is that lieutenant?" Grechov inquired peering at his lower ranking officer.

She paused for a moment, "Please, sir." Brookes pleaded.

Grechov gazed forward into the distance before handing over the keys to Brookes and walking around to the passenger seat. Brookes took a deep breath thankful for not suffering any repercussions for over stepping her bounds.

As the lieutenant drove away she kept her eyes forward, "What the hell was that back there?"

Grechov sat quietly for a moment, "A reminder of who's in charge around here." he groaned.

The two traveled a distance before another exchanging of words, "Hey, take this left." Grechov instructed.

Brookes blindly obeyed her orders until being told to stop in front of a burned party store.

"Here, here. This is the place." Grechov announced.

"Harald's party supply?" Brookes questioned.

"Yeah." Grechov agreed ominously and unbuckled his seatbelt.

Brookes stepped out of the jeep while Grechov approached the burned entrance. The front glass door was busted out. The general pushed the door open stepping on the broken glass cracking underneath each step. A smoke stained bell chimed as he walked inside. Grechov slowly and meticulously scoped the ruined party supplies scattered amoungst the floor and burned shelves.

The entrance bell chimed once again as Brookes entered the building after her general.

She curiously looked at the destroyed store wondering what he could possibly be looking for, "What are you looking for, sir?"

"The right one." Grechov answered quietly stepping forward and breaking a devil mask underneath his boot.

Grechov shoved over a large tipped over shelf onto the ground and ripped away hanging ceiling tiles. Grechov shielded his eye from the dust he caused, but released a sigh of relief after in cleared up. The farthest back wall was covered with hanging masks of all vareity. Brookes gazed on as her superior approached the wall of masks. He picked up multiple masks and tossed them aside after a moments thought.

"Where is it? Where's it at?" Grechov asked growing more impatient.

"Where is what, sir?" Brookes questioned.

"The right one. I need to find just the,..." he paused after ripping burned masks off the shelves, "right one."

At the very back of the shelf was an all white mask in mint condition, free of any burn damage somehow. He reached out and gentally pulled it from off the shelf, held it below his chin and looked at it in admiration. As the general gazed at the mask he noticed something on the floor through the eye hole. It was an identical version of the mask under his foot, except broken in half, filthy, and with burn damage. Grechov squeezed and shattered the mask in his hands and picked up the mask from off the floor. Brookes stood far behind Grechov and watched him place the mask on his face and put his cap back on.

He turned around to face his lieutanant, "Let's go."

Somewhere far away from the Vailstone kingdom Christian, Alisha, and the remaining swordsmen continued wandering through the thick woods.

Bo's tummy began growling once more, "I'm still hungry." he whined.

"Cain went scouting to look for something to eat, remember? I'm sure he'll be back soon. It's only been two hours, right?" Christian asked.

"I'm not sure I'd trust anything an assassin brings me to eat." Vincent added honestly.

"Hey, that assassin helped us out immensely back there. He could have easily just turned and run, but he didn't." Seth added.

"And why is that exactly?" Rufus asked.

"He has his reasons." Seth replied.

Bo sniffed the air, "Hey, I smell fish!" he announced happily wagging his tail.

"Well, your nose is broke cause there ain't no fish here in the woods." Kaz mocked.

At that moment Cain hopped down from a tall tree with a stick that had many fish attached to it. Kaz scouffed as he was proven wrong. Thirty minutes later the group had a small campfire and cooked fish. Alisha, Christian, and Carmon were picky on eating their poorly cooked fish.

"How can you just bite into it like that?" she asked looking at the others.

"It's easy and super yummy. Watch me." Bo added sloppily eating his fish on a stick.

"Yeah, it's not a big deal. I guess." Christian replied hesitantly.

"Oh hush, you've never in your life eaten fish like this before." Alisha exposed.

"Have so." Christian countered.

"Oh yeah? Since when?" his sister asked.

"Um, well, when we went to get the armor of Kamisama." he lied.

Carmon smiled, "Then go ahead tough guy."

Christian dazed off a bit looking at Carmon and her choice of words.

"Well?" Alisha pressured.

"Don't rush me." Christian snapped. He swallowed, took a deep breath, and bit the head off of the fish. The prince suddenly grew nauseous.

"Ya know you're not supposed to eat the scales, right?" Bo added.

"Oh God." Christian hurried away to spit out the fish head.

The six remaining swordsmen sat away from the royal teenagers and ate their fish.

"So what's the plan now? What do we do? Separate and hide?" Wade asked.

"No. You're all branded as kidnappers and terrorists by now. The Vailstone army will track you each down one by one and treat you as such. Best remain together." Cain growled.

"Did you get an idea of where we are yet?" Seth asked.

"No. No landmarks, trails, or roads to be found. Nothing except horse tracks going nowhere" Cain answered.

"And I can't use my phone to locate us unless I get a signal out here." Rufus complained.

"Under the ground...in the forest of darkness, but out here and no signal? We must be on another planet." Wade concluded sarcastically.

"It's getting pretty late already." Kaz noticed.

"Great, stuck in the woods of who-knows-where in the middle of the night. The day keeps getting better." Vincent complained.

"So we'll camp out here tonight?" Rufus asked.

"We don't really have a choice. We'll sleep together and in the morning we'll keep going until we find out where we are." Wade suggested.

"Sleep together?!" Kaz replied shocked.

"Not 'together' together, just around each other together." Wade explained.

"Well, I'm not sleeping naked." Kaz added.

"Somebody's sleeping naked?" Rufus worried.

"Nobody's sleeping naked." Vincent answered.

"Why would you sleep naked? You didn't sleep naked in the hotel with me." Seth asked.

"You two slept together?" Wade asked.

"No, no, no. Just in the hotel." Seth corrected.

"You two got a hotel room together?" Vincent asked curiously.

"Yes, but it wasn't like that." Seth informed.

"I'm not gay." Kaz announced.

"Why does the conversation always seem to be about 'gay' with you?" Seth asked Kaz.

"Nothing's gay with me." Kaz assured.

"Who's gay?" Rufus asked Wade.

Wade shrugged his shoulders and shook his head, "I'm still confused about the naked sleeping in the hotel together."

Cain sat listening to the nonsense long enough, "Enough!" he demonically instructed, "Something more important needs our attention."

"Like what?" Vincent asked.

"I had talked with Cain earlier, before he left to search for the fish and we both agreed that, we have a serious problem." Seth announced.

"Well spit it out. Stop being over dramatic." Vincent hurried.

"We think it was more than coincidence the Vailstone army was headed to the train station the other day. And thought it quiet suspicious how Raziel knew exactly where to find us today before we could even set our plan into motion." Seth revealed.

"A traitor." Kaz stated.

Seth nodded his head, "One of us here had to have tipped off the army AND Raziel. There's no other explanation."

"So how do we find out who the double agent is?" Wade inquired.

"We watch." Cain growled.

"Watch what?" Rufus asked.

"Each other." Cain stated.

An awkward silence fell over each one of the swordsmen as they glanced suspiciously at one another.

In the castle Hikaru sat petting his cheshire cat with Crow and Raziel sitting across from him.

"Sounds like there's more to worry about than just that old mystic now." Crow assumed.

"Indeed. Fire starter is out there burning down the kingdom and now those seven swordsmen have teamed up and are trying to kill you? Hm." Hikaru snuffed, "Well good luck to them."

"They have Christian. I looked everywhere around the rubble, but couldn't find any of them. I'm sure they escaped somehow. They're still out there with him." Raziel informed.

"We don't need Christian anymore. He signed the bill of the 'Dorian Act', I'm in charge now." Hikaru assured.

"We're finding Christian." Raziel sternly informed.

"Then find Christian we shall." Hikaru agreed lesurely.

The three were distracted from conversation once general Grechov marched into the room and stopped to look at them wearing his half mask.

"What is this I hear? Raziel, you were attacked?" the general asked.

"Yes." he confirmed.

"And by whom?" Gerchov asked needing to know.

"It was those sword people, the seven of them." Crow informed making a lame sword motion with his wrist.

"And apparently they have prince Christian captive. Dreadful shame." Hikaru added.

"Um, what's with the mask?" Crow smirked.

"What's with the dress?" Grechov snapped back pissing off Crow. "Where are they now?"

"Apparently they've vanished into thin air without a trace. Our grand duke lost track of them." Hikaru informed.

"I'll find'em soon enough." Grechov assured, " But we can't go in fighting blind anymore. We're not fighting against other men here we're fighting super powers and magic. We need to even the battlefield." Grechov suggested.

"And how do you suggest we do just that?" Hikaru wondered.

"The royal vault." Grechov brought up.

"No. Out of the question." Raziel shot down, "The items and weapons collected in there are dangerous. I collected those from my quests to maintain the peace." Raziel informed.

"And how well is that working out for us?" Grechov asked.

"Pretty damn well mind you. Or have you forgotten most of those artifacts were in the hands of dangerous men before I took them away?" Raziel huffed, "I understand you've been through hell and back Grechov, but don't forget your place." the grand duke warned.

"These people, they are trying to kill us. They plotted an attack against you, kidnapped the only living heir to the throne, and burned half of my face off. Sir," Grechov continued remaining calm, "With these objects from the vault I can march against our new enemies prepared and save our prince, or, I can march our men to the slaughter."

Raziel thought for a moment, conflicted by desire and reason.

"He makes a valid point." Hikaru agreed.

Raziel sighed, "How many would you need?" he asked.

"Aside from myself, I'll select four men." Grechov answered.

"Four men you can trust?" Raziel asked further. Grechov nodded, "Very well. Claim your five weapons from the vault, but Grechov if anything goes wrong I'm holding you accountable. Understand?"

"Understood, sir." Grechov assured.

The general marched down below the castle with two soldiers and lieutenant Brookes. After passing through several sealed heavy safe doors, two rooms of magical enchantments, and a high tech security system they finally reached the royal vault. Grechov stood in front of the locked door and waited. Brookes motioned for the soldiers to unlock and open the door. In that moment the royal vault exposed all of it's secrets to the general leaving him with an ominous smile upon his face.

SPECIAL THANKS

I'd like to thank all who support me & the "7 Blades of Legend" series as well as the Venture universe & brand name. As well as a Special thanks to those who helped finance "Fire Burning" with your generous donations.

Jelle de Leeuw
Christopher Allerdice
Alicia Bluejacket
Tony Canady
Raynelle Torres
Lucky Murphy

Any and all future donataions to help support the publication of "7 Blades of Legend" as well as future titles to come can be made to Paypal account: Venture_universe@yahoo.com

Also, to help keep you informed on the adventures and your favorite characters tune into my Youtube channel: Kyle Canady

(Back of the book text/ information)

The adventures of Prince Christian and the seven swordsmen have only just begun. In the midst of all of the chaos from "The Armor of Kamisama" continue the latest perils to plague the fair kingdom of Vailstone. How can Raziel right the injustice he has committed against Christian and can the prince find it in his heart to forgive him?! Fire starter is furious and determined to exacerbate matters by setting everything everyone holds dear a blaze. Can the seven swordsmen regroup in time and ultimately master the powers hidden with in their swords to stop his vengeance or is all hope lost? Discover new creatures of the north, new allies along the way, and far worse evils to face off against in "7 Blades of Legend: Fire Burning".

Read the tale of "7 Blades of Legend" with an open mind, a terrible misunderstand takes control of friends and family and creates a awful rift between them. Who wins in a clash between heroes?! Can an entire lifetime of doing right be undone by one wrong someone is unwillingly forced into? Which side will you choose? Equipped with the armor of God against seven swords of pure legendary status can a victory really be achieved or is tragedy the destined end result? Join the Venture series universe and read "7 Blades of Legend" and discover the world you never knew existed.